An Ounce
of Lead

pdmac

An Ounce of Lead is a work of fiction. Though actual locations may be mentioned, they are used in a fictitious manner and the events and occurrences were created/invented in the mind and imagination of the author, except for the inclusion of actual historical fact. Similarities of characters or names used within for any person – past, present, or future – are coincidental except where actual historical characters are purposely interwoven. The actions, thoughts, and dialogue of the historical characters featured in this story are fictional and not meant to reflect actual personalities and behavior.

Copyright © 2017 by pdmac

Published by Trimble Hollow Press, Acworth, Georgia

ISBN: 978-1-946495-02-0
eISBN: 978-1-946495-03-7

Cover design by Trimble Hollow Concepts
Cover art by Gulliver Vianei

for Terri Lynn

my Soulmate and Best Friend

A special thanks to Carmen Coyle for her constant encouragement and support, especially in the final editing of this novel.

Contents

Chapter 1

Splayed out on the ground like Da Vinci's Vitruvian Man, Henry Mitchell jerked at the leather straps holding his legs and arms. A shadow spread across his face, and he looked up in terror to see Caleb's maggot eaten body blocking the sunlight, the filmy eyes staring down at him. Just off his shoulder, Diaco de la Fuente's desiccated face, the morion of a Spanish conquistador too big for his skeletal head, likewise studied the spread-eagled inventor and murderer.

Caleb stiffly lowered himself to his knees and leaned directly over Henry, bringing his half-eaten face within inches of the man's horrified stare. Henry twisted away, despite the pain in his head, wrinkling his face in disgust.

"O God, get away. Get out of here."

Caleb reached a boney hand and grasped Henry's chin, forcibly twisting his head to look at him.

A maggot dropped from the eye socket onto Henry's cheek, and he cried out, "Get it off me! Get it off me!"

With a boney finger, Caleb flicked the maggot away and then jerkily stood up. Turning to face de la Fuente, he pointed to the small boxes filled with gold.

Stiffly nodding in understanding, causing the morion to wobble, de la Fuente led the way to the treasure.

"You can't leave me here," Henry wailed. "Please. Please," he begged. "You can have the gold. You'll never see me again. Just cut me loose."

But the two dead men ignored his pleas, instead picking up the small boxes of gold and jerkily making their way deeper into the Dragoon Mountains.

Hours later, with the sun high and hot overhead, the boxes were gone as were Caleb and de la Fuente. All that remained was Henry who licked dry lips and prayed for a miracle.

1

Though the fire was out, grey smoke still curled skyward when U.S. Marshal Mason Sadler stepped down from the Mobile All Terrain Engine or MATE, as the now probably dead inventor, archaeologist, and murderer Henry Mitchell had called it, to survey what was left of Tombstone. The acrid smell of charred lumber infused the morning air.

Standing in the pilot's platform above, Belle Dubois gazed down Allen Street. "I pray no one was hurt. I hope the Theater wasn't burned."

Mason turned his attention from the blackened wreckage to look back up and take in the beautiful, bedraggled woman. For someone who had been bound and gagged, kidnapped, doused with buckets of water, and nearly killed in the rescue, she seemed quite unaffected. Her tousled long blond hair, wild and windblown from the ride back from the Dragoon Mountains, only added to her allure. Her still damp clothes clung to her, especially her buxom chest. Mason caught himself lingering a little longer on that part of her body before forcing himself to look up at her flawless face, now wiped clean of makeup. The pert nose, smooth cheeks, and dazzling and captivating blue eyes were enough to make any man desire her. In fact, every man who saw her did desire her, the Madam of the Bird Cage Theater. That she had wanted him, even during the dark time of his doomed marriage to Elizabeth, made him giddy with anticipation. All the pent-up emotion and desire could now be released. He silently rued the town's destruction as it would most likely postpone his anticipated time with her.

She looked down to see him smiling at her. "What?"

"You look good," he impishly grinned.

Smirking, she shook her head. "I've had better days, though these past two have been fun."

"Fun?" he said, cocking an eyebrow. "You could have been killed."

"I doubt Henry meant it," she shrugged, remembering her hands tied behind her back while Henry pointed the pistol at her head. Part of her was irritated that she had allowed herself to be swayed by the suave archaeologist. She had been distracted by a pretty face wrapped in a nice body with refined tastes and culture. The other part of her was irritated that she had been physically overpowered by the man, that she hadn't been able to defend herself. That she had been captured and bound embarrassed her.

"He murdered Caleb," Mason soberly pointed out.

"And now Caleb's getting his revenge," she quietly replied, remembering Henry spread-eagled on the ground, his feet and wrists staked down while Caleb hovered over him, tormenting him by picking maggots from his own dead flesh and flicking the wiggling cannibals onto Henry's face. Henry had screamed like a little girl. "I never would have believed it had I not seen it with my own eyes."

"Caleb?"

"Yes."

"The dead but not-quite-dead?"

"Yes," she marveled.

"Imagine my own reaction when Caleb cornered me in the church," he said, shaking his head. "That was less than a week ago, late at night when decent folk are in bed asleep. I was heading home and saw the front door to the church swing shut and thought someone was up to some mischief inside the church. Didn't see anyone at first, but I could hear someone moving around. It was when they came to the front so I could get a good look at them in the moonlight that I got my surprise."

"I would've liked to have seen that," she grinned at him. "Were you scared?"

Mason thought for a moment. "I don't know if scared is the right word. I think 'shocked beyond belief' is a better word."

"That's more than one word," she teased.

"I suppose it is," he grinned back. "You hear the tales about the walking dead and ignore them because they're just tales. Then to actually see someone back from the dead…"

"And that one conquistador –"

"De la Fuente?"

"Yes, him. He's been dead for how many years?"

"At least three hundred, probably more," he replied.

"Wonder why he came alive again, if that's what you call it, after all this time?" she mused. "He'd been stuck in that cave with the gold for so long, why now?"

"Who knows?" Mason turned to look at what remained of Tombstone. "Maybe there was some sort of curse associated with the gold." He apprehensively fingered the gold ring in his pocket that Caleb had given him just before they left the Dragoon Mountains to come back to Tombstone. Caleb and de la Fuente remained behind to wreak their own justice on Henry, the man responsible for Caleb's death and stealing de la Fuente's gold. Mason thought it somewhat ironic that the gold de la Fuente claimed was his was stolen from someone else. He had read de la Fuente's journal and the account of the conquistador's journey to the Seven Cities of Cibola and subsequent flight back south where he and his cousin were cornered in the cave just southwest of Tombstone. Hundreds of years later, a crotchety miner named Caleb working a claim no one else thought worthy of a second thought found de la Fuente and the gold.

And who would have believed that at the same time, inventor and archaeologist Henry Mitchell, searching for the very gold that Caleb discovered, ended up having a claim right across the wash from the old miner. What were the odds of that happening? Of course, it really didn't matter now. Caleb was dead and Henry soon would be, if he wasn't already.

Silence settled as the two watched store owners, hotel proprietors, and other business owners sift through the scorched and smoking remains of their respective establishments. Soot-smudged children scampered around the edges of the blackened debris, occasionally chased off by an adult.

"What do you think will happen to him?" Belle asked, watching the men and women scurrying about, business owners unaffected by the fire helping those who lost their livelihoods.

"Henry?"

"Yes."

4

Mason paused to consider. "I imagine Caleb won't be so forgiving. Instead of enjoying his find, he ends up dead because someone else wanted it more. Sort of ironic if you think about it. Henry spends years searching for the gold never finding it, and Caleb stumbles upon it by accident. Poor man never had a chance against Henry." Mason scratched his cheek. "Though now that I think about it, if that curse-of-the-gold thing holds water, maybe de la Fuente and that other conquistador wouldn't have been so friendly had Caleb tried to remove the gold."

"Think they'll kill Henry?" she asked.

"Probably. Staked out like he was, it'll be hard for him to defend himself." The image of Henry splayed on the ground up in the Dragoon Mountains coalesced and Mason found himself wondering what Caleb and de la Fuente were going to do with Henry. And then there was the gold, boxes and boxes of gold. Hopefully the two dead men would hide it somewhere no one would ever find it.

"If I was them," he opined, "I'd kill him and leave him staked out and let the coyotes and vultures take care of the rest."

"How grotesque," she said, curling a lip.

"That's just half of it," he said, turning back to gaze up at her. "If Caleb and de la Fuente can come back from the dead, why not Henry?"

"O my God," she gasped. "I hadn't thought about that."

"If they really wanted to be rid of him, they probably need to let the varmints and critters make off with some of the more important bones, like legs and arms. That way he can't move around."

Belle gave him a queasy look. "What a pleasant thought right before breakfast."

Mason climbed back up and sat down next to her. "Let's go check on the Bird Cage and then see if anyone has any food."

"How about we let me change into something more suitable, first?" she countered then quietly added, "provided my residence hasn't been burned to the ground." Looking behind her at the empty trailer attached to the MATE, she said, "I'm glad Nantan wasn't hurt when his airship crashed."

"He's young and resourceful," he replied, "and lucky. Never gave much thought about what a rifle could do to an airship. Still, I'm mighty glad he and Taboca jumped right in to help. With them trailing Henry in their airships, it made it a whole lot easier for me to track him."

"And then when Nantan started tossing out those bombs," she added, shaking her head with wry bemusement. "When that first one went off so close to us, after getting over the shock, I was wondering whose side he was on. It wasn't until I realized what he was doing that I tried to relax."

"That was pretty clever of him, dropping the bombs in such a way to force Henry to steer into the mountains."

"Wonder how he and Taboca are going to get back to Bisbee?" she asked. "Not a whole lot of room in Taboca's one-seater airship."

"I'm sure they'll find a way," he assured her. "They're machinists... and Chiricahua. By the way, what did they say when you asked to keep this thing?" He looked down at the MATE, the engine pulsing with built up pressure.

Grinning broadly, she announced, "They said I could have it once they were finished with it. They wanted to duplicate it."

"Knowing those two, theirs will have all sorts of extra gadgets. C'mon, let's get you home."

They heard a shout overhead and looked up to see Taboca's airship maneuvering above the town, headed towards Bisbee. Nantan was suspended immediately below Taboca's pilot enclosure in a rigged sling. Nantan held on to the ropes while his feet dangled. He looked like a small boy on a swing.

Grinning, the two Machinists gave a quick wave of recognition. Mason and Belle returned the wave with heartfelt gratitude.

"I hope they come back here soon," Belle said.

"With the MATE still here," Mason observed, "you can count on it."

Belle released the brakes and the MATE slowly chugged forward, the metal treads surrounding the iron wheels leaving teeth marks in the dirt street. Though they received a few stares, most folks were too busy cleaning up to give them much notice. Turning onto 2nd Street, they headed towards Toughnut Street and were rewarded by the still intact Tombstone Lodging House on the corner.

"Thank God," Belle muttered under her breath. Maneuvering the machine in front of the house, she pulled the brakes to bring the MATE to a stop then shut down the engine.

"Aren't you afraid someone might steal it?" Mason teased as he hopped down to come around to help her down.

"If they do, they won't be hard to track," she nonchalantly replied, feeling the strength of his hands on her sides as he easily lifted her up and then down. Brushing a blond strand of hair from her face, she smiled affectionately at him. "You still need to feed me."

"We can find a place right now," he offered. "You look fine." A faint smile gave away his earnestness.

"You're sweet, but silly," she said, reaching up to tenderly caress his beard-stubbled cheek. Standing on her tip-toes, she pulled his head towards her planting a deep kiss on his willing lips.

His strong arms swept her up and returned the kiss releasing all the pent-up passion of the past months. The firmness of her body thrilled him, and he felt her ardor. Lost in each other, it was more than a few moments before they paused to catch their breaths and collect themselves, taking stock of their surroundings, awkwardly acknowledging the passersby who gave them humorous regard.

"I won't be long," she said, releasing him.

"I'll wait," he replied, stating the obvious.

He watched her bound up the steps, noting the stark disparity of her beauty and vitality compared to Elizabeth whose lethargic and doleful existence was more than emotionally draining.

Elizabeth. Was he sad she was dead? A small part of him was relieved while the other part said he ought to feel guilty because she was murdered. Still another part wanted to thank Henry for permanently removing her from his life. Though silently chastising himself for such an uncharitable thought, he rationalized it with the reflection that with her addiction to laudanum and other drugs, it was merely a matter of time before she killed herself. He supposed it came down to the question of who pulled the trigger, yet the result was the same.

While Henry's murdering Elizabeth might have remedied one problem, it led to a far greater one. Mason figured that it was just a matter of time before her father was informed, if he didn't already know, and Reginald Worthington was not a forgiving man, especially as Mason hadn't bothered to telegraph the news. What was the point? Once the agent sent here to checkup on her reported back, Worthington's rage would be unleashed.

Mason knew it would happen sooner or later. It was all a question of when.

Worthington and Mason had never gotten along from the start. It was bad enough when Elizabeth thwarted her father's matchmaking ambitions by marrying well below her station. Then Mason had the audacity to quit the firm to pursue the pedestrian occupation as a common lawman. To add further insult, Mason snatched the man's only child and not only took her away from her pampered and extravagant life but dragged her here to the wild and savage west. It was more than the father could stand. Mason vividly remembered the last words Worthington said to him. Cornering him just before he and Elizabeth boarded the airship to bring them to Bisbee, Worthington leaned in and with a voice of doom said, "If anything happens to her, you're a dead man. Not only you, but your family and anyone else you care about."

Turning to face his father-on-law, Mason curled a lip in a snarl. The man didn't intimidate him like all the other minions who groveled to obey the scion of the Worthington and Son empire. "I don't have a family. They died of yellow fever in New Orleans in 1867. But you already knew that. I was 15 years old when I was forced to live on my own, but I survived. If anything happens to her," he retorted, "it's because you failed as a father and didn't teach her how to survive." He had wanted to add that he was moving out west because he didn't want to encounter the tragic accident that so many of Worthington's adversaries experienced.

Worthington's shocked look was worth the rebuke, but Mason wasn't going to wait for a rematch of wills. Grabbing Elizabeth by the arm, he just about frog-marched her aboard the ship. Her father stormed off, though he did stay to give a stoic wave goodbye to Elizabeth, pointedly ignoring Mason standing next to her.

That was nearly a year ago. During that time, Worthington had sent no less than half a dozen agents to ensure his precious daughter was safe and happy. What frustrated Mason was that he doubted any of the agents told their boss that his daughter was a drug addict.

None of that mattered now. Elizabeth was dead. It also didn't matter the fact that Henry killed her. That thought caused Mason to frown in puzzlement. He still didn't understand why Henry thought Elizabeth was of any importance, to the point of supplying her drugs. And then why bother killing her? Was it to punish him, to make his life even more miserable?

Then the epiphany hit him. Killing Elizabeth was a guarantee that the wrath of Worthington would descend upon him. He would be far too busy fighting for survival, leaving Henry free to plot and plan as needed. But Henry made one very costly mistake. He murdered Elizabeth too soon. He didn't wait long enough for Worthington to find out. Now, instead of heading east with his precious gold, he was staked out in the Dragoon Mountains, waiting death... if he wasn't dead already.

As Mason made a mental note to ride out in a day or two to check on what was left of Henry, he reminded himself that he was going to have to a find another horse to replace the one Henry had killed up in the mountains. While he was contemplating the difficulty of finding another steed as dependable as the one he lost, the door opened to the boarding house and Belle emerged looking refreshed and bright-eyed. Gone was the damp dress, replaced by an elegant high-collared maroon dress patterned in gold and ebony. The tight bodice was waist length, paneled in satin and silk moire ribbon. The sleeves were long with high pleated shoulders. Her blond hair was again swept up to the back of her head.

Even with no sleep for two days, she was stunningly beautiful. Suddenly Mason felt keenly aware of his own manly aroma, as though he'd been out on the trail for a couple of weeks.

"Um… perhaps I should at least shave," he muttered as she walked up.

"You look wonderful." She smiled at him. Studying him for a moment, she felt herself swell with pride. "You were so strong and determined when you stood with your gun pointed at Henry. I could feel his hesitation knowing you could shoot him right between the eyes if you had wanted, even holding me as close as he did."

"Fortunately, I didn't have to."

"I know," she chuckled. "I couldn't figure out what happened when Henry suddenly pitched forward on top of me, knocking me to the ground. When I looked up and saw you and Caleb and de la Fuente dragging him off me, I wasn't sure what to make of it."

"You handled it very well," he said, holding out his elbow for her to slip her hand around his arm.

"You seemed so relaxed with the two of them, so I figured it must be OK." She wrapped an arm around his strong arm, relishing the raw strength of the man. "Well, tall, dark and handsome. Take a lady to breakfast?"

"With pleasure," he gallantly replied.

It didn't take long to find one of the few restaurants still open. The Atlantic was doing a brisk business when Mason and Belle walked in. Though the noise continued, quite a few heads turned to watch them enter, most staring at Belle. As they maneuvered to an empty table, a voice called out.

"Hey Marshal. You missed all the excitement."

"So it seems," he answered, pulling a chair out for Belle to sit.

"Coulda used yer help," another voice rose up in accusation.

"I was busy," he tartly replied. Still standing, he cast a stern glance around the room that had now quieted, the diners paused in their meals.

"Too busy to save our town?"

Mason looked at the man who spoke. He was a partner in Hayes Jewelry store on the corner of Third and Allen streets. Mason then looked around the room as they waited for him to answer. "Not that I owe any of you an explanation," he firmly stated, "but I was tracking down a murderer, the man who killed Caleb and kidnapped Miss Belle here." He was about to add that Henry had also killed his wife but thought better of it.

"Who was it?"

"Henry Mitchell."

There was a pause before the merchant said, "Henry Mitchell? The archaeologist with all those machines of his?"

"That's right."

"He killed Caleb? Why?"

"Caleb had something he wanted," Mason answered, thinking quickly.

"Caleb's claim weren't worth nuthin'," another man, a miner, pointed out.

"Henry didn't want Caleb's claim," he said, noticing the increased attention of the diners. Deciding to play to the audience, he spoke with a bit of flair. "Caleb mined up in Colorado before coming here. While he was there, a man gave him a book. But Caleb couldn't read it.

"Caleb couldn't read?" the merchant said, his superiority obvious.

"The book was in Spanish," Mason explained. "Caleb forgot about it until he came to Tombstone and met Henry Mitchell. Trusting Henry, he gave him the book, only to discover that it was the journal of a man named Diaco de la Fuente, a conquistador." By now, almost all the diners had stopped eating and were in rapt attention. Even the restaurant staff had paused to listen. "But Henry didn't tell Caleb the whole story." He glanced over to the waitress, the teenage

11

daughter of the owner. "Rosalie, how about some breakfast over here?"

He started to pull a chair out, pretending to sit when several voices cried out, "Don't stop now. What happened?"

Mason paused as though remembering what he was saying. "Well, Henry passed off the book as just someone's journal, even offered to sell it for Caleb to some university. What Henry didn't tell Caleb was that the Diaco de la Fuente was one of Coronado's conquistadors who were searching for the Seven Cities of Cibola."

"Gold!" numerous voices, mostly miners, sputtered in unison.

"Now don't go off half-cocked," Mason warned them. "Remember, the stories are mostly just that, stories."

"How do you know what was in the journal?" the merchant challenged.

"Because I read it," Mason calmly replied to an abruptly hushed audience.

"What it say?" several miners demanded.

"Like I said, it's a journal. De la Fuente recorded his travel with Coronado."

"I thought you said it was in Spanish," the merchant again challenged.

"I did. I happen to read Spanish," Mason replied. As the voices bubbled up in questions, Mason held his hands up to quiet them. "OK. Listen. Here's the gist of it all. Henry Mitchell was supposedly an archaeologist and had been searching for the gold from Cibola. But he wasn't an archaeologist. He was a con man looking for the big score. His searching brought him to Tombstone."

"The gold's here?" a voice exclaimed as a miner stood up.

"That's not what I said," Mason shot back, "though that is what Henry believed. He was here because Coronado must have come through here. When Henry discovered that Caleb had de la Fuente's journal, he believed he was on the right track. But he needed to study the journal for any further clues."

"Who's got the journal?" another miner asked.

"Everyone just stop and listen," Mason huffed, frustrated. "I don't know where the journal is," he lied. "Caleb let me read it and I gave it back to him. Henry most likely took it from him after he murdered him. Where it is now is anyone's guess."

"You said you had tracked down Henry Mitchell, that he had kidnapped Miss Belle," the merchant pointed out.

"That's correct," Mason amiably replied. "When I determined Henry had killed Caleb, I set out to get him. Knowing I was on his trail, he kidnapped Belle to make me reconsider. But there's something else you should know," he mysteriously added. "I have reason to believe that Henry purposely set the fire here so that he could make good his escape, thinking I'd have to stay here, and he'd get clean away. Who knows what would have happened to Miss Belle had he got away. She'd probably be dead now."

There was a moment of stunned silence as they absorbed the news followed by a burst of indignation. Mason waved again at Rosalie to come get their order. As she threaded her way around the tables, the merchant's voice rose above the cacophony.

"So where is Henry Mitchell now?"

The room quieted to listen to Mason's answer. "He's dead, somewhere up in the Dragoons. And before anyone goes off hunting for the body," he quickly added, "I searched for the journal and Henry didn't have it on him. It's more than likely he wasn't working alone. It takes money to do what he does and live like he did. Most likely, he probably sent the book off to his partner or partners. So, my word of advice is to be on the lookout for strangers in town supposedly just passing through but stay longer than that. And you'll know it's them if they ask about Henry Mitchell."

"Why was he in the Dragoons?" the merchant asked, his doubt obvious.

"He was originally headed north, probably for the depot in Benson to catch the train, but with the help of two machinists and their airships, we managed to get him turned into the mountains. He was on that machine he called a 'MATE.' It's parked outside the Tombstone Lodging House right now." Casting a smirk at Belle, he quietly added, "If it's still there."

"Think there's gold in the Dragoons, Marshall?" a voice called out.

"Not at all," Mason crisply replied. "Remember, Coronado was searching for the Seven Cities of Cibola. If they ever existed, they were farther to the north, probably Colorado. That was where Caleb picked up the journal. If there was gold in the Dragoons, Henry wouldn't have been headed to Benson."

"Why didn't you bring the body back?" the merchant asked, more of an accusation than interest.

"Because he shot my horse," Mason snapped. "A man who kills another man's horse isn't fit to be buried proper. You should know that."

"Damn right," a voice called out, immediately followed by an increase of noisy agreement.

Turning back to everyone still inside the dining room, he said, "Now if you all don't mind, Miss Belle and I are starving, for we've been up for two days and neither of us has eaten since yesterday morning. Rosalie." Adjusting his chair just a bit more, he seated himself.

Belle leaned forward, impressed. "That was very good. Tell them as much of the truth as necessary."

"I don't need them running around the Dragoons," he softly answered.

After Rosalie took their order and headed back to the kitchen, the room began to clear with a number of miners and others stopping by the table to tell Belle that they were glad she was safe. When things settled down a bit, Mason turned to look at the merchant. "How bad is it?"

"Disastrous. The Cosmopolitan, the Grand and Brown's hotels are all gone. All the saloons, restaurants, and stores from Allen to Fremont and from 5th to 3rd street are nothing but smoking rubble. You should have seen it when Spangenburg's gun-shop went up. Everyone had to clear out in a hurry."

"Anyone hurt?"

"David Neagle had a horse fall on him, and some others got burned by falling timbers. Other than that, everyone seems to be OK."

"How about you?"

"I was lucky," he said standing up. "My store's on 3rd Street. The fire came close, but we managed to get it out before it jumped the street." Laying several coins on the table, he pinched the brim of his hat at Belle. "You two have a good day."

Rosalie carried in their breakfast, placing steak and eggs before Mason and eggs and biscuits before Belle.

"Once I get a handle on what's going on around here, I need to go back," Mason said, cutting his steak.

"You want to go back?" Belle asked. "Why?"

"A couple of reasons," Mason replied. "First, I left a good saddle back there. I wasn't thinking when we left. I should have used the MATE to help me retrieve it. I need to go back and get it before the horse begins to bloat."

"What a pleasant conversation for breakfast," she said curling a lip in disgust. "And the other reasons?"

"I want to check on some friends of ours. I have a feeling that, despite my story this morning, they might be having visitors. And with the trail the MATE left, they won't be hard to find."

"You want to use the MATE?"

"With your permission," he smiled. "I don't have a horse at the moment and by the time I get a new one, we could be there and back. Besides, I don't want to have to buy another saddle."

"Sounds like fun," she smiled back.

With breakfast finished, Belle went to check on the Bird Cage while Mason sought out Mayor Clum and Police Chief Neagle, finding them tiptoeing through the wreckage behind what was once the Tivoli Gardens Saloon.

"Morning Mason," Dave Neagle said, seeing him working his way towards them.

"Morning, Dave, Mayor," Mason greeted them. "Help you find something?"

"We're looking to see what caused it," Mayor Clum answered.

"I can tell you who caused it," Mason said, catching their attention. He related the story about Henry Mitchell, including the kidnapping and shoot out in the Dragoons.

"Damn," Mayor Clum said, shaking his head. "Pity you didn't bring back the body."

"Like I told everyone at the Atlantic this morning, the man shot and killed my horse. A man who kills another man's ride isn't fit to be buried proper. Anyway," he added, "I'll be headed back that way to get my saddle back and if he's not too torn up from the coyotes, I'll bring him back."

Looking Mason square in the face, Dave chuckled. "You look like you've been rode hard and put up wet."

"I've been up for two days," he sheepishly grinned. "I'm going to get some sleep as soon as I make sure everything's good in town here."

"Much obliged, Mason," Mayor Clum said. "Glad you and Belle are OK."

Mason nodded then looked at Dave. "Who'd you recommend for a new horse?"

"Hank Abbott has some good stock," Dave replied. "Lives pretty much due east of here between the Dragoons and the Mule Mountains. The Troop at Huachuca buys from him."

"I know him," Mason nodded. "Thanks."

Hiram Wright pushed open the door to the blockhouse and stepped outside. Lifting his arms in a wide stretch, he breathed deeply the fresh morning air. The smell of coffee spilled out the door behind him, causing him to grin. Maggie was busy about the kitchen cleaning up after breakfast. He heard boys begging to go fishing after they finished their chores.

Hiram cast a slow surveying glance around the small fort, a square enclosure of posts set firmly in the ground, close to each other, each about fifteen feet tall. Directly opposite the blockhouse where he and his family lived was another rough-hewn blockhouse where his brother Ned and his family called home.

Traveling from Denver, they had arrived here at Fort Bonneville in the Wyoming Territory in the late spring when the weather was warm, and the blossoming of the plains had filled their hearts with dreams and grand futures.

In defiance of the mocking, jeers and counsel against staying in the abandoned fort, he and Ned had quickly claimed it as they believed it was situated perfectly to establish a trading post, despite the title of 'Fort Nonsense' or 'Bonneville's Folly.' After all, it had once been a trading post years before; why couldn't it be one again?

The door of the other blockhouse opened, and Ned stepped out, a cup of coffee in hand. Seeing Hiram, he wiggled his fingers in a wave and strolled across the compound.

"Mornin' Hiram."

"Mornin' Ned," he replied.

"I was thinkin' about what we talked about last night," Ned said. "We need to stake out our land claim as far as we can, both sides of the river. There's room here to raise cattle."

"That's fine," Hiram countered, "if we wanna be ranchers. Be a heap lot less trouble to be the middleman. Let other's raise 'em and we can sell 'em."

Ned was about to point out the benefits of cattle ranching when they both heard the noise of engines. They looked up in time to see a strange flying machine skim overhead.

"What the hell?" Ned exclaimed and ran to the front gates, pushing them open then raced out in the open to see the machine slow down to a hover then slowly turn.

Hiram ran up to stand beside him, his mouth gaping wide.

"What is it?" he asked, stunned at the airborne machine that had no air envelope.

The machine was a series of rectangular shapes in the form of a cross, all held up by a number of propellers spinning furiously causing the machine to quiver. There was a single pilot in front.

17

They watched as the airship turned in a wide arc to where the pilot was now facing them. It wasn't until the soft dirt in front of them began churning and spitting followed by the retorts of gun fire that they realized too late the man in the airship was shooting at them.

Turning to flee, they were felled by penetrating rounds that peppered their bodies and continued on up to the gates where Hiram's horrified wife and sons stood framed by the open gateway. Stunned to immobility, she turned too late and crumpled to the ground, her youngest son dead beside her.

The older boy, sensing the destruction had dodged to the side only to turn back to see his mother and brother shredded by repeated rounds from a Gatling gun.

He heard the wail of terror and pain as his aunt stepped out from the other blockhouse, rifle in hand, to see the commotion and was herself cut down.

The older boy curled himself tight and wedged into the corner where the blockhouse and wall joined, shivering in fear, his arms over his head for protection as the airship made repeated passes over the fort, each time spewing its volume of projectiles, splintering and destroying the fort until half the walls had both blockhouses been reduced to rubble.

It wasn't until the sounds of the engine had long faded that the boy uncurled and stood, brushing the bits and chips of wood from his body. Rubbing his eyes with the heels of his palms, he blinked at the destruction.

Walking to the gate, he stared down at his mother and brother, their sightless eyes glazed in death. His head slowly swiveled to gaze out to the open fields beyond the fort where his father and uncle lay sprawled on the ground, his uncle's arm draped awkwardly over his father's head.

Turning, he trudged back to the remains of the blockhouse, digging through the rubble to find a shovel or a spade. Though he was only nine years old, he knew the dead had to be buried. After that, he would have to move on, follow the river south. There were families farther down the river and one of them would likely take him in.

It was late afternoon by the time Mason had worked his way through the town. Deciding to check on Belle, he headed down Fifth Street, passing the still smoking ruins then over across Allen Street. The Bird Cage was doing a brisk business as the miners needed a place to unwind as many of their watering holes had been destroyed in the fire.

Music of *Little Mollie Brown* emanating from the Polyphon assaulted him as soon as he opened the door. The Polyphon Music Box, standing against the wall opposite the bar, was taller than most men. Made of richly carved walnut, it had a glass front that displayed the large metal music disc being played. To play a song, one pulled open the base and selected a music disc. Opening the glass front, one would remove the large disc of the previous song and replace it with the new selection. In order to hear the song, a silver dollar was inserted into the slot on the side of the Polyphon.

Mason glanced over at the bar, custom made of cherry wood with a diamond-dust mirror, to see a crisply dressed bartender in white apron, an older man with broad moustache, serving a drink to Belle, who stood amidst the crush of admirers.

One of them, a miner by the layers of dirt on him, looked up and saw Mason, lifting his shot glass in toast.

"Howdy Marshal," he exclaimed above the music. "C'mon and have a drink with us. Yer a man to thank fer bringin' our Miss Belle back safe."

Belle turned around and smiled affectionately at him. Mason could see that she was as tired as he was.

Walking over to the bar, he nodded at the bartender while those around Belle glad-handed him on the back. The bartender placed a shot glass on the bar counter then poured a shot of the best whiskey in the house.

"You more than deserve this," the bartender said. "This one's on me."

"Thanks Jack," Mason acknowledged and held his glass up in toast. Gazing directly at Belle, he said, "To the most beautiful woman in all the Arizona Territory."

19

Belle blushed as the men cheered and downed their drinks.

"Now gentlemen," Mason said. "If you will excuse us, I'd like to take Miss Belle out to get a bite to eat."

While the coterie of admirers protested, Belle leaned over the bar to tell Jack that she wouldn't be back tonight.

"I'm not surprised," he replied, giving her an avuncular smile. "Get some sleep. We'll still be here when you wake up."

Patting his hand in thanks, she slipped an arm around Mason's arm, bidding adieu to her coterie whose eyes followed Mason with stares of envy.

Once outside, Belle fluttered her blouse and said, "I need a bath more than food."

"Me too," Mason said, suddenly aware of his own piquant odor.

Escorting Belle back to her boarding house, Mason said, "I'll meet you back here."

"I look forward to it," she smiled then kissed him.

As Belle went inside the boarding house, Mason headed up 2nd Street wondering how long was long enough to wait before he came back. If he had his way, he'd be back as soon as he had a bath, shaved and got dressed, which in his case wouldn't take more than twenty minutes. But women needed more time, he reminded himself.

It was as he sat in the round wooden tub that had been hauled into his bedroom that he determined he and Belle would have a real bathtub made of cast iron with clawed feet where one could stretch out. The thought reminded him of the luxury of the home he had in San Francisco when he was married to Elizabeth.

The house was extravagantly large with more rooms and furniture than he could have used in a lifetime, all paid for by her father. The lifestyle of the rich still amazed him. Houses filled with expensive art and sculptures that once acquired were then forgotten, left to hang on the wall or sit neglected on a pedestal to be dusted by the servants. Then all handed down and divided amongst the children who rarely ever turned out like their parents.

As Mason soaped up, he wondered how soon it would be before his father-in-law sent men to kill him. That thought morphed to the kind of men he would send. Those local thugs of San Francisco would stick out here in Tombstone. Most likely, Worthington would send men who would blend in, requiring Mason to be especially vigilant.

Yet he knew one thing was certain. Worthington would not stop until one of them was dead. Mason wondered if he ought to take the battle to Worthington.

It was more than an hour later when Mason stood outside her door, refreshed and smelling like a dandified college boy out on a first date. Shaking his head, he wondered what was different now? Why did he suddenly feel awkward?

The door opened and he sucked in his breath. Belle stood before him dressed in a tight-bodice royal blue dinner dress with a décolletage that showed the hints of ample cleavage. Her long blond hair was curled and fell about her shoulders.

He would have remained there gaping had Belle not playfully laughed and said, "Close your mouth and come in."

"You're stunning," he said with reverent breath.

"Like it?" she asked, twirling around in display.

"The dress is fine," he said. "It's what's in it that is stunning."

"That was sweet," she smiled, coming up and kissing him. "I've had dinner prepared for us here."

She stepped to the side and Mason noticed a small table set for two with another table close by with covered dishes.

"I hope you're hungry," she said, pulling out a chair for him then lifting the cover off a plate and setting it before him.

"Oysters?" he said, surprised then looked at Belle with half-lidded eyes. "I don't think I'll need those."

Mason woke just as dawn was spilling over the mountains. Belle's head nestled on his shoulder, her breath slow and peaceful. An arm draped over his chest.

Twisting his head so as not to disturber her slumber, he searched for a clock and found the mantel clock on the bureau.   It was about 5:20, much too early to get up, especially when he had the beautiful Belle next to him.

His mind drifted to the previous evening's romantic interlude. The dinner had been excellent and was a fitting prelude to the later enjoyments. Once dinner was finished, Bell had collected the plates and set them on a tray outside her door. She then poured two glasses of a fine vintage port and they talked for a while, especially about their future together.

Mason had a second glass of port and before he was halfway through, he could stand it no longer. Placing the half-filled port glass on the table, he stood and reached a hand to Belle, pulling her to standing.

"I think we've talked enough," he huskily said.

"I quite agree," she said, a smile curling the corners of her lips.

"So what should we do?"

"I have an idea," she answered then took a step back and began unbuttoning the front of her dress.

What followed was beyond anything Mason had experienced for Belle was voracious and tender at the same time. It was near midnight before they fell asleep, beautifully exhausted.

He chastised himself for being awake so early, especially since there was nowhere either of them had to be. His mind then drifted to the past few days. Henry Mitchell had truly done him a favor when he murdered Elizabeth.

He frowned with a flash of guilt. Should he really be happy that his wife was murdered? Elizabeth, the pampered, head-strong daughter of Reginald Worthington, the wealthy San Francisco magnate, had been a stunner in her prime. Sadly, she was still in her prime, but her beauty had vanished with her discovery of laudanum. Laudanum has soothed the pains of moving from the glorious balls and festivities of upper crust San Francisco to the crude and ramshackle wild west of the Arizona territory.

The past year here had been a living hell with her. It began the moment he told her that he would quit working for her father.

"You're going to quit?" Elizabeth's eyes burst wide in consternation.

"I hate working there," he said. "I'm cooped up in some stuffy office pouring over stupid ledgers and business deals and I hate it. I'm suffocating."

"But you're making good money and I'm sure it's only a matter of time before Father makes you a partner."

Mason burst a derisive laugh. "Your father hates me. He's hated me from the moment you introduced me to him."

"He doesn't hate you," she unconvincingly replied.

"Good god, Elizabeth. Wake up. With all the time we spend at balls and symphonies and gala affairs, can't you see the way they look at me? It's with pity, but not for me; it's for you. You married so far below your station that your life is ruined."

"No it's not," she stiffly answered. "We'll show them. When you become a partner with father, they'll see."

"Elizabeth," he sighed. "Stop dreaming. Your father will never make me a partner. He barely tolerates me as it is."

"But we're doing so well," she pouted.

"Think so?" he huffed then swept his arms wide at the expensive Victorian Jacobean furnishings in the living room. "Where did all this furniture come from? Your father. We haven't paid for a single item in this house. Why? Because anything you want, your father gives it to you."

"You don't like it?" she frowned, shifting her gaze from the exquisitely hand-carved chimney piece to the monumental sideboard with carved images of fish, game, fruit and other greenery.

"Whether I like it or not is not the point," he sourly said. "You may like living on your father's income, but I don't, and I won't. That's why I'm quitting."

"What do you want to do?" she asked, afraid of his answer.

"I'm going to become a lawman." He folded his arms as if to say the issue was settled

Elizabeth trembled and flopped down into a chair. "A lawman," she repeated, "like one of those common men at some plebian precinct, where the dregs of humanity assemble?"

"No," he half-smiled, "out west, in the Arizona territory."

Her mouth slowly gaped open as she stared at him with horror that soon morphed to cold hatred.

Her father was apoplectic when he heard the news.

"You're a damned fool, man," his father-in-law blustered when he comprehended Mason's plans. They were standing in the billiard room of the extravagant home up on the hillside overlooking the bay. Elizabeth had wisely excused herself and closed the doors, thus removing herself from her father's wrath, all the while hoping he would talk some sense to her foolish husband.

"You've got a fine job with the company, a fine home, and a fine wife. You're on your way up in this world. Why in the blazes do you want to give that all away just to go to some godforsaken hell hole swarming with Indians and Mexicans, just to wear some fool lawman's badge?"

Mason's first impulse was to say, 'Because you're smothering me and my ambitions. Your only child, my wife, is used to having Papa give her everything she ever wanted. I can't do that. I'm not like you. In fact, I don't *want* to be like you. This city is choking me. Your so-called friends with their façade of refinement are all part of an obscene game. If you weren't so rich, they wouldn't even piss on you if you were on fire. Any time I do or say something your daughter doesn't like, she runs back to you and I'm called to stand here to listen to you lecture me.'

Instead, he resolutely replied, "It is what I want to do."

"What the hell for?" Worthington snapped.

"Because," Mason calmly replied, liking the shift in power, "it is what I want to do. It is what I intend to do."

"Don't think you're taking her with you. I won't allow it," his father-in-law imperiously stated.

"You don't have a choice," Mason shot back, his bile rising. "She's my wife and I'll take her where I damn well please."

Worthington was startled to an abrupt silence, unused to anyone contradicting him, let alone raising his voice to him.

"You leave now, I'll cut you off," he threatened. "I'll cut her off. You won't get a penny from me. And when you come crawling back here out of the cesspit of the Arizona territory, you'll have nothing. I won't be here to help you."

"I don't need your damned help and I don't *want* your damned help. We're leaving. And that's the end of it." With that, Mason had jerked the door open to a cold and resentful Elizabeth who turned her back on him and marched off to wait for him in the carriage outside.

When the time came for them to leave, he had agreed to take an airship, though he had wanted to go by train. However, he had adamantly refused to pay for it stating that he had fare for the train and an airship was far too expensive. If they wanted her to go by airship, they could pay for it. And her father did, more by way of insult than olive branch.

Though not as long as by train, the trip to Bisbee was painful. Elizabeth was more than petulant, she was hateful. The few times she did speak to him during the trip, it was to castigate him for the fool's journey they were embarking upon. By the time they arrived in Bisbee, he was half-tempted to send her back.

The airship trip was downright pleasant compared to what happened after the stagecoach dropped them off in Tombstone. Standing in the hot dusty street, their baggage on the ground surrounding them, she had stared malevolently at him and said, "You're going to hell for bringing me here." She promptly sat down on a trunk and refused to move until a buckboard nearly ran her over.

It never got any better after that. Elizabeth politely ignored or refused the invitations of the Tombstone gentry as beneath her attention. After a while, the invitations dried up. But it mattered little, for by then she had discovered laudanum, which the doctors here were only too willing to dispense. After repeated rejections of his warnings, Mason had gone so far as to tell the doctors to refuse to give her any more. But she always managed to find more.

And then she discovered the pleasures of Hoptown's opium. Once that Rubicon was crossed, she no longer cared where she was. But what he couldn't figure out was how she was getting it and how she was paying for it. He had already told all the doctors and everyone in Hoptown that he would not pay for anything they gave her. If they wanted to give her drugs, then they could pay for it.

Then Henry Mitchell showed up and Elizabeth's problems were solved.

Mason's memories shifted to the time her father's agent showed up and Mason had politely informed him that Elizabeth was dead. The agent was horrified, and rightfully so. One could only imagine the fate of the messenger when Worthington was told the news that his only child was dead.

Mason knew that his troubles had just begun. His father-in-law's hatred would be mild in comparison to the vengeance he would wreak, and he had the money to make it happen. It abruptly dawned on him that once Worthington discovered Mason's affection for Belle, Belle's life was also in danger.

Yet his most immediate problem was how to slide out of bed without waking her. Despite his best effort, she awoke when he tried sliding his arm out from beneath her head.

"It's still the middle of the night," she mumbled, blinking up at him. "What time is it?"

"It's about 5:30."

"Why are you awake?"

"I just am," he shrugged.

Rolling on to her back, she yawned and rubbed her eyes with the heels of her palms. "Coffee."

"You sure you want to get up?" he grinned.

"I can always take a nap later," she said, pushing herself up to sit on the edge of the bed.

Standing on the opposite side of the bed, Mason smiled at her. Even with her tousled hair and rumpled nightgown, she was beautiful.

Slipping on his pants and shirt, he buckled his belt and wrapped his gun belt around his waist. "I'll go see if there's any coffee downstairs."

Looking over her shoulder, Belle gave him an appreciative smile.

By the time Mason returned with two steaming cups of coffee, Belle was dressed and sat before the dressing table, arranging her hair.

"Thank you," she sighed, accepting a cup and taking a savoring sip of the dark hot and piquant brew.

"Breakfast will be a little bit," he said, unbuckling his gun belt and hanging it on the hook by the door. "She just started making the biscuits."

"Coffee's fine for now," she replied, setting it down by the mirror. Curling her hair into a bun on the back of her head, she smiled coyly at his reflection. "Thank you for last night."

"Any time," he grinned, bending down to kiss her neck.

Standing behind her, he placed a hand on her shoulders and rubbed his cheek. "Unless you want me to look like a grizzly bear, I need to go back to my place to clean up."

"Don't be long," she smiled and patted his hand.

"I won't." He bent down again, turning her face to his and planted a lingering kiss. "I'll meet you back here for breakfast," he said, locking her eyes with his. "We have lots to talk about."

"Oh?" she coquettishly replied. "I can't wait."

When Mason returned, he found Belle downstairs sipping a cup of coffee, talking with another resident of the boarding house, a lanky young man hoping to work as a reporter for the *Epitaph*.

"Looks like you arrived just in time," Mason said after the introductions.

"I know," he replied, eyes bright with excitement. "Mister Reppy said because I helped out during the fire, he would look to see if he could find a place for me."

"Where do you hail from, Roger?" Mason asked.

"Missouri," he answered with a grin as Missus Hunt entered with a bowl of hot biscuits covered with a towel.

"How you want your steak and eggs?" she asked.

Missus Hunt, a widower, was a slender pleasant looking woman with sandy colored hair. She had been in Tombstone since early 1880. Her husband had been a miner and died when a cave-in crushed his chest.

"Rare and over easy," Mason replied.

"I'll take the same," Roger said, following Mason's direction.

"Just eggs for me please, Missus Hunt," Belle sweetly replied.

With a crisp nod, Missus Hunt placed the biscuits on the table and headed back into the kitchen.

"What brought you to Tombstone?" Mason asked, lifting the cloth covering the biscuits then handing one to Belle.

"I got interested in the newspaper business when Mister Reppy was the editor of the *Jefferson County Leader* in Hillsboro. When I found out that he had moved on to Tombstone, I figured I'd show up and see if he'd let me work for him."

"So you knew him before you came here?" Belle asked, spreading butter on a half a biscuit.

"Not really, just by reputation," he answered. "But when I told him that I was from Hillsboro, he was mighty pleased. I was in his office when the fire broke out."

Mason and Belle exchanged glances, which Roger noticed.

"You know something about it?" he asked.

"Just what I told the folks yesterday," Mason explained. "A man named Henry Mitchell started the fire."

"How do you know that?" Roger asked, though not too dumbfounded to pull out a piece of paper and a pencil. "Is that Mitchell with one 'l' or two?"

"Two," Mason smiled then related the whole story of Caleb's murder and Belle's rescue while Roger furiously wrote, covering his scrap of paper before realizing he needed more paper.

"This is an incredible story," Roger gushed. "Just wait 'til Mister Reppy hears about this."

"I think Mister Reppy is probably more interested in the fire," Belle opined.

"But your story has all the excitement of a train robbery," he replied. "Folks like things like that." Turning to Mason, he said, "Can I sit down with you later this morning and get the whole story again?"

"Probably after lunch," Mason replied, "depending on what's going on."

"Thanks, Marshal," he said, his mouth watering when the door to the kitchen opened and Missus Hunt came in, balancing three plates.

Breakfast finished, the three stood outside next to the MATE. Roger gaped in astonishment.

"It looks like a midget locomotive, except it has conveyer belts around the wheels," he marveled.   "Where's the smokestack?"

Belle pointed to two long brass tubes that ran from the front of the boiler near the crest and along both sides, ending just below the driver's platform.   "The tubes are hollow containers. The front of the tube is open to the air coming from the front of the machine. In the front of each tube is a fan that sucks the smoke up and pushes it out the back. The fans don't need anything to make them spin because they're like whirligigs. When the MATE goes forward, it causes them to spin, which pushes the smoke out the back."

Roger shook his head in wonder. "Who'd have thought to have the smoke come out the back of the engine?"

"It makes it easier to see what's in front," she explained.

"I know. How do you steer it?"

"There are two levers. One controls the right side and the other the left," she said. "They act like brakes and releases. For example, if you hold the right lever back, you stop the right side while the left side still runs. You can turn in a complete circle."

"We really do need to get going," Mason interrupted.

"Do we have enough wood in the tinder box?" she asked. "We'll need wood to fuel the boiler."

Giving her a bemused smile, he stepped up on the wheel tread.

"We have enough to get us there," he remarked. "We can fill up when we get there."

"We're you headed?" Roger asked, his curiosity obvious.

"Get my saddle," Mason explained. "It's still attached to my dead horse. I'm going to use this machine to help me retrieve it."

Roger nodded in understanding.

"Don't you have a newspaper to go help," he reminded him.

"Yup," he said, his eyes lighting up. "Guess I'd better get to work. Pleasure meeting you, Miss Belle, Marshal." He pinched the brim of his derby at Belle then walked off in long strides.

Helping Belle up to the driver's platform, Mason climbed down to the tinder box and started collecting deadwood while Belle worked on stoking the low embers in the fire box. Mason made several trips, depositing armloads of dry mesquite and dead limbs. By the last run, Belle had pressure building and was in position.

"Swing by my place so I can get a length of rope.," he said, sitting next to her.

With a grin, she bumped her shoulder against him. "Ready cowboy? Let's see how fast this thing will move."

"Why don't we wait until we're out of town?"

"You're no fun." She pushed the Johnson bar forward and opened the cylinder cocks. Releasing the engine brakes, she opened the throttle and the MATE lurched forward.

Locking the left side, she caused the MATE to churn in a tight circle. Releasing the brake, they headed back down Toughnut Street and then right on 2nd Street to head towards Mason's room at Pascholy's Boarding House at the corner of 2nd and Safford.

Stopping briefly while Mason ran inside to retrieve a coiled length of rope, they were soon headed out on Contention Road. A mile out from Watervale, they passed John Doling's Tombstone Driving Park as they headed towards the Dragoon Mountains.

"Far more pleasant ride this time, eh?" Mason teased.

"I had to ride in the trailer, and I was all tied up," she said.

"Hmmm… all tied up," he smiled mischievously at her.

She flashed a smile at him. "You think he's still there?"

"I don't know. I just hope Caleb and De la Fuente are gone, with their gold."

He scanned the level terrain before them. The air was clean and the day was breaking glorious in sunshine. Belle steered the MATE along the same path that Henry had taken when he was forced into the Dragoons.

"We need to think about our future," Mason broached.

Belle smiled wide in satisfaction. "Is that a proposal U.S. Marshal Mason Sadler?"

Momentarily confused, Mason grinned when he realized what he had said. "In a way, I suppose, though that's not the way I would have asked. But I'll get around to that shortly," he quickly added when he saw her disappointment.

"So what about our future?"

"The more immediate problem is that my former father-in-law knows by now that his only child is dead. He hated me from the moment he met me."

"Why?"

"I wasn't good enough for his daughter. Didn't come from the right part of society. When I told him I was taking his precious daughter to Tombstone, his hatred hardened even more. Unfortunately, with his daughter dead, he will blame me."

"So what you're saying is that you can expect a visit from some of his employees?"

"Yes," he replied, "and not just me. His hatred will know no bounds and will only be satisfied when I'm dead... me and anyone I love." He paused to let that sink in.

"So I'm in trouble too," she said, matter-of-factly.

"Especially when he finds out that you and I were friends before she died, regardless of the fact that nothing ever happened between us."

"Not that I didn't it want to," she mumbled.

"What?"

"I said 'what do think we should do?'"

"We have to be especially careful and vigilant," he answered. "We need to enlist the help of everyone we can. I have a feeling the people he sends won't care who else gets hurt."

"I'm not going to live in fear," she unapologetically said. "I'll get the Bird Cage folks to help out. We'll get ears on the ground before they show up."

"Wonder if I can get Ringo to help. Seems the sort of challenge he might enjoy."

"And anyone else good with a gun," she added. "Pity Doc Holliday isn't here anymore."

"Last I heard he was up in Colorado," Mason replied. "Anyway, trouble seems to follow him."

Belle slowed the MATE down as they came to the spot where Henry had been forced off the main road into the chaparral by bombs dropped from the airships of Taboca and Nantan, the tread marks plainly visible leading off towards the mountains. Charred earth marked where the bombs hit.

"Last time I came this way, I was a prisoner," Belle observed.

"It wasn't for long though," Mason comforted.

"It was long enough," she said then chuckled. "Not sure what I saw in him. It was funny that I called him Mason when we were together." She gazed at him and patted his leg. "Tells you where my head and heart were."

Mason smiled back at her then shifted his gaze to the front as the trail led into the rugged terrain and into a maze of teetering boulders, steep hillsides and increasing presence of sycamores, oaks, and underbrush.

Belle slowed down even more, twisting her head side to side as she relived the experience of being kidnapped.

When they rounded a large outcropping, they saw the dead steed on its side, flies buzzing around the face.

Belle brought the MATE to a stop while Mason dismounted then helped her down.

"He's gone," Belle exclaimed, staring at the spot not more than fifty feet away where Henry had been spread-eagled on the ground. The four posts were still in the ground.

Mason bypassed the dead horse to crouch down and inspect the posts. "They're not cut. It's as though someone untied him."

He stood up, hands jammed on his hips as he slowly scanned the surrounding trees and vegetation. Looking over his shoulder at Belle, he said, "Leave it for now. Let's see if we can find out where they went."

The trail was marked at first as it snaked its way further into the dense growth. Footprints in the dirt were easy to see and overlapped going back and forwards. Obviously, they were transporting the gold boxes to a safer place. They had not yet traveled a quarter mile when the trail abruptly disappeared. Mason pushed on for another hundred yards but found nothing.

Retracing his steps, he led Belle back to the spot where the trail ended and searched the surrounding terrain. There were few possibilities as the rocks and steep hillsides prohibited deviation from the path.

"Did we miss a turn off earlier?" he said with a frown.

"We might have," Belle replied though unconvinced.

Mason led the way as they headed back to the MATE, slower this time to carefully scrutinize where they might have left the trail. They knew no one had deviated from the trail when they were within sight of the MATE.

"Check around the area here," Mason said, coming to the clearing and walking off in one direction while Belle headed the opposite way.

They spent the next hour combing the area searching for any trace of Henry or the dead men.

"This doesn't make any sense," Mason said, shaking his head, standing in the center of the small oak grove where he had rescued Belle two days ago. "While I appreciate their disappearance, Henry should still be here."

Folding her arms, Belle stared at the spot on the ground where Henry had been staked out. Tilting her head to the left, she said, "Henry was a smooth talker. You think he might have talked his way out of this?"

"I don't see how," Mason replied. "Why would Caleb forgive and forget that Henry murdered him? And I doubt that De la Fuente would be so charitable seeing as Henry was stealing his gold. That's the part that doesn't make sense. Henry should be spread out on the ground, dead, or at least close to being dead."

"On the positive side," Belle offered, "if we can't find them, then perhaps no one else will."

"Perhaps you're right." He lifted his Stetson and smoothed his hair back, settling his hat again. "In the meantime, I got a saddle that needs attention. Swing the MATE around to the other side of my horse while I undo the saddle."

Mason walked over to the MATE with her and retrieved the length of rope. While she tossed more fuel into the fire box, Mason walked back to stare at his horse, shaking his head in disappointment.

"You were a good partner. Pity it had to end like this."

Bending down, he released the cinch strap and pulled it free. He then tied the rope around a front leg pastern, further looping it around the other front leg pastern and repeating the process with the two hind legs then pulled them together as best he could so that in the end it looked like the horse had been calf roped.

Belle positioned the MATE as Mason had asked and waited while he secured the end to the trailer behind the machine. Walking to the other side of the animal, he grabbed the saddle by the horn and the cantle.

"OK. Pull forward, slowly."

As Belle dragged the horse with her, Mason held onto the saddle, finally freeing it when the cinch strap and saddle pad were clear. Giving it a quick inspection, he was pleased that it was still in excellent condition. Placing saddle and blanket in the trailer behind the MATE, he climbed up to sit beside her.

"Ready?"

"More than you'll ever know," she grinned. "We're going to need more fuel."

"Ah yes," he replied. "Forgot about that."

Hopping down, he helped her down and together they collected enough dead wood to fill up the tinder box.

Belle brushed her hands and leaned against the trailer. "So," she said, gazing coyly at Mason. "Where do we go from here?"

"Back to town," he replied, the answer obvious.

"No. I mean us, you and me. Where do we go from here?"

Mason stared at her a moment, his heart and mind racing. Last night had been far better than he had ever imagined, but was he ready for marriage again, so soon after Elizabeth's death?

His rational part took over and he told himself that while he had been legally married, his marriage had ended the day he told Elizabeth they were going to Arizona. What had passed for a marriage this past year was nothing more than two people living together, roommates who hated each other, more than husband and wife. Truth was, he had stopped loving her when she decided her father was more important to her than he was.

If he were honest with himself, he would have to admit that Belle captivated him in ways that Elizabeth never did. Belle was full of the excitement of life, unafraid to experience all she could. If only he had met her first, they wouldn't have to live looking over their shoulders.

But 'if only' was the stuff of dreams. What was here and now was what mattered. Elizabeth was dead and he was not going to berate himself for bringing her here. He had a future, and it was with Belle.

If he were honest with himself, he would tell her that he was head over heels in love with her.

"Um," he hesitated, her piercing blue eyes locked onto his. "Where would you like to go from here?"

Belle stood and turned to him, gently placing a hand on his chest. "I think after last night, it's pretty obvious where I want to go from here."

"Me too," he huskily replied.

"Then why don't you say it," she challenged, her eyes taunting him. "A girl has a right to hear it said."

Mason looked away a moment, took a deep breath then returned to gaze intently at her. "Will you marry me, Belle?"

"Yes, Mason, I will, but there's something you should know."

Mason frown in apprehension. "What?"

"My real name is Katherine."

"Katherine," he repeated with a half-smile. "I'd forgotten about that. I had figured your real name wasn't Belle Dubois, but I never thought more about it."

"I like the way you say it," she said, standing on her tiptoes to kiss him.

"What's your last name?"

"Gilmartin."

"Katherine Gilmartin," he said, nodding with a smile. "I like it. It's a strong name, fitting a woman like you."

"I'll take that as a compliment." She tweaked his nose. "So Mister Marshal Mason Sadler, when?"

"When?" he startled, suddenly nervous.

"Yes, when," she smiled at him. "You've proposed, now it's time to set a date."

Mason cleared his throat. "Uh... whenever's fine with me."

"That's good. I'd hate to think of the gossip if they all thought we were simply living together."

"Like we don't have enough gossip as it is? Who cares what they think?" He stared at her wondering if marriage at this point was such a smart decision, especially with Worthington looking to kill them. But, he reasoned, it didn't matter if they were married or not. Worthington wanted them both dead. Besides, if something did happen to them, he'd rather it be with the woman he loved as his wife.

"So how about right now?" she slyly asked.

Mason cocked an eyebrow at her. "Now? We need to get a parson to do the ceremony?"

"I bet Reverend Peabody might be available."

"We need some witnesses," he pointed out.

"I'll just get one of the girls from the Theater."

Mason thought for a moment. "Wonder if Ringo's in town."

Belle brightened and giggled. "Now there's a combination for the history books. US Marshal marries Bird Cage madam, local gunslinger is best man."

Mason gave her a half-smile when a thought broke through. "This will probably impact our little business at the Bird Cage."

"We'll see," she nonchalantly shrugged. "In the meantime, I've collected a nice little nest egg we can use for a house."

"I've got some too," he said. "We don't need a big place, just quiet enough so we're the ones making the noise."

"Someplace in town?"

"Or maybe out towards Watervale," he said. "We don't want to be too far from work."

"What about your former father-in-law?" she asked, stepping on the tread then onto the pilot platform.

"What about him? I don't see him coming to the wedding."

"Very funny," she smirked. "What I mean is, do we want a place in town where other people can keep a watch, or on our own outside of town?"

"Both have merit," he said. "But I don't want to live like that. While he may be at the top of our list of problems, we have other obligations to worry about too. I want a place where we can be far enough away from folks so we can have some privacy."

"That would be nice, though I don't see that happening," she said. "You're a Marshal and any time something happens, they'll be looking for you."

"True enough," he nodded agreement. "Guess we'd better head on back and find that parson. Besides, I still need a horse."

"So do I," she said, "preferably one that draws a carriage. After all, a madam has to travel in style."

"What about your MATE?" he grinned.

"Not exactly something you can just hop on and ride away," she pointed out. "Anyway, Nantan and Taboca will be borrowing it for a while, so I'll need other transportation." Gazing down at him with a firm stare, she said, "Let's go, cowboy. We've got important business to attend to."

"Yes, Mam," he chuckled, climbing up to sit next to her.

Chapter 2

Harold Tiebot adjusted his tie as he nervously approached the tall twin oak doors to Reginald Worthington's outer office. Pausing, he cleared his throat then pushed open the door.

A petite officious looking woman of middle age dressed in no-nonsense high collar and narrow skirt, her hair in a tight bun at the back of her head, sat behind a wide desk. Just behind her to her left was another set of tall richly varnished mahogany doors leading to Worthington's personal office. She looked up as he entered. Giving him a brief lips-only smile, she said, "He's in conference at the moment. Please take a seat." Assuming she would be obeyed without question, she returned her attention to the paperwork spread before her on the desk.

Harold crossed the room to the row of large, over-stuffed burgundy leather chairs arranged with precision against the wall. He stood for a moment deliberating which chair to select when the tall doors opened. Several men in somber grey and black suits and stiff-collared shirts adorned with impeccably tied cravats emerged. One or two noticed him and gave him a polite, yet reserved, nod of recognition.

When the last gentleman passed through the doors, he closed them behind him. The men wordlessly vanished, and the outer office grew oppressively quiet as Harold seated himself at the edge of a chair in the middle and waited for the secretary to announce him. Instead, she continued her fastidious attention to the papers on the desk, comparing entries in a ledger against listings in a thick register, occasionally making notes on the edges of the ledger.

Wondering if the woman had forgotten him, Harold cleared his throat hoping to gain her attention. Yet she either ignored him or didn't hear him. He cleared his throat again, a little louder this time, but the results were the same. His shoulders slumping in defeat, he scooted back into the depths of the cushions and waited. As he rehearsed how he was going to tell Mister Worthington that his daughter was dead, the rhythmic ticking of the wall clock pierced his awareness, and he unconsciously began to count the seconds as though a convicted man counting down the last seconds of his life.

When twenty minutes had passed, his nervousness could no longer be controlled. Better to get it over with now than keep delaying the inevitable. Standing, he approached the desk.

"Begging your pardon," he ventured, "but I fear the news I have for Mister Worthington is of such grave consequences that I am sure he would want to be notified immediately upon my arrival."

Pursing her lips at the interruption, the woman placed the pen down on the desktop in a slow and deliberate motion. Folding one hand over the other, both on top of the ledger, she stared imperially at him. "And what are these grave consequences that demands Mister Worthington's attention?"

Harold hesitated only a moment. "I believe the news is meant for Mister Worthington's ears first. If you recall, I was here a few weeks ago to receive an assignment from Mister Worthington concerning his daughter."

"Yes," she indifferently replied, "I remember."

"The report I have for him concerns his daughter," he evasively explained. He shifted uncomfortably under the woman's cold gaze.

She was silent for a few moments then reached for the telephone on the right side of her desk. It was an ornate affair with polished oak housing and a brass magneto generator crank on the side. The receiver's ivory handle, mouth and earpieces were separated by silver couplings. Lifting the receiver from the silver cradle on top, she placed it on the desktop then turned the crank several times.

Putting the receiver to her ear, she waited. "Mister Tiebot is here with news about your daughter. Yes sir." Placing the receiver back onto the cradle, she directed a quick glance at the doors to Worthington's office. "You may go in now." She resumed her work as Harold gathered up his courage and pushed through the doors.

When Harold entered, the President of Worthington and Son was standing at the edge of his desk, staring out the window. Reginald Worthington was a tall humorless man with a shock of brown hair greying at the temples. In contrast to the mostly bearded men in his company, he wore a Van Dyke that he smoothed with his fingers when pensive. Even now he had his left arm across his lean stomach propping up his right arm as he smoothed the hairs at his chin. Lost in thought when Harold entered, he continued ignoring him while he pondered.

Worthington and Son had initially been Worthington and Sons as Reginald had an older brother who preferred to enjoy the fruits of their father's labor rather than spend the time either learning or running the business. In marked contrast to his older brother's cavalier approach to his future, Reginald submerged himself into the very core of their father's empire. As time progressed, their father recognized his youngest son's talents and Reginald became his father's confidant even before he entered his teenage years. As the older brother continued to squander his father's trust, Reginald solidified his position as the heir to the corporation, quietly amassing knowledge of the secret and inner-workings of the vast conglomerate.

Reginald was more than obedient to his father's stern and consistent guidance, even to the point of marrying for status. "Marrying for love is a fool's ambition," his father had warned. "Find a woman who knows her place." Yet the most important wisdom was repeated often: "Remember. You are a Worthington. Nothing else matters. To be a Worthington is to accept nothing less than victory. To crush one's enemies is glorious." He had watched his father ruthlessly squash opponents and anyone or thing that got in the way of his ambition.

By the time of their father's abrupt demise, Reginald had learned his lessons well. He had earned a reputation for ruthlessness that exceeded his father's feared reputation, leading some to wonder if the son wasn't responsible for the old man's death. By then, Reginald had all but eliminated his older brother from any claim to the business. With his father finally out of the way, Reginald struck and removed his brother from any ownership apart from the shares their father had bequeathed him.

Yet the bond of family held firm… for a while. Reginald provided his brother a monthly stipend, but as the elder sibling's wanton lifestyle began to incur greater cost and demands, Reginald determined to put a stop to it, a permanent stop. His older brother disappeared not long after, never to be heard or seen again.

That was not too long after Elizabeth was born, before the doctor told him that if he wanted his wife to live, they would have no more children. Reginald had thought long and hard about the doctor's words and determined that the doctor could go to hell. He would continue to perform his functions as a husband, his wife's health be damned. If she died, she died. He could always find another wife, one who would bear him sons.

But his wife defied the odds and survived his coarse ministrations. Yet no children were ever produced beyond the daughter. As the years progressed, his efforts diminished and he turned his attention to the future of his business and the children of his brother. He provided for their welfare, especially his nephew who had all the Worthington traits lacking in the boy's father. It was his nephew's future that he contemplated when Harold slunk through the doors.

Thinking Mister Worthington might not have realized his errand man was in the office, Harold cleared his throat.

Worthington slowly turned to stare at Harold, his look almost reptilian. "What news then?" has asked, his voice emotionless. "Did you give her the money?"

"No, sir," Harold nervously replied.

"No?" he frowned, surprised. "Why not?"

Harold hesitated.

"I said, why not?" he repeated, the chill in his tone making Harold shiver.

"Well, sir," he began. "It's because, uh… it's because, you see sir, I couldn't give her the money because when I found Marshal Sadler in a bar –"

"Sadler!" he snapped. "I told you to deal only with my daughter."

"That's right sir, you did sir, but no one would direct me to her whereabouts, instead pointing me to Marshal Sadler's location. I informed him of my mission and the money, and at first, he refused."

"Typical. The man's a fool."

"Quite right, sir. When I pressed him to direct me to where I might find Lady Elizabeth, I, uh… I was informed, um…"

"Well out with it man," he sternly rebuked him.

Harold swallowed then blurted, "Mister Worthington, sir, I was unable to give the money to Lady Elizabeth, because, sir, your daughter has passed away… that is, she had died, sir."

Worthington's whole body stiffened and his nostrils flared as lips tightened. With a look of cold hatred, he asked, "How did she die?"

"Apparently she died of an overdose of laudanum," he meekly replied.

"Impossible," Worthington sharply retorted. "You are mistaken."

"But sir," Harold began before wilting under the glare of the man's intense stare.

"I said that you are mistaken," he harshly repeated.

"Yes, sir." Harold submissively answered, cowering as though caught in some indiscretion.

"What have you done with the money?"

"It's back in the account, sir."

"You said that Sadler didn't want it?"

"Yes, sir."

"Why not?"

"I don't know, sir. He didn't tell me. All he said was that he didn't want it and for me to return home."

Worthington's icy gaze fixed itself on Harold. "When did she die?"

"A week ago, sir."

"A week ago and I'm just finding out about it now?" he exploded.

"I preferred to tell you in person, sir," Harold quickly explained. "So I hurried back as quickly as I could."

Barely mollified, Worthington simply nodded. "How long before you found out?"

"Marshal Sadler said she had passed away two days before my arrival."

His teeth clenched, Worthington's face solidified into barely controlled rage causing Harold to step backwards. "My daughter dies," he seethed, "and that bastard doesn't have the decency to tell me." Turning his back to Harold, he tilted his head back to stare at the ornately tiled ceiling. "I should have dealt with him when he told me he was leaving." Folding his arms, he said, "Get Clay. I want to see him, immediately."

"Yes, sir." Without waiting for further instructions, Harold fled back through the tall doors and into the less oppressive outer office.

The secretary looked up as he burst through the doors before catching himself and slowly and timorously closing the doors behind him.

Giving him a less than sympathetic glare, she imperiously demanded, "Well?"

"He said to send for Clay," he said, wishing he could flee this smothering place and be free of his obligation so he could return home and get some needed rest.

Oblivious to his discomfit, she said, "Fine. Be sure to file your travel and expense report. Only those meals and lodging necessary to your errand will be accepted."

"I know," he said with a subdued huff. "I've done this before."

Eyeing him as though recognizing him as someone barely above a common worker, she begrudgingly said, "I suppose you have." Returning her attention to her paperwork, she informed him, "You'll be notified when he has need of you again. Please close the doors behind you when you leave."

Clay could have been an attractive man if not for the angry scar that ran from his left ear to the corner of his lips, which gave him the appearance of a constant smirk. Yet his eyes betrayed what might be mistaken for humor for they rarely laughed. Instead, they remained impassively cold, emotionless. He stood before the massive desk in Worthington's office while his benefactor stood off to the side and stared out the window. Running a hand through his shoulder length brown hair, Clay smoothed it against his head, waiting for the chief executive of Worthington and Son to tell him why he was there.

The silence lay heavy for a while until Worthington spoke. His arms folded, he tilted his head back slightly, looking down his nose at the crowds on the streets below. "I want him dead."

"Who?"

"Mason Sadler," came the reply.

"Your son-in-law?"

"Yes."

Clay knew not to ask why but was curious as to what would happen when the daughter found out her father had contracted to kill her husband.

Worthington turned to stare at him. "You have a problem with that?"

"Of course not," he calmly replied. The man did not frighten him like he did so many other people. Besides, Clay knew enough about him to make his life uncomfortable, should it ever become necessary. Until that time, he would perform his role as the muscle, the leverage, to make things agree with the man's whims. Clay didn't care why or who, as long as he was paid.

"I want him to suffer," Worthington stated. "I want anyone he cares about to suffer. I want him to endure pain for a long time. I want him to beg for death."

"He still in Tombstone?" Clay asked.

"Yes."

"I'll take care of it," he replied. "I'll send Braxton. He enjoys that sort of thing."

Worthington fixed him with a sharp eye. "I don't care who you send. I want it done now."

"On my way," he nodded, spinning around and pushing through the doors. Closing the doors behind him, he stood for a moment, musing his assignment. What he remembered of the son-in-law was that he and Worthington did not get along. What he also remembered was that the son-in-law was now a US Marshal. That did put a bit of a burr under the saddle. Still, a job was a job, regardless of the target.

"Well?" the secretary asked, barely hiding her condescension.

Clay regarded her with a cocked eyebrow of disdain. "None of your business."

"But it is my business," she haughtily reminded him. "I'm the one who pays you, don't forget."

Placing both hands on her desk, he leaned in towards her and quietly threatened, "And I'm the one who can make you disappear with no one the wiser, don't forget." Her eyes blinked wide, much to his satisfaction. Standing up, he pretended to brush some invisible piece of lint off the sleeve of his suitcoat. "Be sure my fee is deposited on time. I'd hate for Mister Worthington to have to find another secretary."

While Clay pondered his assignment, Mason and Belle stood before Endicott Peabody inside St. Paul's Episcopal Church. Johnny Ringo stood next to Mason while a tall, curvaceous red-head named High Step Annie stood next to Belle.

The Reverend Endicott Peabody was a solidly built athletic young man who was known to like his claret and good cigars. He had arrived in Tombstone four months earlier and was an immediate hit with the town folk.

"You're not going to preach are you, Reverend?" Mason teased.

"I was thinking about it," he deadpanned. "Not often I get a captive audience. I figure a two-to-three-hour sermon ought to do it."

"Well, you go ahead and preach as long as you like, Reverend" Mason replied, "but we're all leaving in about ten minutes."

Ringo snickered then cleared his throat, assuming an appropriately somber attitude.

Peabody gazed at Mason, knowing that his first wife had died not more than two weeks ago. That Mason was marrying so quickly after the poor woman's death was not his to question. He had heard the gossip about the Marshal and Belle, but it was just gossip. He had talked with some of the girls at the Bird Cage and they unabashedly told him that despite their many efforts, Mason was faithful to his wife, despite the woman's penchant for laudanum.

"Alright then," he smiled. "Let's get started. We all know why we're here."

The ceremony lasted less than the ten minutes Mason had joked about. As payment for his services, a bottle of claret and a box of cigars sat on the front pew.

"You two have a long and loving life," Peabody pronounced with a paternal smile, motioning them to the rear doors.

Standing outside, a teary-eyed High Step Annie hugged Belle.

"She's a fine catch, Marshal," Ringo whispered.

"That she is Johnny," he said with heartfelt thanks. "Appreciate you being here."

"The honor is mine, Marshal."

"Some say that a woman changes a man, brings out the good in him," Mason opined. "Can't say that's true in all cases, but here's hoping."

Ringo grinned at him. "You're a good man already, Marshal. Just keep doing what you're doing."

Mason studied his friend. "Who knows? Maybe one day some fair damsel just might sweep you off your feet."

Ringo's smile faded slightly, and he shrugged. "I don't see that in the cards for me. Anyway, today is about you and

Belle." Glancing at the two women chatting happily, he said, "Is your former father-in-law that vindictive?"

"That and more," Mason soberly answered.

"So she's in as much danger as you are."

"As are you."

"Huh," he said with a half-smile. "Never thought I'd be in trouble being the friend of a lawman."

"Worthington doesn't care about the law," Mason said. "His soul is black and he wants vengeance. The sad thing is that even if he did get revenge, his soul would still be black."

Ringo nodded in understanding. "Here's hoping that Worthington has heart failure and dies... the sooner the better."

"I usually wish the best for a person," Mason said, shaking his head, "but in this instance, I'm feeling less charitable."

"You two can stop being so glum," Belle chastised them with a brilliant smile. Slipping an arm around Mason's arm, she said, "We're going to have a long and loving life, just like Endicott said. C'mon, let's go celebrate."

As Mason and Belle led the way, Ringo crooked an elbow out to Annie who slipped an arm through.

"You two make a lovely couple," Belle said over her shoulder.

"Sort of like beauty and the beast," Ringo chuckled.

"You're a handsome man, Johnny Ringo," Annie said.

"If so, it is only because I am swept away beneath the aura of your loveliness, Miss Annie," he suavely said.

"You talk pretty," she giggled, clutching his arm tight to her side.

They drew a number of stares and raised eyebrows as they paraded down Third Street then onto Allen. Some of the more proper ladies sniffed in aloof condescension as they passed while others less self-absorbed tipped their hats or waved. A few ventured to greet them with genuine friendliness.

Noise and tobacco smoke swirled out the door as they entered the Bird Cage Theater. They were surprised to see Nantan and Taboca chatting with Jack, the bartender, who immediately set about preparing a sangaree for Belle and a shot of whiskey for Mason.

Belle walked over and gave the two Machinists a hug. "I haven't thanked you enough for all that you did to save my life. I'm sorry you lost your airship," she said to Nantan.

"That's OK, Miss Belle," he awkwardly grinned, pleased with the recognition. "Accidents happen."

"It wasn't an accident," Mason said. "I'm glad you weren't hurt. Because of you two, we were able to rescue her and bring a criminal to justice."

"All in a day's work, Marshal," Taboca calmly said then smiled.

"C'mon Annie, let's dance," a miner called out as he pushed his way to where she and Ringo stood. Ignoring Ringo, he reached out to grab her.

"Not now," she sweetly replied, pulling away. "I'm talking."

"You can talk later," he huffed and grabbed her arm.

Ringo gripped the man's arm, causing him to twist up and look at him. "The lady said, 'not now.' She's talking."

"She don't get paid to talk," the miner shot back. "She gets paid to dance and fornicate."

Anger flashed in Ringo's eyes as he launched a right hook that caught the man unaware and sent him sprawling onto the floor.

Rubbing his jaw, the startled miner looked up to see Mason standing over him.

"Mister," Mason coldly snarled, "you're going to apologize to both the lady and her escort, Johnny Ringo."

"Johnny Ringo," the man repeated, eyes bolting wide, jerking his head to stare at the gunslinger. "Geez, mister, I didn't know you was Johnny Ringo." He stumbled up to standing, his head lowered. "I'm sorry, Mister Ringo."

"Not to me," Ringo snapped, "to her. You besmirched her reputation, you uncouth lout."

The miner turned to Annie, his posture like that of a beaten dog. "I'm sorry, Miss Annie."

"Thank you," she said, watching the man slink off along the edges of the dance floor. Turning to Ringo, she leaned in and kissed him on the cheek. "That was really sweet. No one's ever stood up for me like that."

"Well they should," he replied, warm with the overt display of appreciation. Gazing at her, he was struck with her beauty. He knew she was one of the dance girls, but he had not known her to be one of the crib girls. Feeling gallant, he blurted, "Would you like to go for a walk, Miss Annie?" Immediately regretting his words, he prepared himself to be turned down.

Instead, Annie cast a glance at Belle who nodded.

"I'd be delighted to, Johnny," she gushed.

"Take your time," Belle smiled.

"It's getting toward dinner time," Mason said to Ringo. "Why don't you take her to the Atlantic. Tell Rosalie to put it on my tab."

"I can pay for it," he stiffly stated.

"I don't doubt that at all," Mason reassured him. "It's our treat for you two being there with us today."

"You don't have to do that," Ringo said, mollified.

"What kind of friend would I be if I didn't show my appreciation to my friends?" Mason reasoned. "You two go on, have a good time."

Ringo was about to argue again when Annie hugged his arm to her side and pulled him away. "C'mon , Johnny. I'm starved."

With a laugh and a wave of sincere thanks to Mason and Belle, Johnny and Annie pushed through the doors.

"They look good together," Belle observed.

"Now, now," Mason said with a sly grin. "Let's leave them be."

"What?" she grinned back at him.

Mason turned his attention to the two Machinists. "What brings you two here and how did you get here?"

"We used the airship," Nantan snorted a laugh, "me hanging below him like we did going back to Bisbee."

"We came for the MATE," Taboca said. Seeing Belle's look of disappointment, he quickly added, "We won't keep it long. We want to see how it all works, especially the engine steering system. Near as I can figure it from when we talked

50

with Mister Mitchell was that the clutch and brakes are connected to the steering handles. Pulling on one of the handles disengages the clutch, which releases the wheel belt on that side, causing it to slow down while the other side maintains its speed."

"You're boring them," Nantan interjected with a grin then added, "That was fun the other day."

"You're as bad as she is," Mason chuckled. "I'm just thankful it all worked out."

Taboca leaned in to Mason and Belle. "Were there really two dead guys there?"

"He still doesn't believe me," Nantan frowned.

"Yes," Belle answered. "I wouldn't have believed it if I hadn't saw them myself."

Taboca studied her for a moment then straightened, shaking his head. "Wish I could have seen them."

The front door opened, and a voice hailed, "Marshal and Miss Belle."

Turning, they saw Roger wave as he snaked through the crowd.

"Mister Reppy wants me to write about your adventure," he said with all the excitement of a cub reporter. "Said he'd put it in the next edition, front page."

"So you're working for the *Epitaph*?" Belle asked.

"Not yet," he said with determination, "but Mister Reppy said if he liked what I wrote, he'd see what he could do."

"You're in luck," Mason replied, ticking his head at Nantan and Taboca. "These are the two Machinists I told you about."

Roger's eyes widened in glee. "This is terrific," he said staring directly at the two Machinists. "Mind if I ask you some questions?"

Pleased with the attention, both Machinists readily agreed.

"Never had my name in a newspaper," Nantan grinned.

"Why don't you three go someplace quiet," Mason suggested. "Go get something to eat at the Atlantic. Tell them to put it on my tab."

"Thanks Marshal," Roger exclaimed.

"You don't have to do that Marshal," Taboca objected.

"Go on," Belle urged. "Enjoy dinner and tell how you rescued a fair damsel in distress."

"The Marshal did the hard part," Nantan pointed out. "We just dropped bombs."

"Bombs," Roger repeated, his eyes blinking wide. "This is going to be a great story."

As Roger led the way, Belle turned to Mason.

"You're feeling mighty generous."

"That's the least I can do for Nantan and Taboca. And I figure Roger just got here so he's probably watching his money until he gets a job. Wonder if we ought to put a word in for him with Charles."

"What?" Belle asked when she saw him frown.

"I was just thinking that Nantan and Taboca may also be in danger."

"He'd have to wipe out the entire town if he's going to harm everyone who likes you," she said.

"Worthington's the kind of man who would do just that," he replied, downing the last of the whiskey in his shot glass.

Belle was still asleep when Mason quietly dressed and closed to the door to Belle's room at the Tombstone Boarding House. He chuckled softly to himself as he walked down the stairs. Missus Hunt was both delighted and disappointed that Belle had gotten married for it was going to take away reliable income. Mason reassured her that they would remain until they had found or built a suitable home and oh-by-the-way was there a larger room for a husband and wife? Missus Hunt was partially mollified as the rent for the larger room was more.

Stepping outside in the bright clear-sky morning, Mason inhaled the morning breeze coming down from the Dragoon Mountains. Life with Belle was better than he had imagined. He hadn't been this happy in a long time and that worried him.

Casting a slow glance around the streets, he wondered how he could defeat his former father-in-law. Perhaps he and

Belle should disappear. That would keep others he cared about safe. But that was only a temporary fix. Worthington would do whatever he could to track them down and finish the job. The only way to deal with Worthington was to take the battle to him.

And that's the problem. He shook his head in the knowledge that his former father-in-law had far more assets to do his bidding than Mason would ever have. Still... Worthington's villains would have to come here, and here was a lot easier to defend than elsewhere.

Deciding he could use a slow start to the day, he headed over to the Atlantic for a cup of coffee and some breakfast. He was just about to walk across the street when he realized he still didn't have a horse. He didn't have far to walk as he made his way around to the rear of the boarding house before he saw the black metal machine that everyone seemed so fascinated with parked close to the rear porch.

Staring at it, he wondered if Nantan and Taboca would drive it away today then wondered where Taboca's airship was. The last time the two Machinists brought their one-seater airships to Tombstone, John Doling had let them use the open space at the Tombstone Driving Park.

Mason's memory drifted to the time when he had been allowed to pilot Nantan's airship. Nantan helped Mason into the pilot's seat and gave him a quick refresher on the instructions Taboca had provided. After a few jerks and starts, Mason managed to get the airship aloft and headed over the undulating desert.

Except for the noise of the engine, he was surprised at the peacefulness of the experience, like being out in the desert at night, far away from the mining, the stamp mills and the noise of humanity. He remembered the verdant green of the San Pedro River snaking its way north and south. Large sections of trees were cut away for the mills at Charleston and Millville. At one point, a swirl of smoke had caught his attention and he watched a locomotive hauling six passenger cars slow down as it approached Fairbank. Off in the far distance ahead, the Huachuca Mountains filled the vista.

"These things don't turn very quickly," Taboca had called out, "So you need to start maneuvering well before you get to where you want to go."

Mason grinned when he remembered saying, "One more thing... How do we get down?"

"Open the vents and power down the engine."

They had traveled to Henry Mitchell's claim looking for clues to Caleb's disappearance. Wanting not to be seen, he followed Taboca to where the hill blocked their descent. Once down, Taboca leaped out of his seat and shut off the engine before assisting Mason with the same procedure. He then wrapped the front tether line around a large rock and placed several more rocks on top.

"There's enough heat in the envelope for now to keep it filled for a while, but the longer we stay here the envelope will begin to settle and the longer it will be before we can take off again. Fortunately, the sun can help." He went back to the engine box and opened up a thin compartment on the bottom, sliding out a wide folding mirror. Walking to the other side of the ship, he positioned the mirror to reflect the sun's light and heat onto the envelope.

"You want to be real careful not to walk in front of the mirror," he warned him. "It can get quite hot."

Following Taboca's example, Mason had set up his mirror and the two then scrambled over the hill to spy on Henry. Covertly clambering the last one hundred paces, they made sure their shadows did not give them away. When they were just a short distance away, they settled down to watch then finally walked down to Henry's camp.

Henry Mitchell had been the consummate actor, spinning yarns so magical that one couldn't help but be enthralled. It was when Taboca noticed the damage to the MATE that Henry spun his best tale – he was the victim of an attack. Brilliantly played as he worked to throw suspicion away from him.

What bothered Mason the most was that the entire time they talked, he had no clue that Henry had already murdered Caleb.

Mason frowned as he studied the MATE, wondering why a man with so much talent had to resort to crime. Shaking his head, he shrugged at the vagaries of life and headed over to the restaurant.

The place was busy with off-shift miners enjoying a hearty breakfast before heading to their small hovels to get some sleep after a night of digging in the silver mines. A few looked up and nodded with a friendly smile when he entered.

"Here's the famous hero," Rosalie grinned as she sidled up to the table, a cup and coffee pot in hand.

"What are you talking about?" he frowned.

"You rescuing Miss Belle. That reporter, Roger, and them Machinists were in here last night and I heard the whole thing. That must'a been exciting. Roger says it's gonna be in the paper."

"All in a day's work, Mason downplayed. "I'll take my usual and settle up for last night's meals for Ringo and Annie and the others."

"OK, Marshal," she smiled, pouring the coffee.

Mason had barely taken a sip when the door opened and Roger burst in, making a bee line for the Marshal.

"Thought I saw you up," Roger said, his eyes filmy from lack of sleep. "Mind if I join you?"

"Help yourself," Mason replied, motioning to a chair.

"My story is in today's paper," he announced, scooting a chair back and sitting. He glanced up as Rosalie poured him a cup of coffee. "Thanks Rosalie," he sighed. "I've been up most of the night type setting it."

"Looks like you're settling in with the Epitaph," Mason said with a friendly smile.

"After Mister Reppy read my story, he gave me a job on the spot, said I was a natural."

"You want something to eat, Roger?" Rosalie asked.

"Maybe later, Rosalie. I gotta get some sleep. Just wanted to let the Marshal know I was going to make him famous." Standing, he reached in his pocket to pay for the coffee.

"You barely had a sip," she fussed. "That's a waste of good coffee."

"Slow down, newspaper man," Mason drawled. "Finish your coffee."

Casting a glance at the door, he shrugged and sat. "Guess I do have time."

Mason studied him, wondering if he would be a good ally in the fight against Worthington. Could the paper help spread the word? The more he thought about it, the less inclined he was to mention it. The last thing he needed was for everyone in town to be on edge casting suspicion on any stranger that breezed into town.

"So what's your next story?" Mason asked, making casual conversation.

"I was thinking of doing a story on Johnny Ringo. Everyone thinks he's a bad hombre, but he's really a pleasant fellow. I saw him in here last night with one of the girls from the Bird Cage. He was quite the gentleman."

Mason inwardly chuckled at the word 'hombre.' It was the way he said it, like it was an unfamiliar word and he needed to pay attention when he said it. It sounded odd coming from Roger, as though he was desperately trying to fit in. What was strange was that Mason didn't know anyone who used the word, except for the Mexicans in the Mexican part of Tombstone. But then, Roger was young and had the exuberance of one embarking on the adventure of life.

"If you want an interesting story, not that Johnny Ringo isn't interesting," Mason quickly added, "you ought to do one on the two Chiricahua Machinists, Nantan and Taboca that you had dinner with last night. Did they tell you about their baseball team?"

"Baseball?" he repeated with a half-sneer.

"It's the latest sporting event here in Tombstone. We even have the Tombstone Baseball Association. Reverend Peabody's the vice-president. They had a game recently against a team from Tucson. Lost rather badly, so you might not want to print that. But Nantan and Taboca are part of a professional team called the Phoenix Machinists, if I remember right. Who knows, maybe professional baseball will come to Tombstone and you'll be the one who brings it here."

Roger puzzled the possibilities with a concentrated frown. "I don't know," he replied. "I'll ask Mister Rippy what he thinks."

Rosalie returned with Mason's breakfast, sliding the plate of steak and eggs in front of him.

"That looks good," Roger commented.

"You want breakfast?" she asked, giving him a warm smile.

Roger waffled then shook his head. "I really need some sleep." Downing the rest of his coffee, he stood and placed a silver dollar on the table.

"Let me get you some change," Rosalie said, starting to move away.

"Keep it," Roger said, stopping her. "I figure I'll be coming in here for coffee on a regular basis, so how about working up a kind of tab for me?"

"I'll do that," she answered, flashing him a smile.

"Good night," he grinned and walked out.

Mason watched him leave then looked up at Rosalie whose attention still followed Roger. Clearing his throat, he said, "I'll take some more coffee, Rosalie."

"He's a good-lookin' man," she said, before heading off to get the coffee pot.

Belle was up and dressed by the time Mason returned.

"I was wondering where you ran off to," she said, sitting on a chair on the front porch.

"I didn't want to wake you," he replied, noticing she was dressed like a cowhand in pants, shirt, boots and hat. She even had a bandana wrapped around her neck. She looked innocently fetching. "Where you headed?"

"We got some horses to look at today," she reminded him. "I thought we'd take the MATE."

"You had breakfast yet?"

"Had a cup of coffee and some biscuits," she said, stepping out into the street.

"That's not enough," he fussed.

"I'll eat more later. We got things to do." She walked up to him, grabbed his shirt and pulled him down to plant a big kiss. Releasing him, she said. "Let's move 'em out, cowboy," then led the way to the back of the house.

"Yes Mam," he snorted a laugh.

It was mid-afternoon when Mason, perched atop a tobiano paint, ambled down Allen Street, Belle's horse on a lead rope following behind. Belle had returned earlier and was already at the Bird Cage.

Ambling up to the OK Corral, Mason paid lodging for both horses then headed home to clean up. By the time he washed and shaved, his growling stomach reminded him he hadn't had anything to eat since breakfast.

The Atlantic was beginning to get its dinner shift crowd when Mason walked in and headed over to a table by the windows.

"Hey Marshal," a voice called out. "Thanks fer rescuin' Belle. Town wouldn't be the same without her."

"I agree," he smiled, pulling out a chair.

"If it isn't the big conquering hero," another voice spoke.

The room settled to quiet as forks and knives paused in their clatter while the patrons looked at the speaker then to Mason.

Mason looked over to see a well-dressed man with Burnside whiskers gazing intently at him.

"Don't believe I know you, Mister," Mason said, returning the stare.

"I'm new in town," he replied. "Read the extraordinary account in the paper of your infamous exploits."

"I wouldn't trust everything I read in the papers," Mason said with a half-smile.

"I'm sure you wouldn't. How much did you pay him for that glowing account that transcended adulation?"

"I didn't pay him anything and I don't know what you're talking about as I haven't read the paper today."

"I'd be surprised you didn't have a hundred copies back at the house," the man taunted.

Mason coldly regarded him. "Mister. You're beginning to annoy me."

"What? You going to shoot me?" he mocked.

"If I've a mind to."

The man's arrogance suddenly vanished. "You can't do that. I'm a law-abiding citizen and you're a Marshal. You're sworn to uphold the law."

Mason leaned forward, narrowing his gaze at him. "The law says that I'm to deal with public nuisances as I see fit. Right now I'm seeing you as a public nuisance."

"But, but," the man sputtered then snapped his head around at the miners and other patrons who snorted and laughed at him.

"You're not from around here," Mason observed. "Who are you?"

"The name is Jedidiah Wood," he stiffly replied. "I'm a purveyor of expensive goods."

"Like what?" a miner at the next table asked.

"Like watches and the finest jewelry," he condescendingly replied.

"What brings you to Tombstone, Mister Jedidiah Wood?" Mason asked, waving a finger at Rosalie to get her attention.

"Why business, of course," he replied, the answer obvious.

"I suggest you conduct your business and move on. Folks here in Tombstone don't take to strangers insulting its good citizens."

"You can't force me to leave," he said, standing to full height.

"But I can," he calmly replied then turned his attention to Rosalie. "I'll take my usual," he smiled, "and plenty of that good coffee that Roger had this morning."

"Of course, Marshal," Rosalie grinned.

Jedidiah Wood stood glaring at the surrounding patrons who did little to hide their snickering and derision. "I'd watch my back if I were you." he snarled at Mason.

"Spoken like a man who knows what he's talking about," Mason said, leaning an arm over the top of his chair. "You look like the kind who would shoot a man in the back."

Jedidiah Wood's eyes burst wide. "How dare you. How dare you impugn my reputation."

"You want to do something about it?"

Jedidiah Wood looked down at the twin Colts Mason wore low on his hips then licked his lips that had suddenly gone dry.

"Where do you hail from, Jedidiah Wood?" Mason asked, locking him with stern stare.

"San Francisco," he replied, his voice cracking.

"San Francisco," Mason repeated. His first thought was the man standing before him was sent by his father-in-law, but the man seemed too clueless. "Maybe you know my father-in-law, Reginald Worthington."

Jedidiah Wood's mouth slacked open as fear flashed through him. He closed his mouth and swallowed hard. "Reginald Worthington is your father-in-law?"

"Yes," Mason nonchalantly replied, relieved the man was not sent by his vengeance plagued father-in-law. "Do you know him?"

"Only by reputation, Sir," he hastily replied, searching for coins to pay his bill.

Mason watched him as he bustled by, dipping his head in respect as he hurried to leave. Once gone, Mason turned to the group of diners. "I do hope I didn't offend him," he said with a half-smile.

Amidst the guffaws and chortles, a voice asked, "That Worthington fella. He's a mean cuss?"

"The worst kind," Mason said, no longer feeling the need to speak politely of his former father-in-law.

"He gonna be put out when he finds out about his daughter?"

"Like something you can't imagine," Mason replied.

There was a pause before another man, a miner, said, "He gonna send folks here to settle it?"

"Without a doubt," Mason nodded.

"Mebbe ya oughta hightail it somewhere safe for a while," the miner said, "until things settled down."

"His kind don't let things settled down," Mason explained. "He'll be looking for revenge until the day he dies, and longer if he could find a way."

Forks and knives resumed their clatter as the patrons thought about how it would affect their own lives.

"Seems to me," the miner said, "you got no other way 'cept to kill him first."

"Looks the same to me," Mason agreed.

"You goin' to San Fran then?"

"Nope. Got a job here as a US Marshal."

"You just gonna wait fer him to come here?" the miner asked, surprised that Mason was not taking the offense.

"This is my home," Mason answered. "He comes here, he's on my ground."

The miner nodded, liking the answer.

"Besides," Mason continued, "I have good folks like you who keep an eye out for strangers coming through here."

"You can count on us, Marshal," he said, pleased with the show of trust.

"I ain't a gunslinger," another miner pointed out.

"And I'm glad you're not," Mason kindly replied. "I don't want any of you folks putting yourselves in harm's way. You just keep your eyes and ears open and that will be enough."

Mason turned his attention to his meal, hopeful the word would spread. He then thought about the article in the newspaper, imagining that Worthington probably would eventually have a copy, adding more fuel to his fire of revenge. With a sigh and head shake, he knew there was little he could do about it now.

Tobacco smoke and music spilled out the door as Mason walked into the Bird cage Theater. Glancing to his left, he saw Belle, her back to him, surrounded by her usual coterie of admirers. She wore a dress that came off her shoulders, revealing her flawless skin. He couldn't help but smile at her beauty and the fact that she was now his wife.

He wondered if he should be jealous of the attention she commanded yet knew in his heart she was completely devoted to him. That gave him pause as he knew she was in as much danger as he. If they were to survive, they would need to come up with a plan to fight off the foes Worthington would send.

Worthington. The man would never soil his hands doing his own dirty work, especially when he was rich enough to send someone else.

Mason walked to the bar as Jack poured him a whiskey. "Evening Jack."

"Evening Marshal. This one's on me."

"Thank you, Jack," Mason said, lifting the shot glass in toast. "One of these days, I'd like the honor of buying you a drink."

"One of these days, I'll take you up on it." He moved down the bar to attend another customer.

Recognizing the Marshal, the coterie moved away, hoping Mason would soon leave so they could ply their charm once again.

"Bonsoir, talk dark and handsome," Belle said, batting her eyes flirtatiously. "New in town?"

"Just got in," he nonchalantly replied, turning his back to the bar. "Nice place you have here."

"It's the right place if you're looking for a good time." She smiled demurely.

"I think I might like that. I haven't had a good time since, oh… last night."

Sidling up to him, she tenderly touched his arm. "Billy Milgreen is playing poker in the back," she said.

"Is that a problem?"

"Might be," she replied. "Margarita's been flirting with him."

Mason stepped away from the bar to glance at the far end of the Theater where a sultry beauty with creamy bronze skin and long black hair was devoting an unusual amount of attention to a gambler who was doing his best to ignore her but seemed unable to divert his concentration to the card game.

Billy Milgreen brushed a finger at his handle-bar moustache, pushing the whiskers away from his lips as he focused on the cards, yet he couldn't help himself when she leaned in to whisper in his ear. He flashed a grin then shook his head, somewhat unwillingly.

Mason stepped back. "She's a new girl, isn't she?"

"Yes," Belle replied through pursed lips. "I've warned her before about messing with Billy Milgreen. He's Gold Dollar's man."

"Gold Dollar? You mean Little Gertie, that pretty little lady with long golden blond hair who works in the Crystal Palace?"

"The same. All the girls know to stay away from him. Gold Dollar is the jealous type and has threatened anyone so much as looking cross-eyed at him."

"Apparently Margarita isn't afraid of her."

Mason leaned back to watch Margarita plop herself down on Billy's lap. At that moment, the front doors burst open, and a diminutive blond came charging through, making a bee-line to the table to grab a handful of Margarita's hair and yank her off Billy.

The men at the table moved away to watch as Margarita fought back, kicking and scratching, but she was no match for the raging Gold Dollar who pushed her onto the gaming table. In one quick motion, Gold Dollar pulled a stiletto from her garter and plunged it into Margarita's side and chest.

As Margarita's arms flopped to her side and her body settled as though in repose, Gold Dollar fled down the stairs and out the back door.

Startled to action, one of the gamblers yelled for a doctor.

Standing at the main bar, Doc Goodfellow frowned, downed his brandy and pushed through the crowd to examine Margarita. One look told him all he needed to know. "You don't need me," he said, shaking his head. "The girl is dead."

"Better send someone and let Dave Neagle know," Mason said to Belle.

Motioning to one of the bartenders, Belle sent him off to find the Police Chief.

Determining the episode need not interfere with business as usual, Belle directed some of the men to lift Margarita off the table and haul her to the front of the Theater then out the doors to await the undertaker.

Mason watched them as they passed. "She was an attractive woman. Pity her brains didn't match her beauty."

With the body removed, the chatter, music and tobacco smoke resumed, most patrons indifferent to the death though some rued the absence of such a beauty.

Dave Neagle arrived to sort out the facts, sending one of his deputies to find Gold Dollar. "Did you see what happened, Mason?"

"It's pretty much like everyone said. Gold Dollar came in already loaded for trouble. She wasn't carrying anything that I could see as she passed by me. She yanked Margarita off by her hair and the two of them commenced to beating on each other. For as small as she is, Gold Dollar fought like a tiger. Too late, I saw her pull a knife out and stab the victim. She ran out the back when she realized what she had done."

"You say that in court?"

"I'll tell it just as I saw it," he nodded.

"Much obliged." He cast one last glance around the Theater. "Guess I better go see if I can find her before she gets into any more trouble." Pinching the brim of his Stetson at Belle, he headed out to find the soiled dove.

Nantan and Taboca pushed past the Police Chief as they entered, smiling and waving at Mason and Belle.

"What's with the dead lady out front?" Taboca asked.

"Victim of jealousy," Mason said.

"Too bad," Nantan said. "She was pretty."

"The operative word being 'was'," Taboca pointed out then looked at Belle. "Not meaning to rush you or anything, Miss Belle, but when do you think we might be able to take the MATE?"

"You can have her now," she replied.

'We'll take it tomorrow then," he said with a contented smile.

"But before we do," Nantan said, leaning in. "We've got something to show you tomorrow."

"What is it?" Belle asked, intrigued.

"It's a surprise. Come to the Driving Park tomorrow morning and we'll show you our latest invention."

Caroline, a pretty young doe-eyed girl who worked the cribs came over to Belle and whispered in her ear.

"OK," Belle maternally replied. "You stay put for a moment." Turning to Mason, she lowered her voice just enough so he could hear, the two Machinists likewise leaning in. "Caroline says there's a man upstairs calling himself Big Dave Reno."

"Reno?" Mason repeated with a stern frown. "The man's wanted for multiple murders. Last I heard he was up near Dodge City. The man's dangerous and unpredictable."

"The usual?" Belle smiled.

Mason grinned. "Why not. You two," he said to the two Machinists, "keep a watch out here. I'll be out the back door. If he comes through here, get word to me, but don't do anything to stop him. Like I said, he's dangerous."

Downing the last of his Whiskey, he headed out the front doors then waked to the rear door.

Belle turned to Caroline. "Go upstairs and tell Lillie that a bounty hunter is down here looking for Big Dave."

"There is?" she replied, eyes blinking wide.

Rolling her eyes, Belle decided against telling her the truth. "Just go upstairs and tell Lillie what I told you."

"Yes Miss Belle," Caroline replied.

Climbing the steps to the crib alley, Caroline navigated the narrow hallway between the cribs and the exterior wall. Knocking on the door to the crib, she called out, "Lillie?" She heard a scraping of a chair across the floor then Lillie answered.

"Gimme a minute," came the muted response.

Caroline patiently waited until finally the door opened slightly and Lillie popped her head out. "What?"

"Miss Belle said to tell your gentleman that there's a man downstairs asking about him, a bounty hunter. She said to let him know and take him out the back."

Lillie opened the door further and Caroline could see a large black-haired man with a thick handlebar moustache rapidly buttoning up his trousers.

"Didja hear that?" Lillie said over her shoulder at him.

"Sure did," he briskly nodded. "Tell Miss Belle I'm mighty obliged." Giving Lillie a quick peck on the cheek, he grinned. "Thank you, darlin'. Hate to rush off like this."

Lillie quickly dressed and led the way to the stairs, then out to the main floor to the rear stairs by the stage.

"Go down the stairs and past the gamblers. It ain't far to the back door." Standing on her toes, she gave him a quick peck on the cheek.

Giving her a confident grin, he descended the stairs to the basement where the non-stop faro game was in full progress, each man intensely focused on the game and his hand, impervious to all else. Those waiting their chance to play mutely surrounded the table. Pushing through the tobacco smoke-filled air, he turned the corner and paused before the door that led to the outside.

Casting a quick glance over his shoulder, he took a deep breath then cracked open the door and slipped outside into the night. Giving a rapid scan to his surroundings, he grinned to himself that he had escaped another bounty man. That lasted only a moment when he heard the click of a pistol hammer drawn back, and the cold steel of a barrel from a Colt .45 pressed to the base of his neck.

"Big Dave Reno," the voice spoke. "I'm placing you under arrest with the charge of murder. Now the way I see it, you can make this easy or difficult. The easy way is for you to come along peacefully. The hard way is for you to resist arrest and I have to shoot and kill you right here.

"That you, Marshal Sadler?" Big Dave asked, his hands up high.

"It is."

"Now Marshal," Big Dave calmly said. "You wouldn't shoot a feller in the back."

"Not unless I have to," came the quiet reply. "It's not my first choice, but then I expect you know my reputation. You come along peaceful, everything will be fine. But if I have to defend myself, I don't care how I shoot you. And remember, I've got guns in both hands."

"I won't give you no trouble. 'Sides, I ain't got a gun."

"Fortunately, we don't have far to walk," he said as he nudged his prisoner forward. Making their way behind the livery stable towards 6th street, Mason added, "You be real good. I'd hate to have to shoot you."

"How'd you know I was here?" he asked as they headed towards the jail, Mason a step behind.

"Heard there was a bounty hunter in town," Mason lied. "I followed him to the Bird Cage. I wasn't sure where you were in there, but I knew someone would tip you off. Was it one of the girls?"

"I don't know what you're talkin' about," Big Dave innocently said, not wanting to expose Miss Belle for warning him.

"I'm sure you don't," he sniffed. "Open the door," he commanded when they reached the jail, "and keep your hands up where I can see them."

His hands still in the air, Big Dave led the way into the jail where Deputy Harry Solen, a lithe muscular man, sat behind the desk, pen in hand, writing out reports.

"Hullo Mason. Got another one I see. Who's this?" Harry asked, looking up.

"Big Dave Reno. I'm sure there's a warrant for his arrest in that drawer of yours."

"It's been a busy night," Harry commented, retrieving a key ring from the hook on the wall. Casting a cold glance at Big Dave, he said, "C'mon you."

A few moments later, Harry was back, hanging up the keys. "So what happened with Gold Dollar and the other girl?" He pulled open the drawer and pulled out a stack of Wanteds.

"The usual fit of jealousy," Mason replied. "Seems a pretty open and shut case, especially with all the witnesses."

"Here we are," Harry said, pulling out a Wanted with a hand sketch likeness of Big Dave. "Wow. Looks like you hit the jackpot. This one is three grand." He wrote out a receipt slip and handed it to Mason.

"Thanks." Folding the receipt then stuffing it in his pocket, then said, "Listen, Harry. I've a feeling that things might get hot in the near future."

"How?" Harry leaned back in his chair, causing it to squeak.

"With Elizabeth's death, her father is going to want revenge. He blames me for bringing her here and will blame me for her death. Unfortunately, he's the kind of man who won't be satisfied just killing me. He'll kill anyone who he thinks I might like or care about."

"We'll keep an eye out for him," Harry reassured him.

"There's the problem," Mason pointed out. "He won't come himself. He'll send others to do his dirty work. All I'm saying is that we need to pay attention to new folks coming into town."

"I understand," Harry nodded. "I'll let the others know."

"Much obliged."

It was another clear sky morning when Mason and Belle rose early to see Nantan's latest invention. Staring at his reflection in the mirror, Mason saw the bags under his eyes.

"I can't keep doing this," he said, rubbing his eyes, "burning candles at both ends. One of these days I'm going to need to get some real sleep."

Belle, looking as tired as Mason did, simply said, "Coffee."

Dressed, they made their way downstairs where Missus Hunt was already up and setting the breakfast table.

"I need to be gone a couple of days," Mason said, buttering a fresh hot biscuit.

"Why?" Belle asked, not liking the prospect of being alone.

"I am a US Marshal," Mason reminded her. "My territory goes beyond Tombstone."

"When are you leaving?"

"I was going to leave today, but I need sleep. Think I'll wait 'til tomorrow."

"Then I'll just have to leave the Theater earlier so we can be together tonight," she said with a sly smile. "That way I can give you something to think about when you're gone."

"I'd like that," he grinned.

Sitting beside his wife as she expertly steered the MATE, Mason chuckled that she seemed so nonchalant driving around town on the thing. As they cruised out of town towards Watervale towards the Tombstone Driving Park, he remembered Nantan's excitement about his latest invention. Despite their best efforts last night, they couldn't pry his secret from him.

Looking back over his shoulder, Mason made sure their two horses were still attached to the lead ropes anchored to the trailer behind the engine. Off in the distance, Tombstone was waking up. Shift change in the mines was still an hour away.

Pulling up to the stables in the back of the Park, he saw Taboca standing outside the doorway. While Belle shut down the boiler, Mason leaped down and waited to help Belle down. Together they walked over to Taboca.

As they approached, Nantan came walking out of the shadows of the stable.

Mason stopped and stared at the machinist who now stood a good three feet taller than the Marshal. Blinking at the strange contraption strapped to Nantan's legs and back, he frowned in concentration. "What is it?"

"It's a motorized self-propulsion system," Nantan answered, his eyes radiant with excitement.

"What's it do?"

"With this," he proudly replied, lifting an arm from the arm rest and looking down at his invention, "I can outrun a horse, maybe even outrun a train."

"How's it work?"

Mason furrowed his brow as he took in the oddly shaped legs that were nothing more than two bent pieces of metal about five inches wide. The part that rested on the ground was about a foot-and-a-half long and curved up slightly at both ends in a parabola shape. At the rear of the arc, the metal bent sharply and ran straight up, past the attached foot platforms where Nantan's feet rested, then ended just below the back of his knee. There, contained within an elaborate set of straps and joints, another metal bar ran from below his thigh to the machine strapped to his back. His arms rested on two padded armrests.

"It's all controlled up front here," he explained, pointing to a small control panel in front of each hand. "The left side here controls the engine and speed. The right side controls leg movement."

"How do you keep from tipping over?"

"I've got an internal gyroscope that stabilizes the engine. As long as the engine is stable, so is everything else."

"Suppose the gyroscope fails or gets damaged somehow?"

"Well then I'll have to balance as best I can."

"Or come crashing down," Taboca added with a slight smile.

Mason cocked his head to the side, debating whether to ask the nagging question. Curiosity getting the better of him, he said, "Why?"

"Why what?"

"Why this machine? What's the purpose?"

"Because I can," he glibly responded.

Chuckling, Mason shook his head. "Really. What's the purpose?"

"Other than wanting to run fast, I was thinking people whose legs don't work, like those in wheelchairs or bedridden. This could help them get around."

"You'd have to have fifteen-foot ceilings," Mason observed. "And how do you get in and out of it?"

"Ladder," Taboca chimed in.

"I'm still working on the cripple part," Nantan defensively stated.

Mason could hear the engine, but there was none of the steam associated with what he knew engines produced. "What kind of fuel are you using?"

"Acetylene dissolved in acetone."

"What?"

"Acetylene," Taboca repeated. "It burns well, but it can be unstable." He broke out into a broad grin. "We learned that the hard way."

"Yeah," Nantan snorted a laugh. "You don't want to transport it in copper or brass."

Mason thought to ask what happened but decided the scientific explanation was probably more than he wanted to listen to.

"Show him how it works," Taboca encouraged.

On the left hand control panel, Nantan flicked a toggle switch and the engine hummed a bit louder. Waiting for the engine to reach rotation speed, he flicked a toggle switch on the right hand panel and the machine jittered forward, stiffly lifting Nantan's legs before settling into a smoother motion as the engine gained speed. Soon, he was taking long strides around the track of the Driving Park. After a bit, he increased speed into a lope that turned into a run, his stride at least twenty-five feet long. What impressed Mason far more was the speed of the machine that carried him. Nantan was moving faster than any horse Mason had ever ridden.

After a bit, Nantan slowed down, settling into a walk again before returning to where Mason and Taboca stood.

"Well? What do you think?" Nantan beamed with pride as the brought the machine to a halt.

"Very impressive," Mason soberly admitted.

"Is it built to fit you or can anyone use it?" Belle asked.

"Now Belle," Mason admonished, knowing her intent.

"I can adjust the straps to fit different people."

"Now Belle," Mason repeated.

"Might I try it?" she grinned, ignoring her husband.

"Belle," Mason huffed.

"Sure," Nantan replied. "It will only take me a minute to unhook myself. Meet me at the ladder in the barn."

"Do you really want to do this?" Mason counseled.

"Absolutely," she said, following Nantan.

Less than twenty minutes later, Mason stood at the railing of the Park, watching as Nantan gave final instructions to Belle.

"Remember," the Machinist said, "the left side controls the engine and speed. The right side controls leg movement."

"Got it," she smiled. She flicked the toggle switch and the engine hum increased.

"Give it a minute to reach rotation speed," Nantan called out above the noise. "Look at the dial next to the engine switch. When the arrow hits the green zone, you're ready."

Belle watched as the arrow swung out of the red then past the yellow. "OK. It's green."

"OK. Now press the right side toggle to start moving."

Belle flicked the toggle switch on the right hand panel and the machine jittered forward, stiffly lifting her legs. She marched down the track in quirky jerking strides before settling into a smoother motion as the engine gained speed. Too soon, she was taking long strides around the track of the Driving Park.

As she passed by on the first lap, Mason saw the utter glee in her eyes, like a child with the Christmas toy she always wanted.

Halfway through the second lap, she increased speed into a lope that lasted the rest of the lap then turned into a run, her stride looing and fluid, gobbling up the track like a train engine gone wild.

After almost a dozen more laps, she slowed down to a walk before heading over to the three men. Perched three feet above her normal height, she now towered over Mason.

"I like being up here," she grinned, looking down at him. "Sort of gives one the feeling of power."

"How was it?" Nantan asked, his eyes bright with pride.

"It was very easy," she said. "Once I got the hang of it, it took little effort to maintain balance. This is a wonderful machine." She twisted her head to gaze intently at Mason. "I want one."

"Maybe for your birthday," he deadpanned. Turning to Nantan, he said, "While she was out gallivanting around the track, I thought about what sort of uses your machine might have. One use was in a military setting. If you could make some sort of protective armor on the front, it could protect the soldier during an attack."

"And add guns that the operator can fire," Taboca added, rising to the concept, "like Gatling guns."

"You have to crank the handle on a Gatling gun," Nantan pointed out. "It would throw the whole balance off."

"So invent a Gatling gun that doesn't need to be hand cranked," Mason said. "I'm sure between your two genius minds, you could come up with something like that."

Nantan had a faraway look in his eyes. "The first thing is to design a protective armor, something not too heavy, but still give protection."

"Or design it so that bullets are deflected by the angle of the armor," Taboca said.

Soon the two Machinists were in animated discussion while Belle walked over to the ladder in the Barn. Unbuckling the straps, she powered down the engine and stepped onto the ladder.

Mason was waiting for her and reached up, placing his strong hands on her waist and lifting her down.

Her feet firmly planted on the ground, Belle gazed into the eyes of her husband. Stepping up on her tiptoes, she reached up and kissed him.

"This is going to be fun, being married to you," she said, her eyes glistening with adoration.

"And it will be even more fun tonight," he pointed out with a wide smile.

"Hey Miss Belle," Nantan called out as he and Taboca walked over. "We forgot to ask you last night if we could borrow the MATE to retrieve some of Henry Mitchell's machines, especially the IAS."

"IAS?" she repeated.

"Intruder Alert System," Taboca explained. "We have the external cone and sensing rod. We just need to get the rest of it."

"Of course," she replied. "When?"

"Whenever is convenient."

"How about now? We have time," she said, gazing at Mason.

With an indulgent nod, Mason turned to the two Machinists. "How do you want to do this?"

"We'll meet you there," Taboca answered. "I've got my airship here. Nantan will want to run there. We can hook up the machines and head back to Tombstone and drop you off then head off to Bisbee. We can probably have the MATE back to you by tomorrow or the next day."

"There's no rush," Belle smiled at him. "Keep it as long as you like."

"Thanks, Miss Belle."

A little while later, Mason sat beside Belle as she expertly steered the MATE past Tombstone and headed towards the cave not far from the Champion Mines where Caleb once had his claim. Nantan had passed them before they were on the outskirts of town.

Mason quietly pondered the chain of events the secrets of Caleb's cave caused. The poor miner simply wanted to be left alone to work his claim. The man was an odd duck, peculiar in his ways. Though nowhere near yielding the volume of silver the surrounding mines produced, Caleb was able to chisel out a subsistence living, putting what extra he earned in the bank in Tombstone, choosing to walk all the way to Tombstone instead of one of the banks in Charleston less than half the distance away from his claim. 'Banks in Charleston get robbed too much,' he affirmed.

Then Caleb discovered the Conquistadors' gold in another cave inside his claim. It was then the trouble started and trouble's name was Henry Mitchell, a supposed archaeologist. Though Henry's claim to archaeology might be doubtful, that the man was a genius and inventor was beyond doubt. In fact, Mason and Belle now rode in one of Henry's inventions.

Still, what were the odds that Henry's search for the gold from the Seven Cities of Cibola would lead him to the claim opposite Caleb? Once Henry discovered that Caleb had the gold, Caleb stood no chance against the wily inventor.

Mason wished he could have seen the contents of the cave before Henry removed all the gold. He could only imagine how it must have looked with the two dead Conquistadors sitting next to the pile of gold.

Then it was as though everything speeds up. Henry kills Caleb, steals the gold, the two dead Conquistadors come back to life as does Caleb, Henry kidnaps Belle making good his escape while setting fire to Tombstone, Mason enlists the help of Nantan and Taboca, rescues Belle and leaves Henry staked out with Caleb and de la Fuente.

If Mason had heard someone else tell the tale, he would have sworn the man was drunk or drugged… especially the part about the dead coming back to life.

Oddly, that seemed so long ago.

As they descended along the wash between Caleb's and Henry's claims, Mason saw the IAS on its side. Nantan had already dismounted from his legs and was walking the length of the extended lattice of the support tower.

"We're gonna need cables," Nantan called when he saw them.

Taboca's airship slowly descended until it almost touched the ground just beyond the end of the IAS. Jumping out, he tethered the ship to a rock close by then pulled out the heat shield to keep the envelope warm. Walking up next to Nantan, they began plotting the rescue while Mason helped Belle down.

"This is the IAS?" she asked, giving the metal lattice a dubious look. "How's it work?"

"What you see here is the base and extended support for the system," Taboca explained. Pointing to the end, he said, "The cone and rod are attached there. We have those back in Bisbee. Picture the cone like a megaphone a carnival barker uses. Inside the cone is a long rod that sends out an invisible electronic signal. The signal goes in a straight line. When it hits something, it bounces off it and comes back to the cone, which sends the information down the wire in the middle of the support tower down to the machine here." He pointed to the base.

"The base has the parts that decipher the signal," Nantan said. "If the object is stationary, like a rock, nothing happens. But if the object is moving, say like a man on horseback, the machine picks up the difference and emits a loud noise telling us an intruder is coming. According to Mister Mitchell, it can pick up something moving up to almost an eighth of a mile away."

"It's all based on line of sight and movement," Taboca continued. "If you are under the signal, it won't see you. Likewise, the cone rotates side to side, so if you see the cone moving your way and you stand still, it will think you're a rock."

Belle pointed to the small wheel attached to the side of the machine. "Is this what lowers and raises the tower?"

Taboca studied the wheel then the base. "Yes. Too bad the IAS is on its side."

"I don't think Henry wanted anyone else using it," Mason opined. "But, his loss is your gain. How do you want to handle this?"

"We need cable and the other airship," Taboca said. "Using the MATE and the two airships, I think we can sit it upright."

Mason pulled out his pocket watch, flipped open the cover and checked the time. "How long before you can get back with the other airship?"

"We can probably be back in an hour," Nantan called back over his shoulder as he walked over to strap back into his legs.

"Maybe a little more than an hour," Taboca corrected.

Mason looked back at his pocket watch. "It's after ten now. How about we meet you back here at two? That way you don't have to rush and will give everyone time to eat."

"That's perfect," Taboca said. "Thanks Marshal."

As Nantan and Taboca prepared to head back to Bisbee, Mason headed down to cross the wash. A steady stream ran the middle, the overflow from the water the mines pumped out daily.

"Where you going?" Belle asked, catching up.

"Just wanted to take a look at Caleb's claim."

"What do you expect to find?"

"Nothing, really," he replied, leaping over the water then turning to extend a hand to Belle. "Just curious, that's all."

Climbing up the path to the entrance to Caleb's cave, Mason paused outside and turned to look across the wash. Nantan was already in the distance, running in long loping strides. Taboca's airship followed behind him. Mason mused that with Nantan's speed, he would most likely be the first to arrive back at the aerodrome in Bisbee. Whether that was a viable way of traveling was another matter for it still required human effort to make it work. Besides, airships were easy. All one had to do was sit and enjoy the ride.

Stepping into the cave, it was as he expected. Everything was as before, layered in the sand that time and the wind blew in. Even the stones arranged to spell 'Enrique' and 'Oro' were still there

"So this is what de la Fuente did to point the finger at Henry," Belle said, standing next to him.

"So it seems." He cast one last look around the dim cave. The water barrel, Caleb's mining tools, the meager food stocks and his bedroll were all still in place. Except for the layer of windblown sand covering them, it looked as though Caleb would be back at any minute.

"I wonder if de la Fuente is pleased to be freed from the tomb," Belle said, glancing at the mouth of the smaller cave where the stones were arrayed in the spelling pattern.

"Wonder where they've hidden the gold," Mason said. "Let's hope it's never found again."

Belle gazed into his eyes. "I wonder what happened to Henry. You think he'll ever come back?"

"There's gold in the Dragoons," Mason replied with a frustrated sigh. "I suspect he'll be back. My guess is that if he does come back, he'll do it quietly. I'm sure he knows he won't be welcome in Tombstone."

"I'm getting hungry," Belle said, feeling her stomach grumble. "Take me to lunch, sailor?"

"With pleasure," he grinned, taking her hand and leading her out of the cave. Seeing the MATE, he said, "How about letting me drive that contraption?"

"I suppose you ought to learn some time," she chuckled. "We'll need to fill the water tank before we head back to town."

Using the bucket in Caleb's cave, Mason hauled water back and forth while Belle scoured the area for deadwood.

Once powered up, Belle scooted over to let Mason drive. "Not too fast now, Dear. I don't want to mess up my hair."

Flashing a smile, he released the brakes and pushed the throttle and headed up the trail to Tombstone.

"I'm thinking of giving this back to Nantan and Taboca," she said, reveling in ride and wind.

"Why?" he asked, surprised. "I thought you liked this machine."

"It takes too much effort to make it work. Besides, there's a new thing called the automobile."

"Automobile? What's that?"

"It's like a wagon with a steam engine. I read an article where they even had a race in Wisconsin a few years back. The first person to drive from Green Bay to Madison averaging at least five miles an hour won $10,000. Only two machines started and one finished."

"And you want an automobile?" he smiled paternally at her.

"Yes. I bet automobiles are going to replace horse and carriages."

"Nothing can replace a good horse," he said, shaking his head.

"That may be true," she replied, "but you don't have to feed and water and groom and stable an automobile. You don't have to take care of saddles and bridles or pay for farriers and horse docs."

"No," he agreed. "All you have to do is pay for someone to fix it when it breaks down. And it will still require some sort of maintenance and fuel. And I can imagine the headaches the Machinists will have if the automobile becomes a means of transportation. And can you imagine if anyone could afford an automobile like they can a horse? It's bad enough as it is in the cities with all the carriage and tram traffic. Just think about adding automobiles to that? Sounds to me like a headache waiting to happen."

"You're just old fashioned," she said, patting his thigh.

"And what about all the steam and smoke from the engines? You won't be able to see where you're going. At least with a horse, you can go at your own pace and see clearly what's ahead of you."

Belle was about to reply when Mason added, "And what about the mountains around here or anywhere else they have mountains? A horse can go up trails an automobile will never be able to go. So in the end, you'll still need a horse."

"OK, OK, you made your point," she laughed. "But when I'm driving around in the latest automobile and people are pointing and saying, 'There goes Belle in her amazing automobile. We wish we had one,' don't say I didn't tell you so."

"The next thing you're going to tell me," he said with a sly grin, "is that there will be flying machines that go faster than airships."

Laughing, Belle leaned into him and squeezed his arm. "Let's not get carried away now."

Chapter 3

Diamond Dan Braxton stared at the group with his arms folded, waiting for the room to settle. After a bit, his patience finished, he growled, "That's enough. Everybody just button up and sit down." Waiting for them to obey, he leaned back, resting both hands on the desk behind him.

He was a large man, broad shouldered yet trim in physique with a grace of movement that belied quickness when necessary. He had earned his sobriquet due to his fastidious dress and the diamond stick pin he wore in his cravat.

As the room quieted, he began, "We've two jobs. One's in Tombstone, Arizona Territory and the other is right here in San Francisco."

"Good god," a man spoke his disdain. "What the hell's in the Arizona Territory?"

"A man named Mason Sadler," Diamond Dan answered.

There was a pregnant pause before another man asked what most were thinking. "Ain't he Worthington's son-in-law?"

"Yup."

"Uh… does Worthington know about this?" he hesitantly wondered.

"Yup."

There was another awkward pause followed by shrugs and some snickers. "Who cares," the first man observed, "as long as we get paid."

"Exactly," Diamond Dan replied. "We're not here to question why; we're here to perform a… service. We're being paid handsomely for both contracts, so we do them right. As far as the Arizona contract, Worthington's got a special interest in it. He wants the man to suffer, which means we take out those close to him first. He wants this done right, so those of you I send, take your time. Set up the target and when the moment's right, take it out. Save this Mason Sadler fella for last. The rest of you will remain here for the other contact.

Diamond Dan talked first about the San Francisco contract, delegated assignments and sent them off. He waited until there were four remaining members of his team. "You four will take on the Tombstone contract. Ed's got the lead on this one," he said, nodding at an urbane man with thick wavy red hair and mutton chops. "He calls the shots. Get in, set up, make it clean and get out. Remember what our employer wants. Sadler needs to suffer. Make him suffer."

Ed waited for Diamond Dan to finish. "Right. We'll head out tomorrow morning. We head first to Bisbee and set up there. The contract calls for him and anyone he cares about to die. Don't know how many that is or where they are.

"Sadler's got no family other than his wife," Diamond Dan said, "but she's dead."

"What happened?" a powerfully built compact man with short brown hair and full beard asked.

"Drugs," Diamond Dan replied.

"Damn," the man said shaking his head. "No wonder he wants him dead"

"So when we get there," Ed continued, "we find out who's close to him first and then we hit them hard. I'll explain more on the way."

"How long we gonna be gone?"

"Don't know Earl, but figure at least a couple o' weeks." Ed replied. "Save the rest of your questions for later. Meet at the aerodrome at six tomorrow morning."

"We're flying down there?" another man asked. He was small in stature with a receding hairline and looked to be more of an accountant than hired killer. He wore wire-rim glasses.

"Yes, Gordon," Ed patiently explained. "We're supposed to get in there fast without drawing undo attention, and that's the fastest way down."

"Who's payin' for it?" Earl growled.

"Relax, Earl," Ed sighed, rolling his eyes. "You'll get your full share."

"Damn right," he retorted. "Them airships ain't cheap." Casting a glance at Gordon, he said, "You bringing yer usual bag o' tricks?"

"Why yes," Gordon serenely smiled, holding up and patting his briefcase. "They're all right in here."

"Is she comin' with us?" Earl tossed a patronizing look at a curvaceous woman with curling blond hair that spilled down beyond her shoulders."

"Why Mister Earl," the woman coquettishly said, batting her eyelids. Smiling sweetly at him she continued, "I do believe you have slighted me. I'm not sure whether to shoot you right here or wait until you're sleeping like a little baby."

"What?" Earl growled. Before he could take a threatening step towards her, he found himself facing a double-barreled Remington Derringer held in a kid-gloved hand. He looked from the derringer to the woman's face. Her sweet expression hadn't changed, and she smiled at him as though killing him would be a great pleasure.

"Slow down Becca," Diamond Dan cautioned. Turning to Earl, he shook his head with an added sigh. "You're a damned fool Earl. You ought to think before you open your mouth. This here is Becca Morgan, and you'd do well to remember that."

Earl thought a moment then dismissively shrugged. "That should mean somethin'?"

"It ought to," Diamond Dan quietly answered. "She's the one who took out those two prosecutors and the chief of police."

Earl blinked at the revelation, his eyes suddenly wide. "That was some shootin'," he admitted, impressed.

"Why thank you, Mister Earl. For that kind remark, I won't kill you today," she blithely said, securing her derringer in her sleeve.

Not quite sure she was serious or just playing with him, he changed the topic. "'Becca'... is that short for something'?"

"Why how very insightful of you.   It's short for 'Rebecca,' a fine Biblical name."

Ed frowned before interrupting. "You can talk about that later.   Let's get back to what's important.   We all travel as individuals, so make your cover story believable.   Once we get into Bisbee, we head on up to and checkout Tombstone first and find Sadler.   We keep an eye on him for a couple of days and find out who's close to him.   Once I'm satisfied, I'll make assignments.   This should be easy.   Once Sadler and his friends are dead, we come home."

"How about we just take 'em all out at once?" Earl snorted.   "Get 'er over and done with, that's what I'm sayin'."

"Didn't you listen?" Ed huffed.   "Worthington wants Sadler to suffer."

"Hell," Earl sniffed in disdain.   "He ain't gonna know the difference once the man's dead."

"Damn it Earl, just do it like I tell you," Ed snapped.

"You got a problem with that, Earl?" Diamond Dan coldly asked, leaning against the desk and folding his thick arms in front of him.

"Now don't git yer feathers in a ruffle," Earl replied, shaking his head and lifting his hands as though in surrender. "I was just pointin' out another way to git 'er done."

"We'll do it like I ordered," Diamond Dan flatly answered.   Casting a firm eye on the rest of them, he said, "Ed's told you enough already.   You all go and get ready."

As they filed out, Diamond Dan waited until the last one left then observed, "He's going to be a problem."

"So why'd you give him to me?" Ed raised a perturbed eyebrow.

Diamond Dan looked him squarely in the eyes. "Get rid of him.   Make it look like an accident.   Hell, push him out of the airship on the way back if you have to, but he's become a liability.   Get my drift?"

"One hundred percent," he nodded with satisfaction. "By the way, thanks for putting Becca with me."

"She's good," Diamond Dan acknowledged, "but she likes to go her own way.   Be careful with her.   That smile can fool you. She's just about the coldest killer I know, but like I said, she's good and dependable. And she's one helluva shot."

Ed looked at Diamond Dan for a moment. "I heard tell she took out the police chief at a quarter mile."

"Make that almost a half mile," he corrected.

"Damn. What's she using?"

"A Sharps" Diamond Dan replied. "Uses special rounds."

"Sharps?" Ed echoed with some consternation. "How's she going to get it to Bisbee. That rifle's near as long as she is tall."

"You don't need to worry about her," he reassured. "She can take care of herself. You just take care of Sadler. You got maybe a couple of weeks at most."

"Couple of weeks?" Ed sputtered, mentally calculating the travel time there and back. "Doesn't leave us much time to take care of business."

"In this instance, Earl has a point. Worthington wants the man dead. Take out a couple of folks close to him then finish it. No sense stringing it out longer than we have to. Worthington supposedly has someone scoping out Tombstone already."

"Who is it?"

"All I know is that he or she will contact you."

"How do they know we're coming or even who we are?" Ed frowned.

Diamond Dan simply shrugged. "It's all been arranged. You need to wait until they contact you. It will help you get this assignment done quicker."

"Suits me." Ed took a quick disinterested look around Diamond Dan's large office. A tidy desk against which Diamond Dan still leaned sat in the middle of room. A small conference table was positioned close to the wall opposite the tall windows through which the bright afternoon sun poured. Sunlight shafts knifed across the room illuminating Diamond Dan, giving him an apparitional appearance. Ed always found it interesting that Diamond Dan conducted his, um…

'more quiet' affairs right here in his office, right out in broad daylight. "You need any help when we get back?"

"Might," Diamond Dan noncommittally replied. "MacKennagh over in the tenth ward's been acting a little superior lately. Might need to cut him down a notch. We'll see when you get back."

"Glad to help," he said, touching a finger to his forehead in a salute.

Diamond Dan silently nodded. "Remember what I said about Earl. Get rid of him."

The following morning, mixed in the passenger line at the air terminal, they waited to check in their baggage. Ed glanced around, smiling politely at other patrons, pointedly ignoring the faces of the other team members. He struck up a conversation with a well-dressed man with a full beard and smoking a full-bent pipe.

"That's a fine bit of tobacco you have there," Ed observed.

"It's a Turkish blend," the man amiably replied, taking the pipe out of his mouth.

"Do you find it difficult smoking a pipe while traveling?"

"In the beginning," he answered. "But I've got it down to a science now. Manage to keep it lit while I go through ticketing and check-in. All one needs do is ensure there is just the right amount of tobacco in the bowl."

Ed smiled attentively as the man droned on about pipe smoking, tobacco and the number of pipes he had at home. The conversation turned to reasons for travelling to Bisbee.

"I'm going down on behalf of my bank," the man explained. "With the amount of precious ore coming out of Tombstone and Bisbee, one is foolish not to take advantage of the possibilities. Why are you traveling to Bisbee?"

"Pretty much the same reason," Ed replied. "I represent a security firm. We specialize in transportation of precious commodities."

"Do say," the man said, all the more interested. "What is the name of your firm?"

"You will forgive me if I do not answer your question," Ed mysteriously replied. "We are a private company, and our secrecy is our success. When one does not know the means or the method, one does not need to worry about unwarranted attention to shipment of precious cargo. By keeping our company and business arrangements private, we have 100% success rate."

"By Jove that's exceptional," the man exclaimed. "Perhaps we might be able to do some business together."

"That certainly is possible," Ed readily agreed. "If you will give me the name of your company, we will be in touch."

The man reached inside his vest pocket and extracted a business card. "The information is all there. Just ask for me."

"I look forward to it," Ed smiled, reading the name on the card, "Mister Thaddeus Shephard... of Sacramento." He placed the card in his coat pocket. "Have a pleasant flight."

"Perhaps we can have dinner together in Bisbee," the man suggested.

"That would be most acceptable," Ed respectfully nodded.

"Where are you lodging?"

"At the Belmont."

"I'm at the Blair. Perhaps we might visit over dinner in the dining room tonight."

"That would be enjoyable," Ed nodded then handed his ticket to the ticket master.

Ed casually strolled along the corridor, his right hand out lightly touching the rich mahogany walls, the smoothness of the polished wooden surface occasionally broken by carved and curved lines of embellishment. Making his way towards the forward viewing deck, he dipped his head in polite acknowledgement to several ladies passing the other way, most likely heading back to their respective cabins.

Stepping into the wide room, he nonchalantly glanced around, looking for a suitable place to gaze out the tall windows to the land below. The viewing room spread the width of the gondola attached to the giant airship that was slowly making its way to Bisbee. Most of the viewing spaces were taken up, some by families with gamboling children chastised by mothers and fathers to stay behind the brass railing that ran waist high a foot in front of the glass windows. Still, admonitions did little to prevent the smudged handprints on the thick glass.

Looking to his right, he found a spot and maneuvered around chatting travelers to edge up and place his hands on the railing. Taking in the broad vista, he commented to the man standing next to him. "Quite a view."

Earl had already recognized Ed but knew enough to pretend they were strangers. "Yes, it is," he nodded in agreement.

"Traveling to Bisbee?" Ed cordially asked.

"Yes," Earl replied, silently bemoaning the charade and the fact that Ed was checking up on him.

"As am I," he amiably said. "Looking to expand the business. Thought about checking out Tucson, but heard Bisbee was a growing town. What about yourself?"

"Visiting friends."

"Ah," Ed nodded in understanding. "So you've been to Bisbee before."

"No," Earl answered. "This is my first time." Though the words fit, they felt too rehearsed.

"Mine too." Ed smiled as he surreptitiously took in the few people surrounding them. His attention was diverted when the assistant dining room manager appeared in the doorway. He was a middle-aged man, crisply dressed in business attire. He wore mutton chops like Ed.

"Ladies and Gentlemen. If I may have your attention, please. Lunch will be served in ten minutes. At this time, please make your way to the dining room." Having delivered his announcement, he gave a quick bob of his head, spun on his heels and retreated back down the corridor.

While most of the room's occupants converged on the narrow hallway, Ed gave a subtle wave of the hand, telling Earl to stay where he was. Watching as the room emptied, Ed lowered his voice. "I've been thinking of what you said back at Diamond Dan's, about getting it over with once and for all."

"Yeah?" Earl perked up.

"The more I thought about it, the more sense it made. All Worthington really cares about is that Sadler is dead. I was thinking we ought to lay up in Bisbee a couple of days, scout out Tombstone and Sadler then get it over with all at once."

"Now yer talkin'," Earl readily agreed before furrowing his brows. "What about the girl?"

"Becca?"

"Yeah, her. How come she ain't on this airship with us?"

"She has her own agenda," Ed explained, not without some dissatisfaction.

"I don't trust her," Earl sourly replied.

Leaning in, Ed conspiratorially whispered, "Neither do I." Standing up straight, he adjusted his cravat. "Have you seen Gordon?"

"Not since this morning," Earl said. "He's a strange one."

"Yes he is," Ed readily agreed, "but he's quite good at what he does, blowing things up when you need that sort of thing."

"Don't make any sense havin' him here if we're supposed to be quiet about it."

"Exactly," he replied, rolling his eyes. "That's why I want you to take out Sadler. I figure you got the fastest gun, so you got the best chance. We don't need Gordon announcing our presence."

Earl subtly preened at the compliment. "No problem. I'll take him out just as soon as you say the word."

"Good." Ed nodded to the doorway that was now empty. "You'd better get going. I'll see you in Bisbee."

"Pleasure meeting you," Earl said, a little louder than necessary should someone still be lingering in the hallway.

"And you too. Perhaps we'll run into each other again in Bisbee." Ed motioned for Earl to go first then followed him down the long corridor, his hand again lightly brushing the smooth mahogany walls. Staring at the back of his compatriot, he smiled thinking that Earl was much too impulsive. Hopefully that trait would be enough to get him killed in Tombstone.

Mason stood at the bar in the Alhambra Saloon sipping a whiskey as he took in the elegant furnishings. He was amazed at how quickly the Saloon had been resurrected. The owner, Thomas Corrigan, an émigré from Ireland, had been the first to revitalize his establishment on Allen Street after the fire. Corrigan had spared no expense, using the insurance money and more of his own to regain his reputation as the town's most magnificent saloon this side of San Francisco. Just as before the fire, the front part of the large building was the saloon while in the rear were club rooms with gaming tables. Now, the bar itself was the showcase of the Saloon. Wrought from quality walnut, mahogany, and rosewood, all gilded and polished with filigree, carvings, and designs, it stretched nearly the length of the front room. As he admired the workmanship, a well-dressed businessman approached him.

"What do you think?" the man asked, spreading his hands indicating the saloon.

"It's beautiful," Mason readily admitted.

Pleased with the response, the man stuck out his hand. "I'm John Bruce by way of San Francisco. My partner and I are responsible for what you see here."

"Yes," Mason replied with a quick nod and taking his hand, "I know who you are. I've seen you around."

John Bruce smiled at the recognition. "And you are Marshal Mason Sadler. I've seen you around."

Mason smiled at the good-natured gibe. "Pleased to finally meet you."

"Likewise." Turning to the bartender, he said, "Please give the good Marshal whatever he wishes and put it on my bill."

"You don't have to do that," Mason said.

"I consider it a token of appreciation. As you can see," he said, looking around the half-empty saloon, "word is still getting out that we're open. I'd appreciate any spreading the word you might offer."

"Be happy to," Mason replied.

As Mason and John Bruce continued their conversation, Johnny Ringo slipped into the saloon and quietly took a chair not far from the bar. He smirked at what he hoped would be Mason's surprise when he finally turned around and saw him. Another bartender came around and walked up to the table.

"Gimme a whiskey," Ringo quietly said.

While the bartender walked back to get Ringo's drink, another man approached Mason and John Bruce. A well-dressed man he moved with the air of self-importance.

"Afternoon, gentlemen," he acknowledged them, removing his Broadway silk hat and pacing it on the meticulously clean countertop. "I am Amos Stowe, insurance adjuster. I pray that I have not intruded upon a private conversation."

"Not at all," John Bruce cheerfully replied. "What can I get you?"

"Though chivalrous of you, it would be unseemly for me to take advantage of your offer as we have just met." He turned his head in one crisp motion to look at the closest bartender. "A cordial, if you please. A brandy, if you have it."

"Yes, sir," the bartender politely replied. "What kind? Would you like a fruit brandy?"

"Good god, no," he answered, raising an eyebrow in disgust. "A Napoleon or a Cognac if you have it."

"We have Courvoisier."

"Ah, yes. That would be excellent." Turning to John Bruce, he said, "You have a fine establishment here if you can serve Courvoisier."

"This isn't mine," Bruce replied. "Thomas Corrigan owns this. I'm John Bruce. I've been contracted to restore the Alhambra, amongst other buildings."

"You've done well," he acknowledged, giving a quick glance around the room before turning his attention to Mason. "I don't believe I got your name, sir."

"This is US Marshal Mason Sadler," Bruce said, answering for him.

"Ah yes," Amos Stowe said, gazing down his nose at Mason. "I've heard a great deal about you. I also heard that you posted bond for a certain thug named Johnny Ringo," the man said, his superiority obvious.

"That's right," Mason calmly replied, "though I wouldn't call him a thug."

"What would you call him?" he challenged.

"I'd call him a friend."

"A friend?" the man snorted in derision. "A rather strange friend for a US Marshal. I heard that you paid a thousand dollars for his bond."

"It was $500," Mason corrected.

"Looks like you're out $500," the man said, shaking his head at the obvious.

"Why do you say that?"

"The man's a common criminal, an outlaw. You got taken, snookered. I'm surprised that a marshal like you would even consider such a thing."

Mason looked directly at the man. "You don't know Ringo, do you?"

"Only by reputation, and that's more than enough."

"Then you're a fool, mister. A man who lets others make up his mind for him isn't one to be trusted."

"You trust Ringo?" he haughtily demanded.

"I trust Ringo more than half the so-called upright citizens of this town. At least when Ringo gives his word, you know he'll come through."

"Pretty high praise for an outlaw." The man sipped his Courvoisier. "I still think you're out $500."

Mason looked squarely at the man. "Mister, I'm not normally a betting man, but I'm willing to wager another

$500 that says Ringo will pay me back. It might not be this week, this month, or even this year. Hell, I'm willing to wait ten years it that's what it takes."

"You'd wait ten years for someone to pay you back?"

"It's not the paying back that's important to me. It's the knowing. The knowing that he's good for it. It's the measure of a man, knowing that he'll do what he says."

"Suppose he gets killed before he makes good?" the man self-righteously said.

Without hesitation, Mason replied, "Knowing Ringo, he'd come back from the grave to make good."

"Now you're talking nonsense," he sniffed disdainfully.

"Only to someone who doesn't know Johnny Ringo," Mason firmly said. "Besides, truth be told, I don't care if he ever pays me back."

"What? Why?"

"First, it was bond money and when he showed up in court, I got my money back. Second, Johnny may owe me a couple of bucks for the bondsman cost, but I owe him my life. The way I see it, I'm more indebted to him than he is to me."

Amos Stowe slowly shook his head. "I worry when the law and law-breakers sit at the same table. What's this world coming to?"

Mason gazed at the man for a moment before saying, "Where do you call home?"

"San Francisco," he arrogantly replied.

"Nice town," Mason nodded. "I used to live there."

Amos Stowe regarded him with mock horror. "And you left that glorious city to come here?"

"Couldn't wait to get away," he replied. "All that humanity living on top of each other. At least here a man can breathe."

"I suppose that all depends where one lives and works," he condescendingly pointed out. "Were you employed with the constabulary in San Francisco?"

"No," he casually answered. "I worked for my father-in-law." He paused and took a slow savoring sip of whiskey.

When Mason offered no further clarification, Stowe asked, "Well? What sort of trade did was your father-in-law involved with? Perhaps I might recognize the name."

"It was a small affair. I doubt you would have heard of him," he shrugged.

"Come now, sir, no need to be ashamed. We all have to start somewhere. I assume the business was not profitable for you to come here."

"Actually, it was quite successful," Mason mused. "Maybe you may have heard of it, Worthington and Son?"

Amos choked on his drink. "Did I hear correctly? Did you say Worthington and Son?"

"That's right."

"As in Reginald Worthington?"

"That's right," Mason cheerfully replied.

"Surely you're joking," he mocked.

"Why would I joke about that?" Mason asked, cocking his head to stare at him. "If you know my father-in-law, you know one does not joke when it concerns him."

Insight suddenly dawned on Amos. "So you're the one who married his daughter and then ran off to parts unknown. Rumor had it that you were living in Europe."

"Nope. We were right here in Tombstone. Do you know my father-in-law?"

"Only by reputation," Amos said, warily regarding him. Giving voice to his thoughts, he said, "I find it odd that not only would you jettison your life in San Francisco to come here, but that you would associate with known criminals." As soon as he said it, he reminded himself that Worthington was also known to associate with known criminals.

"You're talking about Johnny Ringo?" Mason asked with a sigh.

"Of course. I would think you would have greater care for one in your position." It was said with patronizing aloofness.

"Mister," Mason replied with a tinge of frustration, "I've already told you that Johnny Ringo is a decent man." Out the corner of his eye, he saw Ringo sitting at the table, grinning at him. Johnny gave him a little wave. Hiding a smile,

Mason said, "If you met him, perhaps you'd have a better appreciation of the man."

"My sakes, sir," he blustered. "Why on earth would I want to meet such a despicable character?"

"Now, now," he chided. "Meet him first then make up your mind."

"I will never allow myself to make the acquaintance of that man," he huffed.

"Never?"

"Never!"

"Would you be willing to wager on that?"

"Of course," he adamantly affirmed.

"How much?"

"How much?" he frowned.

"Yes. Would you be willing to wager that $500 you said I lost that you would never allow yourself to be introduced to Johnny Ringo?"

Amos Stowe hesitated and looked briefly around the Saloon. There were a number of men standing at the bar, a few giving him a bemused smile, the others ignoring him or involved in other conversations. There was one man at a table close by, a cowboy by the looks of him, but he appeared lost in his own thoughts. Thinking he had only a day or two left here in Tombstone, he confidently shrugged. "Yes, I would be willing to wager."

"I accept your wager," Mason firmly stated. He looked over to John Bruce. "I call you as witness, Mister Bruce. Mister Stowe and I have laid a wager. Should he avoid introduction to Johnny Ringo, I will pay him $500. If he allows himself to meet Johnny Ringo, he will pay me the sum of $500."

John Bruce smiled and nodded. "I stand as witness."

"When are you leaving Tombstone?" Mason asked.

Amos Stowe grinned broadly in triumph. "Most likely on tomorrow evening's stage."

Mason's shoulders slumped in defeat. "That is unfortunate," he frowned. "I had not counted on you leaving so soon."

"My goodness man," Amos chortled. "What possessed you to make such a bet? You'd better get to the bank to get that $500."

With a sigh, Mason said, "I suppose so." Turning to the bartender, he said, "One more whiskey please."

"No problem, Marshal," the bartender answered with a wink.

Amos continued gloating. "This is the easiest $500 I've ever made. You should have done your research, like a good businessman. Perhaps that is why you chose the law profession. I do not say that out of malice," he hastened to add, "but merely as observation. A good businessman always does his research first. Had you done that, you would have known that I was leaving tomorrow and would not have made such a bet. Unfortunately," he held up his hands in mock sympathy, "there is little doubt that you will owe me $500." He turned his head at the sound of the cowboy at the table scooting his chair back. He watched as the man approached. Amos was surprised that the cowboy was taller than he expected, with the physique and tone of a man who spent his time outdoors.

"Begging your pardon for intruding on your discussion," the cowboy politely said to Amos, "but I couldn't help but overhear the terms and results of your arrangement. The advice you offered to the Marshal was quite sound. A good businessman always does his research. It is an essential trait of every successful businessman."

Amos favorably regarded the cowboy. "You sound as though you have experience, sir."

"In some aspects, yes," he amiably replied. "Any venture worth pursuing demands a certain amount of research." He smiled at him as though in deference to Amos' superior wisdom. "If I am not encroaching upon your discourse here, I would count it a favor if you would allow me to buy you a drink."

"My word, sir," Amos replied, pleased with the offer, "you sound as one with an education."

"I have had that privilege," he answered then looked at the tulip glass that had once contained Courvoisier. "I see that you are a man of refined tastes, preferring the elixir of Courvoisier than the baser libation of an inferior whiskey." Turning to the bartender, he said, "Two Courvoisier please."

Amos blinked as he translated the man's flowery language, both impressed and stunned to hear such words from a common cowboy.

When the drinks came, the cowboy held his tulip glass up. "To your health, sir."

"And to yours," Amos replied, inhaling the bouquet before taking and savoring a sip. "This is most kind of you, sir. By the way, sir, I did not get your name."

The cowboy's eyes suddenly twinkled in mischief. Lowering his glass just below his lips, he said, "The name's Ringo, Johnny Ringo."

Amos blanched then choked on his drink before erupting in a spasm of coughing.

"Glad you were here, Johnny," Mason smiled.

"Any time, Marshal," Ringo grinned back.

"Are you really Johnny Ringo," John Bruce asked the cowboy, his voice tinged with awe.

"In the flesh," he answered, his smile lessening. Turning his attention to Amos who had somewhat recovered, he said, "It appears that you don't like me, yet are quite willing to drink with me."

"I didn't know who you were," he lamely replied.

Ringo's lips tightened as his cold gaze focused on Amos. "So you're saying that if you did know who I was, you'd refuse to drink with me?"

"I.. I," Amos stammered.

"You called me a thug, a common criminal, a despicable character, yet were quite happy to take my offer of a drink. You insult me then drink with me."

"Now Johnny," Mason interrupted. "The man didn't know it was you. If he did, perhaps he might have said something even worse."

Ringo snapped his head to frown at Mason who was smiling. Realizing the joke, he relaxed and chuckled. "You might be right, Marshal."

"Besides," Mason pointed out, "he did say you spoke well, like an educated man."

"That he did," Ringo agreed. Looking back at Amos, he said, "The way I see it is that you owe the Marshal $500. When can he expect payment?"

"Well, uh… I," Amos hesitated.

Believing the man was going to renege on the bet, Ringo leaned threateningly in towards him. "Mister, you might get away with insulting me, but don't think you're going to get away from here without making good on your bet. You were willing to take the Marshal's money when you thought you had won. You want to be on the stage tomorrow? You better make good right now."

Amos gulped, nervously looking at the men surrounding him. None wore a smile. Even the damned Marshal, the one who should have locked up this criminal, was staring at him like it wasn't his concern that Ringo had threatened to kill him. "How… how do I know you're who you say you are?"

Ringo's eyes hardened and a lip began to curl. "You calling me a liar?"

Amos stutter-stepped backwards, his hands up in front of him. "No, no, not at all. Of course not. It was a mistake. I wasn't thinking." He jerked his wallet out from inside his vest, a thin gold chain attached, the other end of the chain disappearing inside his vest. Flipping the wallet open, he counted out five $100 notes and laid them on the bar counter.

Noticing the wad of cash remaining in the wallet, Ringo remarked, "You look to be a very wealthy man."

"I do alright," he said, slapping the wallet closed and rapidly sequestering it. "I, um, I guess I should be moving along." He took another step backwards.

"But you haven't finished your drink," Ringo coolly stated, taking a step towards him. "It's rude to accept another man's drink and not finish it."

Mason collected up the bank notes, folded them and stuck them in his pants pocket. "He's right, you know. You've insulted him once. You don't want to do it again."

Amos remained rooted for a moment, blinking at the realization that the Marshal was quite willing to let Ringo gun him down if it came to that. Shocked at the overt lawlessness of the town, he made a mental note to report this all to his superiors. He might lose the battle now, but wait until anyone in Tombstone ever tried to get insurance again. He'd show them.

Gathering his courage, he straightened up and approached the bar. "You are absolutely correct, sir," he amiably said to Ringo. "I apologize for my ill manners." Lifting up the glass in toast, he repeated, "To your health, sir."

Surprised at the change, Ringo clapped him on the back. "Now that's better. You paid your debt like a man, all fair and square." Lifting his own glass, he clinked it against Amos' glass. "To your health." Both men downed the remaining liquor.

His glass thankfully empty, Amos placed it on the bar top and once again thanked Ringo for the drink as he edged his way out of the saloon.

Once he was gone, Mason looked bemusedly at Ringo. Taking out the cash, he handed it to him. "Glad you were here."

"You made the bet," Ringo replied, holding up his hands in refusal.

"Yeah, but that was only because you were here. I wouldn't have bet had you not been here."

"Still. Your bet, your money."

Still holding out the cash, Mason said, "How about half? You deserve that just for the excellent performance. Isn't that right Mister Bruce?"

"It was a noteworthy performance," John Bruce grinned.

Smiling in response, Ringo said, "OK. I'll take half. But you keep it. You never know when I might need bail again."

Mason snorted a laugh and shook his head. "Hopefully we won't have to do that again."

Ringo flashed him a smile and readjusted his hat. "Guess I better be going."

"Wait a moment and I'll walk out with you," Mason said then turned to John Bruce. "Nice meeting you Mister Bruce. You're making Tombstone beautiful again."

Once they were outside, Mason put on his Stetson while gazing up Allen Street towards the Bird Cage Theater. "Think I might see what a certain madam is up to."

"She's a fine woman, Marshal," Ringo studiously observed. "She's the kind that would never let you down."

Mason immediately understood the inference. Unlike Elizabeth's self-destruction, Belle was thrilled with life and wanted to experience it to the fullest. His doubt was whether she could be satisfied with him.

Sensing his indecision, Ringo quietly offered, "It is obvious to many that she is enthralled with you. A word of advice?"

"Yes?"

"You may have to come up with another plan for catching outlaws in the Bird Cage."

Mason grinned at him. "Shouldn't surprise me you'd know about that. I'd appreciate it if you keep that to yourself."

"No problem, Marshal. If someone's dumb enough to rob a bank then waltz around in public, they get what they deserve."

Mason studied him for a moment. "And that reminds me," he soberly said. "When the stage leaves tomorrow with that insurance adjustor in it, I don't want to hear that it's been robbed on the way to Tucson."

"If it is, you know it wasn't me," he innocently replied.

Mason shifted his eyes to look at him. "Of course not."

"You don't have to worry about me, Marshal. I got your back."

"I know, and I'm mighty pleased you do." He paused momentarily, staring at Ringo as though wanting to say more. Oblivious, Ringo was about to step out into the street when Mason said, "Hold on sec Johnny. I've got something else to say to you."

Puzzled, Ringo turned to face him. "I already said I'd be no trouble."

"That's not it, Johnny. You notice how that insurance fellow got real quiet when I mentioned who my father-in-law was?"

Ringo scrunched his face in thought. "I do recall him being less garrulous."

"Garrulous," Mason repeated with a smile. "You're an interesting man, Johnny Ringo. Don't know many cowboys who would use that word, let alone know what it meant. But the man knew my father-in-law by way of reputation. I'll tell you right now, there is no one in the Arizona Territory who could stop my father-in-law from getting what he wanted."

Frowning, Ringo asked, "What does that have to do with us here?"

"More than you realize."

"So what does he want?"

"My head on a silver platter," Mason replied.

Ringo furrowed his brows. "Why?"

"Because I took his only child away from him, because that only child now lies at Boot hill," he explained.

Ringo nodded in understanding. "He'll send someone here to kill you, and you won't even know he's here."

His lips pursed, Mason slowly bobbed his head in agreement. "But not just me. He'll punish anyone I care about."

Ringo quickly looked down the street to the Theater. "Belle."

"And you," he quietly pointed out.

"Me?" Ringo said then thought about the statement. "I take that as a high compliment, Marshal."

"We'll see how high a compliment you think it is when they come gunning for you."

"I can take care of myself."

"No doubt you can. I'm just giving you a heads up. But just so you know, for each one we take out, two more will take his place. It won't end until either I'm dead or he's dead. So what I'm saying here is that it might be in your best interests to find some other locale to hang around in."

Ringo tilted his head to gaze at him, his normally somber eyes clear and focused. "Can't do that, Marshal. First, I've never run away from a fight. And second, I like here. If he wants a fight, I'll give him one."

Mason gave him a subdued smile of appreciation. "I figured you'd say that."

"What's your plan?"

"Don't have one yet."

"When you do, let me know." Adjusting his white felt gambler hat snugly on his head, he grinned. "Think I'll go find a Faro game somewhere."

"There's probably one over at the Bird Cage," Mason said with a smile.

"I do believe there is," Ringo grinned.

"Annie's a fine lady," Mason observed.

"She's not a crib girl," he blurted.

"Never thought she was," Mason calmly replied. "She's not that kind of girl. She likes her fun but knows when to put a cap on it. Lots of fellas would love to bed her, but she's not like that. Seems to me she's the loyal sort, if you know what I mean."

"I think I do," Ringo nodded.

"She's the kind who only gives her heart once," Mason continued, "and when she does, it's permanent. Neither hell nor high water will change it. It's a good trait to have in a woman. It means she cares more about you than herself."

"Me?" he sputtered.

"Now, Johnny," Mason smiled paternally. "I've seen the way she looks at you. She's smitten."

"Think so?" he frowned, suddenly aware that there was more going on than he wanted to admit.

"I know so. Just be good to her," he said, giving him a friendly pat on the shoulder. "She's one of a kind."

Chapter 4

Sipping a cup of coffee, Mason stood on the porch of Missus Hunt's Lodging House, leaning against one of the columns supporting the roof. The morning sky was cloudless and azure blue. Though cool right now, he knew it was going to be a warm one today.

His hands wrapping the cup for warmth, he gazed down Allen Street, amazed at the change in the city. Despite the ravage of the fire, the town was rebuilding itself, more permanently this time with adobe brick replacing clapboard and canvas.

There were other signs of progress. Some gas company out of New York promised to have gas illumination in Tombstone before the end of the year. And there was the new post office on 5th Street. It wasn't open yet, but it would be in the next day or two. Then yesterday, the Huachuca Water Company put in a fire plug on the corner of Allen and 6th Street. They were going to test the pressure tonight.

He shook his head thinking how much different the town might have been had they water enough to put out the fire that destroyed so much of the business district. Yet the city was like a phoenix rising out of the ashes of its destruction. It was being built stronger and better.

Mason caught a glimpse of someone moving down the street, heading his way. Charlie Parsons, the telegraph operator hustled towards him, waving a piece of paper in the air at him

"Morning, Marshal," Charlie said, walking up.

"Morning, Charlie. What's that you're waving at me?"

"It's a telegram for that Jedidiah Wood fella ya asked me about."

"What's it say?"

Charlie flipped the paper to read it. "Unable to send inventory. Suggest you return immediately."

Mason cocked an eyebrow at him. "That's it?"

"Yup."

Mason pursed his lips musing then said, "Thanks, Charlie. Much obliged."

"What's it mean?"

"Don't know," he replied with a shrug. "Might be some kind of code... or it might be just what it says. He claimed he was a merchant. Sounds like that might be what he is."

Charlie's shoulders slumped in disappointment. "Had another one 'bout the same time fer some fella named Amos Stowe."

Mason grinned as he recalled the wager in the Alhambra yesterday. He was sure Mister Stowe was still smarting from the loss of $500.

"What did it say?"

"Something like, 'Packages arrive in Bisbee Tuesday. Arrange and deliver.'"

His brows furrowed, Mason drifted back to the interaction with the man, remembering he said that he was an insurance adjuster. 'Packages' could mean anything from insurance forms to processing claims. And the way the man reacted when Mason told him about Worthington, said the man was a paper-pusher of upper management, one obsessed with forms and procedures. Bah. With little further thought, Mason dismissed the man as irrelevant.

"Thanks, Charlie. Appreciate you looking out for me."

"That's m'job, Marshal," he grinned. "Anyway I can help."

A gunshot reverberated causing Mason to hand his coffee cup to Charlie as he ran off in the direction of the sound. Turning the corner at Toughnut and Allen, he saw a crowd beginning to form in the middle of 3rd Street up past Billy King's Blacksmith shop. David Neagle came around from Allen Street and the two lawmen approached the crowd.

"What happened?" David demanded as he pushed through the crowd to see a man crumpled on the street, blood pooling from the gunshot wound to his chest.

"Frank Peel shot a Chinaman," a man replied.

"Hell, it's just a Chinaman," a voice said loudly enough to be heard. "Good riddance."

There was a general murmur of agreement when Mason snarled, "A man's been killed. Did any of you see it happen?" He stared at the group who responded with shrugs and head shakes. "If you've nothing better to do than hang around here, go do it somewhere else."

As some of the gawkers began to drift away, David looked over to see Sing Li, the owner of the Chinese Herb Shop next to the blacksmith. The man's usually cheerful face was masked in bitterness.

"Do you know who this is?" David asked.

"Li Chao," he replied, casting wary eyes at those who remained eavesdropping on the question and replies.

"Did you see what happened?" David asked.

"Li Chao and I were talking when a man came in. I do not know this man, but he was drunk. He said that Chinamen don't belong in Tombstone. Li Chao said that the Chinese are important to Tombstone, and we contribute just like every other citizen. This made the man mad, and he cursed at Li Chao who chose to leave rather than argue. The man followed him out. I heard the man threaten him. Then I heard the gunshot."

David turned back to the few who loitered at the edges of the sidewalks. "Did anyone see where Frank went?"

When no one responded, Sing Li said, "I saw him get on a horse and ride north."

"What's it matter?" a voice called out. "It's just a Chinaman."

"That's enough," Mason shot back. "Li Chao was right. The Chinese are a part of Tombstone just like everyone else. It's about time you accepted that." Turning to David, he said, "Who is he?"

"He's supposedly a gambler," David replied. "Comes into town every so often to play Faro. Don't know where he lives. I've had a few run-ins with him before, mostly on drunk and disorderly. Saw him a few times friendly with Curly Bill."

Nodding, Mason said, "I'll ride out and see if I can track him down. What's he look like?"

"About my height," David said.   "Thin, moustache, wears a gambler hat. Has a short scar on his right cheek from a knife fight."

"You will bring him to justice, Marshal?" Sing Li said with surprise.

"I'll do my best."

Sing Li stared at him with appreciation. "I can help if you wish."

"No thanks," Mason politely, though kindly, replied. "This is a law matter. It doesn't need citizen involvement."

Sing Li blinked at the word 'citizen,' surprised and pleased.

Mason turned back to David, "I'll check in with you later."

"Thanks, Mason. Appreciate it." David glanced over his shoulder to see the Undertaker striding towards them. Turning to Sing Li, he said, "I'll need your help here."

Frank Peel's trail was easy to follow. Mason simply trailed the cloud of dust in the far distance heading towards the Dragoons. Mason shook his head and grimly chuckled. Why is it everyone looking to hide heads for the Dragoons? Yes, Cochise managed to elude capture while carrying out successful raids, all the time hiding out in the Dragoons. Fact was, he was still there, buried somewhere in the mountains. Only the Indian Agent Tom Jeffords and the Chiricahua people knew the exact place. But no one would say where. Mason wondered if Nantan and Taboca knew. It was a question he had never thought to ask.

Mason saw the dust settle and disappear just before the Middle Pass road. Frank must have slowed down and headed off to hide. Most likely there was a cabin close by here he would settle for the night and head out in the morning. Mason doubted Frank would ride the Pass road at night. There were too many twists and turns and nighttime was approaching.

Following the freshly chewed up dirt, Mason slowed his pace as the dimming light made it harder to follow Frank's trail. He finally pulled up at the last spot where he thought Frank had been and waited for night to swallow up the landscape.

As darkness settled, Mason scanned left and right, waiting for Frank to reveal himself. He didn't have long to wait as just to his north past the clumps of chaparral, a bit of light flashed in a window then was covered up, light seeping out the cracks in the walls of a long-forgotten cabin. Mason urged his mount forward, crossing a dry arroyo and up a path to a cabin nestled amongst the oak and manzanita trees.

Dismounting, Mason paused long enough to hobble his horse then proceeded on foot, cautiously making his way in the direction of the light. Scouting the surroundings, he lowered himself to the ground to allow the evening to layer itself on the land.

It was close to midnight when Mason rose and crept forward to the cabin. Frank had left his horse secured to the porch post, though the saddle and blanket were in the cabin.

Patting the horse while whispering comfort, Mason loosened the reins and guided the mount back to where his horse rested. Securing the new addition, Mason returned to creep around the cabin, noting one rear window and back door.

Once around the cabin, Mason moved off a bit so that he could have good view and line of sight. Settling back down on the ground, he checked his rifle and six-shooters. Taking aim at the upper part of the cabin, he closed his eyes to protect his night vision the squeezed off a round.

The sound echoed in the night followed by the noise of mad scrambling inside the cabin. Mason waited then fired another round through the front door.

"Who the hell's out there?" a voice from the inside cried out. "What do you want?"

"Frank Peel?" Mason called back.

"Who's askin'?"

"US Marshal Mason Sadler."

"Don't know no Frank Peel. You got the wrong man, Marshal," the voice yelled back. "Ain't nobody here by that name.

"I don't think so. Tom Moses from the Capital Saloon says you owe him money. I'm here to collect."

"The man's a damned liar. I paid him off three days ago."

"That's not the way I heard him tell it." Masson stifled a laugh. The man was far too easy to manipulate. Now if he could bring him in without any trouble.

"You go on back and tell him I said he was a liar. You go on and tell him that."

"I can't."

"Why not?"

"Because he's dead. You killed him."

"I ain't done no such thing," he yelled. "I ain't killed anybody in a long time."

"That's not what I heard," Mason retorted. "I heard you killed Tom Moses and a Chinaman when you were escaping."

"That's a damned lie. I ain't done nuthin' to Tom Moses. I shot the Chinaman because he made me mad and anyway, he's a Chinaman and he don't count. But I ain't done nuthin' to Tom Moses. Why would I do that?"

"So it was just the Chinaman you shot and killed, and not Tom Moses?"

"That's right. Now you go on and clear outta here Marshal and find Tom's killer."

"Frank Peel?"

"Yeah?"

"I'm arresting you for the murder of Li Chao. Come out with your hands high up over your head."

There was a muffled curse inside the cabin as Frank realized he had just confessed to the killing. "But he was just a Chinaman. No jury's gonna convict me of shootin' a Chinaman."

"They will when they see it was cold blooded murder. I think I might wait until Hanging Judge Harper comes to town before we go to trial."

"Why you son-of-a –"

"Now Frank," Mason interrupted. "Let's be reasonable. You come out now and I might be persuaded to go to trial sooner."

"You ain't takin' me in," Frank snapped. "You'll have to kill me first."

"Now Frank, why do you want to do it the hard way?"

"I said my piece," he exclaimed. "You come and get me."

"Alright, boys," Mason called out to his imaginary posse. "I don't want anyone doing anything stupid. Jacob and Stephen, you stay where you are and cover the back. The rest of us will cover the front. We'll set fire to the place once it's light enough to see."

Mason waited, letting the silence permeate. He heard the front creak open followed by a muffled "damn" when Frank realized his horse was missing.

"OK Marshal," Frank called out. "We'll do it your way."

"Not yet," Mason called back. "Wait until first light so I can see where your hands are."

"Damn it all," he fumed. "I'm tossin' my gun out." The door opened and a .45 arced in the air and landed with a thump in the dirt just beyond the porch boards.

"I said first light, Frank, and I mean it. I'm not trusting you unless you come out buck naked."

"Well I ain't comin' out that way," he indignantly shouted.

"Then we wait for first light. Get some sleep in the meantime while the boys take turns watching to see if you make a break for it."

"Why all this fuss for a Chinaman?" Frank called out. "It ain't like I shot a white man."

"You killed a man, Frank. It doesn't matter if he's Chinese, Mexican, Indian, or a white man. You murdered someone and now you have to pay, maybe even with your own life. It's called the law."

"You go to hell," he shouted.

"I'd rather not," he airily replied. "I've sent too many folks down there and I doubt my reception would be a pleasant one. Besides, I have no intention of going there. You, on the other hand…"

"Real funny, Marshal."

"You going to stay awake all night?"

"Don't got much choice, do I?"

"I've already told you we won't do anything until first light. I give you my word. You ought to get some sleep because I doubt you'll get much before the trial. With those beds in the jail, you might as well be sleeping on the ground."

When Frank didn't respond, Mason got comfortable as best he could. He could hear movement in the cabin as though Frank was repositioning whatever furniture was inside, most likely barricading himself for a final stand. With a yawn, Mason relaxed and waited for dawn.

When it was light enough to make out the individual boards in the door and cabin walls, Mason hailed the cabin. "You ready Frank?"

"Just about," came the reply. A few moments later, Frank called out, "Alright, I'm comin' out. Stand where I can see you, Marshal."

"Now Frank, how dumb do you think I am? Don't confuse homely with stupid. You come out with your hands up high." Mason watched as the window shade barely pulled back and Frank covertly peered out trying to discover the Marshal's whereabouts.

"I'll be right out," he said, vainly searching.

Deciding to help him, Mason stood, looking off to his left and right, pretending to silently communicate with his imaginary posse.

Frank said, "How'd you find me?"

"You left a trail a blind man could follow."

The shade eased forward, and Mason raced to the opposite side of the cabin, guns ready.

"Alright," Frank said. "I'm comin' out."

The door jerked open, and Frank lurched out, a six-shooter in each hand, blazing away at the spot he believed Mason to be. A queasy feeling erupted in the pit of his stomach as he quickly realized instead of the Marshal, he was shooting up a large agave.

"Over here Frank," Mason said with a cool smile.

Frank whirled around, guns smoking, fear and anger in his eyes. He snapped his head left to right. "Where is everyone?"

"They got bored and went home," he replied with mock seriousness. "Now throw down your guns."

Frank's fear faded into false confidence when he realized it was just him and the Marshal. The Marshal's fame was in the draw, but they both had guns in hand, and it was just a matter of who could aim and shoot first.

Sensing Frank's new-found confidence, Mason warned, "Don't do it, Frank."

"I don't know what you mean, Marshal." As soon as he said it, he raised his guns, discovering too late that Mason's aim was far better.

A single shot to the chest caused Frank to jerk back then momentarily wobble on weakening legs before he dropped to his knees. Giving Mason a pained look of surprise, he flopped over onto his side, his eyes glazing over with the sheen of death.

With a cluck of the tongue, Mason shook his head and holstered his gun then went to gather up the horses to bring Frank back.

Mason rocked lazily in the saddle as he headed back to Tombstone. Trailing behind him was Frank's horse, with Frank's body slung over the saddle. When Mason arrived in town, he turned onto 3rd Street ensuring that he passed by Sing Li's herb shop.

Word had already spread that the Marshal was back, and Sing Li stood on the sidewalk as Mason sauntered by. Bending his head, Mason pinched the brim of his Stetson in respect to the herbalist. Sing Li returned the gesture with a reverent bow.

Once Mason passed, Sing Li flipped the sign on the door to 'CLOSED' and hurried off to tell Wuhan Mei the good news.

Several days later, three airship travelers were in Ed's room at the Belmont when a soft knock interrupted their discourse. Ed opened the door to the waiting Becca.

"May I come in?" she said with a sweet smile.

"Of course. Glad you're here." He opened wide the door as she breezed past him.

"Good afternoon, gentlemen," she said, glancing around the room. Earl stood in the corner near the window. Gordon sat on a wooden chair by the wardrobe, two hands resting on his briefcase, which lay flat across his lap. Looking back at Ed as he closed the door, she asked, "What's the plan?"

"We wait here for the moment," Ed replied. "Someone is supposed to come by and give us the low down on the situation."

"You said that two hours ago," Earl snarled.

"Patience, Earl," Ed said, not without some irritation. "We've only got here this morning. We've got time."

"I've been two days on that airship. M'legs need stretchin'." He cast a sour look at Becca. "How come you didn't go on the airship?"

"Things that fall out of the sky are never a pretty sight," she replied with a carefree smile.

"Are you saying you don't like to fly?" Gordon asked.

"Let's just say that I prefer terra firma. The more the firma," she said with mock seriousness, "the less the terror." She giggled at her joke, causing Gordon's normally sober face to smile.

A knock at the door silenced them.

Ed opened the door to a well-dressed man who moved with the air of self-importance.

"Good afternoon, lady and gentlemen." Removing his Broadway silk hat, he gave a short crisp bow to Becca then wiped clean the top of the dresser by the door before placing the hat on top. "I am Amos Stowe, insurance adjuster for Worthington and Son. I trust you had a pleasant journey."

"Yes, we did, thank you," Ed replied, closing the door. Once secured, he lowered his voice and said, "What do you have for us?"

"It will not be as easy as expected," Stowe said. "There was a fire last month that wiped out a large part of the town. That said, the town is rebuilding quickly, but folks are wary about strangers not associated with rebuilding. I don't know what individual stories you have but may want to reevaluate them if necessary."

Ed nodded then asked, "What about Sadler?"

"Sadler's got a reputation as a quick draw."

"I can take 'im," Earl snorted in derision.

"All in due time, Earl," Ed reminded him.

"Sadler has a love interest," Stowe continued.

"Already?" Ed repeated surprised. "The man works fast."

"Her name is Belle Dubois."

"She's French?"

"Supposedly," Stowe answered. "She's the Madam at the Bird Cage Theater on the east side of town.

"Involved with a madam," Earl guffawed. "No wonder Worthington is madder than a wet hen."

"Anyone else?" Ed asked.

"Johnny Ringo," Stowe replied, "a gunslinger, supposed to be one of the fastest."

Earl shook his head and laughed out loud. "This don't get no better. The man is hot after a whore and his best friend's a gunslinger. I'm surprised Worthington didn't take 'im out sooner."

"Anyone else?" Ed repeated, ignoring Earl's outburst.

"Those are the main ones, the ones he cares about. If there's anyone else, I'll let you know." Picking up his hat, he gave them a final warning. "Sadler's well liked in town, so be careful."

With the door closed behind Stowe, Ed turned to the others. "Here are the assignments. Earl, you have Sadler."

"Got it," he said with a wide confident grin.

"Becca, you have Ringo."

"A pleasure," she nodded charmingly. "This could be fun."

"I'll take Belle," Ed announced.

"What about me?" Gordon pouted.

"We save you for last," Ed said with a wicked smile. "Scout out the town and see where you can best set up your toys." He then looked each one in the eye. "No one kills their mark until I give the word. Understand? We take our time. Set everything up so that they all look like accidents. There's no rush. I know we all want to get back to civilization, but we're being paid to do a job. Let's do it right."

As they prepared to leave, Ed motioned for Earl to remain behind, waving his hand at him to close the door.

The last to leave was Becca who smiled at Earl. "See you in town, Earl."

Smiling at her with only his lips, he closed the door behind her then turned to Ed. "Yeah?"

"That point I said about taking your time?"

"Yeah."

"Forget about it. The way I see it is we take out Sadler first," Ed said, "sort of like cutting the head off a snake. We take him out, the rest will be easy. But not too quickly. Give Becca chance to work her wiles on Ringo. The man's got a reputation as a gunslinger. Let her get Ringo away from town. That way you won't be distracted when you kill Sadler."

"How long ya figure?" Earl grinned, confident of the outcome.

"Couple of days at most," he reasoned. "She's hard to resist once she gets going."

"No problem," Earl replied with smug satisfaction. "Sadler's as good as dead."

Belle stood at the bar when Annie and Ringo came in, Ringo gallantly holding the door open for her. Annie immediately slipped an arm around his arm. Seeing Belle, she gave her a happy and contented smile.

"You two have a good time?" Belle asked.

"He took me to the river," she gleefully exclaimed. "We took our shoes off and waded in the water just like two kids. It was such fun." She held up a smooth river pebble. "I collected this as a keepsake. That spot will always be special to me." Though supposedly speaking to Belle, she gazed at Ringo with adoring eyes.

"As it will be to me, my lovely lady of the theater," Ringo replied.

Belle noticed his choice of words. Though Annie worked at the Bird Cage, she wasn't a crib girl. Belle liked that about her. She didn't have to sell herself to be successful. Annie was unique in that way for most of the girls here wound up in one of the upstairs cribs. When the time came for them to move on, they had no talents other than those of the crib. The shabby cribs on other side of 6th Street were testaments to those whose lives were inextricably intertwined with the human detritus that had been reduced to begging for favor.

Though Ringo was a gunslinger and gambler, the man had many redeeming qualities. Yet he seemed to move as one in torment as though happiness was an elusive chimera. Seeing him with Annie, Belle prayed that he would find happiness with a woman who was obviously in love with him.

Annie unhooked her arm to talk to Belle while Ringo moseyed up to the bar to order two glasses of wine.

Annie leaned in to Belle. "Johnny wants to take me to dinner and a midnight stroll around town. I know I'm supposed to work tonight, but can I take tonight off? I'll work another night to make it up."

"Of course. Just don't make it a habit," she said with a smile.

"I won't." She shot a glance at Ringo who patiently waited for Jack to pour the wine. "I'm in love, Belle. I've never met a man like him. He's so caring and attentive. He's a real gentleman."

Belle tenderly placed a hand on her arm. "It's nice to see you both happy. Enjoy yourselves."

Ringo walked over, handing Annie a glass of wine. Holding up his glass in a toast, he looked at Belle then let his gaze linger on Annie. "To the two most beautiful ladies in all of the Arizona Territory."

"That was very sweet, Johnny," Belle said while Annie blushed. "Annie says you're taking her to dinner then a midnight stroll."

"She'll be safe with me," he affirmed.

"I have no doubt of that, Johnny," Belle replied then winked. "But will you be safe with her?"

Ringo flashed a grin as Annie blushed again and opened her mouth to defend herself when he said, "I'm sure she has only the most honorable of intentions."

Belle smiled in agreement. "Of that you may have no doubt. Annie is one of the most honest and caring people I know."

"What else is she like?" Ringo asked.

"I think the more you get to know her," Belle replied, her attention on Ringo, "the more you'll like her."

"I find her a most fascinating person," he said.

"I know –"

"Hey," Annie fussed. "I can hear you. I'm standing right here."

Belle grinned. "Why don't you two save the wine for later. Go enjoy yourselves."

Placing her glass on the bar counter, Annie gave Belle a quick peck on the cheek. "Thanks Belle."

Standing outside in the warm later afternoon, Annie slipped an arm around Ringo's arm. "Let's go for a walk, Johnny. I need to tell you something."

Ringo wanted to say something clever, but from Annie's demeanor, he knew better. "Let's get away from the bustle here and stroll ourselves northward."

Squeezing her arm to him, he guided the way along Allen Street, ignoring the glares and stares of the town's proper women.

As they turned on 4th Street, he said, "What is it you wish to tell me, Annie?"

"I want you to know more about me," she replied, "and my family."

"I am your attentive servant, madam," he gallantly answered.

Annie paused for a moment then said, "My father was lynched three years ago for cattle rustling."

"I know about that," Ringo replied. "I also know the sins of the father are not the sins of the daughter."

"Not everybody feels the same way," she reminded him. "When Pa was killed, my Ma and younger brother moved on."

"Where?"

"Back east to kin in Missouri. I stayed here because I didn't want to go back. I figured I could make it on my own here in Tombstone. Besides, there was nothing to go back to. At least here I'm making good money."

"Sounds like you made a wise choice," he pointed out.

They walked in silence for a bit, heading towards Safford Street. Then Annie broke the silence.

"Do you believe someone can come back from the dead, Johnny?"

Ringo blinked in thought before answering. "I used to think it was all hogwash, until the Marshal told me about what he saw. And then when Belle added her version to it, I began to have some doubts as to my steadfast denial. Now, I can't say that I've ever seen anyone come back from the dead. And thinking about my own past, I'm not so sure I want to see any of them again. They all might be a tad angry at me."

"You've killed a lot of men, Johnny?" she quietly asked.

"Not as many as they give me credit for," he softly answered.

Annie nodded then said, "I'm glad you know how to take care of yourself. I wish you had been around when my Pa was lynched. Had you been here he would've had a chance at a fair trial."

'What's done is done," he said. "Can't change what's in the past."

"That's what I say," she readily agreed. "That's why I asked if you believe in the dead coming back, because my Pa came back to see me."

"What did he say?" he asked, more curious than surprised.

"He didn't say anything," she explained. "He just stared and waved his finger like this at me." She held her index finger up and shook it side to side.

"Maybe he was warning you about something," Ringo said. "Did he talk or communicate or anything like that?"

Annie twisted her head to gaze at him with affection. "You don't think I'm crazy, do you." It wasn't a question.

"No I don't. If I was to think that you were crazy then I'd have to say the same about the Marshal and Belle, and I know they're not crazy." He frowned and shook his head. "Now that I think about it, I'm probably crazier than you three."

Annie laughed and squeezed his arm to her side. "You're the best Johnny."

Flattered, he asked, "Have you seen your father since?"

"Just once more. Last week. He did the same thing as before with his finger. It's like he's trying to tell me something, but I can't figure out what it is?"

"Did you speak to him?"

"I tried the second time, but he just stood there."

"What did he look like?"

"He looked like someone who'd been in the grave for a while."

"Mostly skeleton?" he asked, his interest growing.

"Not quite."

"How'd you know it was him?"

Annie shrugged. "I could tell it was him."

"Maybe he doesn't want you working at the Bird Cage," he suggested.

"I don't know why," she said. "He used to enjoy the Bird Cage before he was lynched."

118

"Enjoying it is one thing," Ringo answered. "Having your daughter work here is another."

"But I'm not doing things like the other girls," she countered.

"Maybe he just wants to make sure you don't," he shrugged. "Not meaning to be impertinent," he apologetically said, "but it seems to me he didn't know his daughter very well if he thinks like that."

"I really didn't see a whole lot of Pa. Ma was the one who raised me." Her face softened and her eyes dreamily gazed off into the distance. "We were still living on the farm in Missouri. One day we went into town, and they were having a dance. I begged to come and Ma took me. I had never seen anybody dance before and it looked like such fun. They were cavorting around and laughing and smiling. I decided then and there that I wanted to be a dancer."

"You're a mighty fine one," Ringo complimented. "Every man who comes to the Theater wants to dance with you."

"You're not jealous are you, Johnny?" she smiled sweetly at him.

"Should I be?"

"No."

They stopped and looked out towards the Dragoon Mountains, shadows beginning to stretch across them as the sun settled. The sounds of the mines surrounded them, but here at the edge of town, they didn't seem so intrusive.

"I've fallen for you, Johnny," Annie said, looking at the peaks.

Ringo swallowed hard. "You deserve better than me."

"There ain't anyone better than you," she answered.

"I'm nothing but heartache," he said, staring down at the ground.

"Are you saying you don't have feelings for me?" she asked, a timorous quiver in her voice.

"I'm not saying that at all," he quickly replied, lifting his head to look at her. "I'm just saying what kind of life would it be with me? You need a man who's steady, a man who will provide you with a nice home and a family."

Annie turned to face him, holding his hands in hers. "No Johnny. I need a man to love me. I don't care for all those other things."

Johnny blinked, his eyes moist.

When no words emerged, Annie smiled at him. "That's OK, Johnny. As long as I know you have feelings for me, I'm OK with that for now."

"I do have feelings for you," he huskily replied, "deep feelings... and they frighten me."

"Why?"

"Because I don't want anything to happen to you and I'm afraid that if word gets out that we're together, men will hurt you to try and hurt me." His lips tightened at the thought, and he suppressed a rising anger.

"Then let's go away from here," she blurted. "Run off to some place; start a new life together."

"Can't," he simply said.

"Why not?"

"Marshal needs my help."

"Really?" she frowned.

Deciding that her life was as much in danger as his, he explained the expected danger from Worthington.

"That's why we can't go," he earnestly said. "We need to stay and protect the Marshal... and Belle."

Annie gazed at him with profound respect and adoration. "You really are a wonderful man, to put someone else's welfare above your own. You're one in a million Johnny Ringo." She wrapped her arms around him, kissing him hard.

Mason walked into the well-stocked store of Chinese delicacies, art objects, and incense. Behind the counter, the ruler of the Hoptown, as the white residents called the Chinatown part of Tombstone, smiled as he walked in.

Wuhan Mei was a plump woman taken to wearing purple brocaded silk dresses and adorning herself with rather large amounts of Asian jade jewelry. She smiled constantly and went out of her way to accommodate customers in her shop in Tombstone's Hoptown, especially those customers seeking the blissful enlightenment of laudanum or opium. Yet her smile could be deceiving, for she ruled Hoptown as a stern matriarch. No one did business in Hoptown without her permission. Not only did she rule the Chinese residents of the city, her word and decisions were undisputed law and no Chinese dared disobey.

All the hired housework, yardwork, washing and cooking was done by Chinese labor. The town folk quickly learned that if they wanted Chinese help, they had to bargain with Wuhan Mei. Further, payment was never paid to the worker, but always to Wuhan Mei. However, she guaranteed their work and their integrity. Her guarantee was: "If they steal from you, I will pay."

Wuhan Mei also handled all the drugs in Tombstone, from opium to laudanum to cocaine, though most demand was for opium and laudanum. She also controlled the gambling in Hoptown. Behind her store and in the tunnels beneath were gambling games and other distractions, all policed by Wuhan Mei's special force of Chinese enforcers.

Seeing Mason, she gave him a warm smile. "Ah, it is good to see you, Marshal."

"Miss Mei," he said, pinching the brim of his Stetson. "You're looking well." He walked up to the counter.

"You are most kind, Marshal," she said with a polite bow.

"I understand you asked me to come by. Is there anything I can do for you?"

"Sing Li has told me of your kindness to the Celestials here in Tombstone."

"I brought a man to justice for committing a horrible crime," he said. "I only wish I could have brought him to trial. He needed to be an example to others. Everyman's life is worthy and valuable."

"You are correct," she said, "but not all feel as you do."

"Sadly, that is true."

"But you are not like them. I have declared you a friend of Celestials."

Mason responded with a grave bow and another pinch of the brim of his Stetson. "You do me a great honor."

Wuhan Mei studied him, knowing he could, if he wanted, shut down much of her lucrative businesses. Yet he allowed her to rule this part of the City unmolested. Most likely because she had order and discipline here. Still, he had come as an inferior to a superior. He had manners… and he was quite good looking. Pity he wasn't Chinese.

"I am sorry about Miss Elizabeth," she said, choosing her words carefully.

Mason regarded her with an appreciative smile, knowing she supplied the drugs that were killing Elizabeth.

"She chose her own path," he said. "Those who supplied her with her drugs merely provided a service. It was her choice to indulge or turn away. Can one blame another when one will not listen to reason?"

"Wisely spoken," she said with sincere admiration. "If ever you need help, we will stand with you."

"You are most gracious," he said, "and I will remember your kind offer." With a nod, he turned and strode through the open door. Standing outside, Mason adjusted his Stetson and pondered how he might use this latest boon.

Belle looked in the bar mirror as a well-dressed man with a full beard and smoking a full-bent pipe entered thought the middle doors. Blowing out a slow puff, he stood momentarily surveying the gaming and drinking before making his way to the bar. He moved with the grace of confidence, nodding politely to those he passed.

Smiling at Jack, he said, "A brandy please."

"What kind would you like?"

"I'm in the mood for a fruit brandy. Might you have something appropriate?"

"I've both cherry and blackberry."

"Cherry."

Jack reached behind him for a snifter glass and poured an ample serving.

Accepting the glass, the man caught Belle's eye and he lifted the shifter in salute. "Is this your establishment, gracious lady?"

"Not yet," she smiled.

With a laugh, he swirled the liquor, inhaled the bouquet then took a savoring sip, closing his eyes with warm satisfaction. "By Jove that is an excellent brandy." Staring directly at Belle, he said, "I haven't had brandy like this since that time in Chicago at a little place called Allan's."

Belle perked up and gave him her attention. "Can't say that I've ever been there."

"You'd like it," he said, glancing around the theater. "Doesn't quite have the ambiance that you have here. It's a bit more subdued. But then, that's to be expected from a dour Scotsman." He smiled. "Though last I heard he was beginning to loosen up."

"Now that you mention it," Belle replied, quickly shifting her eyes to see that no one was paying particular attention, "I have heard of a pub called Allan's. I also heard that his sons were taking over the business."

"You heard correctly. And, quite frankly, because the poor man never sleeps. Young Bill is mastering the variety of ales and liquors and distributers, while young Robert handles the accounting side of the business. So far it seems to work quite well."

Belle heard enough to know the man was a Pinkerton agent. "What brings you to our little part of paradise here, mister...?"

"Shephard, Thaddeus Shephard," he said with a flourish. "I'm here on behalf of my bank, a growing institution for a growing community."

"Where might that be?"

"Sacramento."

Belle gave him a feigned look of puzzlement. "You've come all the way from Sacramento, California to Tombstone to establish another bank? I think we probably have enough banks already."

"You may be correct, Miss...?"

"Belle," she replied, "Belle Dubois." *Or is it Sadler*, she smiled to herself.

"You may be right, Miss Belle. But my institution sent me here to check things out. We've heard good reports and thought to investigate for ourselves."

"I think you'll find Tombstone a lively place, Mister Shephard. We're not quite the refined Sacramento, but there is much here that is very attractive."

"What about the criminal element?" he asked, savoring another sip of brandy.

"We are much like any other city grappling with its wealth, but the law here has made significant progress." She cast a glance at Jack who slid a sangaree in front of her. "That was sweet. Thank you, Jack."

Jack nodded and moved down the bar to attend another customer.

"We heard the same and that is why I am here, to learn about Tombstone," Shephard said.

"How long will you be staying?"

Shephard shrugged. "Until I am satisfied this is the right place for us to do business."

"And if it isn't?" Concern crept in as she realized Pinkerton might want to send her someplace else.

"If it isn't," he answered, "then we might have to look for another suitable location."

"As long as silver pours from the mines here," she said, "I doubt you will find a better location."

"You may be right, Miss Belle."

Finishing his brandy, he placed the snifter glass on the bar counter and reached into his pocket to pay.

Belle held a hand up to stop him. "This one is on the house, Mister Shephard. Welcome to Tombstone."

"You are most kind, Miss Belle," he suavely said with a crisp bow. "Perhaps you will allow me the return favor of inviting you and Marshal Sadler to dine with me."

Belle smiled at the invitation. The Pinkertons had done their homework.

"We'd be delighted to dine with you," she amiably replied, wondering how they discovered her romantic involvement.

"This evening perhaps?"

"This evening would be fine. Are you staying in town?"

"No, I'm staying in Bisbee at the moment. When we heard of the conflagration, we thought it best to stay elsewhere. I must admit that I am surprised at the phoenix that has arisen from the ashes. Tombstone looks almost as if nothing had happened."

"You are wise to have made lodgings elsewhere for the time being," Belle opined, "as most of the hotels are booked with carpenters and builders."

"You are right again," he smiled. "Well then, I should get to the telegraph office and let my partners know I've safely arrived. Good day to you madam. I look forward to this evening, say at six o'clock?"

"That would be fine."

With another polite bow, Shephard politely made his way through the crowd and out the door.

Worthington stood at the window, staring out at the streets of San Francisco below, watching the scuttling of pedestrians as they swarmed to places or work or home or the local pubs and restaurants. In the near distance, the harbor pulsed with longshoremen unloading cargo. Farther out, merchant ships, low in the water, waited their turn to pull up to the docks and unload. San Francisco was growing and he intended to own a large slice of that growth.

The door opened and Clay walked it. Standing in front of the desk, he waited to be recognized.

"I'm concerned we do not have enough talent in Tombstone," Worthington said, still looking out the window.

"We have some of our best there," Clay pointed out. "Sending more will only make it obvious what we intend. We can accomplish your desires with what we have in place."

"Nevertheless," Worthington replied, his attention focused outside the office to the streets below, "I want you to employ the Professor."

"The Professor?"

"Yes."

Clay frowned then shrugged. "I'll see if he's available."

"He's available," Worthington coldly intoned.

"As you wish," Clay acknowledged with a subdued sigh.

Worthington turned to stare at him, his face the mask of stone vengeance. "Destroy the city if you have to, but I want him dead."

It was late, later than he wanted to still be awake. Standing at the bar, Mason yawned as he watched the performance. The girls were in fine form tonight, their stocking covered legs kicking high eliciting cheers and whistles from the miners and gamblers.

Looking over at Belle, he smiled to see his wife surrounded by the usual flock of admirers and hopefuls. He was sure that word had to have spread by now that he and Belle were married, or at least involved. But, he reminded himself, that wasn't necessarily a problem for so many men... and women. He shook his head remembering the number of times the girls at the Bird Cage made overt requests, knowing he was married to Elizabeth. Some even went so far as to remind him that Elizabeth was an addict and that he had to be in need, and they would be more than happy to satisfy his need.

But Mason wasn't that kind of man. Once he gave his word, nothing would change it, even living in hell, which is what his marriage to Elizabeth had become.

Then Henry Mitchell came along and did him a favor.

Though reasoning that Henry killed Elizabeth because of Worthington's likely cataclysmic revenge, Mason wasn't sure Henry actually knew anything about his former father-in-law, which made killing Elizabeth puzzling. If Henry had wanted to punish him, he should have left Elizabeth alive and in a drug stupor. That would have been punishment enough.

Mason watched the group of men, noticing a man he hadn't seen before. He had thick red hair and wore mutton chops. He was fashionably dressed in a double-breasted waistcoat obviously cut and made to measure, reminding Mason of the corporate executives who worked for Worthington. A watch chain went from a waist button and disappeared into the vest pocket. He wore a ring on his right hand.

Instead of the usual vying for attention, the man demurely held to the edges of the group, observing and regally nodding when noticed. It wasn't too long before Belle drew him into the group, diverting attention to him. His responses were measured and polite.

During a pause as the girls descended the stage to the waiting men who paid their quarter for a dance, Belle cast a quick glance over to Mason, giving him a wink then returned her attention to her devotees.

Belle's vivaciousness reminded him of the dinner this evening with the Pinkerton agent. The man had come here to check up on Belle and to report that the Agency was quite pleased with her progress. What Mason didn't like was the intimation that if things here were settled down to an acceptable level, they were thinking of moving her to another location.

Mason had argued against that, reminding the agent that Belle had spent a good deal of time working on her persona as well as establishing herself here. No one knew she was an agent, and she was in the perfect spot as a madam to gather information.

"I understand your desire to keep her here," Shephard said, "but the Agency must look to its own best interests. So far, Belle has been a superb asset, but we are concerned that the criminal element in the area may be subsiding."

"Then you don't know Tombstone," Mason tightly replied. "Last year close to $10 million of silver was mined here in Tombstone. We probably have more lawyers per citizen than any town or city in America. Though we like to think of the law as being our arbiter, things here usually get settled with a gun. Speaking of that, how are you fixed for hardware, Mister Shephard?"

The question had startled Shephard and he answered, "I can take care of myself."

Mason stared him in the eyes. "Haven't seen a man yet who can outrun a bullet."

The conversation threatened to get stilted when Belle placed a hand on Mason's arm and interjected, "Maybe you should tell him about Worthington."

"Worthington?" Shephard said, cocking an eyebrow. "That name has significance in San Francisco."

"Then you know that I was once married to his daughter," Mason said.

Shephard's face went blank as he worked to cover this lapse in information.

"I see that you didn't know that," Mason observed. "What you also don't know is that he has never forgiven me for bringing his daughter here."

"You brought her here, to Tombstone?" Shephard said, his jaw dropping.

"Yes. And it is here that she died."

Silence settled as Shephard absorbed the news.

"Mister Worthington's bitterness will no doubt turn to revenge," Mason explained.

"No doubt," he agreed. "This is both good and troubling news."

"How so?" Belle asked.

"We've suspected Worthington for a number of, shall we say, unfortunate accidents to his competitors. Unfortunately, there is nothing that we can tie to him." Shephard's focus narrowed as he sifted the news. "We may need more agents here."

"I wouldn't be too obvious," Belle pointed out.

"By the time you get folks here, it will be too late," Mason surmised. "I wouldn't be surprised if his folks aren't here already scouting out the place."

Shephard tilted his head in thought as he tried to remember the passengers on the airship, yet none came to mind as being suspicious. And that was the problem. The good ones always blend in.

He recalled the dinner on the airship with the gentleman from the security firm, a Mister Edward Church. The man was urbane and an excellent dinner partner. Though reticent of his firm's particulars, he was more forthcoming as to services provided. Shephard wondered if his firm might not be a good partner with Pinkerton. But that was not his decision to make.

Shephard had watched him when they arrived in Bisbee and once the man checked into the hotel, he went straight to business at the first bank he could find. The man then slipped from his mind as Shephard tracked down a stage to take him to Tombstone.

But other than the dinner with Edward Church, there was no one on the airship that caught his attention.

Perhaps I should alert home office," he said.

"Couldn't hurt," Belle agreed.

"Do what you need to do," Mason said, unconvinced it would help.

The meal ended and Shephard caught the last coach to Bisbee.

Wanting to stretch his legs, Mason made the rounds of the city with one of the policemen while Belle changed for work. By the time he returned to the lodging house, Belle was at the Bird Cage.

Casting a side glance at Belle, he thanked his lucky stars that she had decided she wanted him. She was quite a catch in more ways than one.

Downing the last of his whiskey, Mason held a hand over the shot glass stopping Jack from refilling it.

"I'm going for a walk," Mason said. "Let her know, please."

"Be happy to," he replied with a smile.

Once outside, Mason stretched then looked down Allen Street. For as late as it was, the town was hopping. Deciding he would let the city's police department handle the rowdies, he started up 6th Street then changed his mind, choosing to avoid the whore cribs and soliciting women on the east side of the street. Though he understood their reason for being there, it was still painful to see sometimes, especially the women who were past their prime, barely scraping by in a town where wealth flowed like the San Pedro.

Turning north on 5th Street he left behind the noise and bustle of the saloons and night life on Allen Street. The street grew quieter as he walked past the resurrected businesses and homes of the more respectable citizens. It was almost quiet by the time he turned left onto Stafford Street to head towards his old lodgings at Pascholy's Boarding House.

He passed Turnverein Hall and saw the Saint Paul's Episcopal Church just ahead. Crafted from hand formed and sun-dried adobe bricks, it was a fine edifice. Reverend Endicott Peabody had worked a miracle in building that church, raising over $5000 in less than six months. The sad part was that the good Reverend had preached his last sermon in Tombstone this past Sunday. He was heading back east to finish his seminary studies. Many were disappointed Peabody was leaving. The man had established himself as part of the city and was well respected.

As Mason walked on, his thoughts drifted to the time he encountered Caleb and De la Fuente in the unfinished church. He chuckled at the primitive method of communication. It's hard to talk to someone who can't speak or write, one who doesn't speak English, let alone the fact that they're dead… or not quite dead.

How does one explain a person who is dead coming back to walk the earth?

He was abreast of the church when he saw movement at the front doors. Stopping, he noticed the right side door open briefly then close but not completely. The action was repeated several times but with slow and deliberate movements. Taking note that the wind was not strong enough to cause the door to move like that, he headed straight for the Church.

By the time he got to the doors, they were closed. Testing the handle, he found it loose and opened the door.

Stepping inside, he paused and listened. A scuffling noise sounded on the side working its way towards the altar.

With a strong sense of reliving the previous encounter, he commanded, "Whoever is in here, you need to come out now."

There was a long pause followed by a slow scuffle towards him. Holding the door open, Mason stepped outside into the bright moon filled night wanting to make full use of the light to see who the mischief maker was, though having a feeling he already knew. What approached caused him to shake his head and quickly look around to see if anyone was passing by.

"Caleb? De la Fuente? What are you doing here?" Mason asked as the prospector lurched to a halt two paces away, still inside the sanctuary. De la Fuente hovered behind him. Mason did his best not to curl a lip in disgust as he took in the maggot infested cadaver that wavered as it stood before him. The smell of rotting flesh enveloped him, and he involuntarily stepped back.

Instead of answering, Caleb simply stared at him, his head twitching in thought trying to decide what to say. After a few moments, he stepped back and allowed the man behind him to fill the space.

Mason stared at the skull of a man with a conquistador morion that was now too large on its head, the dry skin stretched tight upon the face. Holding up a boney finger, the man pointed in the direction of the Dragoon Mountains where they had last met then made a shooshing motion. He repeated the motion.

Porque está aquí? Why are you here?

De la Fuente waved a boney finger at him then pointed to Caleb and himself. He then marched in place followed by another finger point at Mason.

"*Donde está Henry*?" Mason asked. "Where is Henry?"

De la Fuente pointed back at the Dragoon Mountains.

"*Es muerto*? Is he dead?"

De la Fuente shook his head 'No.'

"He's still alive? *El vive*?"

De la Fuente awkwardly nodded.

"He's still alive," Mason sighed in frustration, "and you left him up there? *Lo dejaste ahí*"

De la Fuente shook his head 'No' and repeated the shooshing motion.

Epiphany hit a like a lead weight. "He escaped? *Se escapé*?"

De la Fuente stiffly nodded."

"*Dónde está el oro*? Where is the gold? Does Henry have the gold?" he asked. "*Enrique tiene el oro*?"

De la Fuente shook his head and pointed to the Mountains.

"*Es seguro*? It's safe?"

De La Fuente nodded.

"*Dónde está Henry?* Where is Henry?"

De la Fuente shrugged his bony shoulders.

His lips pursed, Mason's mind raced with the impossibility of it all. The last thing he needed was Henry and all his inventions coming back to create mischief in Tombstone, especially now when he had to deal with Worthington.

"Thank you for telling me. *Muchas gracias*." An idea began to germinate. Looking at Caleb, he said, "If I need to talk to you, where can I find you?"

Caleb pointed to the mountains.

"The same place where we were before?"

Caleb nodded then cupped his decaying hands at his mouth, pretending to call out.

"I understand," Mason said. "I may need your help."

Nodding, Caleb then held up a hand and mimicked placing a ring on a finger.

"I married her, Mason grinned. "Thank you for the gift."

Caleb tried to smile, but his face contorted grotesquely. He then waved Mason to the door, effectively telling him to leave.

Standing outside the door, he deliberated a few moments more before shaking his head and moving on towards the corner of Safford and 2nd Street where Mayor Clum's house stood. He was halfway down the block when he turned around just in time to see two figures emerge from the church. With a stiff and awkward gait, they crossed the street and disappeared into the barren hills to the north.

When he could no longer see them, Mason turned and slowly walked on

It was in the early afternoon when Clay followed the petite oriental woman through the tall mahogany double doors into the library of the Professor's grand Second Empire style home.

"The Professor will be with you shortly," the woman said in crisp British accented English. "May I fix you a drink?"

"I'm fine, thank you," he politely replied.

"If you change your mind," she said, lifting a slender delicate hand and pointing to a dark walnut bureau with glasses of various shapes and sizes next to numerous crystal decanters, "please help yourself. The Professor has an excellent Courvoisier."

"Thank you."

The woman turned and Clay watched her as she gracefully glided away, her loose raven hair reaching to the middle of her back. The emerald, green silk flower-pattern dress hugged her voluptuous body and he found himself distracted by her overt sensuality.

She turned to close the doors, catching his eyes with a sly knowing smile.

Feeling unmasked, Clay shook his head reminding himself to stay focused. Glancing around the room, he took in the overt display of wealth. A wide crystal chandelier, equipped with the latest in electric lighting, dangled in the middle of a ceiling crisscrossed with thick polished oak rafter ties. The exterior wall leading to the rear veranda that overlooked the gardens was filled with large windows edged in heavy drapes. Directly opposite, bookshelves occupied the wall, floor to ceiling. Yet his attention was drawn to the far wall where a couch and two chairs were arranged on a thick Persian rug before the broad fireplace.

The room had the ambiance of a gentleman's club where one sat with a good cigar and a glass of brandy, reading a book.

The door opened and the Professor came in, the oriental woman following. He was middle-aged, small in stature and walked with a limp. His light brown hair was cut short and parted slightly off center. Unlike so many contemporaries, he was clean-shaven. His eyes lit up when he saw Clay.

"My dear Mister Ballard, how good of you to come by. May I offer you a drink?"

"I'll have whatever you are having," he said with a smile.

The Professor turned to the woman. "Meili, two glasses of Courvoisier."

"Yes, Professor," she demurely replied and moved to the liquor bureau.

"Sit, please," he said motioning to a chair as he levered himself into the chair opposite. "Is this a social call?"

"Business, unfortunately," Clay said, accepting the snifter from Meili. Holding his glass up, he toasted, "To your health, sir."

"And to yours," he grinned, inhaling the bouquet before taking a sip.

Silence settled as they briefly savored their drinks while Meili came around to stand behind the Professor's chair, placing both hands on the back of the thick cushion behind his shoulders.

"Have you been working on any new inventions?" Clay asked.

The Professor smiled in appreciation. "That's what I like about you, Mister Ballard. You have the excellent sense of decorum to not barge into the business at hand like so many of our countrymen do. You appreciate the nuances of relationships. It is a skill and manner that I find lacking and most annoying."

"Quite true," Clay urbanely replied, "especially when one has the opportunity of savoring such a fine libation." He held the glass up as evidence.

"And you are a man with discerning taste, another trait that I admire in a man."

Meili began gently massaging the Professor's shoulders.

Clay looked around the room and nodded. "This room is wonderfully designed to enforce idleness. Sitting here, I can think of nothing better than a glass of Courvoisier, a fine cigar, and a good book."

"Idleness," he perked up. "An interesting word you use, most oriental."

"I'm reminded of the Rivers and Mountains poetry of the Tang dynasty," he casually replied.

The Professor's mouth gaped open. "You are a devotee of Chinese poetry?"

Clay laughed light-heartedly. "I confess I read it in translation. My Chinese is non-existent."

"Do you have a favorite poet?"

"I'm very partial to Po Chü-I," he said, liking the way Meili reacted with newfound respect.

"I prefer Li Po," the Professor stated with a smile, pleased to have found a kindred spirit, "though Tu Fu is likewise excellent."

"Excellent poets," he agreed.

The discussion meandered off into the various poems and lives of the two Chinese poets until Clay redirected the discourse to the present.

"If I may, when I asked if you had any new inventions, you seemed most excited about something. You perked my interest ever since."

The Professor's eye's brightened and he smiled. "Come," he said, scooting forward then forcing himself to stand. "Let me show you."

He limped over to the large bookcase, placing a finger on top of the index volume of the eighth edition of the Encyclopedia Britannica and pulling the top backwards, which caused a section of the bookcase to recede, revealing a landing and a set of descending stairs. Sconces with electric bulbs provided light down to the rooms below.

"Come," he repeated with a beckoning hand. "Let me show you." Holding onto the bannister, he led the way.

The staircase spiraled down, and the Professor had difficulty navigating the steps.

"I built this when I was younger," he explained, "and more fit."

"It is ingenious in its design," Clay complimented.

"You are most kind."

The narrow enclosure opened up halfway down, exposing the Professor's workshop. Lab tables were filled with beakers, bunsen burners, glass and rubber tubing, jars and numerous electronic devices. Yet everything was meticulously organized and arranged.

Bypassing the lab tables, the Professor led the way to doors at the far end of the lab to a set of opaque double doors.

Pausing before the doors, he announced with a flourish, "And now for your viewing pleasure."

Opening one door while Meili opened the other, he motioned Clay inside. Clay peered into a brightly lit room, the size of a large warehouse, with equally high ceilings. In the center was a strange machine constructed in a steel tube framework in the shape of a cross with four wide propellers perched on top at the end of each arm. But instead of facing forward, the blades faced the ceiling.

Approaching the machine, he studied the invention. "What is it?"

"I call it a quadcopter," the Professor proclaimed. "It's based upon Da Vinci's aerial screw utilizing the modified propellers of airships."

Clay walked around the machine, noting the chains that linked the four propellers to the engine in the center. There was another propeller on the back of the longest arm of the cross, facing backwards. Behind this propeller were four vertical fins. At the front of the machine was a pilot's seat.

"How does it work?"

"Allow me to explain," the Professor said. Pointing to the skids upon which the machine rested, he began, "Those are ordinary skids one would find on a sleigh, though they are a bit more reinforced. Upon them rests the quadcopter body, designed in the shape of a cross, with the engine in the center where the arms of the cross intersect. That is done for balance. The propellers facing the ceiling lift the quadcopter into the air, while the propellers in the back move it forward. I steer it left or right using the fins in the back."

Clay's jaw gaped wide. "Ingenious."

Clay walked around to the front, noting that there was a Gatling gun mounted before the pilot's platform with a chain that looped around a cogged wheel where the hand crank should be. The chain then dropped to another cog between two foot pedals. Yet something wasn't quite right.

"Your Gatling gun seems smaller than I expected."

"It's a .32 caliber," he explained. "I made it smaller so the ship could accommodate the weight as well as carry more ammunition. I've found the .32 caliber to be highly effective. I had a chance recently to test its effect in a little out of the way place in Wyoming."

Clay nodded appreciatively. "How does that work?"

"This is the clever part," the Professor grinned. "Obviously I can't use my hand to fire the gun while flying the quadcopter. So I use my feet instead." He climbed up and positioned himself in the pilot's sea, placing his feet on the pedals.

"By pedaling, I perform the same function as the hand crank. The pedals turn the cog, which then aligns the firing pin while rotating the barrel assembly with the bullets. It's exactly the same as a normal Gatling gun but without the need to turn a clumsy handle. That way I can easily change magazines using two hands."

Clay immediately saw the military potential. "Have you approached anyone for sale?"

"I've contemplated a few possibilities, but I need to make a few adjustments before putting bids out."

"May I see how it flies?"

"I was hoping you'd ask," he chuckled. "Meili, let's get the engine going."

While Meili added wood to the firebox, the Professor continued as he scooted himself into the pilot's seat. "I usually use coal to produce enough steam, but for today, I will use wood as it is only for a short demonstration."

137

As the pressure built, the Professor diverted his attention to the dials and switches on the pilot's console.

"OK," he called out. "We've built enough pressure to start."

He slowly pushed two brake levers forwards and the four top propellers began a gradual spinning, gaining momentum. Twisting his head to catch Clay's attention, he shouted over the engines.

"I'm now going to fly."

With the levers pushed all the way forward, the quadcopter began to quiver and hum as the propellers whirled and steam billowed out the exhaust pipes, causing the quadcopter to lift off the ground. He then released the rear propeller brakes, and the quadcopter began moving forward.

For the next several minutes, the Professor navigated his invention in a wide circle, setting it down in the same spot.

Extracting himself from the machine, he motioned to Meili to close down the engines while he and Clay walked into the main lab.

"If we were outside," the Professor explained, "I could show you the full range of the quadcopter and the effectiveness of the Gatling gun. A well-trained pilot can destroy an enemy position in a matter of seconds. Just imagine a whole fleet of my quadcopters attacking an enemy's stronghold."

"You are a man of true genius, Professor," Clay praised.

"You are indeed kind, Mister Ballard." The Professor leaned heavily against a lab table. "While your visit has been most enjoyable, I know you have business in mind. How may I help you?"

"Mister Worthington seeks your help."

"Ah," the Professor nodded. "In what way?"

"He wishes his former son-in-law to suffer a horrible fate," Clay calmly explained.

The professor pondered a moment. "You said 'former' son-in-law. I take it they are no longer married."

"His only daughter has died."

"And he blames the son-in-law."

"Yes."

The Professor frowned. "Surely you have resources to accomplish his desires."

"We do and they are presently in place."

"Then why ask me?"

"Mister Worthington desires it."

"Ah," he nodded with a sagacious smile. "Where is the son-in-law now?"

"Tombstone, Arizona Territory."

"Tombstone... a wild and rugged place from what I hear." Pushing away from the table, he beckoned with his hand. "Come. Let's repair to a more comfortable setting while Meili finishes down here."

Leading the way, he paused mid-limp to press a large black button on a small metal box attached to the pole by the stairs then began climbing the steps.

Expecting to hear or see something, Clay was surprised when nothing happened. He was surprised again when they entered the library to see a lithe, yet well-endowed oriental woman, a bit taller than Meili waiting for them, a tray in hand with drinks poured. Her black hair was curled in a bun at the back of her head, secured by two polished wooded hair sticks. She wore the same flower pattern dress as Meili, except hers was burgundy with delicate flowers of white and gold.

"Thank you, Jingfei," the Professor said, selecting a snifter then settling himself as gracefully as possible in one of the chairs before the hearth, his left leg stiff.

Clay accepted the glass of Courvoisier, noting again the overt sensuality of the woman offering him the drink. With a momentary frown, he wondered if the rest of the Professor's staff might be of the same beauty.

Sitting on the opposite chair, Clay casually remarked, "A very attractive lady."

The Professor looked over his shoulder at the departing Jingfei and smiled paternally. "Yes she is."

"I'm curious, Professor," Clay said. "When I arrived today, I couldn't help but notice that there were no men working here. The grounds keepers were all women, quite lovely by the way. Likewise were those who opened the gates and escorted me to your front door. Do you employ only women?"

"Yes," he replied. "I find their presence most alluring."

"Certainly," Clay readily agreed, sipping his drink. "But don't you think there are some things that are better accomplished by men?"

"Not at all," he replied with a dismissive sniff. "Women are every bit as capable as men. In fact, in many ways they are more capable."

"For instance?"

"Deviousness," he replied with a grin, "and efficiency. If I need something, um, shall we say 'difficult' to obtain, I find women are more deft in collecting what I need. They are subtle and clever. Men tend to be too blustery and constantly needing to prove their bravado. Women are above all that."

Clay was about to object when he remembered Becca. The woman was the most lethal weapon on the team.

"I also noticed that all your staff are oriental."

"Ah, yes," he sighed with pleasure, "a weakness of mine. I find the oriental lass a creature of unparalleled pulchritude." He leaned in towards Clay. "And they are also the most dangerous, a trait I admire and cultivate."

Clay frowned with a half-smile as he thought through the implication. The vision of bedding Meili was suddenly tempered with the image of her with whip in hand.

"Interesting." Clearing his distracted thoughts, he redirected the conversation to his purpose. "Now that you know my reason for being here, may Mister Worthington count on your support?"

"When does he wish my involvement?"

"Immediately."

"Immediately?" the Professor repeated with a frown. Tilting his head and pursing his lips, he said, "Yes, I suppose I might be available. In fact, the desert of the Arizona Territory might be a good location to flex the muscle of the quadcopter."

"I dare say it would," Clay agreed.

The Professor fell silent as he contemplated the necessary steps to get there. "It will take me at least two days to disassemble the quadcopter for transport, another few days to get to Tombstone, then another few days to reassemble. So, let's say a week."

"That would be acceptable," he said.

"I expect to be paid for that time," the Professor pointed out.

"Of course," Clay nodded.

The Professor stared intently at Clay then said, "Tell Mister Worthington that the fee for this will cost him more, much more than previous contracts. After all, I am personally involved in this affair."

"Yes, of course. I'm sure Mister Worthington will accommodate you as you deem appropriate," Clay said. "The important thing is that he wishes his son-in-law to suffer. His words were, and I quote, 'Destroy the city if you have to, but I want him dead.'"

The Professor's eyes lit up. "Destroy the whole city? That sounds absolutely appealing. But that would take more than the single quadcopter I presently have. Pity he couldn't wait a month or two while I built several more. The thought of leveling a whole city with my beautiful machines is simply delicious."

Clay smiled despite himself for the Professor's reaction was like that of a child with a new toy. Finishing his drink, he stood.

"I know Mister Worthington will be pleased to hear of your support."

"Remind him of my fee," the Professor reiterated.

"I will."

Meili crested the stairs and pushed the book back into place, causing the wall to slide forward.

"Meili will show you out," the Professor said with a contented smile, lifting his snifter in acknowledgment.

Following her to the door, he waited as she deliberately opened it.

"Good day to you, Mister Ballard," she said, her voice sultry and inviting then blew him a full-lipped kiss.

Chapter 5

Ed sat in his hotel room, waiting for Becca to arrive. He was beginning to get impatient with their progress. They had been in Bisbee for over a week now and seemed no closer to a cohesive plan. Once Amos Stowe provided his input, he had taken the next airship back to San Francisco.

Grimacing, he shook his head at that fool Gordon who nearly got himself killed when the explosives he planted on one of the roads heading out towards Fort Huachuca failed to detonate. Why the fool decided on that road was beyond him. The only traffic that went that way was the mule teams carrying ore to the mills on the San Pedro. The likelihood of one of their targets heading to the mills or Fort Huachuca was more than remote.

When the charge failed to detonate, Gordon went to check just as a mule team carrying dynamite of all things, managed to position the carriage over the charge. The explosion sent wagon, teamster and mules to oblivion.

Gordon was luckier, but just barely. The explosion ripped most his clothes off his back while peppering his pale body with stones and pebbles. Fortunately, there was no severe damage as he had stumbled on a rock just as the wagon went up. That he was not impaled by splinted wood or iron was also a miracle.

Ed smiled a perverse grin as he thought of Gordon and his discomfort in the simple act of sitting. The damned fool deserved it. Of all people he should have known better.

Fortunately, the subsequent investigation decided that it was an unfortunate accident that occasionally happens with transporting dynamite and that Gordon just happened to be in the wrong place at the wrong time. Unfortunately, Gordon's stupidity put him out of commission for the next few days.

That left Earl and Becca… and him.

Earl was useless and the constant reining him in was getting tiresome. Ed had half a mind to turn Earl loose in the hopes he'd get himself killed.

The door opened and Becca entered.

"You seen Earl?" he asked.

"Last I saw him he was tracking the Marshal," she replied, sitting and arranging her skirt.

"What's your progress?"

"I'm making headway," she said. "The man's got it bad for a little tart in the Theater, so it's taken me a little longer than usual. But don't worry; he's as good as mine."

"When?" he frowned.

"Now, now, Ed," she sweetly said. "Don't rush me. But when I'm finished, he'll be dead and it will look like he did it to himself."

"We don't have much time," he sighed and handed her a telegram. "The Professor is on his way, if he's not here already."

"What?" she snapped, reading the message. Handing it back, she said, "This sounds to me like he doesn't trust us. I don't like not being trusted."

"Neither do I," he tersely replied. "That means we need to step up our timetable. If you see Earl before I do, tell him to go ahead and take out the Marshal, and you can tell him I said so."

"With pleasure," she said, standing. "I'd better get back." Pausing to stare at him, she said, "The Professor here changes nothing. We were given a contract. I expect to be paid for my services. If Worthington thinks he can renege because the Professor is here, he's going to have more to worry about than what to do about his son-in-law. I'm a good shot from a long way off, and you can tell him that." Gathering her dress in a grand display of genteel air, she swept from the room.

Ed watched her leave, pondering his own part. Belle Dubois was a hard nut to crack. It was obvious that she and the Marshal were bonded; married was the appropriate term. Whereas the Marshal's moves were hard to track and inconsistent as he had an entire county to monitor, Belle was either at the Theater or home, though she ventured at times with Mason to look at properties between the Dragoons and Tombstone. The attraction of the chaparral was beyond him, as was the desire to live in a boomtown like Tombstone, no matter how hard they tried to add refinement.

The problem was getting Belle away from Mason or the Theater long enough to finish her off and then dump her body where Mason would see it.

Frowning, he wondered if giving Earl free rein was such a good idea. Suppose he actually killed the Marshal before the lawman had a chance to see his friends and loved ones die. Then again, Earl was impetuous and with a little luck the Marshal would solve the problem for them.

Belle saw the obvious when Annie came into the Bird Cage. The girl was not the ebullient dancer all the men wanted to dance with. In fact, Annie's demeanor as of late bordered on sadness.

"I thought you and Ringo were going on a picnic today," Belle said.

"He's with that woman," she morosely replied. Heaving a pained sigh, she said, "I don't understand. I thought we had something special, something permanent."

"Maybe you still do," Belle comforted. "I've seen the lady, and she's nothing like you. He'll get tired of her soon enough and realize he had what he wanted all along back here."

"You think so?" she asked, half-heartedly.

"Without a doubt," she encouraged.

The door opened and Mason strode in, giving Belle a broad smile.

"You're back early," Belle exclaimed, crossing to meet him and leaping into his arms, planting a deep kiss on his lips.

Setting her down, Mason laughed. "Good to see you too."

"Miss me?"

"Every minute of every day," he assured her then saw Annie. "Hey Annie. How are you?"

"She's having man problems," Belle explained.

"Oh? Ringo?"

"Yes," Belle said. "Seems a new lady in town has captured his fancy."

"Someone new in town," he repeated. "What's she like?"

"She's real pretty," Annie said, curling a lip.

"I think you ought to find out who she is," Belle suggested with a smile.

"Can I have a drink first and talk with my wife? I haven't seen her for almost a week." He stepped up to the bar where Jack had already placed a shot of Tennessee whiskey. "You're a good man, Jack. Whatever she's paying you, it's not enough."

"I quite agree," he said with a slow smile.

Stepping out onto the boardwalk in front of the Bird Cage Theater, Mason frowned when he saw Ringo come out of a restaurant across the street, arm in arm with a young lady whose proper dress and demeanor seemed an odd contrast to Ringo's swaggering bravado. She was a pretty curvaceous girl with curling blond hair that cascaded beyond her shoulders. Upon stepping out onto the sidewalk, she opened a small sun parasol.

Ringo saw him, waved then started to guide the young woman over to him. Mason waved at him to stay and crossed the street to meet them.

"Hey Marshal," Ringo grinned. "Like you to meet the newest addition to Tombstone. This is Miss Delilah Kelley. Delilah, this is the best lawman in the entire United States, Marshal Mason Sadler."

"Maybe not the best," Mason demurred then gave her a polite smile. "Second best would do."

Delilah flashed a captivating smile. "Pleased to meet you, Marshal." Delilah looked to be not more than twenty-two years of age with the fair and smooth skin of youth. She carried herself as one who was confident without arrogance. Mason was momentarily uncomfortable by the woman's penetrating gaze, as though memorizing his face.

"What brings you to Tombstone," he asked, breaking the spell.

"My father," she said. "He thinks Tombstone would be an excellent location for a woman's clothing store, a more upscale clothing store, and sent me to decide its viability."

"So he sent you alone?" he said, an eyebrow raised while marking the choice of words. Not the normal language one hears in Tombstone. "This is still a pretty rough town."

"Oh," she smiled sweetly, "Johnny will protect me."

Mason looked at Ringo and saw that he was smitten. He also noted that Delilah called him 'Johnny' and not 'Ringo' or 'Mister Ringo.'

"How long you been in town, Miss Kelley?"

"I arrived just a few days ago. I had the good fortune of bumping into Johnny almost as soon as I stepped off the stage."

"That's right, Marshal," Ringo chimed in. "I saw her standing there looking around, so I walked over and asked if she needed help."

"I told him I was looking for someone who knew the town," she said, continuing the story, "and could help me come to a decision. Although he appeared a bit rough at first," she teased him, gently wrapping a hand around his arm. "He was so gallant that I couldn't help but be captivated."

Watching the two, Mason felt like he was intruding, yet he wanted to be polite. "Where do you hail from Miss Kelley?"

"A tiny little town called McArthur in Ohio," she sweetly answered. "But Daddy moved us to Kansas City a few years ago when he saw that business was stronger than poor little McArthur. I do so miss that little town."

"McArthur," Mason repeated. "I've been there, just once, passing through. Ate at a place called Shirley's on South Market Street right off Main Street just a block or two away from the depot. Been there forever. Excellent food. Do you know it?"

Delilah hesitated for just a heartbeat before saying, "Why yes. Delightful little place. She made the best rhubarb pies I've ever had."

Nodding in agreement, Mason asked, "Is your father still in Kansas City?"

"That's right. I think he's getting tired of the big city and misses McArthur. When he heard about the silver mining in Tombstone, he said, 'Delilah, that's the place we need to go.' So here I am, checking it out. And I have the good fortune of doing it in the company of this handsome cowboy." She hugged Ringo's arm to her.

Ringo said nothing, blushing instead.

Chuckling, Mason said, "Well, enjoy your stay here, Miss Kelley. I commend your choice of escort. You will find no one better."

Ringo flashed him a look of deep-seated thanks. "I think we've taken up enough of the Marshal's time, Miss Delilah. How about we find ourselves some horses and take a ride?"

"That would be delightful, Johnny" she gushed. "Pleasure meeting you, Marshal."

"And you too, Miss Delilah." He pinched the brim of his Stetson in respect. Mason remained where he was and watched them walk away, happily engaged in conversation. Delilah was showering Ringo with overt and focused attention as though he was more than just an escort.

And that worried him, for he indeed had been to McArthur, but there was no restaurant named 'Shirleys' there. He had made that up. He doubted Delilah had ever been to McArthur. What game was she playing? Why was she so enamored with Ringo?

Mason had a bad feeling and whenever he had a bad feeling, someone got killed. He needed to warn Ringo but doubted the man would listen. He was in too deep. Perhaps he should have Belle talk some sense into him. Just as he stepped onto the street a voice growled off to his right.

"That's far enough, Marshal."

Mason turned to find a powerfully built compact man with short brown hair and full beard staring menacingly at him. A six-shooter strapped to his side, his hand hovered over it. He stood on the street a step away from the boardwalk, about ten paces between them.

Frowning, Mason cocked his head slightly. "Do I know you?"

Recognizing the posture and outcome, town folk hustled out of the way, clearing the area behind both men. Several ran off to find Sheriff Johnny Behan or any of the town's policemen.

"No, but you soon will," the man taunted.

Turning to face him, Mason said, "Before we commence to shooting, mind telling me what this is all about? After all, a condemned man ought to know why."

With a smug smile, the man said, "I suppose that's fair. A man oughta know who killed 'im."

"Appreciate it."

"Name's Earl. Yer father-in-law sends his respecks."

"Ah," Mason nodded, "thought it might be something like that." Frowning again as though puzzled, he said, "Though it's a might odd you standing here. The men Worthington sends usually shoot a man in the back, like the cowards they are. I'll give it to you, Earl. You're not a coward like all the others. Why you stand right out in the open and challenge a man like a real man should."

"Yer right," Earl grinned with satisfaction. "I ain't like the rest o' them."

"No you're not," Mason complimented. "And I certainly do appreciate you coming here to face me like a man. We both know only a coward shoots a man who doesn't have the chance to defend himself. If I'm going to die, I'd like to face my adversary head-to-head, like real men." He slowly and carefully raised then lowered his right hand. "I'm just going to unfasten the hammer loop." Pulling off the small leather retaining loop from the hammer, he raised his hand. "Mind if I ask another question?" He lowered his hand and relaxed.

"You sure are a talker," he grimaced. "What now?"

"Just wondering if there's any more of you here. I mean, after the shooting's over, there's nothing left to do here."

"Almost," he sneered. "Got a few other folks t' take care of, folks kinda special to ya. Worthington wanted it done all proper like, with you bein' the last t' go. But I figured it different. Why waste all that time? Yer all gonna be dead just the same."

"Sound reasoning," Mason acknowledged. "So how many would that be left to do the job?"

"Damn it all t' hell, Mister," Earl scowled. "You got the mouth runs. What's it matter t' ya who's left?"

"Call it curiosity," he shrugged. "Just like to have some answers before it's over. You've been man enough to face me. I figured you'd be kind enough to fill me in."

Earl's arm was beginning to stiffen and he quickly shook it to get the blood flowing again. "There's four of us down here. Once yer all dead, we're outta here. OK? That's all I'm gonna say. Let's get this over with."

"Fair enough," Mason calmly nodded. "So when you say four, does that count you?"

"Damn it all," Earl burst. "Quit yet stallin'."

"Ah well," he sighed before politely adding, "Now then, you just let me know when you're ready."

"Oh, I've been re–" Earl began but was abruptly interrupted when the bullet from Mason's six-shooter plowed its way between his eyes, snapping his head back, his body following in a spasmodic arc as it jerked backwards to finally flop sprawled out in the dirt street. Earl's gun was still in the holster.

Mason remained immobile for only a moment before walking to stand over the body. Six-shooter still in hand, he flipped open the loading gate, aligned the cylinder and pushed back the ejector rod, pushing out the empty shell, which dropped to the ground next to the dead man. Reaching to his belt, he withdrew a bullet and replaced the spent round. He looked up just as Police Chief David Neagle crossed the street.

"Hello David," he said, holstering his Colt.

"Hey Mason. I saw the whole thing," he said. "Wasn't going to interrupt as I saw he wasn't about to be dissuaded." He gave him a quick smile. "Knew you'd take him down."

Mason returned the smile with a pensive half-smile. "One of these days I won't be so quick. Even the best of us can't fight time. Hopefully I'll have hung up my guns well before then." Looking down on Earl draped upon the road, blood and brains staining the dirt, he observed, "Have you see this guy before?"

David studied the dead man for a moment. "Can't say that I have," he replied, shaking his head.

"You know why he was sent here to kill me," Mason said.

David shook his head. "Your father-in-law."

"My former father-in-law."

David pursed his lips. "There'll be more."

"There already are. Four of them, well… three now."

"Here? Now?" David's eyes hardened.

"Yes. I've an idea about two, but the other one…" he shook his head.

"Which one?"

"Well," Mason mused a bit before answering. "I've nothing other than my gut, but that young lady who's taken such a shine to Ringo isn't telling all. She's up to something. Won't do any good trying to tell Ringo. He's bitten."

"You think she's here to kill you?" he asked, his doubt apparent.

"That's just it, David," Mason frowned. "Earl here confirmed what I suspected all along. They were sent here to not only kill me, but those close to me."

"Belle?"

"That would be my first choice."

"Any ideas?"

"There's this new fellow, red-headed, well-dressed, mutton chops, hangs around the Bird Cage. He spends his money freely enough. Not sure where he's staying, but I don't trust him."

"Good enough reason for me," David answered.

"Howdy, Gents," a slender man dressed in black announced as he walked up.

"Charles," the two lawmen replied in unison.

"You're here fast," David chuckled.

"Good news travels fast," Charles Tarbell, the City Undertaker smiled back.

"Good news for whom?" Mason wryly observed.

"Me for one," Charles easily answered, "and for whichever one of you is still standing after the um... altercation." Holding up a cloth tape measure, he shook it slightly at David. "May I?"

"Be my guest," he replied.

While Charles bent down to measure the body to get the coffin size right, Ringo came up, Delilah clutching is arm in tight affection.

"That was some fine shooting, Marshal," Ringo congratulated him. Looking back and forth between Mason and Delilah, he explained, "We saw folks starting to scatter and I knew something was up and then I saw it was you and I told Delilah here, I said 'Watch this.' That's what I said, didn't I?"

"He certainly did," she readily agreed. "Why I've never seen such speed before. You were lightning fast, Marshal."

"So you've witnessed such things before, Miss Kelley?" Mason asked, noticing the way she studied him, especially the way her eyes were drawn to the holster and the Colt tucked snugly inside it.

Delilah was caught flat-footed for only a moment. "Only in carnivals and traveling shows. Johnny said you were the fastest man in the West."

"Johnny was just being his humble self," Mason answered. "He's every bit as good."

"Really?" she gushed, squeezing his arm tighter.

For some reason, Delilah's overt affection struck Mason as less than genuine. And then there was that brief flash of satisfaction when she saw Earl stretched out on the street.

"I'm not sure watching a man get killed is such a pleasant experience for the lady," David said, gazing pointedly at Ringo. "Perhaps you should escort the lady to a more appropriate venue."

"Oh I've seen dead men before," Delilah brightly interceded. "Why one time when I was living in McArthur, I saw a poor unfortunate man hit by a train. My goodness you should have seen the mess after that one."

Mason and David exchanged a quizzical glance, both thinking the same thing. The woman was more than unaffected by the shootout; she seemed to relish it.

By now, a few bystanders edged over to satisfy their own morbid curiosity. David glanced around before asking, "Anyone recognize him?"

Several shook their heads. One, a miner, studied the corpse a bit more intently before answering, "I seen 'im talkin' to a little feller t'other day walkin' past Blond Mary's cribs."

"What did this gentleman look like?" David inquired.

"He were a city-type fella. Had this satchel he kept holdin' to his chest, even when he walked off."

"Anything else?" David prodded as the others began to drift away.

"Eh…" The miner scrunched his face in thought. "Wore one o' them bowler hats." He curved his hand over his head as demonstration. "That's 'bout all I ken 'member, honest t' God. I gotta git t'work"

"Fine," David nodded. "Thanks for your help."

As the miner ambled off, David shooed away the rest. Turning to Mason, he ticked his head towards the Bird Cage Theater. "What say you and I take a walk?"

"Sounds good," Mason readily agreed.

Turning his attention to Charles who had finished measuring and was about to head back to the mortuary, he said, "You can deposit his personals at the jailhouse, Charles."

"Of course," he obsequiously replied. "Gentlemen," he bobbed his head then pinched the brim of his stovepipe hat to Delilah, "and lady."

"We'll leave you two lawmen to take care of business," Delilah sweetly said. "Johnny promised to take me riding."

"That I did," Ringo grinned. "See you two later." With a cheerful salute, he guided Delilah onto the boardwalk.

Mason watched them until his eyes rested on Ben Gilstrap, a part time miner who spent most of his days in a blind drunk, just as the two passed behind him as he leaned unsteadily against an awning post just outside the door to Rafforty's saloon.

"You need to go home, Ben," David chastised him.

Ben stared at the two lawmen a bit then said to Mason, "Saw him with another fella."

"What?" Mason frowned

"Said I saw that fella yonder you shot with another fella." He ticked his head at Earl who had been loaded onto a wagon and was heading to Charles' mortuary.

"What did he look like?"

Ben wiped a hand across his smudged forehead. "Sure gonna be a hot one today."

"When's the last time you ate?" Mason asked.

"You're wasting your time on him," David warned then turned to watch the wagon lumbering off. "I'll telegraph folks in San Francisco. Maybe someone's heard of Earl there."

"Thanks."

David shot a look at Ben then at Mason. "I wouldn't hold onto much coming out of him."

"Ben has his moments," Mason said, smiling kindly at Ben.

"I'll let you know if I hear anything," David said, shaking his head as he walked off.

Mason turned his attention back to Ben. "Like I said before, when was the last time you ate?"

"I ain't hungry," Ben replied, licking his dry lips.

"You have to eat sometime, Ben. You can't drink your way through life."

"Been doin' fine so far." He blinked and scrunched his eyes as though trying to wake up.

"You said you saw Earl, the man I shot, with another man? What did he look like?"

Ben licked his lips again. "Sure gonna be a hot one today."

"Ben," Mason sternly spoke. "You either tell me what you saw, or I'll go find someone else who saw it."

"Now don't go off half-cocked, Marshal," Ben sputtered. "I'll tell you what I saw. Just that it'd be nice to have a drink while I'm tellin' it."

Mason frowned at the man. "C'mon then. You can eat while you drink."

Ben's face split into a wide grin. "That's mighty kind of ya, Marshal."

"Let's head over to the Atlantic," he said, turning to head off to his favorite restaurant.

Ben hustled to take up the stride beside him when realization hit. "They ain't got nothin' to drink there."

"You eat first and if I like what you tell me, I'll spot you a beer."

"That's better," he nodded.

"So what was the man like," Mason asked as they walked.

"He was a little fella, kinda baldin' and wore spectacles. Had this satchel with him. He's that same fella who got hisself blown up by that dynamite wagon."

Mason's lips tightened as his suspicions about the man who just happened to be at the wrong place at the wrong time were confirmed. Listening to Ben as he talked, Mason decided a trip to Bisbee was next on his list. With Earl dead and the little man a likely accomplice, only two more of Worthington's rogues remained... That is if Earl was telling the truth.

"Hey Marshal," a voice cried out.

Mason turned to see Roger waving a pencil at him as he bustled over.

"Hello Roger," he said with an indulgent smile.

"I just heard the news. Amazing story. Can I have a few moments of your time?" Roger hovered the pencil over a piece of paper, ready to transcribe the event. "Did you know the man?"

"No," Mason said. "Never saw him before."

With a pained expression, Ben looked at Mason then at Roger then back to Mason. "Lunch then beer?" he reminded the Marshal.

"Of course, Ben," Mason kindly replied then turned to Roger. "Come with us and you can finish your story. My treat."

"Don't mind if I do," he grinned.

Once inside and after they ordered, Roger returned to the gunfight.

"Why do you think he wanted to shoot it out with you?"

Mason pondered the question, wondering if he should pass along what Earl had said. Perhaps he should enlist the help of the townsfolk. It might help tracking down the others of Earl's team.

"He was sent here by my former father-in-law," Mason said.

"Your father-in-law?" Roger repeated. "Why would your father-in-law send someone here to kill you?"

"Because he believes that I am responsible for his daughter's death."

"What was her name?"

"Elizabeth."

Roger furiously scribbled. "Maiden name?"

"Worthington."

"Worthington," he said as he wrote the name. "Where does he hail from?"

"San Francisco."

"San Francisco," he said and wrote. "Never been there. Nice place, I understand. So what happened to his daughter?"

Mason paused, deciding just how much to say. Everyone in Tombstone knew she was an addict. They didn't know she had been murdered.

"She died of a drug overdose," he answered, "and I'd appreciate it if that was not in your story."

"But it's important to the story," Roger objected. "It's all part of the who, what, where, when and why. It's the reason the gunslinger was here in the first place. "

"I suppose," Mason replied, unconvinced.

"Are there more coming or here already?"

"He said there were four here. I have a hunch about one, but the other two are a mystery."

"Who's the hunch about?" he eagerly asked.

"Not going to say, especially if my hunch is wrong. No sense in blaming an innocent man."

"Yes," he acceded. "I suppose that's fair. So tell me what you know about the man you killed."

"You make it sound like I started it," Mason said, cocking an eyebrow.

"I didn't mean to," he apologized. "I know it was self-defense. Did you discover anything about him?"

"Just that his name was Earl and that he was sent here by Worthington to kill me. Now let's eat," he said as the waitress placed three plates on the table.

The Bird Cage Theater was its usual cacophony of the Polyphon Music Box, loud conversations, gambling disagreements, all covered in layers of tobacco smoke when Mason walked in and headed to the bar, giving a friendly nod to Jack behind the bar, wiping a glass clean.

"Tennessee whiskey, Jack," Mason said with a smile.

"Knew you would be here, so I had one waiting for you," he said, lifting up a shot glass from behind the bar and placing it on the bar top in front of him.

"Thank you, Jack."

The music in the Polyphon ended and Ed Wittig's five-piece band filled the void with dance music. Mason leaned back against the bar, the shot of whiskey in his right hand as he gazed out at the raucous dancing and boisterous music. He smiled watching the men and Bird Cage girls cavorting on the dance floor through the haze of cigarette smoke. Looking up at the cages above, he wondered how the ladies were faring. Usually, customers who rented a cage for the evening understood the ground rules. $25 was for the privilege of sitting in the cage for the evening. Anything more cost extra, including the girls. But every now and then a cowboy or miner would want more than they paid and Belle would have to gently remind them.

And then there were the not-so-gentle reminders like the time the curtains opened, and Belle tossed the obstinate and quite drunk miner over the side to land on the dance floor below. It was a wonder the man didn't break a leg or an arm or shoulder. The startled dancers paused for only a moment then laughed uproariously as the dazed man wobbly staggered to his feet, quite unsure of where he was or how he got there. The dancing recommenced as the miner was firmly escorted out the building.

Belle's reputation was further entrenched as a no-nonsense, though quite beautiful, madam. After the miner-tossing incident, as it became known, she had little trouble with men renting the cages. Thus, Mason was puzzled as to what or who required her presence upstairs. She still had her coterie of admirers, but whenever Mason showed up, they knew enough to drift away and leave the two alone.

Belle descended the steps from the upstairs cages, paused to look at the Polyphon as if deciding to check the coin box, changed her mind and swirled towards the bar where Mason stood watching her.

"A sangaree please, Jack," she said with a sigh.

"Coming up, Belle," he smiled in reply.

"So?" Mason wondered.

"Nothing serious," she shrugged. "He wanted to know if it was possible to rent the crib for a number of nights."

"And he had to talk to you? He couldn't have asked one of the girls?" He looked up to see the curtains pull open and a lankly man with thick wavy red hair and mutton chops leaned forward to glance down on the dance floor. Mason shifted his gaze away from the man, pretending to watch the same dancers yet out of the corner of his eyes he saw the man switch his attention to where he and Belle stood. Mason pretended to take a quick look at the occupants in the other cages, noticing each time he looked up, the man shifted his face and attention to the dancers.

"Why Marshal Mason Sadler," she teased. "Are you jealous?" She picked up the sangaree Jack set before her on the bar counter.

"Of course," he calmly replied. "It was hard enough fighting off Henry Mitchell. Don't want to have to do that again."

"But it was such fun," she said, batting her eyes in innocence, sipping her sangaree.

"For you," he dead-panned. "All you had to do was ride in the back in the trailer. You even got to go for a swim."

"That's not funny," she chided, though smiling. "After he dumped that second bucket of water on me, I couldn't stop chattering. I'm surprised you couldn't hear me. I wrapped myself up as best I could in that dirty canvas. I got a little warmer by the time you finally showed up."

"Well," he pointed out, "I didn't want to interfere with you having such a good time." He noticed the red-haired man was still watching them. "Do you have a name for the gentleman upstairs? He seems awfully interested in you."

Belle turned to look up just as the man turned his face away. "His name is Ed. He's usually down here with the others. A polite gentleman and educated. Still, he's not my type."

"What is your type?" he asked, giving her a sly smile.

Leaning into him, she smiled invitingly. "I think we already know the answer to that, Marshall Mason Sadler."

"Let's keep it that way," he said with affection. Staring at her, his focus was on the man above. "I don't like the way he keeps looking over here. I think we need to find out more about him."

"I'll send one of the girls."

The doors opened and Nantan and Taboca plowed in, laughing. Seeing Mason, they bustled over.

"You two are in good spirits," Mason observed.

"We had a race and I won," Nantan explained.

"He cheated," Taboca said with a laugh. "He got me with the old 'your shoe's untied.'"

"Where did you race?" Belle asked, giving them a warm smile.

"On the way here from Bisbee," Nantan said. "We had just climbed up and over Mule Pass when he challenged me to a race."

"How far was the race?" she innocently asked.

"The first one to Tombstone," Nantan laughed.

Mason's jaw dropped. "You ran form Bisbee to Tombstone?"

"Yup," Nantan said with a giggle.

Mason frowned as he studied him. For someone who supposedly raced more than 20 miles, he didn't look tired. "How long did it take you?"

"Less than an hour to get from Bisbee to here."

"What?" Mason exclaimed. "That's impossible. That's more than 20 miles an hour. No human being can run that far that fast."

"He could if he had the right equipment," Taboca winked.

Dumbfounded, Mason continued to stare at them until the epiphany hit. "Your running machine," he said to Nantan.

"Yup," he replied with a grin. "Taboca and I built another one for him. Tonight was more of a test run. We held back a bit, not sure of what to expect. But we're pleased with the results. We'll probably run back to Bisbee tomorrow and see if we can increase the speed."

"Aren't you afraid of falling?" Belle asked.

"That's the biggest concern," Taboca agreed. "We've been lucky so far. I imagine falling at 20 miles an hour would be something like falling off a moving train. It might not kill you, but it's gonna hurt like hell." Realizing his slip, he looked quickly at Belle and said, "Sorry."

"I've heard worse," she chuckled, "but that was very polite of you to say that."

Nantan folded his arms and feigned a glare at Taboca. "Him gottum bad tongue. Me smackum upside head." He then gave Taboca a playful swipe at the head.

Snorting a laugh, Taboca shook his head. "He always makes me laugh when he talks like that. It just sounds so stupid, it's funny."

"What's stupid," Nantan said, "are people who actually think we talk like that. We're machinists, the best machinists in the entire Arizona Territory. You'd think by now folks would know who and what we are."

"Some folks will never come around," Mason pointed out. "That's their problem." He leaned in and lowered his voice enough to be heard over the dancing. "Have you two seen the man in the crib above, the one with red hair?"

Both machinists turned their heads to look above. Ed saw them and returned the gaze. He broke off when Nantan waved at him.

"Can't say that I've seen him around," Nantan said.

"If you do," Mason said, "Let me know where and when."

"Sure, Marshal," Taboca said. "Is he a problem?"

"Don't know yet. Just a hunch."

From the corner of his eyes, Ed watched them, noting their camaraderie. He hadn't seen the two young men before. They looked to be Indians and that puzzled him. He was surprised their kind was let into places like this. He would need to find out more about them.

His interest was interrupted when a gunslinger entered. Ed knew the man was a gunslinger by the way he walked. Besides, he already knew what Johnny Ringo looked like. He watched as one of the dancers, a girl called High Step Annie, extracted herself and ran over to him.

"Johnny," Annie exclaimed, grabbing and squeezing his hands. "It's so good to see you."

"You too," he said, staring into her eyes.

Belle recognized the look and turned to Annie. "Why don't you take a break for a bit."

"Thank you, Belle." She slipped an arm around his as he led her outside.

Standing on the sidewalk, Ringo cast a glance at both ends of the street, deciding neither looked good, so he escorted her down Allen Street and turned on 5th.

"Everything OK, Johnny?" she asked.

"Everything is perfect," he replied.

They walked in silence for a bit before Annie said, "I've missed you."

"I've missed you, too."

"Then how come I haven't seen much of you?"

Ringo paused before answering. "A man has to know for sure. Sometimes we do things that don't make sense, but it does to us."

Annie frowned at him. "I don't know what you mean, Johnny."

"You've seen me with Delilah," he explained.

Annie's lips tightened and her face hardened. "Yes."

"She's a pretty woman, educated, going places."

Her shoulders slumped as she braced herself for the news. "I suppose."

They were at the end of the street and Johnny stopped and stared out in the evening darkness then shook his head. "But she's not for me."

Her spirits soaring, Annie took a breath. "What do you mean?"

"I mean," he said, turning her to face him. "She's got a lot of excellent qualities, but there's something missing."

"What?"

"Those feelings a fellow has when he's with a girl and when he's not with her, she's all he thinks about... like I am when I'm with you."

Her eyes brimming, she threw her arms around him and kissed him hard and passionately. "I love you, Johnny. Wherever you go, I want to go with you. I don't care where it is. I just want to be with you. We don't need no fancy house or finer things. As long as I'm with you, I know we'll be happy."

Ringo smiled devotedly. "You might make an honest man out of me yet."

Annie leaned back to stare into his eyes. "I want to marry you, Johnny. I've never felt like this before. I know you're the one for me. I will love you beyond the grave and back."

"That's a pretty far piece," he smiled, "but I'll take it."

Mason stood next to Belle as the performance of *Uncle Tom's Cabin* raged across the stage. The Theater was packed, and the audience enthralled as the drama's heroine, Eliza, was struggling across an imaginary river with a live bloodhound braying at her heels. The dog was obviously well-trained yet added to the suspense.

Suddenly, an intoxicated cowboy, believing Eliza needed help, leaped to his feet, drew his pistol and shot the poor dog.

The loud bang shocked the audience only for a moment before their sympathies for the imperiled heroine abruptly transferred to the deceased canine. While the director, a porcine man in tweed, hurried to remove the carcass so the show could go on, miners, cowboys, and gamblers close by the young cowboy rose up and proceeded to thrash and pummel the unfortunate miscreant.

As fists and feet found their target, Mason waded in, several waiters adding needed muscle.

"Back off now. Leave him alone. Back off."

By the time Mason had restored order, the young man was bloodied and bruised, though still quite inebriated. Hoisting him up to standing, he dragged him away from the angry mob and out the front door.

"A mere inconvenience," the director called out above the din then dramatically added, "The show must go on. Please take your seats everyone so we can find out what happens to our suffering heroine."

The audience needed little urging and quickly settled. Outside, Mason dragged the cowboy to the jailhouse.

"What happened to him?" Deputy Harry Solen asked when Mason pushed open the front door.

"Got into a little trouble at the Bird Cage," Mason said then went on to explain what happened. "Figured he'd be safer here than somewhere else in town. He's still drunker than a skunk, so I'm thinking he might not remember much of what happened tonight. You might remind him when he sobers up. He'll have to make good on that dog he shot."

Shaking his head, Harry took the man's feet while Mason held him up by his arm pits and they carried him into one of the cells and placed him on the bed.

"He'll also be fined for carrying a weapon in town," Harry said. Gazing down at the man whose face was scrunched in pain, he said, "And folks wonder why I don't drink much. If I ever get like this, you do me the favor and just shoot me, because getting like this means I've lost all self-respect."

"Don't be too hard on the young man, Harry," Mason smiled. "He's young and he'll learn some time. Besides, he got carried away by good acting."

"I suppose. Speaking of acting," Harry said. "That blond package calls herself Delilah is over the top. Don't see what Ringo sees in her, or she in him for that matter."

"What do you mean?"

"Even I can tell Delilah is putting on a show. I just can't figure out why. It's not like Ringo's loaded. Besides, I saw her with that fella with the wavy red hair and mutton chops."

"Ed?"

"If that's his name," Harry said. "It was quick, but they talked like they knew each other."

"When was this?"

"A day or two ago. Saw them duck in the alleyway behind Peter's Restaurant and Lodging House just before dinner. They talked then she came out first while he went round and came out on Toughnut between Peter's and the Russ House."

Mason's lips tightened. "Thanks Harry. I'd appreciate you keeping an eye on those two. They're up to no good."

"I figured as much." Hearing the cowboy groan, he sniffed and shook his head. "I'll let him suffer for a bit to teach him a lesson then send for the Doc when I get a chance."

Bisbee's residents were already at work when the firm knock on Ed's door woke him. Scrunching his face, he started at the mantel clock on the dresser. It was almost nine o'clock. He had slept later than usual.

The knocking persisted and he called out, "Just a minute."

Slipping on his trousers, he slipped the suspenders over his shoulders then opened the door.

"That damned whore," Becca snarled as she stamped her way past Ed.

"What are you talking about?" he asked, rubbing his eyes.

"Ringo," she snapped. "That whore of his has him wrapped around her little finger." She flopped down on a chair. "After all that time invested in setting up the hit, she snatches him right out from under me."

"Start from the beginning," he said, stifling a yawn.

"I thought I had Ringo all set, but he dumped me last night. Said his heart belonged to that tramp in the whore house."

"So take them both out," he said, the answer obvious.

"No," she emphatically replied. "I'm going to take him out and let her suffer." Leaping up, she coldly nodded. "And I know how I'll do it."

Without a word, she stalked past him and out the door.

Belle was at the bar talking to Jack when Ringo walked into the Theater looking for Annie. Seeing him, she gave him an affectionate smile.

"I'm glad you two worked things out last night," she said. "You two deserve each other."

"I'm getting the better end of the deal," he grinned. "She around?"

"Powdering her nose," she smiled, knowingly.

"Ah. I'll wait."

Jack slid a shot of whiskey in front of him. "My treat, Mister Ringo."

"Mister Ringo," he grinned. "So formal, but thank you."

Annie came up the stairs and her eyes lit up. "Johnny." She breezed across the empty dance floor and sidled up next to him, wrapping her arms around him.

Downing his whiskey, he placed the empty shot glass on the counter then gazed at Annie with longing and devotion.

"I have to do something in a little bit. Delilah isn't taking 'no' for an answer, and I've got to set things straight. She's going to come by in a bit and we're going to talk. I wanted you to know so that you know what I'm doing and if tongues should say otherwise, you'll know the truth."

"You're a good man, Johnny," she gushed. "I know you love me and so it doesn't matter what other people might say. You'll always be mine."

"That I will, Darling." He kissed her on the forehead. "I'll be back before you know it." Turning to Jack, he said, "Save me another one of those. This time make it a Tennessee Whiskey."

With a wave and a wink, he gave Annie another hug and a kiss on the lips then headed for the door, his walk that of a contented man.

Lounging comfortably in his private railcar, the Professor slid back a window curtain to stare out at the Chiricahua Mountains in the distance as his train moved off to the siding at Dragoon Station. The vast open space between the train depot and the mountains caused him to shake his head. While he admired the ruggedness of the terrain, he was already missing the pulse and life of San Francisco. Still, he had a job to do. Besides, this would give him a chance to put the quadcopter to the test.

Glancing up at Meili, he said, "Let's arrange for suitable transportation before we unload. But let's find an appropriate place to set up first, somewhere where we won't be noticed."

"Yes, Professor," she said. "What about Tombstone and the Marshal?"

"We have time," he said. "Let's find a place first. We can send out our scouts while we're putting the quadcopter together. If the Marshal is already dead, it doesn't matter. If he's still alive, we can monitor him while we run the trials."

He stood up and limped past the plush couch and headed towards the back door. Once outside, he scanned the flat desert out towards the Chiricahua Mountains then slowly twisted his head, shading his eyes with the palm of his hand, until his gaze rested on the Dragoon Mountains.

"Let's try there first," he said, ticking his head at the Dragoons, "somewhere on the east side of the mountains. It looks to be relatively quiet."

"As you wish," Meili said, kissing him on the cheek.

The Professor grabbed her hand as she was about to step away. "Remember," he warned. "This is a man's world out here. Not everyone appreciates strong women. Some say they do but only to a point. We don't want to draw undue attention to ourselves. Let's be docile and discreet."

"Of course, Professor," she demurely replied.

"But that doesn't mean we have to put up with their insults," he said with a smile. "Revenge is mine, saith the Lord. In this case, revenge is ours, silent and deadly."

"I wouldn't have it any other way," she sweetly smiled

As they stood on the platform, a railroad worker strutted by, noting the number of attractive oriental women. The man wiped a greasy arm across his forehead and leered at Meili before turning his attention to the Professor.

"Hey mister. You got a travelin' whore house here?"

The Professor curled a lip in disgust then forced a smile. "No. These ladies work for me."

"I bet," he said with a lascivious grin.

The Professor shot a glance at Meili and whispered in Chinese, "You can take him out first."

"With pleasure," she answered, giving the man a polite smile.

"You gonna be here long?" the man asked.

"Long enough to unload," he said. "I'll need to turn her around."

"Cain't do that here," he informed him. "You'll have to back 'er up and head on up to Hatch Junction and turn her around there."

"How far is that?"

"It's 'bout two hunnerd miles from here. Take you better part o' two days to get there, turn 'er around, and get back."

"Thank you," he said, dipping his head in a polite nod. "You have been most informative."

"Any time," he quipped then walked off.

"Once we unload," the Professor said to Meili, "send the train on to turn around. I want an escape route in case we need to leave in a brisk departure."

He watched her descend the steps to take charge of the other ladies. Inhaling a slow deep breath, he decided it was too hot to stand on the platform. Besides, he really ought to check on the quadcopter. It had taken more time than he realized to disassemble and pack up the flying machine. Hopefully putting it together wouldn't take as long.

And then there was that little part of the Gatling gun. He smiled broadly, wondering if there was a town not too far away that he might destroy. It didn't have to be a big town; just one not too many folks would miss.

Annie stalked back and forth across the dance hall, ignoring calls to dance. Belle noticed and called her over.

"What's wrong?"

"Johnny didn't come back last night," Annie fretted. "He said he would be right back, but he didn't come back."

"Maybe something came up," Belle offered.

"Uh uh," Annie adamantly said, shaking her head. "Johnny wouldn't go anywhere unless he told me where he was going. That girl's done something to him. I swear she has."

"Now we don't know that," Belle said, trying to calm her.

Annie clenched her fists. "I swear if that woman so much as touched a hair of his head, I'll kill her."

"Stop talking like that," Belle said. "You don't know what's happened or if anything has happened. I'm sure we'll find out soon enough. He'll probably come walking right in here saying his horse threw a shoe or something like that."

While her words did little to assuage Annie's fears, she nodded, hoping for the best. "I've never loved a man like him before. I don't know what I'd do if anything ever happened to him."

"Let's not jump to conclusions," Belle counseled. "You're expecting the worst. If nothing's happened to him, all your fears are for nothing."

"And if something has happened to him?" she challenged.

Belle gave Annie a maternal pat on arm. "All I'm saying is to wait and see. I'm sure there's a reasonable explanation."

"Suppose he ran off with her?" she said, eyes wide with fear.

"Now you're being silly," Belle replied. "What did he tell you yesterday?"

"That he loved me… that he wanted to marry me."

"And you think that would all change overnight?"

Annie stood facing Belle, her brows bent in a deep furrow. "I suppose not."

"I *know* not," Belle countered. "I've seen the way the man looks at you. He's not interested in anyone else."

"Then where is he?" Annie pleaded. "I'm going crazy."

"I'll ask Mason to see what he can find out," Belle offered. "If anyone can find him, Mason can."

Chapter 6

His mood stoic, Mason rode along the freight road that went east from Tombstone to Morse's sawmill far up the canon in the Chiricahua Mountains. The day was warm, and he lifted his Stetson and wiped his forehead.

When the news came this morning that Johnny Ringo was dead, Mason was filled with a great sadness. Deciding not to tell Belle or especially Annie the news until he found out more, he had saddled up, gathered a couple of other men and ridden out of town as soon as he found out.

Jim Morgan, a teamster hauling a load of lumber down to Tombstone had come to tell him. Jim said he found Ringo propped against the giant live oak by Turkey Creek. Jim now rode alongside of Mason on a borrowed horse from the OK Corral.

"I stopped by that oak tree, you know," Jim said, explaining what he had found, "the one with them five trunks' comin' outta it. I stop there regular like just to set a spell and eat m'lunch. It's close to the creek and there's this flat rock you can sit on. Wull, I stopped my wagon and was fixin' to git my lunch when I seen 'im. Didn't know who it were at first, so I says, "Howdy" but he didn't give no answer. So I gets my lunch and as I'm walkin' up on 'im, I seen who it was and that he was dead and so I come high-tailin' it here to find you."

Two more men rode with Mason and Jim. Ted White and Bill Knott agreed to come along to act as a coroner's jury. It was mid-afternoon by the time they approached the place where Ringo was. Crossing the creek, Mason followed the road around a bend before heading up away from the road to the small clearing. As they approached, Mason could see Johnny Ringo leaning back against the tree, his head sunk down on his chest.

Coaxing his steed closer, Mason dismounted a short distance away, looping the reins around the branch of a nearby tree. The others did the same, hanging back to allow Mason to inspect the ground and dead man before they came up.

Mason stood for a moment to take in the scene. Johnny's white felt hat, stained with blood, lay at his feet on the ground. His right hand, still holding his six-shooter, was on his lap, caught in the watch chain on the left side of his vest. His rifle stood firmly propped against the tree.

Mason came closer and saw the brain-mess scattered on the tree trunks behind the dead man. The back part of his head was a gaping jagged wound where the bullet had passed out. Looking to the side, he saw the hole in Johnny's right temple. Frowning, he drew closer scrutinizing the entry wound.

Reaching for the gun on Ringo's lap, he pulled back the hammer halfway then flipped open the cylinder gate. Slowly turning the cylinder, he pushed back the ejector sending out an empty shell. He repeated the process only to discover that the other chambers of the cylinder had been loaded.

Standing up, it was then he noticed that Ringo's coat and boots were missing. Wrapped around his feet were strips of his torn t-shirt. When Mason stared at the two gun belts Ringo was still wearing, something puzzled him. One belt had cartridges for his rifle. The other was for his six-shooter, but it was on upside down and all but two of the shells had tumbled out of it onto the ground.

At first glance it looked like Johnny might have finally killed himself, yet Mason knew better. The man may have been morose at times, but this latest venture with Worthington gang had energized him.

And then there was Annie. Ringo acted like a man in love. He had never seen Ringo that starry eyed. Something wasn't right.

"Looks to me like suicide," Ted flatly stated. "Whatcha think, Marshal?" he asked as Bill and Jim examined the body.

Mason was silent for a bit before shaking his head and saying, "Something doesn't make sense. Where are his boots and coat? Where's his horse?"

Bill was inspecting the entry wound when he said, "Strange. Don't see no powder burns. If the man killed himself, there oughta be powder burns."

"Still think it's suicide," Ted reaffirmed.

"Look here fer yerself," Bill objected. "There ain't no powder burns. When a body gets shot close up like, there's always powder burns."

Ted obliged and walked over to give a cursory look. "So there ain't no powder burns. Look at the back o' the man's head. It's obvious he done it to himself."

While Ted and Bill argued the finer points of powder burns, Mason walked around the grounds looking for any telltale signs. It was as he studied where Ringo had tied up his horse that he noticed the other set of hoof marks. Someone else had been here and he had a nagging suspicion he knew who.

"I agree with Bill," Mason said, still examining the hoof marks. He back-tracked them until they crossed the creek. Returning, he went up to the body and reexamined the bullet wound.

"But that'll mean an inquest," Ted complained. "It ain't like we got ourselves a whole lot to go on. I say we call it suicide. Jim? What's your call?"

"I'm with you on this," he said, ready to get back to work. No one cared about a dead outlaw, especially one with this man's reputation. "Besides, we can always change it if we hear someone claiming to have killed Johnny Ringo."

"That's pure foolishness," Mason countered. "Anyone can make the claim. You going to investigate every time someone says so?"

"C'mon Marshal," Ted objected. "There's not a whole lot we can do here. The man's dead. I know he was a friend of yours, but he's dead."

"I won't have the man's name dishonored by claiming it was suicide," Mason stubbornly stated. "There's another set of tracks here where his horse was tied," he said pointing to the ground by the tree.

"Those could be anybody's," Ted said. "It rained here a day or so ago, so who knows whose prints those are."

"OK," Mason said, "then what about the man's feet? If it rained like you said, the pieces of his undershirt wrapped around his feet ought to have some sort of dirt on them. They're clean."

"He coulda come here after the rain," Jim said.

Realizing he was going to get nowhere with either Jim or Ted, he asked Bill. "What's your take on this?"

Bill slowly shook his head. "Seems to me like there's more questions than answers. We can call it suicide and be done with it, or we can call it somethin' else. Either way, we're gonna hafta do somethin' with the body. We cain't just leave 'im here."

"Before anyone touches anything," Mason commanded, "we all agree that there's no powder burns on the skin, and that the underclothes on his feet are clean."

"Don't see how that's important for anything," Ted shrugged, "but sure, I agree."

"Jim?"

"Yeah, sure. Let's get him covered before he starts to stink. Don't none of us got a shovel, we'll probably need to cover him up with rocks."

"Just enough to keep the critters away," Mason said. As he stood gazing down at the dead man, a man few called friend, melancholy filled him. "I want him to have a decent burial later."

Stripping Ringo of his gun belts and six-shooter, they stretched him out on the ground and began retrieving rocks to pile on top of the corpse. In a little while, the body was covered enough to keep unwanted pests away. The four of them stood side by side for a moment staring at the temporary grave.

"Reckon one of us ought to say something?" Jim asked.

"You knew 'im best, Marshal," Bill said to Mason.

Mason's melancholy hadn't left him, and he said, "I'd rather wait until he's buried proper. I'll say something then."

Jim had fashioned a crude cross from two branches and stepped in front of Mason to place it at the head of the grave when he spun around and banged against him. The sound of a rifle shot followed immediately. Mason staggered back while blood poured out from Jim's chest as he sunk to the ground. The other two immediately dove for cover behind the piled up gravestones. Two more shots ricocheted off the stones.

"Still think it was suicide?" Mason bluntly asked, his pistol drawn. "Can you see where it's coming from?"

"No, dammit," Bill retorted. "Somewhere across the creek, but I ain't stickin' my head up to find out." He hunkered down even lower.

"Jim's a goner," Ted blurted, looking at the glazed over, unseeing eyes.

Mason cast a quick glance at the dead teamster then picked up the crude cross Jim had fashioned. Staring hard at Bill, he said, "You're not carrying."

'I'm a businessman, not a marshal," Bill sourly countered. "Didn't think I needed a gun comin' here."

"Take his gun," he said, indicating the six-shooter in Jim's holster, "and when I tell you to start shooting, you start shooting." Taking off his hat, he placed it atop the upright part of the cross. Handing the hat and cross to Ted, he said, "When I tell you to poke this hat up, I want you to stick it up at the other end there. Not too much, just enough to draw fire. I'm going off the other side."

"You sure?" Ted asked, wide-eyed.

"Just do what I tell you," Mason sternly replied. Flicking back the cylinder gate, he spun the cylinder ensuring all chambers were loaded. He then shifted his gaze to where the horses were tied and where his rifle was, still in the saddle holster. Scooting away to the opposite end, he crouched, ready to sprint across to the horses. "Do it now."

Ted poked the hat up and a moment later it flew off immediately followed by the sound of a rifle shot. Mason was up in a flash and racing across the open to the horses. He jerked to a halt to hide behind a tree a few paces away.

No sooner had he stopped than the sound of a bullet whizzed by to where the shooter expected Mason to be.

"Now Bill!" he called out.

Bill had crawled to the end of the cairn, pistol in hand. "I see 'im," he exclaimed. "He's up the side of the hill behind the rocks, about two o'clock."

"Start shooting," Mason demanded. "Keep him occupied while I get my rifle."

Bill obeyed and shot off a few rounds, all hitting well below where the gunman was. "He's a good 300 yards away," he called back to Mason.

Mason was already running with Bill's second shot. Reaching the horses, he yanked out his Winchester and cocked it. Quickly taking his bearing, he watched where Bill's rounds were kicking up dirt up the side of the hill. It was then he saw movement farther up the side. The gunman appeared to be overly confident because he didn't bother to fire and hide. He was lodged behind a good-sized boulder that gave him some protection while allowing him to steady his aim. The man was looking at them as he carefully reloaded, occasionally glancing down as he withdrew bullets from his belt.

Silence settled momentarily as the gunman sized up his quarry. Mason watched him nestle the rifle on top of the rock and take aim at him.

"You got some left, Bill?" he quietly asked.

"Still three in the chamber," came the reply.

"Now's a good time to use them. Aim high. Take your time."

Mason positioned himself behind a tree and tucked the Winchester into his shoulder. He popped his head out and jerked it back in one quick motion. It was enough to get a bullet zinging by.

Bill fired off a shot, took note of where it kicked up dirt and aimed higher. "I'm getting closer," he said firing a second round. It was when he fired the third round that the gunman's bullet kicked up fragments off a stone next to his face. "Dammit," he bellowed. "I'm bleedin'."

It was when Bill fired his third shot that Mason had gambled. He stepped from behind the tree and took quick aim just as the gunman fired at Bill. Squeezing the trigger, he felt the gun buck then watched as the gunman's head lurched backwards and the rifle point aimlessly in the air.

"Stay here," he commanded. He started forward, but the gunman, though hit, was not ready to give up, and pulled out a pistol and fired off shots as he scrambled up over the hill.

As the assailant struggled to put distance between them, Mason calmly took aim, but the attacker was clever and used the dips and rocks to his advantage. Too late, Mason realized the man was getting away. Instead of giving chase by foot, Mason spun around and ran for his horse.

"You two get yourselves out of here," he commanded. "Take Jim with you." I'm heading after him."

Not waiting for a reply, Mason leaped onto the saddle, quickly checked his handguns and stuffed the rifle in the saddle holster. Flicking the reins and giving the flanks a kick, Mason and steed lunged forward splashing across the creek to give chase.

His attention focused on the chase, he noticed too late the movement to his left when his quarry, bent over the saddle, lashed his horse and sped away.

Turning, Mason slowed his mount down, knowing a horse can only run so far so fast. At the speed the man was moving, his horse was as good as wasted in another mile or two.

Becca's arm hurt like hell. The bullet had torn a chuck out of her left shoulder and the galloping and jarring of the horse wasn't helping. Though blood still seeped onto her shirt, layers were drying and coagulating a russet brown. Yet adrenaline pumped through her, diminishing the pain enough that she could ride, and shoot if necessary.

That the Marshal was chasing her more than irritated her. That he had shot her made her angry. But what made her furious was that he was still alive, and it could ruin her reputation.

She felt her steed's strength beginning to ebb and she knew she would have to either find a replacement or hold up somewhere and wait for the Marshal. Yet the thought of waiting for him didn't sit well as she was a stranger in his territory. She would have to get to Bisbee and find a doc who didn't ask questions.

Up ahead, she saw the outlines of a ranch house and a corral with several horses. Shooting a glance over her shoulder, she couldn't see her pursuer, so she quickly decided a new horse was about due.

Slowing down, she heard the dog barking as she drew up to the fence. Dismounting, she glared at the animal and in one swift motion drew her six-shooter and shot the poor creature, which gave a final yelp as it tumbled over dead.

The door burst open, and a man emerged aiming a rifle at her.

"What the hell you think yer doin'? You shot ma dog. Why the hell you'd shoot ma dog?"

"I don't have time to explain," she said, firing a shot that caught the man in the forehead, sending him back through the open doorway.

Taking the bridle off the spent horse, she placed it on another mount and pulled herself up, thanking her parents that they taught her how to ride bareback. Kicking the horse to action, she barreled out of the corral and headed on to Bisbee, praying that Ed was there to help find a doc.

Mason heard the gunshot and urged his steed to a quicker gait. By the time he arrived at the ranch house, the woman was standing outside the doorway, hands gripping the man's feet, struggling to haul him out of the house. Two young children numbly watched from inside.

The woman stopped when she heard Mason ride up. Shielding her eyes with her hand, she stared mutely at him.

"I'm US Marshal Mason Sadler," he said. When she didn't respond, he added, "I'm tracking a man who came by this way. Did he do that?" He ticked his head at the prone man behind her.

"It don't matter," she replied, her voice tired. "He weren't any good as a man or a husband."

Mason stifled an irritated sigh, not sure if the woman was in shock from the death or the fact that she was now free. "Did you see who did this?

"Took one o' the horses and went off that way." She pointed in the direction of Bisbee. "Left that one there behind." She pointed to the sweat-flecked mount whose flanks were still heaving.

"Was it a man or a woman?" he queried.

The woman shrugged, looked down at her husband then back at the horse.

"Not sure which one t' do first," she mumbled. "Horse needs attention, but I don't want him lyin' here like this. I got children inside."

Torn between resuming the chase and helping the widow, Mason knew it was still a ways to Bisbee. Slipping down form the saddle, he walked over to the man, grabbed his ankles and dragged him out to the side of the house.

"Thank you, Marshal," she said then turned to the two youngsters in the doorway. The oldest was not yet four years old. "Getcher things. Once I get the horse cleaned up, we're leavin'."

"Where you headed?" he asked.

"Bisbee then back home to Missouri. Got kin back there." She wiped her hands on the front of her dress.

"I'll need you to stop by the sheriff's office in Bisbee and write a statement."

"Ain't no good at writin'," she explained, walking over to the horse.

"You just tell the sheriff and he'll write it down for you, Missus…"

"Riley," she replied.

"Will you do that for me, Missus Riley?"

"Suppose I could," she said.

"You got any other livestock?" Mason asked as he mounted.

"Nope. Sold the last bit o' stock to pay the bank." She walked over to the water pump and cranked the lever, filling a bucket to take to the horse.

"Sorry about your loss," he said.

"I ain't," she replied, the tiredness in her voice beginning to slough away.

With a polite nod, Mason wheeled around and headed off to Bisbee.

Becca had to change horses once again, hopefully for the last time. Her arm was beginning to stiffen, and she needed a doc to sew her up. Up ahead was a gate to another ranch. Slowing down, she stared up the road between the fenced pastures to the distance ranch house, noting that there were men outside working the corral.

Deciding she couldn't take the chance, she eased back slightly on the gait and hoped the animal would last until she reached Bisbee.

It was as she came upon the edges of the Mule Mountains that her horse stumbled, causing her to roll as the animal crashed to the ground. Picking herself up, she grimaced as she clutched her arm, staring at the poor creature whose labored breaths said it would die here.

Turning her back on the horse, she plodded into the mountains hoping perhaps she might find a stream or bit of water. Her thirst was growing, and the dry dust of the day thickened her lips. Fortunately, the tethered airships hovering above the city provided a guide like a beacon in the night.

When Mason came upon the dead horse lying on its side, he knew his prey was not far in front. It would now be a matter of tracking his, or rather her, footprints. Mason had no illusion about who it was ahead of him. He shook his head wishing that at a time like this he could wreak justice on his own.

Standing up in the stirrups, he gazed out over the landscape yet could not see anyone in the distance. Knowing she had to get to Bisbee, he mulled whether to track her or wait for her in town. The easiest would be to wait for her in town and get some help from the sheriff.

Settling back down in the saddle, he turned away from the pursuit and headed around the foothills of the Mule Mountains. Besides, the afternoon was moving along, and it would be dark soon. He doubted she would be back in town before dark and the thought of her in the mountains in the night gave him satisfaction.

Becca stayed low as she watched the lone rider move off from pursuing her and headed around the mountains to Bisbee. She knew what he was doing. He was going to wait there for her.

Waiting until he was far enough away, she stood and began retracing her steps. There was a cabin not too far back. If she could at least wash and bandage the wound and find another shirt, she could then find another horse and head north, away from Bisbee.

Night was falling as Becca crouched near the towering ocotillo and watched and listened. The curtains were drawn at the windows, but there was light coming from inside. She could smell smoke which meant that someone was cooking. Her stomach growled at the thought, reminding her she hadn't eaten.

Waiting until night had darkened the sky, she stood and approached.

"Hullo in the cabin," she called out. When no one answered, she called out again. "Hullo in the cabin. I need help."

"Go away," came the muffled reply. It was a woman's voice.

"I'm alone and injured," Becca said. "I need help."

There was a long pause before the door cracked open and light and a Winchester spilled out.

"You alone?" the woman demanded.

"Yes."

"What happened?"

"I've been shot."

The door opened wider and light from behind the woman silhouetted her in the doorway. Leaning out, she cast a slow glance around.

"You'd better come in."

"Thank you"

Becca walked past the woman and into the cabin. Though small, it was cozy and well-built with a separate room as a bedroom. The aroma wafting out of the cast iron oven caused her mouth to water.

"What happened to you?" the woman asked.

Becca turned to her host. She was slender and pretty, fair complexioned with strawberry blond hair. She looked to be no more than twenty years old.

"I got shot."

"Why?"

"I took a dislike to a fella and he got to me before I got to him," she cryptically replied. "You alone?"

"My man's in Bisbee."

"Then I probably shouldn't be here when he gets back."

"Won't be back until the morning," she replied, leaning the rifle against the wall by the door. "Sit down and let me take a look." She pointed to a chair by the stove.

"Smells good," Becca said, gingerly unbuttoning her shirt and pulling it off her shoulders.

"You're welcome to some," she said with a polite smile as she focused her attention on the wound. "You're lucky. It's not too deep. It'll leave a scar, but you'll be OK." She dipped a clean cloth into a bowl of water and began dabbing the blood away.

Becca flinched.

"Sorry."

"Don't be," Becca said. "You're mighty kind to help me."

"Not at all," she said, dabbing, rinsing the cloth and wiping the blood away.

"You said your man's in Bisbee?"

The woman paused mid-dab and furrowed her brows at Becca as though debating how to answer. "Yes."

"What's he doing?"

"Probably drinking and whoring."

Becca stiffened then snarled, "What kind of man leaves a person by herself in the middle of nowhere?"

"The kind of man that don't care," she answered.

"You two married?"

"Common law," came the response. "At least that's what he calls it."

"Why do you stay here then?"

"Just waiting for a good excuse to leave."

"What's your name?" Becca asked.

"Del. It's short for Adeline. What's yours?"

"Becca. It's short for Rebecca."

Del stared down at Becca. "If I didn't know any better, I'd take you for a man at a distance, wearing britches like that." She purposely left out the part of the two six-shooters in the gun belt around her hips

"They're comfortable," Becca said. "Why should men get comfortable clothes and women be forced to wear things that make them look silly."

"I agree," she said, "only I can't find a store that would sell me a pair." She wrapped a clean bandage cloth around the wound. "That'll do for now. We'll need to change the bandage later on."

She turned to grab a potholder and opened the oven. "It ain't much, but it's filling." She pulled out a cast iron frying pan brimming with cornbread. "There's chunks of bacon and rabbit and peppers in it," she said. "There's butter on the table."

"Smells good," Becca complimented.

Del sliced the cornbread into pie-shaped pieces and dished two out for Becca. "Usual, I take out a couple slices for him, but lately he ain't hungry after he's been drinking."

"Sounds to me like you need to move on," Becca said between bites.

"I'm aiming to," Del replied then ticked her head at the coffee pot on the stove. "There's hot coffee if you want it. Help yourself."

Becca looked around and saw two tin cups on a shelf by the stove. Retrieving both, she poured two cups, handing one to Del.

"Where you headed?" Del asked.

"North," she replied, knowing the thrust of the question. The thought of taking her along had advantages. The Marshal would be looking for a woman traveling alone. Having Del with her might make it easier to evade. An epiphany hit and she smiled thoughtfully at her hostess.

"How keen are you on your man?"

"Not at all," Del said, curling a lip. "Like I said, I've been waiting for the right time to leave."

"Suppose something happened to him, something bad... say like he was shot or something like that?"

"Make it all the easier to leave," she said, slabbing butter on a piece of cornbread.

'I have an idea," Becca said, "but I'll need your help. I need a place to stay for a bit until I can heal up a bit more."

Del was quick to understand. "Here's as good a place as any. Don't get many visitors."

"Your man will need to find another place to stay."

"He can rot in hell for all I care. And besides, he ain't my man. I only say that when I'm alone and a stranger happens by."

Becca nodded, grasping the inference. "What time does he usually come home?"

"Midmorning, after he's slept off the drink. More coffee?"

With her arm patched up and food in her belly, Becca began to relax. "How did you end up here?"

"Came here from Waco wanting to jump on the silver mining. They weren't hirin' when we came, and Lloyd figured we could make it ranchin'. Found this god-forsaken piece of dirt and been here ever since."

"How long have you been here?"

"Two years... two god-awful years, scrapin' to get by. And when we do get money, he spends it."

"How'd you end up with him?"

Del's lips tightened and her face hardened. "My Pa owed a debt. He sold me to pay for it."

Becca dropped her knife. "He sold you?"

"*Indentured* was the word he used. It's highfalutin' but it means the same. I refuse to marry him, but he got his way with me none the same." She turned away to look at the window as though peering through it. "When he started whorin', it gave me a break. I hated him touchin' me."

"Well," Becca cheerfully said. "I think we can take care of that little problem tomorrow."

Del gazed at her with warm eyes. "Got only one bed, but it's big enough for two."

Becca blinked then smiled. "That'll be fine."

Belle held Annie in her arms as the young girl silently struggled to make sense of it all. Ted White had come by and told Belle the news that Ringo was dead as was Jim Morgan. Mason had gone after the murderer.

Belle had waited to tell Annie the news as the dancer had been gone for a while searching for clues to Ringo's whereabouts. She had passed Ted coming out of the Bird Cage. He said nothing, instead giving her a look of pity.

Annie's eyes had welled up with tears when Belle relayed Ted's story, yet her first words were, "Poor Jim. He's got a wife and young ones." Pulling back from Belle's comforting embrace, her face hardened and her eyes burned with anger. "That woman did this to him," she declared.

"Now, Annie," Belle cautioned. "You don't know that for sure."

"I know it in my heart," she said. "She's gonna pay."

Belle hung onto Annie's arm, preventing her from leaving. "Not so fast. You still have a job here. The best thing to do is to take a breath and plan. You don't even know where to start."

Annie fumed but knew that Belle was right. "It's not fair," she said through gritted teeth.

"Of course it's not fair," Belle agreed. "But if we're going to make her pay for her crime, we have to think and plan."

"We?" Annie said when she realized Belle's intent.

"Of course, 'we,'" she replied. "You don't think I'd let you do this by yourself."

"I beg your pardon," a male voice interrupted.

So intent was their attention to each other that they had not noticed Ed standing close by.

"I do not mean to intrude," Ed commiserated looking at Annie, "but I couldn't help but overhear the tragic news that someone dear to you has died."

"The man I love was murdered," Annie fiercely replied.

"My goodness," Ed said, startled. "How terrible."

"And I know who did it."

"Now Annie," Belle warned.

"Who?" Ed asked.

"A hussy named Delilah."

"How do you know?" Ed said with curiosity.

"She'd been after him ever since she came to town. She knew he was my man and when he went to tell her he wasn't interested in her, that he wanted only me then she killed him."

"My word," Ed replied, aghast.

"But she can't run forever," Annie said. "Ted White said the Marshal winged the person who shot Johnny and was chasing her to Bisbee."

"Annie," Belle firmly said, interrupting, wanting her to stop.

"Well it's true," Annie adamantly said.

"If the Marshal had injured her," Ed consoled, "you can be sure he will capture her, and she will be brought to justice." He gave her an empathetic smile. "I think Miss Belle here has the right approach. Instead of rushing out unprepared, why not wait until the Marshal has returned?"

Belle cast him a glance of thanks as Annie took a deep breath and sighed.

"Go freshen up," Belle told her. "By the time you get back, maybe Mason will be back."

"You think so?" she said with hopeful eyes.

"You never know."

As Annie walked away, Ed leaned in and said, "You are good for her, and for all the other girls who work here. You're very caring and understanding."

"That's very kind of you to say that," she replied.

"The Marshal's a good man," he continued. "I can see why you are so enamored with him."

"Yes he is," she answered, wondering why he was so interested."

"Mister Anderson," a voice boomed out. "Fancy meeting you here."

Ed and Belle turned to see Thaddeus Shephard saunter over, pipe in hand.

"Mister Shephard," Ed pleasantly smiled. "How are you?"

"You two know each other?" Belle asked, surprised.

"I had the pleasure of meeting Mister Anderson on the flight from San Francisco to Bisbee. We shared a pleasant meal and conversation together. I haven't seen him since we landed. How's business?"

"Fine," Ed replied. "And yours?"

"Excellent," he grinned, "excellent. With the amount of silver mined in Tombstone alone, we should be doing a thriving business in the very near future."

Belle was about to excuse herself when Ed asked Shephard, "Have you heard the news? Johnny Ringo has been killed."

"I am afraid I am unfamiliar with the name," Shephard replied. "Was he a friend?"

"No," Ed answered, disappointed with Shephard's lack of interest. "He was the love interest of a woman here. It sounds to me like the eternal tragedy of a lover's triangle."

"Ah," Shephard nodded. "Those things happen."

"If you'll excuse me," Ed said by way of extracting himself, "I've business to attend to at the moment. It's good to see you again, Mister Shephard. Perhaps we can have dinner in the next week or two."

"That would be most acceptable," he grinned, shaking his pipe at him in a friendly wave.

As the door closed behind Ed, Shephard turned to the bartender. "Mister Jack, a cherry brandy if you please."

"Right away," Jack said with a professional smile.

"Enjoying your stay here, Mister Shephard?" Belle asked.

"An interesting situation you have here," he replied, accepting the snifter, swirling the brandy. Inhaling the bouquet, he took a small sip, savoring the thick flavor.

"Anything new?" she innocently asked.

"Nothing," he said with some frustration. "There's nothing on the woman named Delilah or on Mister Anderson. It's obvious they're using fake names, but there's nothing that I've been able to use to corroborate criminal activity. For all we know, they could be who they say they are."

"I don't trust him," she said.

"We have bigger problems at the moment," he said then sipped his cordial.

"What?" she asked.

"I received word that the Professor left San Francisco about a week ago, heading this way. I've instructions to look for him."

"Be careful," she warned. "He doesn't play nice."

"I know. I've lost two friends trying to bring him to justice." Lifting the snifter higher, he swirled the liquid again, watching the drops clinging to the sides. "Be careful yourself," he cautioned. "If the Professor is here, there's a reason and it's never a good one."

It was either early or late. It was all a matter of perspective Belle thought as she walked along Allen Street towards home. At three o'clock in the morning, it was way too early to be up and much too late to be awake.

Passing by the resurrected saloons and hotels and other businesses, she smiled at the steady business the saloons maintained. This town liked to drink.

Nodding to the occasional man not too drunk to recognize her, she silently mused as she walked. She hadn't heard from Mason since yesterday morning and that concerned her. Though she knew what he was doing and where, it gave her no comfort for she also knew he was pursuing a dangerous murderer, which most likely was Delilah.

Though she knew that Mason loved her and was committed to her, it didn't mean she didn't feel a little twinge of jealousy. Delilah was a beautiful woman and if she could fool Ringo into a trap, she could do the same to Mason.

Passing Haye's Jewelry Store, she turned left on 3rd Street, unaware of a man lurking in the shadows behind the store. He was swift and silent as he came up behind her and wrapped her neck in a choke hold. Though her hands went up to try and pull the arm away, darkness filled her eyes and she went limp.

Ed immediately let go when she went limp and dragged her to the space between the store and the next house.

"Help me carry her to the wagon," he said to a smaller man who had remained in the shadows.

Gordon limped from the darkness, still tender from the ill-timed dynamite blast. Grabbing hold of Bell's feet, they carried Belle further into the space at the rear of the buildings then to the waiting wagon next to the blacksmith shop on Toughnut Street.

"Where are we taking her?" Gordon wheezed, unused to physical labor.

"To the cabin."

"Our hideout?" Gordon exclaimed, worried.

"You have a better idea?"

"Why kidnap her in the first place?" he asked

"Becca may be in trouble," Ed said. "We use her as leverage and when the Marshal comes to rescue her, we kill them both."

"I'll set up booby traps," Gordon announced, pleased with the opportunity to show off his, so far unused, talent.

"That would be an excellent idea."

Lifting her into the wagon, they placed her on her side then gagged her and tied her wrists to her ankles behind her.

Pulling a tarp over her, they climbed to the seat where Ed released the brake and flicked the reins to the two mules.

Slowly heading west on Toughnut Street, they passed Missus Hunt's Lodging House then turned right on 2nd Street.

They were not yet out of town when Belle came to, discovering herself bound and gagged. She snarled to herself bemoaning that this was the second time she'd been caught unawares and bound and gagged. Squirming to slide out from beneath the tarp, she succeeded in wedging herself against a corner and shimmying up to where she could see over the wagon's side. Twisting her head, she watched as Tombstone dwindled in the distance.

Seeing the two men up front, she grunted to get their attention.

Gordon turned around. "She's awake."

"You can go ahead and take the gag off," Ed said.

Gordon climbed into the wagon and pulled the gag out of her mouth.

"Thank you," she said with a deep breath. She looked at Gordon then cocked her head to stare at the back of Ed's head. "Who's your friend here, Ed?"

"His name's Gordon. Say 'hello' Gordon."

"Hello," Gordon repeated.

"He's an expert on blowing things up."

Belle cast a look at him in the dimming moonlight. "Weren't you the one who was nearly killed on the road to Charleston?"

Ed snorted a laugh.

"Are you just learning," Belle innocently said, "or are you just bad at what you do?"

Ed chortled while Gordon indignantly said, "It was circumstances beyond my control."

"Of course," she sweetly answered. "Where are we headed?"

"A nice little place where we can settle down and wait for your Marshal to come save you," Ed said.

"Why kidnap me?"

"Because Mister Worthington wants your man to suffer," Gordon answered.

"Shut up Gordon," Ed snapped.

"Why?" Gordon said, feeling confident. "It's not like she can do anything about it." Staring at her, he said, "Once I set up my booby traps, your lover boy will be as good as dead."

Belle slowly shook her head and started chuckling.

"What?" Gordon frowned.

"You two have no idea what you're dealing with," she said. "I'll bet you ten to one that neither of you will be alive a week from today."

"What are you talking about?"

"Don't pay her any mind," Ed sniffed in disdain. "She's just trying to frighten you."

"That's good advice," she lightly laughed. "Please, don't pay me any mind. But don't say that I didn't warn you."

"Shut up," Ed warned.

"You sound nervous, Ed," she taunted. "I thought you said there was nothing to worry about." She turned her attention to Gordon. "Did Ed tell you that the Marshal is the fastest gun in the West? Did he tell you that Earl challenged him and never got his hand on his gun before the Marshal whipped out his .45 and drilled the poor man right through the forehead."

"I said shut up," Ed snarled.

"Now you sound scared, Ed. That's not good leadership. Fear in a leader instills fear in a subordinate. Poor Gordon here's beginning to shake like an autumn leaf."

"I am not," Gordon retorted with a quiver in his voice.

"See?" Belle said. "He's scared and he ought to be. When the Marshal finds you, he's going to kill you both."

"Why don't we just kill her and be done with her?" Gordon said, his apprehension growing.

"Spoken like a real man," Belle mocked, "a real man who would shoot a person in the back because he's got no guts to confront him face to face."

"I said shut up," Ed snarled and leaned back to backhand her across the face.

Belle's head twisted sharply at the impact, and she winced as she worked her jaw to relieve the pain.

"See there Gordon?" she ridiculed. "There's a real man. You need to take lessons from Ed. You need to tie up your victims first then hit them when they can't strike back. That's a real man."

"I said shut up," Ed growled, lifting his arm to strike her again. When she didn't flinch, he glared at her and refocused his attention forward.

"What are we going to do?" Gordon asked.

"We're going to do what we planned. You're the expert demolitions man –"

"That's debatable," Belle chuckled.

"Ignore her," Ed coldly said. "Stay focused. When we get to the cabin, you set up your traps and we wait. Won't be long before he discovers she's gone."

"How's he going to know where she is?" Gordon asked.

"I left him a note," Ed grinned.

"You really *are* dumb," Belle snickered.

"Why?" Gordon blurted.

"You kidnap me and then tell him where to find me?" she said, her tone full of derision. "Are you two in training? When does the real team show up, you know, the professionals?"

"When we're finished with you," Ed sneered, "you're going to wish you'd never been born."

"Oooh, I'm so scared." Belle heaved a longsuffering sigh. Turning her attention to Gordon, she asked, "After you set traps around the house, how are you going to protect it from the sky?"

"What" he startled.

"Don't listen to her," Ed tersely warned.

"That's right Gordon," Belle said with feigned earnestness. "Listen to Ed. He's got all the answers. Be sure to thank him when you get shot first."

"What do you mean about the sky?" Gordon asked, frowning with growing worry.

"Have you forgotten about our Machinist friends and their airships?"

"Airships?" His mouth gaped open at the thought of a rescue coming from above.

"By the way, you do know they're Chiricahua. They can track a polar bear in a snowstorm. And they're clever. You'll never know they're there until you wake up and they're standing right next to you. And then there are the bombs. Fascinating devices they drop from the sky."

"She's lying," Ed snapped. "Put the gag back in her mouth. I'm tired of her blabbering."

Gordon climbed back into the wagon bed to replace the gag. "She keeps turning her head," he complained as he struggled to stuff the gag in her mouth.

Ed pulled back on the reins to halt the wagon. Turning to glare at her, he said, "You got a choice, lady. You either keep your yap shut, or we do another chokehold and put you out, this time for a lot longer."

Belle quickly considered the results knowing the consequences of an extended chokehold. "Oh alright," she huffed. "I'll be good," then softly mumbled, "for a while."

Dawn was rimming the mountains in iridescent reds and golds when Ed drove the wagon off the trail, crossing a dry arroyo and up to a cabin that looked to be long abandoned, nestled amongst the oak trees.

Dismounting, he cast a cold glance at Belle. "You talked big on the way here. We'll see how big you talk when your lover boy gets here and your whole world comes crashing down on you." Snapping his head to stare at Gordon, he said, "Get your toys out and make this place into a fort. No one gets through. Understand?"

"You do what you're good at," Gordon lectured him, "And I'll do what I'm good at." He felt better now that the sun was up and he could get to work.

Belle paid attention as Gordon lowered the rear wagon gate and began unloading boxes and containers. "What'cha got there?"

"The tools of my trade," he loftily replied. "Once you see my creations, you'll regret the moment you mocked me."

"Humor me," she said as Ed walked inside the cabin.

"Well," Gordon smiled and pointed to fours crates. "These contain variations of the cemetery gun."

Belle nodded. "Do these swivel too when the trip wire is hit."

"That and more," he serenely replied. "Instead of one bullet per gun, mine are like little cannons that spray razor sharp projectiles, giving new meaning to dying by a thousand cuts."

Belle's lips tightened at the imagery, and she silently prayed Mason would discover the trap before it was too late. "What about the other boxes?" she asked.

"Those are step bombs," he replied.

"Step bombs? How do they work?"

"Aren't you the inquisitive one," he sniffed.

"Can't help it,' she shrugged. "Call it professional curiosity."

"You two quit jabbering," Ed snapped as he emerged from the cabin and walked up to the wagon. Staring hard at Belle, he said, "I'm going to free your legs. You make a run for it and I'll wing you in the leg. Then I'll do such a bad job patching you up that you'll bleed to death, only it will take a couple of days, and the pain will be unbearable."

"My, my," she replied with cold aplomb. "And to think that I once thought you might be a gentleman."

"That's the least of your worries," he answered then turned his attention to Gordon. "Get a move on. I suspect it won't be long before the Marshal shows up and I want to make sure our surprise is ready and waiting when he comes."

Becca was up at first light. Though tired, her shoulder hurt and her sleep had been restless. She looked down at Del whose long hair spread across the pillow. Her breathing was slow and peaceful. She looked so innocent asleep.

Slipping out from the thin cover, Becca stood and slowly moved her arm, working out the stiffness. Putting on her trousers, she again wished she was somewhere civilized so that she could take a long bath and put on clean clothes.

She looked back at Del and chuckled to herself. Del's innocence was a façade. The woman was more streetwise than she let on. Becca was surprised she stayed here until she learned that Del had been secretly sequestering money. Every time Lloyd came home from a night of whoring, Del would wait until he fell asleep then search through his pockets and take a small amount of whatever he had, but always never enough to be noticed. After two years, Del had managed to save almost $100, which was one of the reasons she was still here.

Becca studied Del's face and body. The woman was very pretty and had the kind of body men loved – young and firm. Had she wanted, she could've made good money in the cribs in Bisbee, if leaving here was that important. But that would have meant degrading herself and why should she have to debase herself in order to get what she wanted?

Stiffly sliding her arm through a sleeve, Becca fingered a button on the blouse Del had given her to wear last night. It was clean and had a fragrance she couldn't quite place. At first, she had been worried that the wound in her arm would bleed through and stain the sleeve, but by the time she changed the bandage, the bleeding had stopped.

"You're awake," Del said and yawned.

"Didn't mean to wake you," Becca said.

"That's OK. I'll make us some coffee."

Del flipped off the cover and sat on the edge of the bed, rubbing her eyes. She wore a thin linen nightgown with the sleeves cut off. Pushing herself to standing, she padded over to the stove and opened the door to the firebox. Stirring the coals, she added a bit of kindling followed by larger pieces of mesquite.

Soon, the bouquet of coffee filled the cabin.

Becca opened the door and breathed in the morning freshness. It was a clean smell, unlike San Francisco with its mixture of ocean and factories and humanity. While she liked the bright cloudless days and wide-open spaces here in the Arizona Territory, she missed the pulse of San Francisco teeming with people and the overlapping noise of business and living.

"What time do you expect him back?" she said over her shoulder.

"He's not even awake yet," Del scoffed. "Don't figure on him coming back here 'til mid-morning. Here ya go." She handed Becca a cup of coffee.

"Thanks." Becca sipped the hot brew as she pondered her next steps. It would do no good to try and contact Ed. Most likely the Marshal was still in town waiting for her. Yet she needed to get some clothes and money, which were in her hotel room.

Turning to Del, she said, "Once we take care of... what was his name?"

"Lloyd."

"Once we take care of Lloyd, I'm going to need you to head into town and get some of my things. And then I'm going to want a bath. You have a wash tub?"

"Of course," she said, the answer obvious.

"Didn't mean to imply anything," she apologetically said. "I thought you would." She fluffed her blouse. "This blouse smells good."

"I take that one to the Chinese laundry in Bisbee."

Becca immediately understood. This blouse received special treatment. "You're very kind to let me wear it. Was it a gift?"

"I had a suitor before Lloyd. He bought that for me. I don't wear it 'cause it makes Lloyd mad. It looks good on you," she said with a smile.

"It will look good on you again," Becca promised.

By mid-morning, Mason knew he had to move on. Annie had a right to know what happened to Ringo, if she didn't already know. After alerting the sheriff's office, he had gone to a number of lodging houses asking about Delilah, but none of them had her as a guest, even after he described her. Frustrated, he went to the airship terminal and asked about her, receiving the same response.

It was as he was leaving the terminal that an idea sprouted and he headed off to the Machinists Union Lodge on Brewery Street. Opening the main door, he smiled at his good fortune when he saw Taboca coming into the lobby.

"Morning, Marshal," Taboca greeted him with a broad smile. "What brings you here?"

"I'm hunting a killer and I need your help."

"Of course," he replied.

"I need to borrow one of your airships to help me search."

"No problem. They're over at the terminal in the Machinists hanger."

"Hey, Marshal," Nantan called out as he walked into the lobby. "What are you doing here?"

"He's hunting a killer and needs our help."

"Alright," Nantan exclaimed. "What do we need to do?"

"He's going to borrow one of our airships," Taboca answered.

"He can use mine," Nantan offered. "Taboca can help in his, and I can use my motorized self-propulsion legs."

"He's been itching for an excuse to use them," Taboca said, shaking his head and grinning.

"Who we looking for?" Nantan asked.

"A woman. Good looking with blond hair. I got a shot at her at a distance, so she's wounded."

"Who'd she kill?"

"Johnny Ringo."

Nantan's joviality evaporated. "I'm sorry, Marshal. I know he was a friend. You can count on us to help."

"I knew I could. That's why I'm here."

"Where are we looking?" Taboca asked.

"Mountains outside of town. She was headed this way last night, so I expect her to try to get into town to get to a doctor. If I wounded her bad enough, she could be lying out there somewhere. Either way, I want to find her."

Taboca led the way, and they headed out the lodge, down Brewery Street and over to the airship terminal on the south of town. The Machinists terminal was at the far end.

Entering the terminal, Mason saw the two mini airships, their air envelopes deflated.

"Don't worry," Nantan assured him. "They won't take long to fill. All I have to do is fire up the fuel boxes and we'll be ready."

"How long with that take?"

"A little more than half an hour." He gave a cheery wave and went over to a large wall cabinet and began hauling out his invention.

While the airship envelopes inflated, Taboca gave Mason a quick refresher.

Pointing to the control board and two levels in the pilot's position, he said, "Remember, all you have to do is keep in mind a few basics. The ship can only go forward, left, right, up, and down. The levers on each side of the pilot's seat here are for steering. Pull the left lever and push the right, you go left. Pull the right and push the left, you go to go right. The two levels up on the control board are just like a carpenter uses. You use those to help keep the ship balanced and level."

He then pointed to the tube that went from the engine compartment to the envelope. "The heat from the engine goes into the envelope and heats the air-gas mixture. Because the back end gets heated first, it tends to stay the warmest. Just like the last time, you'll feel the rear end rise up on you, sort of like a bucking horse, though not quite as strong. When that happens, just open the vents and it'll settle. Keeping the ship level is a combination of opening and closing the vents."

"I remember," he nodded.

"Here," he said, handing him a set of glasses with colored lenses. "You can use Nantan's glasses."

Mason slipped the glasses in his top pocket while he waited for the ships to be ready. He watched Nantan position the legs of his contraption next to a low platform followed by placing the engine on the platform itself, close to the legs.

"We've made some improvements," Nantan said, waving a hand at him to come over. "Before, the arms were stiff, and it made running unnatural. We now have arms that move just like regular arms. The controls are in the hand pads."

"We thought about what you said about body armor," Taboca said. "We're still experimenting, but we can't find anything light enough that will give protection yet let the operator still move quickly. What we've found is that adding armor slows down the machine. And if we put it only on the front, it throws it off balance."

"I'm sure you two will figure it out," Mason said with a smile. "If you put an angle on it, the armor might not need to be so thick."

"What do you mean?"

"When a bullet hits a hard object, it deflects or bounces off in another direction. You could make the armor in the shape of an arrow. That way you could use thinner armor."

Taboca frowned in concentration. "That might work," he agreed.

"If you make it out of wood then add a thin coat of metal, it would be lighter than just metal," Mason added.

Taboca's eyes lit up. "What an excellent idea."

"You want me to wait until you two are ready," Nantan asked, "or can I go ahead?"

"She's dangerous," Mason warned. "I think it better we go together."

While Mason and the two machinists waited for the envelopes to fill, Becca and Del sat in the shade of the porch. Belle checked her guns while Del sipped a cup of coffee. The Winchester leaned against the door mantel behind her.

Becca noted her new friend was surprisingly calm, early on chatting merrily about her life and where she grew up. When it came to Lloyd, her tone changed and impatience surfaced.

Just as Del had predicted, Lloyd came riding up on a brown and white paint that looked to be well fed and cared for.

"Who are you?" he asked Becca as he dismounted.

"Where'd you get the horse?" Del interrupted with a frown.

"Won her last night. M'luck's changin'. Knew it would." Wrapping the reins around the hitching post, he stood and stared at Becca. "Who are you?" He then noticed the blouse. "And why you wearin' her blouse?"

"It's a long story," Del said, standing. Picking up the rifle, she said, "There's something out the back you need to see."

"What?"

"You'll see. We can't make any sense of it."

As they walked behind the cabin, Lloyd cast a long glance at Becca, liking what he saw. "Where you from, little lady? You look like someone I seen before."

"Who knows?" she amiably replied. "You might have. Have you been to Tombstone lately?"

"Ain't been there since we got this place," he said walking closer to her and giving her a leer.

Del stopped and pointed. "It's just t'other side of that ocotillo."

Lloyd walked around to find a freshly dug depression. Two shovels lay off to the side. Frowning, he turned to see Del standing a little distance away, cradling the Winchester in her arms.

"Your whorin' days are over," Del said, shifting the rifle to both hands.

"What?" he sneered. "You gonna shoot me."

"No," Becca interrupted. "I am."

Her hand flashed up and she fired, the bullet penetrating his forehead, sending him reeling backwards towards the depression.

Del walked up next to her, handing the rifle to her while taking the gun from her hand and moved over to stand above Lloyd. Giving him a look of hatred, she fired a shot into the man's chest where the heart had already stopped beating.

Walking back to Becca, she handed her the gun back then returned to Lloyd where she dropped to her knees and rifled through the man's pockets.

"Looks like he did better'n he was letting on." She held out a handful of silver dollars.

"We'd better get him covered up," Becca counseled. "Then we need to get started."

"Started on what?" Del asked, grabbing his wrists and dragging him into the depression.

"Once we finish here," Becca said, scooping a spade full of dirt and tossing it over the dead man, "you need to ride into Bisbee, buy some men's clothes that will fit you and another horse. You got enough bullets for the rifle?"

"Got plenty. What about a saddle?" She dumped a shovel's worth of dirt on Lloyd's face.

"Saddle's expensive. Besides, you already got a saddle on the one horse. Don't want folks getting suspicious."

"One of us is gonna have to ride bareback," Del pointed out.

"I'll do that. Rode bareback growing up. Besides, you'll need a place for the rifle while you're riding."

Del paused and stared down at the half-filled hole. "Never thought I'd be so glad to see him dead."

By the time Becca and Del shoved the last bit of dirt over Lloyd, Mason and Taboca were airborne over the Mule Mountains, working slowly in widening loops. Down below, Mason watched as Nantan stretched his mechanical legs, covering wide distances in long strides.

Their searching proved vain until Taboca noticed a rider in the distance coming towards Bisbee. Getting Mason's attention, he pointed and together they swung the airships around and headed to intercept the lone rider.

Mason's pulse quickened when he determined the rider was a woman with light colored hair. Yet he intrinsically knew it wasn't Delilah for the woman rode with a relaxed gait, showing that she had not been wounded. Lowering his airship for a better glimpse, he let his disappointment settle when she looked up at him. Increasing the engine power, he rose into the sky to join Taboca.

"It's not her," he shouted.

Taboca replied with a shrug the called back. "We'll need to head back to refuel."

Nodding in understanding, Mason swung the airship in a wide arc and headed back to Bisbee.

Del saw them before she was halfway to Bisbee. She knew who they were looking for. Maintaining her pace, she serenely made her way towards town, waving cheerfully when the one airship descended to get a better look at her. She grinned when she saw his disappointed look followed by them departing back to the airfield.

Riding into town, she stopped at the first mercantile shop on Main Street. Looping the reins around the hitching post, she walked in

"May I help you, Miss?" the owner asked. He was a middle-aged man with a clipped handlebar moustache.

"I'm looking for men's clothes," she sweetly replied, "about my size."

"Your size?" he said, raising an eyebrow.

"It's not for me," she said, flipping a hand at him. "My brother's coming in from back East and I want to surprise him."

"And he's about your size," he said with a smile.

"We were twins. I imagine him being a man and all, he might be a little bit broader and more muscled by now, but I'd rather the clothes be too tight than too loose. He's a little on the vain side."

"Ah," the merchant nodded with a smile. "I have a cousin like that. I've plenty of trousers and shirts. What about undergarments?"

"I'd just as soon let him decide for himself," she blushed.

"Of course," he replied with a laugh.

Selecting a shirt, trousers and belt, she watched as he wrapped them in brown paper and tied a string around the package.

Paying for her purchase, she stepped out onto the sidewalk, wondering where she could buy a horse. Walking back inside, she asked the merchant, "Where might I buy a horse?"

"There's a few places in town," he said. "You might try one of the corrals or stables. They usually have a horse or two folks want to sell. The closest one is on Howell Street."

"Much obliged," she said with a smile.

It was when she was negotiating the price of a horse at the corral that a man noticed the mount hitched outside.

Storming into the corral, his head snapped side to side as he searched for someone. "Where's the fella that rides that horse outside?" he demanded.

"That's my horse," Del calmly said, sizing him up. He was a hefty man, with a week's worth of beard stubble. His teeth were stained from tobacco.

"No it ain't," he countered. "That's my horse."

"Well now," she sweetly answered. "How can that be if I'm riding it?"

That seemed to confuse him for a moment as he struggled to respond. "How'd you git that horse?"

"It's my husband's horse," she said. "I'm using it to run some errands."

"He stole it from me," he growled.

"Really? When?"

"Last night," he replied. "We wuz playin' cards –" He caught himself before he revealed the real cause of his loss.

"Last night? That's odd," she said glancing at the corral owner who had a hand on his pistol in case of trouble. "He's not left the ranch this past week."

"That's a lie," he burst.

"Mister," the corral owner intoned, concerned he might be losing a sale. "The lady said her husband was with her last night. I don't like strangers callin' a lady a liar. If you got a problem, you best take it up with the sheriff and leave her alone." His hand rested on the pistol grip for emphasis.

The man's lips tightened, and he glared at them then whirled around and marched out.

"You best let yer man know whats' goin' on," he advised.

"I will," she said. "Thank you."

Paying him the cost for the mare, she climbed back into the saddle. Once settled, he handed her the lead rope and she headed out of town, back to where Becca waited. Had she looked back when she edged past the outskirts, she would have seen three men on two horses following at a distance.

One man riding double was the irate gambler whose horse she now rode.

Mason was impatient to take back to the skies. "I know she's out there somewhere."

"We've finished adding coal to the fuel box," Taboca said to him. "She'll burn hotter, so you'll have to watch the rear end and adjust."

Nantan was in his running machine waiting by the hanger bay entrance.

By now, Mason was familiar with the airship and slid into the pilot's seat. "We'll check the same area," he called out. "If you see anything suspicious, go after it and we'll follow. Remember. Be careful. She's a killer. Don't put yourself in danger."

Once airborne, Mason led the way out of the hanger towards the northwest side of the mountains. He had barely reached observation level when he saw the woman riding north. Three men on two horses were at a distance behind, apparently trailing her.

Getting Taboca's attention, he motioned him to hang back. Nantan noticed and slowed his pace so that he trailed well behind the riders, though itching to startle them by racing past them.

Becca stood in the doorway watching as Del cantered up to the cabin.

"Got everything," she said, hitching both horses to the outside post then noticed Becca staring past her shoulder. Turning, she saw the airships in the distance.

"Something's not right," Becca frowned. "You talk to anybody in town?"

"There was a man at the corral who claimed this was his horse," Del explained, stepping inside and unwrapping the package. "That was it."

"Get changed while I watch the outside." Winchester in hand, Becca stepped back inside and went to the window, pushing open the shutters, giving her a view of the front side of the house.

She saw the men on horseback cautiously approaching from the south. Sizing up the distance, she rested her elbow on the window frame and took aim at the two men on the horse who had stopped for them to dismount. Squeezing the trigger, she was rewarded when both fell backwards off the animal.

By the time the other rider heard the retort and saw his friends tumble to the ground, it was too late, and he felt his chest explode and he too fell to the ground.

Becca wasted little time and rushed outside.

"Where are you going?" Del called, sliding boots on her feet.

"We got two more horses to use, with saddles," she shouted back.

By now the two airships were closing the distance and by the time Becca had the horses in hand, the airships were almost on her. With no hesitation, she raised the rifle and fired at Mason's airship, hitting the envelope.

Mason heard the shot followed by escaping gas and he veered off to the east, struggling to control the descent. Taboca immediately increased the heat to his ship, sending it skyward and out of range.

As Becca raced back with the horses, Mason's airship plummeted to the ground, finally crashing a little distance from the Swisshelm Mountains. Circling overhead, Taboca watched Nantan cover large distances in gaping strides as he hurried to help the Marshal.

By the time Nantan arrived, Mason had managed to worm his way out of the pilot's carriage and from under the collapsing envelope and was hustling far enough away from the smoking wreckage.

"You OK, Marshal?" Nantan blurted.

Mason brushed the dirt from his clothes. "I'm fine," he said though clenched teeth. The fire from the engine box spilled out and the ship was consumed in flames. "I'm sorry about your airship. Seems like I'm bad luck to be around with airships." He edged closer to ensure the fire did not spread beyond the airship.

"I was going to say we can fix it, but that's a bit late now," he grinned. "Want me to give chase?"

"From a distance," he said. "I don't want either of you getting hurt."

"You going to be OK?" he asked, wisps of smoke curling out the exhaust pipes of his machine.

"I'll be fine." He looked up to see Taboca's ship descending to hover a few feet above the ground.

"We can do like Nantan and I did when we went from Tombstone to Bisbee," he called out to Mason. "Hang on to the bottom. We can get there faster that way. I'll fly low."

Looking dubiously at the airship, Nantan reassured him. "Don't worry. Just hang on tight. It'll be faster this way. You can get your horse and we can track them down, me on my legs, you on your horse, and Taboca in the air."

"Probably should have done that the first time," Mason mumbled to himself.

"What?"

"I said we need to take the time to make sure the fire doesn't spread."

Circling the blackening mass, Mason noted the wind and the surrounding chaparral and began clearing a path around the burning debris. By the time he was satisfied, he rued the time spent here and not chasing Delilah.

Casting another worried glance at Taboca's airship, he decided he needed to act. "Let's go."

Taboca's airship rose enough for Mason to grab hold of the undercarriage where he looped a leg around the outer frame.

"You hang back and out of trouble," he said to Nantan.

"I will."

As Taboca's airship gained altitude, Nantan turned to retrace his steps and track their prey.

Becca watched with satisfaction as the airship crashed in the distance. She was smug and satisfied when no smoke billowed.

"You ready?" she said to Del who emerged out of the house, dressed in men's clothing. Becca smiled at her. "You look good."

"Feels good," she replied, stuffing the rifle in the saddle holster then adding ammo boxes to the saddle bags. She placed a bag of coins in the opposite saddle bag. Holding onto a lead rope, she climbed up. Seeing a single airship headed back to Bisbee, she grinned, "That should hold 'em for a while." Gathering the reigns, she gazed back at Becca. "Where we headed?"

"North," Becca answered. "We need to put as much distance as possible between us and the Marshal." She kicked the steed's flanks and her horse broke into a trot.

"Then where do we go?"

"We got to get out of this state as soon as we can. Then we head west to San Francisco."

"San Francisco," Del repeated with excitement. "Never been there."

"You'll like it," Becca grinned. "All sorts of interesting people."

In the distance behind them, Nantan loped along at an easy clip, keeping them far enough ahead to follow but not too close to be seen. Casting a glimpse at the afternoon sky, he knew he would have to turn around soon before night settled. He looked back over his shoulder and saw Taboca's airship in the distance. Slowing his pace, he decided to wait for his cousin to catch up. Once night came, it would be anyone's guess where they went.

Chapter 7

The Professor eased back on the throttle and the quadcopter slowed down as he lined up on the target in the distance, a large billboard with a crude outline of a building hastily painted on it. As he approached the target, his legs spun the pedals that worked the firing mechanism of the Gatling gun at the front of the ship.

Bullets started spewing forth, churning up the desert before the target and continuing as he sped forward until they began hitting the wood, splintering it into fragments and chewing it to destruction.

One magazine finished, he paused mid-spin, extracted the magazine and replaced it with a fresh one then resumed firing. He was halfway through the magazine when he saw that his rounds were going over the target. That meant he had to circle around and begin another pass and that frustrated him.

The quadcopter ought to be able to hover better. The problem was the repeated firing of the Gatling gun caused the ship to vibrate.

It was as he was circling to make another run that he saw them in the distance, two riders heading towards his camp. Deciding he didn't need too many curious eyes, he curved back around and sped back to camp, landing his machine in the middle of his compound.

"Two riders approaching. Find out who they are and what they want," he told Meili.

"Yes, Professor," she smartly answered then strode off.

The Professor walked off to his tent while a team of women efficiently pulled a desert themed camouflage canvas over the quadcopter, effectively hiding it from view.

A short while later, the tent flap opened and Meili returned with Becca and Del. "They're friends," she informed him, "part of the team sent to take out the Marshal."

209

The Professor sat at a large dining table, drinking a glass of brandy and smoking a cigar while a number of oriental women busied themselves with setting the table for an evening meal.

"And what are the names of our friends?" he said with a welcoming smile.

"I'm Rebecca," Becca said, "and this is Adeline, though we prefer to be called Becca and Del."

"How quaint. Meili," he said turning to his assistant. "Two more for dinner, please."

"Yes Professor."

"Professor?" Becca said, immediately recognized the name. "What brings you out to this little bit of heaven?"

The Professor chuckled and waved for them to sit. "We share the same employer with the same objective." Noticing her favoring her arm, he said, "Are you alright?"

"It's nothing."

"She got shot," Del volunteered. "It isn't bad, but it'll leave a mark."

"I have full medical supplies here. Would you like one of my ladies to take a look? They're quite proficient, you know."

"That's OK," Becca demurred, noting the absence of every other ethnicity except Chinese.

"Really," he smiled. "I insist."

"I'm really fine," she repeated then saw the firmness in his eyes. "Alright. I suppose."

"Excellent. Meili, would you see if Daiyu is available?"

"Yes Professor."

Becca watched the very attractive woman walk to the tent flap and issue orders to find Daiyu. Meili wore leggings that were tighter than normal trousers, and a thin silk jacket embroidered at the sleeves and neck. The effect was fetching yet practical as it allowed easy movement.

"I take it that our quarry is still at large?" the Professor said.

"Yes," Becca answered. "He's got some machinists helping him. They're using small airships out of Bisbee."

"Interesting." He smiled at the thought of doing battle with airships, though it would be hardly fair. Still, it would give him a chance to practice some gunnery in the air. The thought of watching a flaming airship plummeting out of the sky gave him amused satisfaction.

"And the Marshal?" he asked. "Is he the one who...?" He nodded at her injured shoulder.

"Yes," Becca grimly replied. She had never been injured or hurt in all the assignments she'd completed. This was the first time she had failed in her mission, and it grated her. Though she knew she should escape and fight another day, especially with the Professor here, her professional vanity would not let her rest. Besides, she had a reputation to think of. If word got out that she had failed, her future employment would be jeopardized.

"He's looking for me," she said, "so he's bound to come this way. The airships will give him away."

"Which way do you think he will come?" the Professor asked, more out of courtesy than interest. He already had a security perimeter set up around the camp with guards and trip wires that sent up fireworks. It was impossible for anyone to get within a half-mile of the camp without him knowing it.

"He knows I was headed this way. My guess is that he will head north to the depots and ask about me. When he gets nothing, he'll head south on this side of the mountains, assuming I'm holed up somewhere in the mountains."

The Professor politely smiled as he listened, glancing between Becca and Del, who seemed enthralled with the tent and its furnishings.

"You'll forgive my probing," he said. "Your name is known to me as a reputable assassin, but I understood that you worked alone."

"Del is a friend who I found along the way," she explained. "We share the same temperament and I've taken her as a sort of understudy until she's ready to go out on her own."

"Very noble of you," he said with a quick nod.

The tent flap opened and Daiyu entered. She was young, in her late teens, and very pretty with thick black hair and doe eyes that constantly appraised. Wordlessly, she approached Becca and stood before her, staring at her shoulder then to her face.

Seeing the doubt in Becca's eyes, the Professor said, "She may be young in years, but there is no one I trust more in the medical profession than this wise physician. Go with her and let her tend to your injury."

Reluctantly, Becca allowed herself to be led away while the Professor chatted amiably with Del.

"Tell me Miss Del," he charmingly said. "What brought you to the Arizona Territory and how did you end up riding with Becca?"

"I was forced to come here," she said, then explained about the contrived arrangement.

"Barbaric," he empathetically commented.

"Then Becca came along," she said. "She got shot by the Marshal and was looking for a place to hide for a while 'til she healed. Her showing up was a God send. She was looking for a place to get better and I was looking for someone to help me escape. We hit it off instantly. When Lloyd came back the next day, we shot him and rode on. That's when the Marshal started chasing us in that airship, so she shot him down. But he ain't hurt. Saw him hangin' on the bottom of that other airship, headin' back to Bisbee."

"My goodness, what a tale," he smiled.

Becca came back in smiling, moving her arm. "She's good, not like a lot of those sawbones who the first thing they think is if an arm or leg is wounded to cut it off."

"Oriental medicine is so far advanced beyond our feeble efforts that it will take centuries to catch up," he opined. "I prefer the civilized method of medicine compared to the quacks and fakirs that pass for western medicine. But that is a topic for another time. Dinner will be served soon. Perhaps you both would like to wash up."

Becca and Del exchanged glances.

"There is hot water for baths in another tent," he explained, "and if you wish I can get you some new clothes."

"I like my clothes right fine," Del said, folding her arms. "These ain't even two days old."

"As you wish," he said, holding up his hands in defeat.

"By the way," he said. "You are welcome to spend the night here before resuming your escape to the north and away from this barbarous place."

""I'm not going anywhere," Becca firmly spoke. "I had a job to do, and I intend on completing it."

"I admire your tenacity," he said with a hint of condescension. "But really, you've had your chance and now it is my turn."

Becca bristled at the inference of incompetence. "There's still the other two. You might be wasting your time here."

"With all due respect, my lovely interlocutor, if you were unable to complete the mission, I have serious reservations that the other two would accomplish what you failed to do, especially as your skills far exceed theirs."

Though flattered at the compliment, she suppressed the umbrage at his manner. "I've not finished yet. I always complete an assignment, no matter how long it takes."

"Then allow me to suggest we act as partners," he smoothly replied. "I am paid for my services regardless of who is responsible for the man's demise. I believe between the two of us we can outsmart one Marshal."

Mollified, Becca smiled. "Agreed. It might help if we knew where the other two are and if they've made any progress."

"What are their names and what do they look like?"

"Ed and Gordon," Becca replied then described the two men. "Last I knew, they were in Tombstone working on the others close to the Marshal."

"I do not care about any others," he said. "My obligation is to remove the Marshal. We waste time on distractions."

"I quite agree, though I've already killed Johnny Ringo."

"And he is?"

"A gunslinger of some renown in these parts. He was a friend of the Marshal."

"A friend?" he said, surprised. "The Marshal has an odd taste in friends. He sounds like an interesting man. Pity we have to kill him."

"What about Ed and Gordon?" Becca asked.

"I'll send someone to inquire to their whereabouts. What was their responsibility?"

"Ed was to go after the madam of the Bird Cage Theater. She's the Marshal's lover."

"Another amusing tidbit," he chuckled. "The man sounds positively fascinating. And Gordon? What was he to do?"

"Blow things up," she replied. "He was our fall back in case we ran into trouble."

"I see. I'll send someone to locate them. In the meantime, I suggest we concentrate on the Marshal."

The front tent flap opened and was held back from the outside as several women carried in trays with the evening meal.

"Ah, dinner is served. I believe you'll find this chop suey quite extraordinary as the meat is tender rabbit. There is also an excellent wine to go with it."

"Wine?" Del gasped with pleasure staring at the dishes as they were placed before them. Her mouth watering at the enticing aromas, she looked up at the Professor. "You eat like this all the time?"

"I'm afraid so," he shrugged.

Del turned to Becca. "Do you eat like this too?"

"Maybe not as grandly as the Professor," she said, "but yes, I dine in the best restaurants."

Del took one encompassing gaze at the opulence if the tent and the food then said, "This is what I want and I aim to get it." Turning to Becca, she added, "I'll be your best pupil. Teach me how to do what you do."

"I'll do my best," Becca answered, watching as the lid was removed from the plate.

Mason was glad to be back on firm ground and in the saddle. While Taboca went back up to look for Nantan,

Mason headed north to Tombstone. It was time to tell Annie what had happened to Ringo.

He watched Taboca's airship slowly moving north, realizing it would be impossible to track Delilah once night set in. Still, he had an idea where she was headed. He was puzzled as to who the other rider was travelling with her.

He had gone by the cabin where he had seen Delilah before she shot him out of the sky. Three bodies were sprawled on the ground not far from the cabin, dead from gunshot wounds. Doing a quick search inside the cabin and finding nothing of interest, he mounted and headed home. He'd telegraph the sheriff in Bisbee about the dead when he got to Tombstone.

By the time he arrived, night had settled, and Tombstone was in full raucous mode. Hitching in front of the Bird Cage, he went in and was surprised that Belle was not at her usual place.

"Where's Belle?" he asked, walking up to Jack behind the bar.

"Haven't seen her all day," he replied, his concern obvious.

"Annie?" Mason asked, his mind distracted by Belle's absence.

"She knows," Jack replied. "Ted came by and told her."

Quickly nodding, Mason bolted out the door and headed home, ready to bound up the stairs when Missus Hunt saw him.

"A man said to give you this, Marshal," she said, handing him a sealed envelope.

Mason ripped open the envelope and read the note. Gritting his teeth, he spun around and headed back out the door. His frustration mounted as he knew his horse needed to eat. Leading him over to the OK Corral, he took off the saddle and impatiently waited while the horse was fed and watered.

He knew where they had taken Belle. His first instinct was to rush there to rescue her. But his survival sense also told him it was obviously a trap. He was curious why they

215

would tell him where she was, knowing that he would sense a trap.

By the time the horse was fed and watered, the moon was up, lighting up the night. Putting a dry saddle blanket on his steed, Mason threw on the saddle, cinched it up and headed out to find Belle.

He was north of Watervale when he saw odd movement off amongst the ocotillos. Swinging down out of the saddle, he pulled out a .45 and called out, "Show yourself."

The movement transformed to three figures jerkily walking towards him. The glint off the morion told him it was Caleb and de la Fuente. He didn't know who the other was until he came close.

"Ringo?" he sputtered, his mouth gaping.

Johnny Ringo stood before him, a gaping hole in the back of his head. Flies swirled around him, and he flapped a hand to brush them away. Maggots were already working the edges of the wound.

"How did you…" Mason fumbled.

Ringo pointed to the other two.

"They got you?"

Ringo nodded.

Collecting himself, Mason took a breath then asked, "Did Delilah do this?"

Ringo nodded and his placid face twisted into anger.

"Do you know where she is?"

Ringo shook his head.

Caleb waved a hand to get Mason's attention. Pointing to Mason then to his wedding ring, he then pointed off towards the cabin where Belle was held.

"You know where Belle is? *Sabes dónde está Belle*?" Mason said.

Caleb nodded.

"How many are there? *Cuántos hay*?"

De la Fuente held up two boney fingers.

"It's time to free her," Mason announced.

Caleb raised both hands and patted the air, cautioning him then curled a hand telling him to follow them.

Reins in hand, Mason followed the three dead men as they spasmodically made their way towards the cabin. Crossing the arroyo, Caleb stopped and pointed to the ground, carefully edging his way around something in the road.

Mason kneeled and felt the ground, feeling the edge of a metal plate. Immediately knowing what it was, he stepped back and staked his horse a distance away before rejoining the others.

Caleb slowly led the way, carefully avoiding the road mines. They were still a distance away from the cabin, but light illuminated the covered windows, giving Mason a beacon to follow.

A little further up the trail, Caleb abruptly and stiffly bent down, gingerly touching something above the ground.

Mason couldn't see what it was until Ringo's cold dead hand grabbed his wrist and guided it down to the wire that spanned the distance across the road.

"Stay here," Mason whispered, involuntarily shivering at the touch of the dead man's hand.

Following the wire to the side of the road, he found the cemetery gun hidden behind a rock formation. The gun was larger than he had expected, mounted to a swivel on a tripod. Carefully fingering the trigger mechanism, he worked the wire loose until it came free.

Curling the wire in small loops like a lasso, Mason retraced his steps then placed the wire on the side of the road.

"Any more?" he quietly asked.

Caleb nodded then pointed to the surrounding rocks and trees.

"Any more leading up to the cabin?"

Caleb shook his head.

"Then we wait. You all need to find a safe place to hide."

Turning around the three dead men moved back down the road, Caleb leading the way. Their movements reminded Mason of three crippled blind men.

Leaving them to find a safe spot, Mason redirected his attention to the cabin. Working his way to the cabin, he positioned himself at the edge of the porch at the corner of the building and waited. He could hear voices inside and gave a silent prayer of thanks when he recognized Belle's voice.

Maintaining his silent vigil, thankful the night wasn't cold, Mason struggled to listen to the conversations, but the voices were muffled. Yet every now and then, he would hear Belle say something followed by an irate response, causing him to chuckle.

Mason then worked his way to the rear of the cabin, discovering the wagon and the mule staked close by. Rummaging in the wagon, he found several burlap sacks and rope. Collecting the booty, he worked his way around the cabin to the other side of the porch and waited.

As the night wore on, the voices and conversation diminished. Mason knew it was just a matter of time before they would need to settle down to sleep. It wasn't too long before he was rewarded as the door opened and light burst into the night silhouetting a figure.

"Be sure to watch where you're going," a voice called out from the cabin. "I've got traps everywhere."

"I know what I'm doing," the man in the doorway answered. "You just watch our hostage there."

Closing the door, he stood on the porch under the overhang to let his eyes get adjusted to the dark. He then moved towards Mason, stepping off the porch just before the end and walking to where the mesquite and cactus edged the clearing around the cabin.

Mason waited in the shadows by the cabin as the man unbuttoned his trousers to relieve himself. When the man finished and was preoccupied with fixing his trousers, Mason silently crept up behind him, pulling out his .45, grabbing it by the barrel and slammed the pistol butt into the man's head, knocking him out cold.

Dragging him back to the rear of the cabin, Mason tied his hands to his ankles behind him and secured a burlap sack over his head and shoved him under the wagon then returned to wait for the other kidnapper. Returning to the corner spot by the front of the cabin, Mason didn't have long to wait before the door opened.

"Ed?" a man's voice called out. "Ed?" There was a pause then a repeated nervous beckoning. "Ed? This isn't funny. Ed?"

A hand extended from the doorway, a kerosene lamp in hand.

"What's the matter, Gordon?" Belle taunted from inside. "Looks like Ed deserted you, left you here to fend for yourself. If I were you, I'd hightail it out of here too."

"He's just messing with me," Gordon unconvincingly replied. "Ed? That's enough. Get back inside here. We need to take turns getting some sleep. Ed?"

"He's gone," Belle smugly said. "Looks like you're on your own. By the way, I imagine Ed probably didn't get too far before the undead got him."

"Undead?" Gordon sputtered, his voice squeaking. "That's utter nonsense."

"Suit yourself," she said, "but I've seen them. One's a conquistador from the time when Coronado went through here. Mean as a snake. Angry too at being woken up. We've had a number of miners disappear only to find their bodies with the heads cut off a couple of weeks later."

"Shut up," Gordon pouted. "Ed?"

"Why don't you go look for him?" Belle said. "I'm not going anywhere, especially with the way I'm tied up. Go ahead. I'll wait." She snickered. "What's the matter Gordon? Scared?"

"Shut up."

"A brave man like you? Scared?"

"I said shut up." He turned and the door closed behind him.

A few moments later, the door opened, and Gordon emerged, a gun and lamp in his hands.

"That's not going to help, Gordon," Belle called out to him. "You can't kill them. They're already dead."

"Keep talking lady," he snapped. "Your stories don't scare me." He took a hesitant step onto the porch.

"They ought to," she said. "You'll find out soon enough."

"If you don't shut up, I'm coming back in there and gagging you."

"Oh OK, have it your way. I'll just be real quiet." She lowered her voice so that he could still hear her. "I won't say anything. I'll just be real quiet sitting here minding my own business. I won't talk about the undead or the things that go bump in the night or the little fact that Ed's gone. I wonder where he went? I mean, he was here just a minute ago and poof, he's gone. Sort of makes you wonder what's out there. But you want me to be quiet, so I'll just sit here pretending nothing strange is going on."

"Will you shut up," Gordon said through clenched teeth. He took a hesitant step onto the porch.

"Why are you so mad?" Belle innocently asked. "I'm being quiet. You can barely hear me. And anyway, I'm just taking to myself so it's not like I'm bothering you. I'm merely wondering why Ed left you to fend for yourself. What did he know that you don't? Did he discover some secret treasure and decided to keep it all to himself, leaving you here to take the blame for kidnapping me?"

"Lady," Gordon snarled. "When I get back, you won't be able to talk for a week." He took another step out, holding the lamp high and scanning the surroundings.

"How romantic. Are you taking me on a trip?"

Ignoring her, Gordon slowly made his way towards the corner of the building.

Hidden on the side of the cabin, Mason watched as the brightness of the lamp approached. Hunkering down close to the ground, he tightened his fingers around the grip and waited. Just as Gordon came into view, Mason reared back and cracked the barrel against Gordon's shin.

Gordon cried out in excruciating pain, dropping both pistol and lamp. As he dropped to the ground, all he saw was a shadow rear up and the butt end of a pistol come crashing down on his head.

Grabbing him by his arms, Mason dragged him into the cabin.

"Hello Sweetheart," Belle cheerfully greeted him. She sat in a chair, securely bound by ropes around her ankles and middle. "I'd offer to help, but I'm a little tied up at the moment."

Mason strode over, bent down and kissed her long and passionately.

"I missed you too," she grinned as he stood up to untie her.

"You had me worried," he said, loosening the last of the knots.

"I'm glad you came when you did," she chuckled, standing. "I was beginning to run out of material."

"So I heard," he smiled. Grabbing Gordon, he hauled him onto the chair. "Tie him up while I get the other one."

Mason returned with Ed thrown over his shoulder. Seating Ed in another chair, he readjusted the bonds, securing him to the chair. He then placed a burlap sack over Gordon's head.

Turning, he headed to the doorway and called out, "It's OK. You all can come on in."

Belle gave him a quizzical look. "You brought along help?"

"Some folks you know," he smiled then ticked his head at the two men in the chairs. "Learn anything?"

"I think Delilah's real name is Rebecca. Ed talked about a woman named Becca who was in trouble. Also, just before these two kidnapped me, Shephard came to see me. Said the Professor was in the area. He went off to search for him. I was headed home when these two interfered. Ed is the leader of the group. Gordon is a munitions man. From what I could determine, there are only four of them. You already took care of Earl, so we still have Becca, or Rebecca, to find."

"She's not far from here," he said. "She's got another with her and they're heading north on the other side of the Dragoons. She killed Ringo."

"That's what I figured," she nodded. "Poor Annie. The girl is head over heels in love with him. Pity."

Three figures huddled at the doorway causing Belle to startle when she saw the gunslinger in the middle. "Johnny Ringo?"

She shot a glance at Mason who splayed his hands and shrugged. "Don't ask me how, because I haven't the faintest idea how this all works. But I'm mighty glad they were here to help. They're the ones who warned me about the traps."

Turning to Caleb and de la Fuente, he said, "I can still use your help. I need to know what's happening on the other side of the mountains. I'm looking for a woman with blond hair. She's wounded, probably in the arm or shoulder. There's another person riding with her. He's dressed like a man, but I swear I saw long hair, so it might be a woman dressed as a man."

Mason realized that Caleb understood, but de la Fuente did not yet comprehend. "*Necesito tu ayuda.*" He then repeated what he had told Caleb.

The two undead nodded and spasmodically walked out into the night, the light from the kerosene lamp reflecting on de la Fuente's ill-fitting morion.

Turning to Belle, he asked, "Do you know how many traps he might have set up?"

"I don't know. We'll have to get him to clear them."

"We'll do that first light. I can't afford to have anyone come by here and get killed because of these fools. In the meantime, I suggest we make ourselves comfortable and wait for our two guests to come around."

He cast a glance at Ringo who stood stiffly to the side, his arms folded, the flesh of his hands a cold white. Flies continued swirling around the gaping hole in his head and he swatted at them when they flew in front of his face.

Mason wanted to say something, but what does one say to a man who was robbed of his happiness? Picking up the looped gun belt on the table he pulled out the pistol, a short barrel Peacemaker .45. Checking the action, he unfolded the belt, noting the bullet loops were filled with ammunition.

Shoving the pistol back in the holder, he handed the rig to Ringo. "Here. You might want this. It's not your own gun, but it's a Peacemaker and that should help."

Ringo's stony lips curled into a barely perceptible smile as he strapped the gun belt around his waist. Taking the gun out, he twirled it in his dead hands, then shoved in back into the holster, nodding thanks at the same time.

Ed's entire body felt heavy as though his strength had fled him. He tried to move his hands, but they felt bound together like stuck magnets. He heard the voices, but with his head stuffed inside a grain sack, it was difficult to make out what they were saying and besides, the sack itched like crazy. Suddenly the sack was ripped off his head and he winced as the abrasive fabric pulled against his skin. Blinking in the dimly lit room, he groggily looked to see the Marshal sitting in front of him, his legs crossed, a six-shooter in hand resting on his lap.

"Finally waking up, I see," Mason calmly said, slowly spinning the cylinder of the six-shooter.

Ed frowned then slowly took in his surroundings. It was the same cabin where not too long ago he had held Belle prisoner. Light from two kerosene lamps on a rough-hewn table off to the side flickered shadows across the room. Other than a fireplace in one corner, there was little else in the room except for four chairs.

Mason sat facing him. Belle, with an 'I told you so' grin, sat next to him. On the chair to his right, sat Gordon, the little munitions man. His head was likewise stuffed in a grain sack, his body limp as he slowly breathed as one in a deep sleep.

"Hullo Marshal," Ed said, his tongue thick, as his mind slowly cleared. The ache at the back of his head still pounded and he blinked at the dull throbbing pain. There was a faint foul odor coming from behind him as though something had died. "How'd you manage to get by Gordon's bag of tricks?"

"I had a little help," he said with a faint smile.

His head clearing, Ed's confidence returned. He'd been in worse situations before and Worthington's lawyers always managed to set him free. "I'm not telling you anything."

"I didn't expect you would." Mason continued slowly spinning the cylinder of his .45. "So I'm thinking of how I can legally torture you to exact a confession."

Ed's eyes blinked wide. "You can't do that."

"Says who?"

"You're a lawman. You've got to take me in. I know my rights. I demand to see a lawyer."

Mason glanced around the room then looked at Belle. "Do you see any lawyers in here?"

Belle looked around the room then shrugged. 'No."

"Looks like there aren't any lawyers available," Mason said with feigned disappointment. "But we can remedy that. The way I hear it, anyone can become a lawyer if they're older than 21, provide evidence of good moral character, and can pass an examination by a judge."

Mason turned to Belle. "Are you over 21?"

"Yes," she demurely replied.

"Can you provide evidence of good moral character?"

"Yes."

"What is it," Mason asked.

"I'm the madam at the Bird Cage Theater in Tombstone," she answered.

"That's good enough for me," Mason nodded.

"What?" Ed burst.

"You be quiet," Mason warned. "I'm not finished."

"But you're not a judge," Ed objected.

"I'm a duly appointed US Marshal, charged to enforce the laws of this nation," Mason calmly replied. "As there are no judges available at this location, I have assumed the responsibilities and authority of a judge."

"You can't do that,' Ed snapped.

"I just did," Mason pointed out. "Now you be quiet or I'll have to gag you. I've got to now give the applicant an examination."

Turning his attention back to Belle, he asked, "What is your name?"

"Belle Dubois," she answered.

"Where do you live?"

"I live in Tombstone, Arizona Territory."

"What's two plus two?"

"Four."

"Looks like you passed," Mason grinned. "Congratulations."

"What kind of examination is that?" Ed blurted.

Ignoring him, Mason said, "The defendant here requested a lawyer. Are you willing to represent him?"

"Yes, your honor. And we'd like to plead guilty on all counts."

"I didn't agree to that," Ed shouted.

Still ignoring him, Mason frowned as though pondering the plea. "I need to make a decision, so I think I'll ask my friend behind you to help me."

Ed turned his head to the side to look. The foul odor grew as a man jerkily passed by him and made his way to stand next to Mason. Ed's eyes bolted wide in recognition. "R… Ringo? But you're supposed to be dead." He stared in morbid fascination at the gaping hole in Ringo's head.

Ringo stopped to stand by Mason, staring down at Ed whose shock had transformed to revulsion.

"That's right," Mason nodded in agreement. "Delilah killed him, just like you planned. She played up to him, stole his heart, then killed him… not even blinking an eye."

"I had nothing to do with that," he pleaded, looking away. "I only know he was killed by what other folks said."

Ignoring his pleas, Mason's eyes narrowed to fix their intense focus on him. "How many more of you are there?" he coldly demanded.

"I don't know what you're talking about," he replied, repelled by the dead gunslinger standing by Mason.

Mason stopped spinning the cylinder and cocked the hammer back on his six-shooter. "Mister, I'm going to ask you just once more. Now you think about your next answer, because if I don't hear what I want, I'll start at your knees first." He pointed the barrel at Ed's left knee. "Then for each wrong answer, I'll blow a hole in another joint in your body. I'll keep doing this until I get bored. Oh, I won't let you die, but when I'm through, you'll wish I did."

"You can't do that," Ed exclaimed. "You're a Marshal. You just can't take the law into your own hands. This whole court is a sham."

Ringo held up a hand to get Mason's attention.

"Yes?"

Ringo nodded and pointed to the other man who was beginning to stir.

"You want me to start with him instead?"

The dead gunslinger stiffly nodded.

"OK, why not. Go ahead and take his hood off."

Ringo lumbered over to the other man. Grabbing ahold of the grain sack with a maggot filled hand, parts of the boney fingers just beginning to show, he jerked the sack off then jittered and jerked his way back to stand next to Mason.

Gordon scrunched his face as he worked to gather his bearings. His eyes grew large when he saw Ringo. Hunching his shoulders as in apprehension, he then willed his eyes away from the dead man to Mason and then to Ed. His heart racing, fear spilled across his face, and he looked to Ed for help.

"Your friend here says I should start with you," Mason calmly said.

"No I didn't," Ed shot back

"St- start what?" Gordon nervously asked, just now realizing his hands and feet were tied.

"Answering my questions. I put it to him that for each wrong answer, I would shoot him in the leg, then work my way up to the arms. He didn't like that and said I should start with you."

Gordon's head snapped in cowering fear to stare hatefully at Ed. "You bastard."

"He's lying," Ed protested. "I never said that."

"He's already pleaded guilty to all the charges," Mason explained.

"No I didn't," Ed sharply interrupted. "And you haven't even charged me with anything."

Mason blinked as though realizing he had forgotten something. Gazing at Belle, he said, "How about kidnapping, murder and plotting to commit murder?"

Belle cast a quick glance at Ed who stared back at her with hatred in his eyes. "My client agrees and we still plead guilty."

"You bitch," Ed snarled.

"You are out of order, Sir," Mason firmly stated. "The court fines you $100. You will refrain from further outbursts or the court will be forced to implement immediate justice."

Mason turned his attention to Gordon. "You see, justice demands that at least one of you pays for the crimes. The penalty for kidnapping and murder is death by hanging. Since we don't have a scaffold here, I'll have to carry out the sentence myself. That means I'm going to execute one of you and send the other one back to Worthington with a message. The question is, which one of you do I shoot, and which do I let live? Decisions, decisions." He trained the six-shooter on Gordon. "You look like a man who wants to live."

"O god, please don't shoot me," Gordon begged. "I'll tell you everything."

"Shut up you damned fool," Ed snarled.

"Now, now," Mason cautioned him. "Let the man talk."

Gordon's eyes snapped back and forth between Ed and Mason, his fear of dying overcoming his fear of Worthington.

"Perhaps you need a little help," Mason suggested. He whipped the six-shooter to the right and squeezed the trigger. The gun bucked and flashed, the smell of burned powder filling the room. Ed cried out in pain as the bullet tore into his shoulder just above the collar bone. Blood flowed out as he gasped in quick breaths.

Ignoring Ed's distress, Mason turned to Gordon. "He's not hurt that bad. He'll live... at least for a while." Abruptly leaning back as though having an epiphany, he pushed his Stetson back off his forehead. Looking up to Ringo, he said, "You know, we could make it more interesting by having this one answer the questions," pointing to Ed, "and for each wrong answer I'll shoot the other one."

Belle stifled a laugh then regained her composure, folding her hands on her lap.

"O God, no!" Gordon burst, quickly realizing that Ed would purposely answer incorrectly so that he would be the one who survived to go back to Worthington. "I'll tell you everything, I swear."

"OK," Mason shrugged. "We'll try it your way. How many of you are there?"

"Don't say a word," Ed seethed, grimacing in pain.

Letting out a sigh of exasperation, Mason said, "Am I going to have to shoot you again?"

Before Ed could reply, Gordon announced, "Four."

"Four," Mason repeated, nodding in thought. "Who are they?"

"There's us two," Gordon quickly answered. "A man named Earl, strong sort of fellow with short brown hair and full beard. You killed him when he challenged you to a shootout. Dumb bastard got what he deserved. He was a blowhard."

"Damn you," Ed snapped. "What's the use in telling him? Can't you see he's gonna kill us both anyway?"

Gordon's eyes blinked wide at the revelation.

Mason tilted his head as though pondering the option for the first time. "Hmm. I hadn't thought of that, but it doesn't suit my needs. I need someone to take a message back to Worthington. Killing you both sort of complicates that, don't you think?" Looking directly at Ed, he said, "You're beginning to get on my nerves. Now shut up and let the man finish. You interrupt once more and I'm going to have to shoot you again, and my aim might not be as steady this time."

The pain in his shoulder reminded Ed that the Marshal would not hesitate to make good on his threat.

"The other one's a good-looking woman with blond hair, goes by the name of –"

"Delilah," Mason answered.

"That's one of the names she uses," he said. "Her real name is Becca, short for Rebecca."

Mason's eyes hardened and he asked, "If it's me Worthington wants, why bother killing Ringo and kidnapping Belle?"

Gordon took a deep breath. "Worthington wanted you to suffer. That meant taking out anyone close to you."

Mason's lips tightened as he knew Belle was still in danger for one of Worthington's assassins was still at large. He no longer had time to waste. "The woman called Becca. She's riding with another individual. Who is it?"

Gordon's face turned blank. "I... I don't know of anyone else. There were just the four of us who came here. Ed here's in charge of the team. If she's riding with someone else, maybe Mister Worthington sent another person."

Belle leaned over to Mason and whispered, "Remember, the Professor is somewhere close. She might be riding with one of his people.

Mason nodded then turned his gaze back to Gordon. "Worthington never deals directly with his dirty work. Who sent you here?"

"Diamond Dan Braxton," Gordon answered. "A big fella, wears a diamond stick pin. He's a ward boss in San Francisco."

"I know of him," Mason said. Tilting his head, he frowned in thought. "There's got to be someone else between Worthington and Braxton."

"I only know Braxton," Gordon apologetically replied. "He's the one who gives us our assignments. We go to his place in the 6th Ward."

"Chinatown?" Mason asked.

"Just outside of Chinatown on California Street," Gordon explained.

"Why don't you just give him the address," Ed sneered, "make an appointment for him, you damned fool."

Mason shot a sharp glance at Ed. "That's another outburst in my court. This time I can't overlook it and will be forced to make a ruling." He paused for effect then said, "Looks like you lose."

"You can't do this!" Ed exclaimed in a rush. "You're a US marshal. You can't kill me. You've gotta obey the law. You have to take me in."

Shaking his head, Mason heaved a dramatic sigh. "What is it with you people? You knowingly and willingly break the law, to include murdering innocent people in cold blood, and when you get caught, you suddenly want the law to protect you." Standing up, he focused his attention on him. "This time it's not going to work. I condemn you for kidnapping of Belle Dubois and the murder of my friend Ringo."

"But I didn't kill Ringo," he protested.

"Now you're quibbling," Mason replied. "Whether you planned the operation or pulled the trigger, it's the same in my book of law. I now pronounce sentence." Turning back to Ringo, he asked, "Your verdict?"

Ringo held out a withered arm and pointed the decaying thumb downwards.

Belle waited only a moment before stretching out her arm and thrusting a thumb down.

Mason frowned at her and said, "I'm not sure as his lawyer you're allowed to vote, but in this case I'll make an exception and consider you part of the jury." He then turned to Gordon. "Would you like to add your vote to the total?"

"Oh," Gordon trembled, his prospects of surviving suddenly increasing. "I completely agree with you."

"Makes it unanimous," Mason said.

Ed glared in fury at Gordon. "You son of a –"

The words died on his lips as Mason's six-shooter again bucked in his hand, the muzzle flash spewing out death, the bullet piercing Ed through the heart. Ed reacted to the shot by jerking backwards causing him to fall back onto the floor, still seated in the chair.

As Mason calmly walked over to view the body, he half-cocked the hammer and flipped open the cylinder cover. Turning the cylinder, he pressed back the ejector rod and dislodged the spent casings, replacing them with bullets in his gun belt. Satisfied Ed was dead, he walked over to stand before Gordon.

"You get to live, for now. If I ever see you again, anywhere, you're a dead man. We clear?"

"Yes, Marshal," he said, bobbing his head with relief.

"You're going to deliver a message to Worthington for me. You tell him that I'm coming for him. You got that? I'm coming for him."

"Yes, Marshal. I got it."

"I want you to talk to Braxton first. You tell him I'm coming after Worthington. I got no issue with him. He was merely performing a service, fulfilling a contract. No hard feelings. Tell him what you saw here and let him know; I have more friends like Johnny Ringo."

Gordon shuddered, his head bobbing.

"Now I'm going to cut you loose. Before you go, I want all your traps cleared from around this cabin. My friend Ringo here is going to see that you do it right. I wouldn't cross him if I were you. He may be dead, but he's got a temper on him and I'd say that right now he's pretty mad."

Gordon nervously stared at Ringo. "Is he really…"

"Dead?" Mason finished for him. "Quite. Your friend Becca made sure of that."

"But… but, how…"

Shrugging, Mason walked behind him and untied his hands. "Right now, that's the least of your concerns. You better pray that he doesn't lose his temper and decide to do something you may regret."

His feet unbound, Gordon popped up to standing, rubbing his wrists. "You don't have to worry about me, Marshal. I'll do like you asked."

Mason spun the cylinder on his six-shooter and sternly warned, "Remember what I said? I'll probably be in San Francisco in about a week. You better be clear of there because I'd hate to have to make good my threat about killing you." *If Worthington doesn't kill you first*, he thought to himself.

It was early morning by the time Gordon finished disabling his traps. Needing no urging he fled on foot, anxious to be away from the place. Casting one last glance over his shoulder, he saw the three of them standing under the porch awning, watching him. Ed lay prone in the dirt before them. Gordon's nervousness remained until he was out of pistol range then gradually decreased. Following the Marshal's directions, he headed west hoping to see train tracks before the day got too hot.

Waiting until he was far enough away, Mason shifted his gaze down to stare at Ed then back up to Belle and Ringo.

"If you can come back from the dead, so can he," Mason pointed out. "We need to make sure he never comes back."

Ringo made a slicing motion at his throat.

"Cut off his head?" Belle questioned, curling a lip.

Ringo nodded.

"That's disgusting."

"He may be right though," Mason said. "We need to completely destroy him."

"Why not just burn him up? Cremate him?" she suggested.

"That's another good idea," he agreed.

"I like that one better," she said. "We have kerosene in the cabin. Let's dig a shallow grave and place him in it and then cremate him."

Mason looked at Ringo who nodded.

"Belle and I will do this," Mason said to him. "I need you to go find Caleb and de la Fuente and see if they've found anything."

Ringo stared at him for a moment then pointed to the wounds in his head followed by using his fingers as a gun. He repeated it a few more times.

"Becca shot you," Mason said, attempting to understand.

Ringo nodded then slowly, but firmly poked himself in the chest.

"I understand," Mason grimly replied. "Becca is yours."

Ringo gave a firm head-bob.

"She's all yours. Remember," he cautioned. "We don't want her coming back either."

Ringo stiffly nodded and lumbered off to find Caleb and de la Fuente

Belle discovered a spade in the wagon and went to find a suitable spot to bury Ed. Mason walked up just as she thrust the blade into the hard ground.

"Why don't you let me do that," he said.

"I'll let you," she readily agreed, handing him the shovel.

"What is it with you and everybody wanting to kidnap you?" he said with a grunt as he, forced his weight onto the shovel.

"Just want to keep your life interesting," she cheerfully replied.

"It's interesting enough with just the two of us doing nothing."

"Now, now," she teased. "You'd get bored if I didn't get kidnapped every now and then."

Pausing with his foot on the blade, he flashed a smile. "Somehow I can't see life with you as ever being boring."

"And I intend to keep it that way," she said. "I'll go get the kerosene."

When she returned, Mason took the can and pointed to the wagon and the mule that was now hitched. "We're going to need help. While I finish up here, why don't you head back to town and wire Nantan and Taboca. Tell them to bring whatever toys they might think useful. Meet us back here."

"You want anyone else from town?" she asked.

"Outside their jurisdiction," he replied.

"I know," she said. "Just a thought."

"I don't doubt any of them would be more than willing to help, especially Davy Neagle. But they know the law. Besides they've enough trouble on their hands dealing with the drunks and partiers in town."

"I'll be back as quick as I can." She gave him quick kiss then added, "Don't do anything silly until I get back."

"I'll be good," he grinned.

By the time Mason dug a shallow pit and dragged Ed over and dumped him in it, Ringo had returned with Caleb and de la Fuente. The three men staggered close but still a safe distance away to peer into the grave. Dousing Ed with kerosene, Mason stepped back, struck a match and tossed it on the body which immediately caught fire.

While Mason stood and watched as the flames consume the clothing then the flesh, the other three stood far enough away to avoid the flame. Occasionally they would move to the other side when the wind shifted, and the smoke and the smell curled towards them.

As the fire petered out, Mason stirred the ashes and bones, separating the skull from the rest. Shoveling it out, he carried it over to a grouping of rocks and placed it on one of the smoother stones. Then in one strong arcing motion, he slammed the shovel's iron blade onto the skull, splintering it into pieces.

"That should hold him for a while," he stated. He then turned to Caleb and de la Fuente. "Did you see anything?"

Caleb shook his head, making an arcing motion with his hand.

"Too far away?"

Caleb nodded.

"We'll wait until Belle returns," Mason said. "If you want, you three can go scout some more, but don't compromise yourselves, especially you," he said gazing at Ringo. "I know you want vengeance, and rightfully so. But we don't want Becca getting away. Patience. She'll be yours when the time comes."

Ringo stared at him then nodded. Turning, he took the lead as the three men staggered away.

As they disappeared amongst the chaparral, Mason hustled down the road to where he had left his steed staked down. Climbing up in the saddle, he eased the mount towards the cabin. Dismounting, he led his horse to the rear of the cabin where a well had been sunk though the iron handle looked like it hadn't been used for a long time. Going back into the cabin, he found a useable cooking pot, returning outside to bend his efforts to coax water out of the well, the creaking and groaning of the pump disturbing the otherwise silent morning.

Nothing happened for the longest time, and he wondered if it wouldn't be faster going back to Tombstone, but he could feel movement and pressure in the pipe, causing him to pump faster. Finally, water burst from the mouth and spilled into the pot. It was refreshingly cold, and he cupped his hands to grab a mouthful.

Placing the pot on the ground for his steed, he shook the water from his hands, feeling the coolness of water on the body, musing how Ringo and the others would never know thirst again. Neither would they experience the warmth of a woman's touch. He wondered what their existence would be from now on. De la Fuente had been dead for over 300 years. Was he cursed and that was why he was still here? Was he condemned to roam the earth until the curse was lifted? If so, who lifted the curse? And why was he cursed in the first place?

Mason's questions were frustrated because none of them could talk. Though they understood what he said, they could only communicate in yes or no answers. And de la Fuente only spoke Spanish.

Mason thought about the ancient conquistador, the morion jiggling on his desiccated head making him look comical. Here was a man who had traveled with Coronado and had answers to all sorts of questions, especially as to where the Seven Cities of Cibola were. Mason smiled in thought as he wondered if he might be able to figure out where those cities were.

But he had other things to worry about at the moment. Knowing it would be some time before Belle returned, he decided he could use a bit of sleep. Tethering his steed in the shade, he placed the filled pot close by, took off the saddle and headed back to the cabin.

It was still cool inside though he knew it wouldn't last once the heat of the afternoon sun arrived. Placing the saddle on the floor, he arranged the table against the door so that anyone pushing the door open would cause it to make noise as it scraped across the floor. Satisfied, he stretched out on the floor, resting his head on the smooth leather. Tilting his hat over his eyes, he was soon asleep.

While Mason settled into some well-deserved rest, on the other side of the mountain, the Professor was putting his latest invention through a series of test runs. Not wanting to be too visible, he purposely kept his craft from hovering above the mountain crests. As he flew in a slow circle, he pondered the problem of the inability to go backwards. He could hover in a stationary position, but to get to an original position meant he had to go in a circle.

It was as he was circling back to the center of the tent compound that he noticed several riders heading to camp. Two he recognized as members of his household. The third was a man, his hands tied behind him.

Settling the machine into position, he powered down the engines. Limping away from the quadcopter, the Professor frowned as he noted the newcomer to the camp.

"What have we here?" he asked as the two scouts helped Shephard down from his mount.

"We found him spying on us," the one scout said. She was a little taller than the professor, svelte with luxurious black hair. She wore leggings and a leather vest over a silk blouse. "He was using this." She handed him a compacted spyglass.

"My, my," he chuckled, extending the spyglass and peering through it at the surrounding mountains then at the man. "A competitor perhaps?" he said collapsing the instrument.

Peering intently at him, the Professor was surprised the man showed no fear. "Come, good sir. Do you have a name?"

"Shephard, Thaddeus Shephard, of Sacramento City Bank, at your service." He bowed as best he could despite his hands being tied. "Might I request these bonds be removed?" He twisted to the side to display his hands.

"Of course, Mister Shephard," the Professor graciously acknowledged. "Yingtai, would you do the honors, please?" he said to the scout who produced a small blade from the pocket of her vest and was about to slit the ropes when she decided to untie then instead.

The Professor eyed him with an indulging smile. "What brings you to this little part of paradise, Mister Shephard?" He opened and closed the spyglass.

"Investment, sir," he grandly stated. "My bank sent me here to measure the prospect of the silver mines."

"Which is why you are here?" the Professor said, opening the spyglass.

Shephard leaned forward and lowered his voice. "I heard whisperings of a strange machine that flew and decided to investigate. I must say, your machine is incredible, a unique measure of genius."

Flattered, the Professor acknowledged the compliment with a tilt of his head. Turning to Yingtai, he said, "Have them set another place for lunch. Mister Shephard will be joining us as our guest."

"Delighted, sir," he grinned. "I'm reminded of a verse of poetry.

When someone visits our thatch house, I
Call the kids to straighten my farmer's cap,
And from the sparse garden, gather young
Vegetables – a small handful of friendship."

The Professor startled and his mouth gaped. "You know Tu Fu?"

"Why yes," he replied, charmed that the verse was recognized. "Are you a fan of Rivers and Mountains poetry?"

"My favorite poetry," he exclaimed.

"My word, sir," Shephard gushed. "You are an amazing individual, erudite and a man of science. May I be so bold as to request a tour of your marvelous flying machine?"

"Of course," the Professor readily agreed. He started to limp towards the quadcopter when Shephard stopped him.

"Might I be allowed to retrieve something from my saddle bags?"

"What?" the Professor questioned, cautious.

"My pipe," he smiled. "I find it most refreshing to indulge in a bit of fine tobacco while listening to men of science expound on the latest advances."

"He also had this," Yingtai interrupted, handing the Professor a Sheriff's model Peacemaker .45. "We found it in his saddle bag."

"A precaution," Shephard explained, "though I confess I'm not much good with the thing. I'm an investment banker, not a marksman." When he saw the doubt in the Professor's eyes, he said, "My partners insisted I bring it when it was decided to send me here. I'm afraid they indulged their knowledge of the untamed west from dime store novels. Thus, I keep it wrapped in my saddle bag. I see no sense in courting trouble."

The Professor took the gun and inspected it, flipping open the loading gate and rotated the cylinder. "Doesn't look like it's ever been fired," he observed.

"Lord willing, I intend to keep it that way. It's in the same condition as when it was issued to me," he said. "And I pray to return it in the same condition."

Closing the loading gate, the Professor handed the gun to Shephard who in turn handed it to Yingtai.

"Would you be so kind as to return it to my saddle bag where you found it," he said. "And may I impose upon you to retrieve my pipe and tobacco from the other saddle bag?" He turned to the Professor. "If you are a pipe smoker, I would be pleased to share some of my tobacco. It's a superb Turkish blend with a smooth taste and quite aromatic."

The Professor eyed him with a curious smile. "You're an interesting man, Mister Shephard."

"As are you, sir," he replied watching Yingtai gracefully glide over to his mount. Turning to the Professor, he said, "I'm afraid I did not get your name, sir."

"I am called the Professor."

"Ah," he nodded in understanding, "an appropriate appellation."

When Yingtai returned, she was carrying a small cotton bag, secured by a drawstring, and handed it to Shephard.

Shephard opened the bag and withdrew a light brown beautifully carved meerschaum pipe.

"A beautiful pipe," the Professor commented.

"Thank you," Shephard said. "It was made in Eskisehir." He looked expectantly at the Professor, awaiting recognition. When none came, he said, "I take it you are not a pipe smoker?"

"I prefer a good cigar," he replied.

"Ah yes, of course. As a man of science, a fine cigar would be easier to enjoy while working, *n'est ce pas*?"

"*Mai oui*," he smiled in reply. "*Vous parlez français*?"

"*Bien sûr.*"

Elated to find someone so refined, the Professor led the way to the quadcopter, explaining the machine in French, while Shephard languidly strolled beside him, filling his pipe with tobacco, asking questions.

By the time they were finished, the Professor was more than impressed for Shephard asked probing and intelligent questions. As they walked back to the dining tent, Shephard changed the dialogue to English.

"I must say, Professor. Your flying machine is most intriguing. My bank sent me here to determine the efficacy of the silver market. But I surmise that your machine would be a far better investment than silver. Have you thought of buyers or investors for your work?"

Pleased with the appreciation, the Professor thought of the possibilities of investors. He could make a substantial amount of income by marketing and selling his invention... and do it legally. The thought amused him.

"Until recently, I had only given cursory thought to the marketing of my quadcopter. It still needs refinement. However, your comments have reawakened those thoughts. Perhaps we can discuss this over lunch."

"Excellent," Shephard suavely smiled. "Then perhaps you would be so kind as to show me how the machine works and the accuracy of its weapon."

As the Professor held open the tent flap, Shephard entered, immediately noticing Becca and Del already seated at the large dining table with four place settings. At the narrower part of the table, the two women sat across from each other. They looked up at him, caution in their eyes.

"Good afternoon, Ladies," he suavely acknowledged. Glancing around the luxuriously apportioned tent, he also noticed the women serving the meal. Casting a glance over his shoulder at the Professor, he said, "Surrounded by such pulchritude. You are indeed a fortunate man."

"Quite so," he grinned in return. "Allow me to introduce my other guests. This is Miss Rebecca, or Becca as she likes to be called."

"Madame," Shephard bowed, noticing the woman was doing her best to hide the fact that she favored her left shoulder.

"And this is Adeline," the Professor continued, "or like her friend's penchant for diminutive, she prefers to be called Del."

"*Tres enchante*, Miss Del," Shephard replied, noting the woman's awkward smile, realizing she hadn't a clue what he had said. Del reminded him of a child in a toy store, eyes wide with awe. It was obvious she was in a world beyond her experience and imagination.

Shephard and the Professor seated themselves and the servants gracefully placed the meal before them. Shephard smiled merrily as the wine was poured. Lifting the glass, he swirled the liquid and inhaled the bouquet.

"A Bordeaux," he said with contentment, inwardly smiling at the Professor's surprise.

"You know your wines," the Professor said with admiration. "It's from –"

"Ah, ah," Shephard admonished with an impish grin while wagging a finger. "Let me see if I can guess." He inhaled the bouquet again then sipped the full-bodied flavor. "I would guess a Chateau Latour, 1855 or '56."

The Professor's mouth gaped as he stared at Shephard. "My God man, are you that well versed in wines?"

Shephard laughed lightheartedly. "It's really a process of elimination. First, I enjoy a good Bordeaux. Second, I would expect nothing less than a quality wine, a Premiers Crus, from a man of your tastes. That reduces the number of wines to five estates. From there it is rather simple."

The Professor grinned broadly. "I hope the meal likewise meets your expectations."

"I do not doubt it will," he replied then turned his attention to Becca and Del. "And what brings ladies of refined taste to the wilderness of the American west?"

"Just passing through," Becca answered.

"And where are we headed?"

"San Francisco," Del volunteered.

"Ah yes," Shephard nodded. "A delightful city.   And what line of work are you in?"

Assuming Shephard was a friend of the Professor's, Del said, "We're runnin' from the law."   She startled then frowned when she felt Becca kick her leg.

"Oh my," Shephard said then politely smiled. "I'm sure whatever it is, your involvement is innocent."

"Oh, I don't know about that," Del snickered, receiving another kick.

Smiling graciously, Shephard held his wine glass up to the Professor. "This is truly an excellent meal, worthy of the finest restaurants in Europe." Switching to French, he said, "I trust these two are not part of your business."

"Do not worry," he replied, also in French. "They have nothing to do with my enterprises.   They showed up yesterday. I am merely offering them temporary lodging while the woman with the blond hair gets healed." He pondered revealing more than necessary, especially his association with Becca's benefactor.

"That is good," Shephard continued, lifting his glass in toast and taking a sip.   "It would complicate business dealings were such characters involved. You are a true genius and I wish to see you succeed."

Acknowledging the compliment, the Professor likewise lifted his glass. Gazing at the two women, he realized he needed them gone if he was to successfully broker backing for his inventions.   He then debated whether fulfilling Worthington's demand was such a good idea. Yes, he had been handsomely paid, but with a bank's backing and other investors, he could make one hundred times more than what Worthington provided.   Perhaps it was time to bet on a different horse.

Looking across at Shephard, he couldn't help but chuckle to himself at the thought that this latest venture would be an honest enterprise. The thought of him making money via legitimate means was intriguing.

Catching Meili's attention, he called her over. Continuing in French, he said, "The two women can spend one more night here. Then send them on their way."

"Yes Professor."

"One more thing," he added, lowering his voice and causing her to bend forward to hear. "Our other guest claims to be with the Sacramento City Bank. Verify that."

"Yes, Professor."

Standing, she glided smoothly to the back of the tent for a brief conversation with another woman.

Chapter 8

Shephard sat on his horse with two of the Professor's escorts saddled close by, all far enough away while the Professor powered up the engine and the blades started slowly rotating. As the propellers gained momentum, the ship quivered before slowly rising off the ground. Once the machine ascended high enough, Shephard and the escorts rode out to watch the Professor maneuver the machine then attack the hastily erected house in the distance.

Extending his spyglass, Shephard followed the movements of the quadcopter until it finally lined up on the house. Pausing in mid-air, the Professor pulled back on the bolt then pushed the throttle forward.

The ship gained speed as it approached the target. A hundred feet from the house, the Professor began peddling, causing the Gatling gun to begin spewing its deadly contents, splintering and chewing up the boards of the house. He then made two more passes, the final pass causing the house to fall in on itself.

Once back and settled within the safety of the compound, the Professor shut down the engine and emerged, quite pleased with himself.

Shephard, grinning broadly, walked up and gently placed a hand on his shoulder. "That was an amazing display of firepower. I am prepared to query my bank as to the possibility of investing in your venture. In fact, whether they are hesitant or not, I am prepared to invest my own resources in your venture. What say you?"

"I agree," he happily nodded, envisioning the significant monetary gains.

"Excellent," he said with a sigh of contentment, opening his pipe pouch. "I am curious, Professor," he said as he withdrew his pipe and tobacco. "I understand the need for secrecy and seclusion. Is that why you came all the way out here instead of closer to home?"

The Professor hesitated in response then said, "Yes, that's exactly it. The more remote the better. Less prying eyes around, though you did manage to find me." He frowned as he reasoned out the likelihood of word getting out. "How did you manage to find me?"

"Like I mentioned before," he replied, lighting his pipe. "I was in Tombstone and some cowboy was sitting in the restaurant claiming he had seen a flying machine that didn't have an air envelope. At first I thought the man had too much to drink, but it was early in the day and the man seemed quite sober. While others scoffed at the idea, I warranted it needed further attention. After the attention given him was diverted, I covertly asked the man where he saw the machine. He seemed quite willing to tell his story as I appeared to be the only one who believed him. He said in the Dragoons. I secured the services of a horse and saddle and here I am."

Deciding it was possible someone could have seen him the last time he flew, the Professor accepted the explanation.

Wuhan Mei's usual smile disappeared as she cast a piercing glare at the older man when he told her the news. A Chinese woman had ridden into town and sent a telegram. Who did this newcomer think she was? No Chinese in Tombstone so much as breathed without her say so.

"Stop groveling Huang Fu and tell me what happened."

"I saw her, Miss Mei," the older man said, bobbing his head. He reached for the broom to begin sweeping the floor. "She rode right by me, nodded at me then went to the telegraph office."

"Is she still there?" Wuhan Mei demanded.

"I don't know," he replied. "When I saw her go into the office, I came straight here to tell you."

"Go find out who she is and why she is here."

They were interrupted when the woman in question entered the store. She wore leggings and a leather vest over her silk blouse. Her Stetson fit snugly on her long black hair that fell to the middle of her back.

"Welcome to my humble shop," Wuhan Mei said with a polite smile. "You are new to our community."

"I have come to pay my respects, Madame Mei," she said with respect. "I am Yingtai."

Wuhan Mei acknowledged the obsequious bow with an indulgent smile then eyed the woman's attire. "You have the manners of a proper Chinese woman, yet you a have adopted the curious dress of the round eyes," she said, "and a man's clothing at that."

"It is easier to work in these clothes, Madame Mei," she explained.

Casting a hard stare at her, she said, "No Chinese work in Tombstone without my permission."

"I already have a job, Madame Mei."

"In Tombstone?" she bristled, cocking an eyebrow.

"No, Madame Mei. I am from San Francisco. I am here on business," she replied.

"The business here in Chinatown is my business," she said, smiling with only her lips.

"Yes, Madame Mei," the woman said, bowing respectfully. "I work for a man called the Professor. He sent me here to send a telegram about a certain individual."

"I have not seen this man in town."

"We have a camp on the other side of the mountains."

"Which mountains?" she asked.

"They are called the Dragoons."

"This man, the Professor, what does he do?"

"He is an inventor. He has invented a flying machine that does not use an air envelope."

"A flying machine," she mused then studied the young woman. "You came to Arizona so he could fly his machine?"

"No. We are here looking for a man, a US Marshal named Mason Sadler."

Wuhan Mei stiffened. "What do you want with him?"

"The Professor was sent here to kill him," she confided.

Wuhan Mei folded her chubby arms and shook her head. "You will bring trouble down on your house if you pursue this path. The Marshal is a respected man and a dangerous enemy. He is wise and clever. Already he has killed many men seeking to kill him. Why do you wish his life?"

"I do not know, Madame Mei," she replied. "All I know is that a man named Clay came and once he left, we packed all of the things for the airship and came here."

Wuhan Mei studied the woman a moment then said, "Obedience is a virtue; blind obedience is dangerous. How is it that this Professor sent you to send the telegram?"

"I am a valued member of his household," she answered.

"But not valued enough to know the reason why you are here."

"I am sure Meili knows," she said. "She has been busy and has most likely forgotten to tell me."

"Meili?" she said with a frown. "Who is Meili?"

"She is the Professor's deputy and most trusted advisor."

Wuhan Mei tilted her head slightly and frowned with puzzlement. "The Professor is Chinese?"

"No, Madame Mei. He is a round eye, but everyone in the household is Chinese."

"How many?"

"There are twelve," she answered, "in accordance with the zodiac. There are eight of us here in Arizona."

Wuhan Mei's frown deepened. "He has twelve Chinese women as his household?"

"Yes Madame Mei, all very attractive."

Wuhan Mei's face spilt into a broad smile. "He is no fool then."

"It's not like that, Madame Mei," Yingtai sputtered.

"Of course not," she replied with a knowing smile, which abruptly vanished. "You tell your Professor that the Marshal is a friend of Chinatown. We will do nothing to help you harm him."

"I did not come here to ask for your help, Miss Mei. I stopped by your store because I did not want to return so soon."

Wuhan Mei politely smiled at the woman. "Stay as long as you wish. But when you go back, warn your Professor that the Marshal is a friend of Chinatown. We will not allow him to be harmed. You tell your Professor and the others in the household. The Marshal is a friend of the Chinese."

"Yes, Miss Mei."

The loud chugging of the MATE woke Mason as Belle maneuvered the machine up the trail to the cabin. Perched on his mechanical legs, Nantan loped beside her in easy strides, while above them, Taboca hovered in his single-seater airship.

Stretching the stiffness out of his body, Mason opened the door and stepped out to stand under the porch overhang. He smiled as Belle drove up yet noticed the bags under her eyes. The woman needed sleep. Despite her exhaustion, her eyes were bright with excitement.

She wore leggings that hugged her shapely legs, and a blouse that accentuated her feminine assets. Mason found himself distracted by her innocent sensuality and, once again, silently thanked Henry Mitchell for his role.

Henry Mitchell... Mason knew he should feel guilty that Henry had murdered Elizabeth. But the truth was, being married to Elizabeth had been hell on earth, especially the last year as he watched her descend into the depths of addiction to both laudanum and opium. The once beautiful and gregarious Elizabeth had morphed to a shriveled shell of a mean and bitter crone.

Watching the beautiful Belle descend from the MATE, he pondered the former marriage to Elizabeth. He had analyzed the reasons for the marriage to the point of numbness. Yet the reasons that emerged constantly repeated: he was infatuated; he believed her to be refined and cultured; she was from a wealthy family; she wasn't like her father; they would have a fairytale marriage; he would be successful in the business world; they would live happily ever after.

The only reason that ended up being true was that he had been infatuated.

Elizabeth was the girl from the other side of the tracks, the good side. That she found him attractive and captivating confounded him and he did his best to live up to her expectations, even accepting a position with her father's company.

Her father, THE Reginald Worthington, hated him and did nothing to hide his disdain from the moment they met. That his daughter refused to consider anyone else for marriage, infuriated him to the point of threatening to cut her off. Her obstinacy matched his and their rows became almost legendary, at least amongst the servants. But Elizabeth was his only child and in the battle of wills, he blinked first.

Early on, Mason saw the signs of what their future would be like. Elizabeth was a spoiled child, demanding and getting everything she wanted. So intent on appeasing her, he neglected who he was, to the point of sitting behind a desk in an oppressive office, shuffling worthless papers, suppressing the screaming inside him yearning to be somewhere, anywhere outside.

Then one day a plump officious oaf in sideburns and condescending tone informed him that the report he had been working on would need to be redone because the proper forms had not been utilized. Despite pointing out that the data was all correct, Mason was firmly, yet politely told to redo it, using the proper forms.

Muzzling the urge to throttle the pompous fool, Mason politely acknowledged the mistake and waited until the man left then pushed back from the desk, retrieved his hat and walked down to sign up as a US Marshal.

Both Elizabeth and Worthington were apoplectic when he informed them of his career change. Neither forgave him for bringing Elizabeth to Tombstone.

Though his marriage suffered, his contentment with his position and authority blossomed. He was finally happy doing what he was meant to do. It was an inverse proportion: the happier he was in the job, the lower Elizabeth plummeted.

Then Henry showed up and finished the job.

Now Henry was gone, and Mason was fighting for his life.

Nantan came bounding up, grinning his usual good-natured smile. Settling his mechanical legs, he looked around for a place to sit, deciding on the roof of the porch as the best choice.

"So what's the plan?" he asked, perched on the edge of the roof and looking down as Mason stepped out from beneath, doubtful the roof could hold him.

"I'd like for Taboca to take a look while Belle gets some rest," he said.

"I'm fine," Belle objected.

"I'm sure you are," he replied, "but we've got time and you've been up all night."

"What about Delilah?"

"I don't think she's gone far," he said. "My guess is that she's probably close by, looking to complete her mission."

"But she's wounded," she pointed out.

"Not too wounded to ride hard and shoot," he countered.

Taboca brought the airship down close to the outer clearing, hovering a few feet off the ground as Mason and Belle walked over.

"Take a look on the other side of the mountain," Mason said. "Stay low and out of sight if you can."

"Can do," he smiled. Throttling the engines while increasing the heat to the envelope, the airship rose and soon disappeared over the ridge.

Looking at Belle, Mason smiled. "Go ahead and get some sleep. I've got a feeling it's going to be a long night."

"What about you?"

"I snoozed waiting for you."

"Cheater," she teased, wrapping an arm around his. "What do you expect to find?" she asked as they walked back to the cabin.

"Earl said there were four of them. I count five, adding the one riding with Delilah. That means Earl couldn't count or there are more here than what he knew about."

"Shephard said the Professor is also in the area," she pointed out.

"I don't know anything about him."

"He's an intelligent criminal," she explained, "and a brilliant scientist and inventor who offers his services to the highest bidder, those services not always being legitimate. He's managed to avoid indictment so far, which is why Shephard is out here following him. Oh, and while I think about it, he lives in San Francisco."

"That pretty much tells me all I need to know," Mason said with a pensive nod. "We have to assume Worthington is the reason for him being here."

"Unfortunately, I think you may be right." She stopped him, staring up at his face. "He's going to be a lot harder to overcome than the others."

"I know," he replied with a half-smile. "It just means we're going to have to be smarter. Besides," he added, walking on and pointing to Nantan perched happily on the porch roof, "we have geniuses of our own."

"I've got some of Nantan's explosive toys in the trailer," she said.

"Good," he said, pleased. "We'll make good use of them."

While Belle settled as best she could using Mason's saddle, Taboca guided his airship over the ridges of the Dragoons, searching for anything unusual. It was when he cresting a ridge not far from the Middle Pass that he was surprised when he saw a machine slowly ascending from amidst a large grouping of tents.

Instinctively lowering his ship below the crest, he watched in amazement as the machine rose then hovered, using no air envelope but four separate blades spinning furiously. At the rear of the machine, a single propeller pushed the machine forward, the pilot using fins behind the rear propeller to steer it.

Yearning to rush over there and learn all he could about the invention, he forced himself to stay the course and watch. The machine moved forward, picking up speed. His pleasure abruptly turned to worry when he saw the Gatling gun spewing its destruction and splintering the house in the near distance. The machine made two more passes and the house collapsed upon itself.

Waiting until the machine returned to the camp and lowered to land in the middle, Taboca powered up and headed back to the cabin, deciding to follow the Middle Pass to keep out of sight.

Landing in the clearing by the cabin, Taboca tethered the airship to a nearby tree, letting the engine run while he hustled up to Mason and Nantan who were walking towards him.

"I saw an incredible sight" Taboca said then related the information about the quadcopter. "It has a Gatling gun on the front because the last thing I saw was the pilot shooting a house and destroying it. I couldn't see how he fired the gun, but there was only one pilot."

"Horizontal propellers," Nantan enthused, fascinated by the machine. "How can we get a closer look?"

Before Mason could answer, movement behind him caught Taboca's attention and the machinist's eyes widened in apprehension. Turning, Mason saw Caleb and de la Fuente stumbling out from the woods towards the cabin.

"Where's Ringo?" he called out.

Caleb replied with a stiff shrug.

Frowning, he turned back at Taboca, he asked, "If you shut down your airship, how long will it take to get ready again?"

"I can leave the engine running on low to keep heat to the envelope," he said, warily regarding the latest arrivals. "I'll need more fuel to fly."

"We can get those two to help. I've come up with a plan and will need everyone's help, including them," he added, thumbing over his shoulder.

It was early evening when Yingtai returned. She immediately went to Meili to relate the message from Wuhan Mei. The Professor saw them and called her over.

"Did you receive a response from the bank?"

251

"Yes, Professor," Yingtai replied. "Mister Shephard is an employee there. He is one of the owners."

The Professor brightened at the news, pleased that Shephard had already committed to investing in his invention.

"What about Ed and Gordon that Rebecca mentioned?"

Yingtai shrugged. "I could find nothing about them other than they had been seen in town."

The Professor frowned. "Nothing other than that?"

"No Professor. The man called Gordon was involved in an accidental dynamite explosion, perhaps a week ago. He was not seriously injured. No one has seen either of them for several days. However, when I was in town, a woman driving a strange machine drove into town. It looked like a small locomotive, but it didn't need railroad tracks because it had these metal belts that went around the wheels allowing it to go in any direction it wished."

"Interesting," he replied, his attention perking up. "Who was driving this machine?"

"The woman called Belle. She is Marshal Sadler's woman and she seemed quite happy."

"Happy?" His interest in the machine evaporated. "That can only mean Sadler is not dead. Most likely he's taken care of Ed and Gordon." He twisted his head to gaze at Meili. "This is not good. With the present financial possibilities, I think we may need to reassess our position here."

"I agree," she replied, placing a hand on his arm.

"There is one more thing, Professor," she said. "I went to pay my respects to Madame Wuhan Mei."

"Who is she?"

"She is the Celestial Madame of Tombstone," she explained.

"Yes," he nodded. "That was appropriate."

"She warned that the Marshal is a friend of Chinatown and they would protect him."

The Professor's eyes hardened. "How did she know about the Marshal?"

She hesitated and lowered her head. "I told her."

"You told her?" he exploded.

"She had to," Meili interrupted. "Wuhan Mei is the madame of Chinatown. Yingtai could not refuse to answer her questions."

The Professor's lips tightened. "I know, I know. I understand. What else did she say?"

"She said that we pursue the Marshal to our peril. He is a dangerous man. But more importantly, he is a friend of Chinatown. They will come to his aid if necessary."

Scowling, the Professor pursed his lips.

"There is yet one more thing. Professor," Yingtai said.

"Now what?"

"When I was riding back, I swear I heard an airship, but it sounded like it was right above me. I looked around but didn't see anything."

Knitting his brows in concentration, he then turned to Meili. "You come with me."

Spinning on his heels, he limped with determination to the tent where Becca and Del were housed. Without bothering to let them know he was there, he was about to pull the tent flap open when Meili brushed past him.

The two women were examining Becca's wound when they looked up to see Meili enter followed closely by the Professor. Becca quickly closed her blouse, giving him a dirty look.

"You're going to have to move on," he announced. "I can't have the Marshal coming here."

"I thought you were supposed to kill him," Becca said, raising an eyebrow.

"I've more important things than chasing after a US Marshal," he tartly replied.

"But you've been paid," she curtly pointed out, knowing he did nothing without upfront money.

"That's not your problem," he retorted.

Becca studied him for a brief moment then sneered, "You're going into business with that banker that stumbled in here. You've been hustled by a better hustler."

"You would do well to watch your mouth," he warned. "Remember where you are. If I wanted, I could turn you over to the Marshal and no one would be the wiser."

Becca's mouth shut tight as she stared angrily at him, knowing she was in no position to argue. She would wait until she got back to San Francisco and tell Worthington. He would take care of this arrogant bastard.

"I want you gone after breakfast," he stated then stormed out.

"What are we gonna do?" Del asked.

"We're going to head north like we originally planned," Becca stated. "Once we hit the railroad tracks, we head west towards Tucson. Once we get to Tucson, we can get an airship to San Francisco."

"An airship costs money," Del pointed out. "We don't have enough."

Becca chewed her lip as she mulled their prospects then gave voice to her thoughts. "The Marshal thinks we're heading north. Suppose we head south to Bisbee. He wouldn't expect us to go that way. I still have my things there. We could take an airship out of Bisbee and he'd be none the wiser." She paused then smiled. "I wonder if we could get the Professor to help us."

"How?"

"Come with me," she said then led the way to the Professor's tent.

Pushing the door flap open, she saw the Professor and Shephard lounging on thickly padded field chairs. Shephard tapped the tobacco in his pipe while the Professor airily waved a cigar emphasizing a point in their discussion. They looked back when Becca and Del entered.

"Yes?" the Professor scowled upon seeing her.

"We need your help," Becca sweetly said.

Heaving a long-suffering sigh, he asked, "How?" Becca shifted her glance at Shephard. The Professor noticed and said, "He knows."

Giving Shephard the same sweet smile, she said, "The Marshal expects us to travel north. We intend to go south instead. But we want him chasing us north."

"So what are you asking?"

"Find us some different clothing. Send two of your girls, dressed similar to us, north after breakfast while Del and I head south."

"South to where?"

"Bisbee."

"Isn't that from where you fled?"

"Exactly," she smiled. "He wouldn't expect us there."

The Professor mused a moment then said, "I can accommodate the clothing and sending women north. However, you'll have noticed that none have blond hair like yours, so the ruse will likely be discovered before they got too far."

"All we need is a head start," she confidently replied.

Giving her a regal nod, he said, "It will be as you wish." Glancing over at the ever-present Meili, he said, "Find some appropriate clothing for them."

"Yes, Professor," she replied then looked at the two women. "If you will follow me, please."

Shephard waited until the women departed then said, "Is that wise, Professor?"

"It was necessary," he nonchalantly replied. "I need to rid myself of their presence here. Sending two riders north for a mile or two seems a small cost to send them on their way."

"Ah," Shephard smiled knowingly. "Cleverly done. Suppose the Marshal shows up?"

"I shall inform him of their destination," he answered with an innocent shrug.

Shephard snorted a laugh. "Well played, Sir. Well played."

Mason looked up at the star filled sky, paying special attention to the position of the Big Dipper in relation to the North Star. It was almost directly below the North Star which meant it was a little after four o'clock in the morning as Mason and the others made their way down the Middle Pass coming out of the Dragoons. The night was illuminated by a half-moon allowing Belle to navigate the MATE along the dirt road. Perched beside her, Mason strained as he studied the road ahead without the benefit of the head lamp. Limping behind her, Caleb and de la Fuente did their best to keep pace. Deciding the pace was too slow, Nantan had stretched his long mechanical legs and was already nearing the plain at the base of the mountains. Taboca hovered high above them, positioning himself over the camp that was marked with gas lit lamps spaced at intervals along the perimeter.

"I wonder what happened to Johnny," Belle said.

"I hope he's not going off on his own," Mason replied. "We have the element of surprise on our side. Let's hope it stays that way."

Nautical twilight was upon them, and they could make out the edges and shapes of the nearby trees and rock formations.

"We need to hurry," Mason warned, "if we want to catch them still asleep."

Belle increased the speed, leaving Caleb and de la Fuente staggering furiously to keep up. Once out of the mountains, Belle slowed to a crawl as the team assembled.

Nantan came up and said, "I'd not be surprised if they know we're here. The noise from the engine carries in the night."

"Can't be helped," Mason said. "You know what to do. You hang around the perimeter to the north. I expect once the action starts, Delilah and her friend will head out fast."

"I got it," he grinned, anxious to test his legs out.

"This isn't a game," Mason reminded him. "They're likely armed."

"I'll be careful," he answered then headed out onto the plain to circle east then north around the camp.

Looking up, Mason could make out the silhouette of Taboca's airship. Casting a glance at Belle, he said, "We give him twenty minutes to get situated, then we move in."

Circling high above the camp, Taboca stared down at the circle of flickering Rochester lamps that illuminated the tarp covering the quadcopter. Desperately yearning to see the machine up close, he hoped that once the action stopped, he could land and study the man's invention.

It was when he saw the light from the MATE burst on, that he leaned over and started dropping the multi-spiked bombs, watching the flash of explosions when they detonated down below.

Enjoying the destruction like a teenager lighting firecrackers, he reached behind him for another bomb, lofted it into the air and watched its descent only to realize too late it was heading straight for the quadcopter.

The perimeter guard heard the MATE as the machine's engines cranked up. Calling out a warning as she strained to determine the engine's approach, she stumbled back, blinded as Belle reached forward and engaged the dynamo switch just below the pilot board and a burst of bright eye-searing light shot out from the carbon arc lamp in the front, brilliantly illuminating everything in its path.

Moments later explosions rocked the camp as Taboca dropped small brass globe bombs with a series of spikes embedded into them. His accuracy set fire to the fuel shed. And then one hit the tarp covering the quadcopter.

In the blazing light of the fires and the carbon arc lamp on the MATE, the camp erupted in a cacophony of running and yelling. Shots were fired, but Belle yanked on the left brake, rotating the MATE's headlamp across the camp. She then yanked back on the right brake, the treads of the machines chewing up the ground as the searing light of the headlamp swept across the camp. She repeated the sweeping motions, digging the MATE into a small trench. Then with one flip of the dynamo switch, the light went off.

Having turned away and shut his eyes when Belle activated the light, Mason's night vision was clear as he raced into the camp, bypassing the perimeter guards who stumbled and blindly groped their way in a daze. The flap to the largest tent in the camp opened and he watched as a man emerged with a rifle. The man saw his quadcopter in flames, and he cried out.

"My quadcopter."

Mason took note of the man and circled behind him, catching him as the man approached the wreckage.

The Professor felt the muzzle of a pistol at the base of his skull behind his ear.

When the explosions started, Becca leaped out of the cot, quickly drawing her boots on. "Let's go," she commanded.

Del needed no urging and had her feet jammed into her boots. "How did you know?" she asked, wondering why Becca wanted them to sleep in their clothes.

"No time to explain," she said. "Call it a hunch. Make for the horses."

Cautiously pulling the tent flap back, she saw the melee of the Professor's servants and guards struggling to gain control of the camp. Leading the way, they headed for the make-shift corral at the north end of the camp. Quickly saddling two steeds, they pushed through the perimeter, whipping their horses to speed.

They were yet a quarter mile from the camp when to their right, a large figure began giving chase, and it was gaining on them.

Nantan felt giddy as his long strides not only kept pace but allowed him to reel them in as he worked to intercept them. Then he realized he hadn't quite thought about what he was going to do once he caught up with them. Yet it was the thrill of the chase that spurred him on, and he figured that if he could knock them off their horses that would be enough.

Becca's fear increased as she realized he was closing in on them, and she whipped her mount to a gallop, leaving Del behind her. Looking back over her shoulder, she watched the man in the strange contraption pull alongside Del then push her from the saddle. Del struggled to hang on but when the man bumped against the horse and pushed again, Del went flying into the dirt, careening over and over until she ended up in a crumpled heap.

Becca's first instinct was to go faster, but she knew the horse wouldn't last. Then an epiphany hit, and she slowed down to a trot, allowing the man in the machine to catch up.

Just as he was about to come abreast, she kicked the horse into a gallop. The man responded and he caught up.

Just as he again pulled abreast of her, she jerked the reins to the right, knocking into the man, which caused him to stumble. She watched in satisfaction as his legs tangled and he crashed down, sliding and rolling, unable to get up.

Reining in her mount, she retraced her path past the man, who was alive, but in a daze. Ignoring him, she went back to check on Del. Part of her said to leave her. Del would only be a burden and slow her down. Yet there was the beginning of a friendship and Becca had few friends. Besides, the man sent to track them was injured and not likely to be a bother.

Approaching Del, she dismounted and ran to her young friend. Dawn was just below the horizon and in the dim light she could tell Del was still breathing. Glancing quickly around, she saw Del's horse close by.

Leaving her own horse by Del, she walked over, took hold of the reins and led the animal back to where Del's scrunched face told her that her friend was in great pain.

"Can you move?" Becca asked.

"It hurts," Del groaned.

"I know it does," she replied. "Can you move?"

Del stretched out an arm then cried out in pain. Breathing rapidly, she grunted, "Go. Just go. I'll only hold you back."

"I don't want to leave you here," Becca soothed.

"It hurts too much to move," she replied.

"You have to try. Let me help you." She reached down to pull Del up by her armpits.

Del cried out in pain. "My leg's broke and so is my arm. Just leave me. I'm not going anywhere."

Her lips pursed, Becca gently lowered her to the ground. Shooting a glance over to the man on the artificial legs, she saw him struggling to sit. Deciding when his friends would come to his aid, they would look after Del too. Del had a better chance here than riding with her.

Becca dropped to her knees beside her friend and kissed her on the forehead. "Someone will be along for that man back there. They'll likely take care of you too. You get yourself better. Don't worry about what's going to happen. You've done nothing wrong. When you're healed, wherever you are, I'll find you. Then we'll go off like we planned. It'll be better then."

Through the grimace of pain, Del looked up at her. "I'll hold you to that."

Becca lingered for a moment longer then stood and mounted her horse. "I'll find you wherever you are."

Giving her one last hopeful look, she spurred her steed to a canter.

While the women in the Professor's camp struggled to put out the fires, Mason frog marched the Professor into the nearest tent where a kerosene lamp had been lit and a man, wearing a loose silk robe sat on the cot, tamping a bit of tobacco into a pipe. He looked up when they entered. He gave Mason a flicker of warning and a barely perceptible shake of his head.

"My word," Shephard exclaimed. "What's going on here?"

"Stay where you are mister," Mason said, "and keep your hands where I can see them." He then twisted slightly so that Shephard could see the US Marshal badge.

"Not to worry, Marshal," Shephard replied, holding up his hands.

Mason eased the Professor away from him and leveled the six-shooter at him. "Where is she?"

"Where is who?" the Professor seethed.

"Delilah. Where is she?"

"I assure you, there is no one named Delilah here."

"An attractive blond."

"Rebecca?" Shephard volunteered.

"That might be a name she's using," Mason said.

Shephard shifted a look to the Professor then back to Mason. "I knew this might happen. This good man here offered sustenance to a woman who was injured. Only too late did we learn that she was not what we were led to believe."

"And you are?"

"Thaddeus Shephard, of Sacramento City Bank. I am here at the behest of my bank to study the marvelous flying machine this gentleman has invented."

"That's wonderful," Mason deadpanned. "Now where is she?"

Casting a grateful glance at Shephard, the Professor relaxed. "I do not know, Marshal. When I discovered her possible criminal past, I demanded she leave at first light today. You are welcome to search the camp."

The tent flap opened and Meili burst in. Seeing Mason with the gun pointed at the Professor, she hesitated.

"It's alright, Meili," the Professor said. "The Marshal is looking for Rebecca."

"She's gone," she answered.

"Where?" Mason demanded.

"She rode north with that other woman."

"What other woman?"

"There was a woman named Adeline with her," the Professor said. "I know little about her." Turning to Meili, he asked, "Is everything under control?"

"Yes. The fires are under control. The fuel shed is still burning but it is contained. However," she said, giving Mason an icy stare, "the quadcopter is damaged."

The Professor glared at Mason with indignant righteousness. "By what right do you come here and destroy my property."

"By right of the law," Mason shot back. "You were harboring a known murderer. Your own questionable past and dealings with the law gave me authority."

"What?" Shephard said, shocked.

"It's not what you think," the Professor hastened to assuage him.

The tent flap pulled aside, and Belle entered, flashing Mason a confident smile. "So this is where you ended up."

"Delilah, or Rebecca, or whatever name she's using is headed north with a woman named Adeline. See if you can alert Taboca to see if Nantan intercepted them, while I continue my questioning of the Professor and ..." Mason paused as if struggling to remember his name.

261

"Thaddeus Shephard," Shephard filled in, "of the Sacramento City Bank."

"A banker?" Belle frowned, feigning puzzlement.

"I'll explain later," Mason said. "She's headed north. We need to stop her before she gets too far."

"Right."

The tent flap closed behind Belle as Mason holstered his six-shooter. "I want to talk to you two separately," he said to the two men then focused on Shephard. "You first."

Waiting for the Professor and Meili to leave, Mason moved closer to Shephard. "What's going on?" he quietly asked.

"We discovered the Professor's airship when a lad stumbled into Marston, Wyoming a while back with tales of a flying machine that killed his family and destroyed an abandoned fort at Bonneville. We sent someone to investigate and found the tale was true and the carnage indescribable."

"So now you want to pretend the murders never happened?" he said, his lips pursed.

"Wyoming's a tough place to homestead. Accidents and misfortune happen all the time," he indifferently pointed out. "The government is extremely interested in the Professor's airship. They're willing to look the other way in this and his other shady dealings in order to get their hands on the quadcopter. We can't afford for another country to steal this invention. It could revolutionize warfare as we know it."

Mason sifted the news then heaved a sigh. "OK."

He was about to turn to interview the Professor when Shephard grabbed his arm. "Remember. Neither you nor Belle know me. As far as you're concerned, I'm a banker with the Sacramento City Bank."

"We understand."

Moments later, the Professor returned to the tent. Shephard remained seated on the cot, puffing away on his Meerschaum pipe.

"I've learned all I need to know from Mister Shephard," Mason said to him. "It seems you are in a legitimate business dealing this time."

The Professor slid his eyes to Shephard with a look of gratitude.

"Damage to your airship?" Mason inquired.

"It's not as bad as I thought. I can repair it."

"I know two machinists who will want to take a look at your machine," he said.

"They're welcome any time."

Belle popped a head in and said, "Nantan's down. He needs help."

Nantan was sitting up when they arrived, Taboca helping him unstrap. Taboca's airship hovered nearby. They looked up as Belle and Mason reined in and dismounted.

"Nothing broken but my pride," Nantan cheerfully announced. He was covered in purple bruises and wide swaths of scrapes and shallow cuts where layers of skin had peeled off.

He pointed to where Del lay on her back, her horse close by. "I don't know about her, though. The blond woman with her headed south towards Bisbee."

"You sure you're OK?" Mason asked.

"I'm fine," Nantan said. "I'm going to hurt for a while, but I'm OK."

Mason walked over to stare down at Del.

Squinting in the sunlight, Del looked up at the Marshal. "You're too late," she hoarsely gloated. "She'll be gone by the time you get there."

"Get where?"

"Wherever you think she is."

Mason took a knee beside her. "Where is she?"

"You're too late," she repeated with a moan, closing her eyes.

"You need help."

"I'm the one that did it," she mumbled.

"Did what?"

"All the killin'. She's innocent."

"You killed Ringo?"

"Yeah," she answered with labored breath.

Mason lips tightened and he shook his head. "And Frank? You killed him too?"

"Yeah, him too."

"And Belle and Nantan?"

"Yeah. I killed all of 'em."

Belle heard her name when she walked up. "Ask her if she's killed President Chester A. Arthur too."

"The woman's obviously delirious. She needs a doctor."

"I'll go back and see if the Professor can rig up a contraption to bring her back to town."

"I'm headed to Bisbee. I think she's backtracked and looking to fly out from there. I'll meet you back in Tombstone."

"It's a date," she grinned, giving him a kiss.

They looked over to watch Nantan awkwardly stand, his cousin fretting over him. Seeing them, he waved then limped over to the airship.

Becca's hopes soared with each mile she got closer to Bisbee. She chuckled as she passed by Del's homestead, remembering the shallow grave where Del's former common-law husband now resided.

Coming around the Mule Mountains, she eased her horse through the traffic of miners, businessmen and pedestrians. To the south of town, she could see the airships tethered and waiting for passengers. She smiled knowing it was just a matter of minutes before she would be on board, sailing for home.

Coming up to her hotel, she looped the reins around the hitching post, wishing she had time to bathe and properly clean up. She was tired of all this desert dust crusting on her skin.

"Good morning, Miss Delilah," the man behind the counter greeted her. He gave her a curious glance at both her attire and overall run-down and beaten look. But most of all he noticed the six-shooter strapped to her waist.

"It's been a long couple of days," she pleasantly said. "My key please."

"Of course."

Key in hand, she climbed the stairs, walked down the hallway and went to unlock her door only to discover the door already unlocked. Slipping her gun out, she quietly turned the handle and opened the door. Spreading it wide she peered in to find nothing amiss. Pressing the door all the way open, she did another scan of the room and again found nothing awry.

Sliding her gun back into the holster, she was about to step in when she was thrust forward causing her to sprawl onto the floor. Recovering enough to reach back for her gun, she felt the crushing weight of a booted foot on top of her hand.

"You're hurting me," she huffed.

The boot stayed on her hand while whoever it was removed the gun from her holster. Once liberated of her firearm, the boot was removed from her hand. As she turned to sit up, she heard the door close and the bolt slide home.

It was then she inhaled the overpowering stench of decaying flesh.

Looking up, she stared at the man, his hat slung low over his eyes. He looked familiar but she couldn't place him.

"Who are you?" she coldly demanded.

The man raised his head to gaze at her with lifeless eyes.

Becca stared in disbelief at the apparition standing before her. "J... Johnny?"

Ringo slowly nodded.

"But... but... you're supposed to be dead." Her mouth gaped wide as he removed the hat from his head, exposing the gaping wound. It was then she noticed that his flesh had that pale waxen look of a dead man.

Yet it was the barrel of a .45 pointing directly at her that got her attention.

Blinking in confusion, she gathered her wits.

"I didn't mean to, Johnny," she pleaded. "I was forced to do it. They were blackmailing me," she explained, struggling with a plausible story. "Really. My life was at stake... So was my family's. I had to make a choice. You gotta believe me." She leaned forward, edging her hand toward the knife in her boot.

Ringo held his pistol steady as he took a step closer.

Becca's entreaties continued. "You gotta believe me. It was Worthington who made the decision. I had to do it. I had no choice. You just have to understand."

Ringo's hand began to lower and Becca waited for her opportunity. His hand was almost to his side when she went for the knife. But Ringo had anticipated her move and with a flick of the wrist, fired, catching Becca in the same shoulder Mason had injured.

The knife flipped away from her hand to slide across the floor stopping below the bed as she twisted from the shock that sent her collapsing against a small bureau. Blood flowed from the wound, and she grimaced in pain.

Ringo teetered over to stand above her. Then in lumbering awkward movements, he lowered himself to his knees, bringing his face within inches of hers.

She tried not to stare into his lifeless eyes or the blackened mass of rotting flesh and brain. The malodorous reek of the decay of death caused her to turn away.

Grabbing her chin, he twisted her head around then pressed his dead lips against hers. She struggled to withdraw, but his grip was powerful and unrelenting.

In her struggle to avoid his face, she failed to notice that he had raised his pistol. When he released her from the kiss, she felt too late the cold steel barrel pressed to her temple. Her eyes widened in profound shock just as he pulled the trigger.

She slumped over onto her side, blood pouring from her head.

Ringo stood, stared at her for a moment then retraced his awkward steps to the door. He could hear footsteps running down the hall. Holstering his gun, he staggered over to the bureau where the Rochester lamp perched. Setting the glass globe aside, he unscrewed the top then poured the contents over Becca and the bedding.

Retrieving the matchbox, he stood in the doorway, stuck a match and flicked it onto Becca. Her body instantly caught flame that spread to the bed.

Tossing the matchbox near the body, Ringo turned and limped down the hall. He was in the back alleys by the time the fire alarms clanged. It wasn't until he crested the hills outside the city that he turned to see the smoke billowing from the hotel.

Oblivious to the dance band and whirling dancers inside the Bird Cage Theater, Mason stood at the bar watching Jack pour a shot of whiskey.

"You look like a man who could use more than one of these," Jack observed, sliding the glass across the bar top.

"It's been a long day," Mason sighed. Raising the glass, he glanced over to see Belle at the end of the bar, merrily holding court with the usual coterie of admirers who either didn't notice her grand wedding ring or chose to ignore it.

The shot glass held mid-air, he stared in fascination at his wife. The woman who so recently had been kidnapped under the threat of death was cheerfully chatting away as though nothing of consequence had occurred.

Mason shook his head and grinned. Staring at himself in the mirror behind the bar, he looked like he had been rode hard and put up wet. Belle? She looked just as stunning as ever. How she managed to go from bound captive thrown in the back of a wagon to assaulting an armed compound to the fetching Bird Cage Madam all in less than twenty-four hours was beyond belief. And to listen to her, it was a fun day.

Downing the warming liquor, he placed the glass on the bar for a refill. While Jack poured, Mason once again looked at his wife, wondering when it would all end, the constant looking over their shoulders. But he knew the answer.

It wouldn't end until Worthington was dead, or they were.

Mason pondered his next steps. Of the four sent here to kill him, two were dead for he had personally seen to that.

He had sent one back to Worthington with a warning. That still left Delilah… or Rebecca.

When he discovered that Delilah had escaped and once he was sure Nantan wasn't injured too severely, he had sent Belle back home and headed to Bisbee. He was halfway there when he saw smoke coming from the other side of the Mule Mountains, which meant there was a fire in the city. Assuming Delilah had set it as a distraction while she headed to the airship terminal, he spurred his horse to the terminal, expecting to find her waiting.

Yet when he arrived and searched the passenger manifests and walked the passenger waiting lounge, Delilah was not there. He rechecked the manifests and took his time working the lounge, all to no avail. It wasn't until the last airship departed late in the afternoon that he had to accept that Delilah had slipped away.

Mounting his steed, he grimly made his way over the mountains and out onto the plain, following the road to Tombstone. It was dark by the time he arrived at the OK Corral and stabled his horse. Knowing Belle was probably at work, he went home and cleaned up enough to be presentable then stopped at the Atlantic for dinner.

Walking in, he heard his name called and looked over to the table by the window to see Roger waving at him.

"Dine with me, Marshal," he called out.

Giving him a friendly nod, he pulled a chair out and plopped down.

"You look tired," Roger said.

"Had a long ride," he replied as the waitress sauntered up.

She was a pretty girl in her teens and made moon eyes at the handsome man. "What'll you have, Marshal?"

"Steak, rare, potatoes, biscuits and gravy… and coffee."

"Right away, Marshal," she said with a warm smile, her gaze lingering almost to awkwardness before she turned and sashayed away.

Roger's face split into a wide grin. "She's taken with you, Marshal."

Oblivious to the girl's attention, Mason cocked an eyebrow and twisted his head to look at her. "She's almost young enough to be my daughter."

"Some men like 'em young," he pointed out.

"That's disgusting," Mason retorted with curled lip. "Besides, I already have the most beautiful woman in the world."

"That you do, Marshal," Roger readily agreed. "So, what's been happening that's caused you to be so tired? Chasing outlaws and criminals?"

"You might say that," he replied, debating just how much he wanted to relate. Part of him was willing to indulge the newspaperman, but most of him wanted to simply enjoy the meal in quiet.

"Who was it?" Roger persisted.

Deciding to leave most of the story out of it, especially Belle's kidnapping and subsequent rescuing, the help of Caleb and de la Fuente, and the attack on the Professor's camp, he said, "A woman named Delilah –"

"That lovely blond lady who I saw in the company of that notorious gunslinger named Johnny Ringo?" he interrupted.

"The same," Mason said. "But her real name is Rebecca."

The waitress brought Mason's coffee, slowly placing it before him. Shooting glance at Roger, she perfunctorily asked, "More coffee?" before returning her attention to Mason.

"Yes, please," he answered.

Ignoring him for the moment, she stared at Mason and said, "My name's Rebecca."

"What a coincidence" Roger chortled while Mason stiffened.

"What's a coincidence?" she asked, looking at Roger then back to Mason.

"The Marshal's tracking down a dangerous murderer named Rebecca."

The girl's face went white. "It's not me," she stammered.

"Of course not," Mason said, flashing Roger a stern stare. "You're too sweet to be a criminal."

The effect was instant, and the girl relaxed, taken with the compliment. Pursing her lips at Roger, she walked away, forgetting Roger wanted more coffee.

Roger watched her saunter away for only a moment. "So tell me more about this Rebecca person. Who did she kill?"

"Johnny Ringo."

Roger's jaw dropped. "Johnny Ringo?" he repeated. "How do you know it was her?"

"Let's just say I have it on good authority."

"An eyewitness?"

Mason pondered his response. Ringo was certainly a choice eyewitness but being the victim of a murder and the eyewitness would be difficult to use in court, especially as the witness was... not quite dead.

"Yes," Mason reluctantly replied.

"Who?"

"Now Roger," Mason gently chastised. "This is an ongoing investigation. I can't reveal my sources or give away information that might aid the murderer."

"I understand," he said. "What can you tell me about this Rebecca woman?"

"Not much. You probably know as much about her as I do." Mason was surprised when Roger flushed though quickly recovered as though caught in some indiscretion.

"I know nothing about the lady," Roger said with a little more conviction than necessary. "I only saw her from afar, usually in the company of Ringo."

"I met her once or twice," Mason said, "and like you, always with Ringo."

Young Rebecca brought their meals and placed them on the table. "Is this Rebecca woman dangerous?" she asked, her eyes on Mason.

"Very," he replied, his attention on the steak.

"You will be careful, won't you?" she said, concern in her voice.

"I always am," he replied, slicing a piece of meat and plopping it into his mouth. His shoulders settled as he savored the prime cut of meat. "This is heaven," he said, closing his eyes.

"More coffee?" Roger asked, holding up his cup.

While the young Rebecca retrieved the coffee pot, Mason redirected the conversation to more mundane matters occasionally asking questions about Roger's past. By the time the meal ended, young Rebecca discovered to her grieving disappointment that Mason was married. To make matters worse, he was married to the madam of the Bird Cage Theater.

Watching the Marshal and the newspaperman walk out together, Rebecca determined that the Marshal needed to be rescued from his ill-fated marriage and she was just the woman to do it.

But here at the bar in the Theater, Mason was ignorant of young Rebecca's girlish crush and dreams. Downing his third shot of whiskey, he felt the stress of the day slough off and suddenly realized he was very tired.

Catching Belle's eye, he pointed to himself then wiggled his fingers imitating walking toward the door.

Excusing herself from the admirers, she came up to him. "Going somewhere, tall, dark and handsome?"

"Home. And if the object of everyone's desire and lust is not too busy fending off the multitudes of suitors, the Marshal would love to have his gorgeous wife accompany him."

"Hmmm..." she said, placing a finger on her cheek, pretending to consider. "I think she may be ready. She's more tired than she's willing to admit."

The evening was boisterous as Mason and Belle walking arm in arm down Allen Street. The street was filled with miners, cowboys, gamblers and the ever-present music that spilled out of saloons as the doors opened and closed with regularity.

Belle squeezed Mason's arm. "I love living here with all this energy of life. I don't ever want to leave."

"No one says we have to," Mason replied. "I like it here too. So, if we're going to stay here, we need to think of the future. I won't be a US Marshal forever and I need to plan for what I want to do. I'm not a farmer and I'm not going to be a bartender."

"How about a businessman?" she replied.

Mason involuntarily bristled, thinking that Worthington was a businessman and he wanted to be nothing like his former father-in-law.

Belle noticed and stopped, reaching up to tenderly touch his cheek. "You're nothing like him. We can be rich and honest at the same time."

"Perhaps you're right," he said as they resumed walking. "We ought to invest now then, while there's still opportunity."

"We can talk about it tomorrow," she said then yawned. "I'm really tired."

They were coming up on Missus Hunt's boarding house when Belle noticed movement by the MATE.

"Someone's by the machine," she whispered, maneuvering Mason towards the hulking metal engine.

"Ringo?" Mason blurted when the gunslinger stepped out in the light. "Where have you been?"

Ringo lifted an arm up and pointed south beyond the city.

"Mountains?" Mason said with a frown.

"Bisbee," Belle announced.

Ringo nodded.

"Did you see Rebecca, I mean Delilah?" Mason asked, his interest immediately aroused.

Ringo nodded then made a slicing motion at his throat.

"She's dead?" Mason asked, his hope rising. "You kill her?"

Again Ringo nodded.

"Where is she?" he queried, knowing that if Ringo could come back from the dead, so could Rebecca.

Ringo pantomimed striking a match and throwing it then swept his hands up imitating a something catching flame.

"Fire?" Belle offered.

"You burned her?" Mason said then abruptly realized the cause for the smoke in Bisbee. "You burned the hotel, too."

272

Ringo shrugged indicating it couldn't be helped.

"Well, I just hope no one else was hurt." Though concerned about the fire, Mason was relieved that another problem was eliminated.

Ringo pointed to Mason then to Belle then to her ring.

"Married," Mason said.

Ringo stiffly nodded then pointed to Belle.

"Wife?"

Ringo nodded again then made an arcing motion with his hand.

Mason frowned in concentration. "I don't know what you mean."

Ringo pointed again at Belle and held up two fingers. When Mason continued to stare dumbly at him, Ringo pointed to Belle's ring then Belle then held up two fingers. He repeated the movement several times.

"I think he means I'm your second wife," Belle interjected.

Ringo's shoulders settled as he nodded. He then held up one finger.

"Elizabeth," Mason said.

Again Ringo nodded.

Mason cocked an eyebrow his eyes widening. "She's not coming back from the dead, is she?"

Ringo shook his head and waved his hand dismissively.

"Thank God," Mason said, relieved.

Ringo again held up one finger then pointed to Mason.

"Elizabeth."

Ringo shook his head, thrusting his finger at Mason.

"I hate charades," Mason said in frustration.

"Man," Belle chimed in.

Ringo nodded, turning his attention to her. Holding up one finger, he pointed at Mason then made a slashing movement at his throat.

Belle thought for a moment then said, "Worthington."

Ringo's head bobbed in jerks of satisfaction. He then held up his hand, palm facing up and pretended to write.

"You want us to write Worthington's name," she said.

Ringo's arms flopped to his sides as he gave a final nod.

Grinning at Mason's bewildered stare, she said, "I was always good at charades."

"I won't even pretend to understand how you figured that out," he said.

"I'll get some paper and a pencil."

Ringo waved at her to stop then held up three fingers.

"You want three pieces of paper to write three names?"

Ringo replied with a jerky nod while Mason scrunched his face vainly trying to comprehend how Belle so easily understood.

"What other two names do you want?" she asked.

Ringo pointed to himself and Mason.

"Got it," she grinned. "I'll be right back."

While Belle ran off to write the three names, Mason gazed at his friend. "I'm sorry about all this, Johnny. This is my fault."

Grimacing, Ringo wagged a finger at him telling him he was wrong in no uncertain terms.

"They came for me," he continued. "When Elizabeth died, Worthington wanted me dead. But he also wanted everyone I cared about to also suffer."

Ringo held up a hand to stop him. He patted himself on the chest then pointed to Mason before crossing his middle finger over his index finger indicting that he and Mason were 'tight' as friends.

"I'm still sorry Johnny. You're a good man and deserved more than this."

Ringo again wagged his finger at him.

Belle returned with three separate pieces of paper with a single name written on each one.

Accepting the paper, he folded each one separately then jabbed them into his pants pocket. Ringo then pointed at Belle and Mason and jabbed a finger downwards.

"You want us to stay here," Belle said.

Ringo nodded.

Mason frowned when he suddenly realized what Ringo had in mind. "You're going after Worthington?"

Ringo folded his arms and nodded.

"You'll never make it," Mason warned. "It's one thing to be here where you can hide in the mountains and be seen by folks who understand, like Belle and me. Once you start heading west and it gets crowded, folks will notice and you'll be hunted down."

Ringo didn't budge, but simply stared at him with lifeless eyes.

"On the other hand," Belle interrupted. "Worthington wouldn't be looking for Ringo."

"You're not helping," Mason chided. "I'm worried about Ringo. It's bad enough Worthington sent someone here to do this to him," he said, waving a hand at him.

Belle rested a hand on Mason's arm. "Let him go. It's only fair that he have a chance for revenge for what's been done. Besides, what does he have to lose?"

Ringo took off his pistol belt and pointed to the empty cartridge loops.

"I've got ammo upstairs in my room," Mason replied.

Ringo folded his arms, waiting.

Shaking his head, Mason said, "I'll be back in a minute." He returned with two boxes of .45 ammunition, handing the boxes to Ringo. "You be careful."

Ringo held up a thumb.

"We'll see you when you get back?" Belle asked.

Ringo turned to her. Wrapping his arms and hugging himself, he then pointed down the street.

"Don't worry," she reassured him. "We'll take care of Annie."

With a wave of his hand, Ringo lurched into the night.

Chapter 9

Gordon rubbed his hands as he waited in Diamond Dan Braxton's office. He startled when the door opened and Diamond Dan strolled in, giving him a quizzical glance.

"What are you doing here?" Diamond Dan asked, placing his derby on the curled arm of the mahogany coatrack.

"Everyone's dead," Gordon nervously replied. "The Marshal's still alive."

"Yes, I know," he said, seating himself behind the wide desk.

"You do?" he blinked in surprise.

"Yes, I do." Resting his elbows on the arms of the chair, he templed his fingers. "How is it that you are still alive?"

"I was there when he shot Ed," Gordon confessed. "We had kidnapped Belle –"

"Who's Belle?"

"His lover, his girlfriend. We heard the Marshal had wounded Becca, so we knew we had to act fast. We kidnapped Belle and brought her to a cabin by the mountains. I set traps all around the cabin, cemetery guns, foot traps, others. It was the middle of the night, but we knew he would try and rescue her. Once he tripped one of the traps, we were going to kill the woman."

"What happened?" Diamond Dan asked.

Gordon slowly shook his head in amazement. "He got by all my traps and caught us by surprise. He then shot Ed and sent me to give you a message."

"Me?" Diamond Dan said, surprised.

"Yes. The Marshal said he was coming for Worthington. He said to tell you first that he has no beef with you, that you were just fulfilling a contract."

Diamond Dan mulled the news then asked, "He coming by himself?"

"No," Gordon replied, licking his lips. "He's got friends, and these are the kind of friends you can't defeat."

"What?" he scoffed. "Why?"

"They're already dead."

Diamond Dan stared at Gordon then snarled, "What the hell are you talking about?"

Gordon cast a quick glance around the room before lowering his voice. "Becca killed Johnny Ringo, but he's not dead. I saw him with my own eyes." He raised his hand to his head. "She shot him in the head. I saw where she shot him. But he's not dead. I mean, he's dead, but he's not dead."

Diamond Dan frowned as he stared at his diminutive explosives expert. The man was obviously scared about something. But he didn't need him spreading this whopper of a story, especially here in Chinatown. The Chinese were superstitious enough without adding walking dead to the mix.

It was obvious that the Marshal had more help than they realized or knew about and that could mean trouble if the law was federal. He didn't need federal agents and lawmen snooping around his territory. It was costing him more than enough paying off the San Francisco police. Sadler was doing him a favor by sending him a warning.

Diamond Dan chuckled at the man's audacity. He was telling him to mind his own business and things would be fine. He had to admire that about the man. He had beaten one of his best teams and was now willing to let bygones be bygones.

Shaking his head, he turned his attention back to Gordon. Whatever happened out there in Tombstone had frightened the little man enough that he was now useless.

"Alright, Gordon," he expansively said, getting up and coming around the desk. "I've got the message. You're free to be on your way."

He escorted the nervous man to the door when Gordon paused and gazed up at him. "I swear I'm telling you the truth. He's got the dead helping him."

"I'm sure you are," he smiled, clapping him on the back.

Opening the door, he watched as Gordon stole his way out of the office, casting furtive glances as he pushed through the door of the outer office. Looking to his right, Diamond Dan caught the attention of a man lounging in an overstuffed chair, pretending to read a newspaper.

Their eyes met and Diamond Dan curled a finger at him.

"Timothy, lad," he said with a smile as the man walked up to stand beside him. "Our friend there has outlived his usefulness. Dump him down at the wharves."

"Yes Sir," he nodded. Folding his newspaper, he went to stalk his prey.

Diamond Dan inhaled a deep breath, nodded at the rest of the group in the outer office and returned to his own office, closing the door behind him. Walking to the windows, he gazed out as he mused this latest tidbit.

Worthington was in trouble, especially now that Gordon would be dead before he had a chance to warn him.

Diamond Dan half-smiled at the danger of his decision. To cross Worthington was to cut one's own throat. But there was something about the brazenness of the Marshal's statement; 'I'm coming after him."

Very few men could claim to have stood up to Worthington. Sadler had now done it more than once. He admired that about the man, and any man who would stand up to Worthington deserved a chance. Besides, he never liked Worthington anyway.

Abruptly he tilted his head as a thought passed. Why not tell Worthington what Sadler threatened? It would do wonders to see Worthington rattled and nervous. Worthington would then demand protection, which could be provided at a greatly increased cost.

Hurrying back to the outer office, he motioned to another man. "Go catch Timothy and tell him to hold off until I say so."

"OK, Boss."

Diamond Dan grinned as the man ran after Timothy. This might actually work out quite well. He could charge Worthington an exorbitant fee then let Sadler in to finish the job.

Snickering, he returned to his office, quite pleased with himself.

Gordon smoothed his shirt as he nervously approached the tall twin oak doors to Reginald Worthington's office. Pausing, he licked his dry lips then pushed open the door.

Worthington's secretary, a petite officious looking woman of middle age dressed in no-nonsense high collar and narrow skirt, her hair in a tight bun at the back of her head, sat behind a wide desk. She would be attractive had she not the perpetual visage of scorn. She looked up as he entered, giving him a cold stare of long-suffering indulgence.

"Sit," she commanded. Assuming she would be obeyed without question, she returned her attention to the paperwork spread before her on the desk.

Gordon glanced around the room to the row of large, over-stuffed burgundy leather chairs arranged with precision against the wall. He stood for a moment deliberating which chair to select when the tall doors opened. Two men in somber grey and black suits and stiff-collared shirts adorned with impeccably tied cravats emerged. One noticed him then immediately dismissed him as no one of consequence.

When the men wordlessly vanished through the main doors, the outer office grew oppressively quiet. Gordon sat at the edge of a chair by the wall and waited for the secretary to announce him. Instead, she continued her fastidious attention to the papers on the desk, comparing entries in a ledger against listings in a thick register, occasionally making notes on the edges of the ledger.

Frustrated that he was kept here like some recalcitrant schoolboy waiting to see the headmaster, he cleared his throat hoping to gain her attention. Yet she either ignored him or didn't hear him. He cleared his throat again, a little louder, but the results were the same. His shoulders slumping in defeat, he scooted back into the depths of the cushions and waited.

As he rehearsed how he was going to tell Mister Worthington that the Marshal was coming here to kill him, the rhythmic ticking of the wall clock pierced his awareness and his frustration grew as he sensed he was wasting time here when he should be looking out for his own future.

When twenty minutes had passed, his nervousness and frustration could no longer be controlled. Standing, he approached the desk.

'I'm, I'm here... uh, I need to speak with Mister Worthington," he said.

"Of course you do," she tartly replied, her eyes on her work."

"It's important."

"It always is," she sighed then lifter her head to fix him with an icy gaze. "And you are?"

"I'm Gordon," he meekly replied, fidgeting under her stern eyes.

"Does Gordon have a last name?"

"No... I mean, yes, but I... it's... I don't use it. I have a message for Mister Worthington from his son-in-law."

The secretary stiffened, looking down her nose at him. Sizing him up for a few heartbeats, she said, "What is the message?"

"It's for Mister Worthington," Gordon stubbornly said.

"I determine what is for Mister Worthington," she crisply asserted.

Gordon stared at the imposing woman, wondering why he felt so intimidated. The woman was smaller than he was. Yet he knew why she caused him to feel awkward, insignificant. She was the gate-keeper to one of the most powerful men in San Francisco, if not the entire United States.

Hs mouth suddenly dry, Gordon licked his lips. Deciding he would have fulfilled his task by relaying the message, he blurted, "The Marshal said he's coming for him."

"Pardon?" she said, momentarily losing her composure.

Liking the reaction and the giddy feeling of putting her in her place, his voice grew stronger. "The Marshal said not to bother sending anyone else for he aims to come here and settle it once and for all."

Her lips tightened and she blinked in consternation then reached for the ornate telephone on the right side of her desk. Lifting the receiver from the silver cradle on top, she placed it on the desktop then turned the crank several times.

Putting the receiver to her ear, she waited. "Sir, a Mister Gordon with no last name is here with news about your former son-in-law. Yes sir." Placing the receiver back onto the cradle, she directed a quick glance at the doors to Worthington's office. "You may go in now." Her head turned and her gaze followed him until he pushed through the doors.

When Gordon entered, the President of Worthington and Son was standing at the edge of his desk, staring out the window, his left arm across his lean stomach propping up his right arm as he smoothed the hairs of his Van Dyke beard. Having known the man only by reputation, he was immediately intimidated by the imposing humorless man who seemed lost in thought. Wanting to relay his message and get the hell out of there, Gordon cleared his throat.

Worthington slowly turned to stare at him, his look almost reptilian. "What news then?" has asked, his voice emotionless. "Is he dead?"

"No, sir," Gordon nervously replied.

"No?" he snapped, his lip curling to a snarl. "Why not?"

Gordon hesitated.

"I said, why not?" he repeated, the chill in his tone making Harold shiver.

"Well, sir," he began. "It's because, uh… it's because, you see sir, the Marshal, your son-in-law –"

"He's no longer my son-in-law," he coldly intoned. "Get on with it man. Brace yourself and tell me what I want to know."

"Sir, the Marshal bested all of us sent down there to take care of him. He killed Earl in a shootout, bypassed all my traps and killed Ed."

"Stop babbling like an incoherent fool," Worthington commanded. "Get to the point."

Summoning up his courage, Gordon said, "He's coming for you. He told me to tell you he's coming for you."

Worthington's nostrils flared and his lips tightened. The haughty mien flittered for a mere instant before cold determination settled.

"Thank you," he said, giving Gordon a look that said he was dismissed.

Needing no urging, Gordon bustled though the doors and out the main doors before taking a deep breath as he stepped outside into the humid air of San Francisco. Relieved to be released from the oppressive offices of Worthington and Son, he felt free as though a great burden lifted.

Taking a quick glance up the block, he decided to see Diamond Dan again and ask for his share of the contract. After all, he did the best he could. It wasn't his fault Ed couldn't manage the team. Whistling a tune, he set off down the street, failing to notice Timothy emerge from the shadows.

Night had slipped into the alley ways when Lester Branaugh stumbled his way through the kitchen, past the cooks furiously stirring meats and rice in woks, past lesser cooks slicing and dicing vegetables or artfully carving garnishes, past the pot lickers, past the waiters picking up patron's meals to finally lurch out onto Duncombe Alley. Rubbing his filmy eyes, he licked dry lips, craving something to satisfy his overwhelming thirst. Despite the tantalizing smells of the kitchen, thirst occupied his urges. Beer would be marvelous right about now, but his funds were severely depleted from the cost of escaping the cruelty of daily existence in the opium dens behind the kitchen.

Clearing his throat caused him a fit of coughing spasms. Wiping his sleeve across his mouth, his mind was clear enough to know that he needed money. That meant finding employment somewhere, anywhere... either that or begging. His last venture of begging produced a few coins and a beating by some Irish hooligans who boldly informed him he was on their turf.

Bruised and humiliated, he had scuttled away. Deciding to search for work, he found employment in a warehouse along the wharf, cleaning and sweeping. The foreman, needing longshoremen, had taken one look at Lester's withered frame and knew the man wasn't strong enough for anything beyond the simple labor of sweeping. Still, business was good, and Lester was hired.

The first week was hell for Lester as he struggled to control his addiction with the problem that he wouldn't be paid until the end of the week. His incoherent ramblings as he swept and cleaned caused others to steer clear. He saw their undisguised disdain, but it mattered little to him. When he received his first week's earnings, he fled back to the safety of the opium resort on Duncombe Alley.

He was frugal in the beginning, spending only enough to satisfy his cravings, yet leaving him lucid enough to return to work. But as time wore on, his cravings exceeded his income and his work suffered until the foreman called him in, handed him pay for the work performed then let him go. Since then, he had tried to find work, but no one would give him a chance.

Hacking a cough again, Lester glanced around this back alley of San Francisco's Chinatown. His mind fuzzy, he wanted a drink, but a sense of purpose escaped him and he stood vacantly staring down the alley towards the opening that spilled onto Jackson Street.

Money... he needed money. Thrusting his hands into his pockets, he vainly searched for coins, withdrew his hands then repeated the search as though some errant coin would magically appear.

A voice in his head reminded him that water would satisfy his thirst, to turn around and go back into the kitchen and ask for a glass of water. But another voice argued the last time he did that, they yelled at him in that incomprehensible language and chased him out of the kitchen. Besides, beer quenched a thirst far better than water ever did.

With single-minded determination, he shuffled forward looking for someone to alleviate his pecuniary deficiency.

He knew better than to ask the Chinese. Their answer was always the same: "Get a job." Some even added, "Stop opium." And then there were those whose undisguised looks of disdain made him angry. Who were they to think they were better than he was?

Obliviously muddling along as he passed the other kitchens, their own patron opium addicts slipping through the doors, he stared straight ahead, the faint incense from the joss houses perfuming the thick malodor of unwashed bodies.

Turning right onto Jackson Street, he lumbered past the tailors and the cigar and overalls factories, as he headed towards Stockton Street, searching for a face other than a Chinaman. He passed a tailors' shop then an empty lot when he saw them standing by the corner of the tin shop, two men, white men. His focus redirected to them and he hurried his stumbling.

"Begging your pardon, gentlemen," he stated as he staggered up. "Might I implore you to aid me in my quest for nourishment?"

"Well look who we have here, Bryan," the one man sneered, raising a condescending eyebrow at Lester. He was a large man with mutton chops and a fedora. Folding his arms, he stared down at him. "We've been looking for you, Lester."

"W... why?" he stuttered, not recognizing either man.

"Tell 'im, Bryan," the man said.

"You owe Slim Carl some money," Bryan said. He was a head shorter than the other man, thinner, with the arrogance of a man who had no real power but what was given him by those stronger than he. "Me and Eliot here come to collect."

"I... I don't know what you're talking about." Lester started to back away, but Eliot reached out a beefy hand and grabbed his shoulder.

"You made some bad choices. You bet against Cincinnati and everyone who knows baseball knows the Cincinnati Red Stockings are the best team in baseball. But then, I don't expect you to know much about the sport."

"I... I," Lester mumbled, struggling to remember making a bet.

"Listen to 'im, Bryan," Eliot snickered. "The man's tryin' to think of an excuse why he hasn't paid Slim Carl." Still gripping Lester's shoulder, he sniffed and curled a lip. "You stink of opium." Shaking his head, he clucked his tongue. "Seems to me you need some remindin' of how you spend yer money. Slim Carl says to remind you."

"Now, now wait just a minute, gentlemen," Lester pleaded as they lifted him by his armpits and dragged him to the vacant lot between the tailor's and the tin shop. "I just need a little more time."

"You got no more time," Eliot growled as they dragged him behind the tailor's shop.

Once in the darkness and shadows behind the shop, Eliot straightened Lester to standing. "What are we gonna do with you?" he said, dusting at imaginary lint on Lester's shoulders.

"I –" Lester began then doubled over as Eliot let fly a gut-wrenching punch to his stomach.

Dropping to his knees, Lester wrapped his arms around his stomach, the pain wracking his emaciated body.

Grabbing a handful of hair, Eliot jerked Lester's head back while Bryan swung a fist and whacked him in the jaw, sending him reeling to the ground.

Shaking his hand at the pain for the strike, Bryan walked beside the moaning Lester and delivered a kick to his ribs. He was about to deliver a second kick when a cough behind them caused him to spin around.

The light from the streetlamps on Jackson Street cast silhouetted a man in a cowboy hat slung low over his face. His duster rippled in the light wind.

"What the hell do you want?" Eliot snarled, hands by his sides, ready to knock some sense into this intruder.

Ringo pointed a gloved finger at Eliot and then at Bryan then motioned for them to leave.

"You want us to leave?" Eliot snorted a laugh. "Mister, why don't *you* just leave if you know what's good for you."

Ringo repeated the hand motions, this time a bit more firmly.

"Mister, you just got yourself in a heap of trouble," Eliot said, facing him head on. Bryan followed suit and the two stood menacingly waiting.

Hat low over his head so that they could not see his eyes, Ringo turned to face the two men. Pulling back his duster, he revealed the .45 pistol in the holster.

"You expect us to be scared of a two-bit man with a two-bit outfit," Eliot scoffed.

In one jerky motion, Ringo withdrew the pistol and shot him through the forehead, sending him reeling backwards. As the man tumbled to the ground, Ringo leveled the barrel at Bryan.

"Don't shoot, don't shoot," he pleaded, hands high. "I'm unarmed."

Ringo kept the barrel pointed at him.

"You just made a big mistake, Mister," Bryan threatened. "That was Smooth Eliot you just shot. He's the boss of this neighborhood and he works for Slim Carl. Once Slim Carl finds out, you're in big trouble."

Ringo tilted his head as though pondering the tidbit of information then fired, the round penetrating right between the eyes.

Walking over to the two bodies, he gave each one a brief glance then holstered his gun.

"Jeez, Mister," Lester blurted, shocked yet relieved. "Thanks."

Pushing himself to his knees, he looked up at his benefactor. "He's right, you know. Once Slim Carl finds out, there's gonna be trouble to pay."

Ringo said nothing, instead reaching a gloved hand down to help Lester to standing.

"Thank you, my friend," he said, catching his breath while still holding onto his stomach. It was then he sniffed and crinkled his nose. "Damn but it stinks back here."

As they walked to the street, Lester noticed the stench moved with his rescuer. "I don't mean to be ungrateful, and I certainly don't want to offend, but you smell worse than I do."

Ringo simply shrugged and reached into his pocket and unfolded the paper, holding it up for Lester to see.

Scrunching his eyes in the dull light he read aloud, "Worthington. Your name is Worthington."

Ringo shook his head and reached into his pocket then pulled out another piece of paper, unfolding it and held it up for Lester to see and pointed to himself

"Ringo," Lester said. "Your name is Johnny Ringo."

Ringo nodded.

"My name is Lester. Thank you for saving my life."

Stuffing the paper with his name back into his pocket, he waved the paper with Worthington's name on it at him.

"You're looking for somebody named Worthington?" Lester said.

Ringo awkwardly nodded.

"OK. Where does he live?"

Ringo silently folded the paper and stuck it in his pocket. Poking himself with a finger, he tapped the fingers and thumb of his other hand, imitating talking while he shook his head.

"You can't talk?" Lester asked.

Ringo nodded.

"Jeez, Mister, that's sad. What happened?" he asked before realizing what he said. "Oh, sorry. I didn't mean it."

Ringo pulled out his .45, slowly spun the cylinder to punch out the spent shells, replacing them with cartridges from his gun belt.

Lester's thirst returned and he licked dry lips. "My good sir," he said, carefully regarding the gunman. "I'm a bit down on my luck and am in need of a drink. Might I impose on your generosity to spot me a pint?"

Ringo pulled out the paper with Worthington's name, pointed to it then held up his index finger.

"You want to find Worthington first," Lester said, his hopes dashed.

Ringo reached into his pocket and pulled out a silver dollar. Pointing to the printed name, he then waved the silver dollar at Lester.

His hopes rising, Lester nodded. "This Worthington fellow, what can you tell me about him?"

Ringo rubbed his fingers together, indicating wealth.

"He's rich," Lester said then blurted, "O my God. Reginald Worthington?"

Ringo nodded and sighed as he slid the gun back into the holster.

"Why do you want to find him?" he nervously asked.

Ringo pulled out his six-shooter and pretended to shoot.

"You're going to kill him?" he said aghast.

Sliding the gun back into the holster, he nodded.

"Are you crazy? The man's protected by an army of professional killers. You won't get within a mile of him before he discovers you."

Ringo stiffened and jabbed a finger at Lester then at the written name. He then flashed the silver dollar.

Lester's thirst began to overcome his fear. Besides, he could get a beer for a nickel and spend the rest at the opium den.

"I'll help you find him," he finally said, "but I'm not a killer. You're gonna to have to do that on your own. Once I take you there, you give me the money and I'm on my way. OK?"

Ringo nodded that the arrangement was satisfactory.

"He's got offices downtown somewhere. I don't know where he lives, so it'll be easier to find his workplace. I think it will probably be easier to do what you want to do with him there."

Ringo tilted his head and frowned.

Lester shrugged, licking dry lips. "He's probably more protected at home thinking anyone dumb enough to want to kill him would go there first. Besides, anyone can walk into his office."

Ringo nodded as though it was not important.

"C'mon," Lester said, the thought of the silver dollar giving him cause. "I think I might know where we can find his office." As they walked off, Lester noted Ringo's staggering walk. "Are you injured?"

Ringo shook his head, pressing the pace.

It was an hour later, having been rebuffed by too many pedestrians who turned their noses up at the two piquant vagabonds that they finally discovered the whereabouts of Worthington's business headquarters. Lester led the way, chattering endlessly to fill the void of his mute friend.

Standing in the shadows across the street from the tall stone edifice, Lester pointed to the lights flickering in the top story of the building.

"His offices are probably up there. He could be there or he might be home. Either way, this is where you want to be."

Ringo nodded then handed Lester the silver dollar.

Accepting the coin, Lester smiled. "Thank you, my friend. Good luck to you." He stuck out his hand.

Ringo stared at it a moment, then reached out a gloved hand and grasped his hand in a firm grip.

"If you survive this," Lester said, "go on back to where you rescued me. I'll find a way to hide you."

Ringo nodded, gave Lester a quick hand wave then turned to face the building, the name 'Worthington and Sons' blazoned across the front.

Casting a quick glance around, Lester walked off leaving Ringo to his fate. Pledging to hide him if he succeeded was an easy promise for he knew once Ringo got inside the building, he was as good as dead.

As was his habit these days, Reginald Worthington was still in his office, long after peers would have headed home. That was what separated him from everyone else. He had stamina and the drive to succeed where others were merely content to rest on what they had. Not him. He wouldn't be content until he owned everything and everybody, and all his enemies were crushed.

Sitting in his richly apportioned chair, he reread the telegram and smiled in arrogant satisfaction. For all of Mason's bravura, he was still in Tombstone. Yet Worthington's smugness was empty of real joy, for Mason still lived. That the man had managed to somehow overcome the various elements sent to eliminate him said that Mason was more than a worthy opponent. Worthington nodded with begrudging respect.

Sending men and women to kill him was becoming expensive, especially as the man refused to die like any normal person would. There had to be a better way, something he wouldn't expect.

Then it dawned on him that Mason was playing a game with him. He was lulling him into a false sense of security. He would strike when Worthington had let his guard down. But Mason failed to take into account that Worthington still had spies in Tombstone, whereas Mason had no one here. Two could play this game.

Worthington smiled at his own cleverness. He was, after all, a patient man. He would use the same delaying tactic Mason was employing against him. Leave him alone for a while; let him relax, thinking it was over. Mason's claim that he was coming here was all pompous brag.

He glanced up at the somber petite woman dressed in proper high collar and narrow skirt, her hair in a tight bun at the back of her head, who stood obediently at the side of his desk. Her countenance seemed to brighten when responding to him. He was of the belief that she was secretly in love with him, which was only to be expected. After all, he was a Worthington.

"Miss Hale," he said with the air of superiority. "Inform the gentlemen in the outer office that I will no longer need their services."

"Of course, Mister Worthington," she replied.

With a crisp yet graceful turn, she crossed the room and opened the door. Lounging in the outer office were two burly men dressed in somber suits. One sat in a chair by the wall. The other leaned against the doorjamb of the main doors. They looked up when the door opened.

With a gaze of authority, she lifted her head to stare down her nose at them. "Mister Worthington has asked me to inform you that your services are no longer required."

"For the rest of the evening?" the man at the doorjamb asked.

"Permanently," she replied.

"Are you sure?" the man in the chair frowned.

Miss Hale turned to glare at him before slowly enunciating, "Of course I am sure. You may inform your employer that he is free to submit his final statement at his earliest convenience. Good evening to you, gentlemen."

She stood before Worthington's door like a guardian gargoyle, imperiously waiting to be obeyed.

The two men exchanged glances. The man in the chair shrugged and pushed himself to standing. With a grin, he ambled over to the man waiting at the doorjamb.

"Fancy a pint?" he asked with a smile. "No sense wasting a good night like this."

Miss Hale waited until the door closed then walked over to twist the deadbolts of the two door locks.

Satisfied, she was almost to the door of Worthington's office when she was interrupted by a knock at the main doors. Supposing one of the security guards had forgotten something in the office, she grimaced in irritation, retracing her steps.

Flipping the deadbolt knobs to unlock the door, she stutter-stepped backwards at the man in a black duster standing before her, his black felt gambler hat low over his eyes.

She went to push the door closed but was thwarted when he stuck his boot in the opening. "What do you want?" she indignantly demanded. "You can't just come barging in here like this. You need an appointment. Come back tomorrow."

She tried again to close the door but her strength was no match for his and he effortlessly pushed the door open and stiffly walked in. It was when he brushed past her that she noticed the smell, like something had died.

"My God man," she decried. "You reek. You can't come in here like some unkempt common wharf scum."

He ignored her and continued his jerky walk towards the door to Worthington's office.

She raced around him, positioning herself between him and the door. "You can't go in there. I won't allow it."

Stopping, he pulled back the duster, exposing his six-shooter.

"I'll call the police," she said, her voice rising along with her fear.

Resting a hand on the gun's handle, he motioned her to move with the other hand.

"I swear I'll scream," she threatened. "The police are right outside, right now."

He pulled the pistol out of the holster, cocking the hammer as he raised the barrel and pointed it at her face.

Refusing to back down, she hunched over and half-closed her eyes. "I won't let you," she meekly stated.

With a quirky shake of his head, Ringo flipped the six-shooter in his hand and crashed the cylinder and handle part of the gun into the side of her head, sending her reeling to the floor. He stood over her for only a moment as she lay unconscious. Satisfied she was still alive, he opened the door to Worthington's office.

His eyes focused on the opening door, Worthington stood behind his desk, his hand inside the top right drawer reaching for the small pistol inside.

Ringo entered, pistol drawn. Finding his target, he shifted the barrel, aiming it at his quarry.

"What do you want?" Worthington haughtily demanded.

Gun steady, Ringo staggered forward until he stood on the opposite side of the desk. Reaching into the pocket of his duster, he withdrew a folded piece of paper and slapped it down on the desk.

Leaving the drawer open, Worthington reached for the paper and opened it. "Johnny Ringo," he read then looked up at his adversary. "I don't know who this is or what it means." He flipped the paper at Ringo.

Ringo pointed to the name then jabbed a gloved finger at himself.

"You?" Worthington said with a half-sneer. "You're Johnny Ringo?"

Keeping his head low, Ringo nodded.

"And that's supposed to mean something to me?" Worthington's hand slowly made its way to the drawer.

The barrel pointing at Worthington's face, Ringo cocked the hammer then reached up and removed his hat.

"Good God," Worthington blurted, seeing the gaping wound in Ringo's head. It was then the smell permeated his senses. It was a foul odor like that of a dead animal. He stared at Ringo and at his emaciated face, marveling that the man was still alive. "You should really see a doctor."

Noticing Worthington's hand just about to reach into the drawer, Ringo dropped the barrel and shot, nipping the finger of Worthington's index finger.

"Damn you," Worthington bellowed, clutching his bleeding finger. Pulling a handkerchief from his coat pocket, he wrapped it around the bleeding finger. "What the hell do you want? Why don't you say something?"

Ringo repeated the same hand and slashing motions that he used with Lester to explain his inability to speak.

"You're dumb?"

Ringo nodded, pointed to his head then thrust a finger at him.

"What?" he said, clutching his finger. "You blame me for that? I had nothing to do with that."

Ringo reached into his pocket again and pulled out a second folded piece of paper, tossing it on the desk.

The pain finally lessening in his finger, Worthington unfolded the paper. Reading the name, his nostrils flared in anger and fear for he understood why Ringo was here.

"I'll make you a deal," he said. "Whatever Sadler's paying you, I can double it, triple it. I can make you very rich."

Ringo flicked the gun to motion him away from the desk.

"You don't understand," Worthington pleaded, willing the pain in his hand to go away while he stood behind the desk, his hand lowering to the drawer. "I can make you a very wealthy man. Just name a price."

Ringo fired again, this time penetrating clear through Worthington's hand.

Yelping in pain, Worthington reached for the gun with his left hand only to feel the explosion of pain as Ringo fired a round through that hand as well.

"Damn you to hell," Worthington howled. "I'll kill you for this. Your life won't be worth two cents when I'm finished with you."

Ringo swiveled the six-shooter and fired again, hitting Worthington in the shoulder just below the shoulder blade then followed in rapid succession shots to the other shoulder and both thighs.

Worthington crumpled to the floor while Ringo lurched around the desk, pushing spent shells out of the cylinder and onto the floor. Standing over the helpless magnate, he slowly pulled a cartridge from the belt and slid it into the cylinder then turned the cylinder to the next empty hole and repeating the process until six cartridges were firmly seated and ready.

His breathing labored, his wounds seeping blood and staining his expensive suit, Worthington stared up at Ringo, raging hate in his eyes.

"Oh my God," a woman's voice blurted.

Ringo looked back to see a horrified Miss Hale standing in the door, a purple-black lump on her temple.

As she turned to flee for help, Ringo raised his arm and shot her in the head, propelling her forward to sprawl on the outer office floor by her desk.

"You go to hell," Worthington spat.

Ringo turned his attention back to man who sat propped against the wall, his arms draped by his sides and his legs splayed out in front. As he stared at him a thought came to mind.

Pulling open the remaining drawers, Ringo spilled the contents on the floor. Lumbering over to the bookshelves, he yanked them off the shelves and tossed them into piles on the floor. He then disappeared into the outer office, side stepping the prostrate Miss Hale, where he repeated his ransacking of the books and papers, and yanking files out of the filing cabinets.

Returning to Worthington's office, he unscrewed the top off a kerosene lamp perched on a bookshelf, splashing the contents over the papers and onto Worthington's clothes, careful that he didn't inadvertently douse himself.

"You bastard," Worthington groaned, vainly trying to evade the splashes of kerosene oil.

Satisfied Worthington was sufficiently drenched in kerosene, Ringo staggered to the outer office, unscrewed another lamp and sprinkled the contents over Miss Hale, the furniture, and the piles of books.

Pausing to survey his handiwork, he then careened into Worthington's office to reach up and turn off the gas lights in the walls. He then opened up the gas on one light just enough to be barely noticed.

Making his way to the outer office, he paused in the doorway to stare at Worthington. With a stiff wave of his hand, he turned to retrieve the matches in Miss Hale's desk drawer.

"You won't get away with this," Worthington called out. "Think about what you're doing. My offer still stands. I can make you very rich."

Ignoring him, Ringo lurched back to the doors separating Worthington's office form the rest of the world, matches in hand. Standing in the doorway, he flicked a lit match onto a pile of books and watched as the pile caught fire and the flames spread following the trail of kerosene.

He remained framed in the doorway until the flames began crawling towards Worthington. Turning, he limped to the main doors, impervious to the screeching wails of the magnate of San Francisco.

By the time Ringo was headed back in the alleys of Chinatown, he could hear the fire alarms erupting throughout the city.

Clay sat behind the desk, leaning forward, staring at the headlines of the front page of the Daily Morning Call. Worthington was dead, a victim of a horrible fire that destroyed his offices and much of the company's current records. The fire burned the buildings on either side and would have continued had not someone determined to shut off the gas to all the nearby buildings.

Leaning back in his chair, he shook his head and sniffed as he half-grinned at the irony. Worthington had spent thousands upon thousands of dollars to kill Mason Sadler, and the man succumbs to a fire in his own building.

Swiveling his chair so he could gaze out the window, Clay rubbed his chin as he pondered Worthington's obsession with killing Sadler. The score so far was Sadler- 5, Worthington – 0. If he was a betting man, he would be compelled to bet on Sadler. Yet Clay knew beyond a doubt that Worthington's death was no accident. How Sadler had managed it was a puzzle, especially as the Marshal was still in Tombstone.

The unfortunate part was with Worthington dead, Clay was out half of his commission. But, he shrugged, that was the nature of his business. Besides, there were others who needed his services. It was time to put an end to Worthington's contract.

Chapter 10

Belle watched Annie as she was led out onto the dance floor. That she followed instead of her usual pulling the man to the center of the room and breaking out into the raucous dancing that earned her the name 'High Step Annie' spoke volumes. The once sparkling eyes and enthusiastic embrace of life were gone, replaced by a brooding melancholy. Her partner noted the obvious difference and no matter his efforts, she wouldn't respond. Finally, in desperation, he said something that resulted in her stiffening and slapping him in the face before stalking off the dance floor and heading for the doors.

Belle intercepted her when she passed by the bar. "What happened?"

Annie came to an abrupt halt and fumed, "He said that I needed to get over it. Johnny was a no-good gunslinger who deserved what he got, that it was time for me to move on."

"That was cruel," Belle commiserated. "It's obvious he didn't know Johnny."

Annie twisted her head to look over her shoulder, glaring at the man who had laughed off the slap and was back in line waiting his turn to dance with another girl.

"Why don't you go home," Belle suggested.

"It's too quiet there," Annie said, heaving a sigh, "and lonely. At least here there's noise to keep me distracted."

"I understand," Belle said with a sympathetic smile. "You don't have to dance if you don't feel like it, but you do need to make an effort to be nice."

"He deserved that slap," she protested.

"I'm not talking about him," she replied. "He should be slapped for making a comment like that, early and often."

The flippant comment caused Annie to smile. "OK, Belle. I'll try."

"That's my girl." She gave Annie's hand a warm squeeze.

It was mid-morning when Mason strolled along Allen Street, musing about Shephard and the Professor. The Professor's machine was indeed a marvel and a terrifying weapon for war. But was his invention enough to warrant forgiveness of past egregious actions? Apparently the US Government thought so. No sooner had the Professor packed up and moved his machine to the railroad landing in Benton when word came down, and in no uncertain terms, told lawmen across the nation to leave the Professor alone.

Mason shook his head wishing the US Government would tell Worthington the same thing: 'Leave Mason Sadler alone.'

Hearing his name, he looked up to see Charlie Parsons, the telegraph operator, bustling towards him.

"Morning Charlie."

"Morning, Marshal," he greeted him, holding up a telegram. "It might be nothing, but I thought it a might curious."

"What's that?"

"That newspaper fella, the young one working at the Epitaph."

"Roger?"

"That's him," he nodded then leaned in confidentially. "He's got a telegram here from some man named Clay Martin in San Francisco."

"San Francisco," Mason repeated, more than curious.

"Yup." He waved the telegram at him then held it in two hands to read. "Says here, 'Your benefactor has died. You're on your own.'" Looking up, he frowned and said, "I thought he was a Missouri boy."

"So did I," Mason mused.

"Seems a bit hard," Charlie remarked, "his benefactor dying and all, and to be told you're on your own."

"Yes it does," Mason agreed.

"Course that does seem puzzling," Charlie continued. "Didn't know he had a benefactor and if he did, the man couldn't have been much of one. I heard Roger was barely making ends meet with what the newspaper paid him."

"Newspaper is a tough business," Mason commented.

"Hey Marshal," a voice called out.

Mason looked up to see John Bruce marching towards him. "Morning, Mister Bruce."

"Didja hear the news?" he said, his voice brimming with excitement. "Worthington is dead."

"What?" Mason blurted. "When? How?"

"I just found out this morning. I was checking up on the bar I had shipped from San Francisco for the Crystal Palace. One man had a newspaper with him." He handed the newspaper to Mason.

Mason read the headlines blared across the top. "Reginald Worthington DEAD!" He quickly read the story, curling a lip at the obsequious eulogy for the man. It said nothing about Elizabeth other than she was living in Tombstone with husband Mason Sadler, a US Marshal. Worthington had died in a fire under suspicious circumstances. Also dead was a Miss Eunice Hale, Worthington's secretary. The fate of the business empire was in question as Worthington had not designated a successor.

Mason scanned the paper for any other relevant news concerning Worthington. Not finding any, he handed the paper back to John who held up his hands.

"You keep it," he smiled. "Figured you might want to frame that."

"Thank you for letting me know," Mason said, still absorbing the possibility that he might finally be free of Worthington.

"Anytime," he said. "Better get back before those oafs put it in upside down." With a wide grin, he strode back towards the Crystal Palace, passing a woman an attractive brunette, hustling toward the Marshal and the telegraph operator.

"Marshal," she called out.

Mason and Charlie looked up to see one of the Bird Cage girls.

"Hello Nola," Mason said with a smile.

"Miss Belle sent me to fetch you. Said to meet her at High Step Annie's room. Something bad has happened."

Turning to Charlie, Mason said, "Thanks for the insight. Appreciate you keeping me informed."

"Any time, Marshal," he replied with a satisfied grin. "Guess I best get this thing delivered."

While Charlie strode off to deliver the telegram to Roger, Mason followed Nola to the house. Nola headed off back to work as Mason stepped into the foyer of the boarding house. Bounding up the stairs, he moved down the hall until he came to Annie's room. Belle was standing over Annie's body when Mason walked in.

"What happened?" he asked, his voice muted. He gazed down at the pretty woman who seemed in peaceful slumber lying atop the covers of the bed, except for the blood trail that spilled over the covers by her hands.

"She slit her wrists," Belle said with a sigh.

"I can see that," Mason said. "Why?"

"I think it had to do with Ringo."

"She killed herself because Ringo was dead?" he said, cocking an eyebrow in doubt.

"I can think of no other reason," she replied. "The girl had fallen helplessly in love with him. She was never the same when she found out he had been killed."

Mason stared at her, shaking his head. "What a waste. I better let Charles Tarbell know he's got a body here."

"Maybe not," Belle blurted, putting a hand on his arm. "I have an idea."

Frowning, Mason said, "What's your idea."

"Let me clean up her arms first and then you can help me load her into a wagon." She glided over to the pitcher and water bowl, pouring a generous amount into the bowl.

"What are we going to do with her?" Mason said, watching in morbid curiosity as she soaked a towel and wiped the dried blood from Annie's wrists.

"You'll see." Glancing back at him watching her, she chided him. "Don't just stand there gawking like an oaf; go get a wagon."

Shaking his head, he chuckled as he headed out the door. By the time he returned, Belle had cleaned up Annie's wrists and changed her blood-stained clothes.

"You'd be a good undertaker," Mason commented. "Give Charles a run for his money."

"No thanks," she replied. "I like my customers alive." Pointing to the legs, she commanded, "Grab a hold."

"Where're we taking her?"

"To the wagon," she replied with an impish smile.

"Very funny," he said, rolling his eyes. "Then where?"

"Find Caleb and de la Fuente."

"They're in the Dragoons."

"I know," she answered.

"What do you expect them to do?" he asked as they struggled to carry Annie down the stairs. "This girl's heavier than I realized."

"I don't know what all goes on with people like Caleb and de la Fuente," she said, "but they must do something or have some special power because Ringo is walking around because of them."

"And you think they can rescue Annie?" he said

"It's worth a try," she replied with a hopeful shrug.

"We don't even know where Ringo is," he pointed out as they placed her in the wagon.

"I expect he'll come back here when he's finished doing whatever he's doing," she said, climbing up onto the seat.

"How about you let me drive," Mason wryly commented. "Folks are beginning to question my manhood with the way you carry on."

"Why Marshal Mason Sadler," she sweetly said. "You're not bothered by a little gossip, are you?"

"Gossip I can handle," he said. "It's the looks of pity that irritate me. They don't know you like I do. And besides," he frowned, taking up the reins. "Isn't it about time you stop getting kidnapped all the time?"

"What? And spoil all that fun," she teased, "especially when they tie me up." She gazed at him with half-lidded eyes.

Snorting a laugh, he shook his head. "I don't even know how to respond to that one."

"Then drive on Marshal Sadler. We've got a body to deliver."

It was late afternoon when they split off from the road that went through the middle pass, working their way up the trail that the MATE had carved out when Henry Mitchell had led them on his wild chase.

Mason reined in the mules when they came to the clearing where Henry had been staked out what seemed so long ago. Dismounting, Mason came around to help Belle down.

"I'd give a month's pay to know where Henry ended up," he said, scanning the clearing and surrounding trees and rocks.

"I'm beginning to think we may see him again," she replied, walking over to the spot where Henry had doused her with a bucket full of water to keep her from revealing their location. "After all, Caleb and de la Fuente still have the gold."

"You may be right." Walking to the center of the clearing, he called out, "Caleb? De la Fuente?"

His calls were answered by silence. Overhead, a vulture crested the warm wind currents and drifted away.

"Caleb. De la Fuente," he again shouted, the sound of his voice quickly absorbed by the surrounding hills, trees and chaparral.

"What do we do if they don't show up?" Belle asked.

"We wait," he answered, his eyes relentlessly studying the nooks and trails. "I know they're here somewhere." Walking to the edge of the clearing, he called out, "Caleb. De la Fuente."

When the silence again filled the afternoon, he walked back to the wagon to peer at Annie who seemed in peaceful repose. "If they don't show up soon, we're going to have to take her back."

"How're we going to explain her in the back of the wagon?" she asked, walking up to stand beside him.

"Good question."

"We could always say we were taking her for a drive," she said, gazing up at him with innocent eyes.

Smirking, he shook his head. "Somehow I don't think that will work." Looking out over the wagon, he added, "I hope they come soon. I'd hate to leave without giving her a chance."

"Worst case," she pointed out, "is that we bury her here like you did Ringo. Then we keep trying to find Caleb and de la Fuente. They helped Johnny."

Gazing up at the sky, he said, "Then I suggest we begin collecting rocks before it gets too dark."

Dusk enveloped the mountains when Mason and Belle paused to gauge the pile of stones.

"I think we've collected enough," Mason said. "Let's go ahead and get her out of the wagon."

Belle glanced around once more, her disappointment showing. "I was hoping they'd show up before now and we wouldn't have to do this."

Mason gave her a resigned shrug then unhooked the tailgate. "There's nice spot over at the edge of the clearing where we can place her."

Carefully lifting Annie out of the wagon, they carried her over to where a tall oak was flanked by red-bark manzanita trees. Laying her on the ground, Belle dropped to her knees to arrange Annie's dress.

Mason watched for a moment then twitched his head at the sound of a dried branch snapping. Looking back beyond the wagon, he saw Caleb and de la Fuente pushing their way through the low mesquite and towering ocotillo.

"They're here," he triumphantly announced.

Belle bounced up and ran to greet them. "Finally. Didn't you hear us calling you?"

Caleb shook his head.

"How did you know we were here?"

Caleb replied with a shrug.

"We need your help," she continued, motioning them to where Annie lay.

When they approached and stopped to stare down at Annie, Belle turned to Caleb and said, "Can you make her like you?" She turned to Mason and pointed to de la Fuente.

Understanding, Mason said, "*Puedes hacerla como tu?*"

Caleb looked to de la Fuente who hunched his shoulders and spread his hands, effectively asking why.

"She's Ringo's girlfriend," Belle explained.

"*Ella es la chica de Ringo,*" Mason said.

De la Fuente nodded in understanding. When Mason and Belle stood waiting, he flipped his hands at them, telling them to go away.

"Thank you," Belle said, touching his arm without thinking, the desiccated skin sending chills up her arm.

Mason and Belle climbed aboard the wagon and Mason flicked the reins. Dusk had given way to night and as he guided the wagon back the way they came, Belle looked over her shoulder to see Caleb and de la Fuente watching them. She strained to see them until they disappeared in the distance and darkness.

The next morning, Belle rose early and dragged Mason out of bed.

"C'mon. I want to see if she's still there."

Blinking in groggy sleepiness, Mason stared out the window. "It's not even daylight yet. What time is it?"

"Never mind that," she grinned. "Get dressed. I'll fire up the MATE and we can get there and back in time for breakfast."

Gaping a cavernous yawn, Mason rubbed is eyes and sat on the edge of the bed as Belle bustled out, leaving closing the door with a thump.

By the time Mason was dressed and downstairs, Belle had the MATE running and waiting outside the front of the boarding house. Climbing aboard, he turned to look at Belle.

"Coffee," he said. "You don't expect a man to go traipsing around the countryside without a cup of coffee first."

"You're going to have to wait," she said, patting his thigh. "First things first."

"You're so cruel," he moaned. "Besides, first things first means coffee."

"Later," she grinned, giving him a peck on the cheek. She released the brakes and the MATE lurched forward.

An hour later, she steered into the clearing, immediately noting Annie was not there.

"They did it," she gleefully exclaimed.

"You don't know that," Mason soberly objected. "They could have simply carried her body away somewhere where she'll be found years from now."

"You are such a grouch in the mornings," she said, playfully patting his arm.

Setting the brakes, she leaped down and went to the spot where they had placed Annie last night. There was no evidence that they dragged the body to another location.

"So do we call then and see for sure?" she said, hoping Annie was close by.

"I think we need to let the dead rest a while," he counseled. "Let's be satisfied that she is no longer here. When they're ready to let us know, they'll come tell us."

"You sure?"

"Yes, I'm sure. C'mon. Let's go home, get some breakfast, and start a new day together.

Belle gazed up at him with affectionate eyes. "I'd like that, especially the starting a new day together."

Reaching a hand down to help her up, he said, "Now that Worthington is no longer a threat, maybe we can settle down to a life as husband and wife. We need to move out of the boarding house to a place of our own."

"I agree," she replied, releasing the brakes. "I have a place in mind."

"Oh? Where?"

"A place in town, not too far from the Theater." She pushed the throttle and the MATE sped up.

When she continued to drive without telling him more, he said, "OK. Where in town not too far from the Theater?"

"It's on Fremont Street."

"Fremont Street," he frowned then cocked an eyebrow. "You don't mean…"

"Wyatt Earp's former house," she said with a sly grin.

"Uh," he replied, giving her a skeptical glance, "I'll have to think about that one."

Mason slid the chair back from the lunch table in the Atlantic Restaurant and sat down opposite a startled Roger who quickly regained his composure with a bright smile.

"Afternoon, Marshal."

"Afternoon Roger. How goes the newspaper business?"

Before he could answer, young Rebecca sashayed up, her adoring attention on Mason. "What can I get you, Marshal?"

Mason looked at the steak and potatoes on Roger's plate. "I'll have the same as Roger has. Cook the steak rare. And coffee."

"You got it, Marshal." She winked at him and walked away, her hips swinging.

"The girl's got it bad for you, Marshal," Roger grinned.

"Much too young for my tastes, even if I was single." He leaned back with a contented sigh, gazed out the window then back to Roger. "So now that Worthington's dead, what are you going to do?"

"Well, I'm not sure what I'm –" he began then caught himself. His mouth went dry and the fork in his right hand shook.

"I'm disappointed in you," Mason said, locking his eyes on him. "Here I thought you were a hard-working clever young man when all along you were working for Worthington. I must admit that you were very convincing."

"It's not what you think, Marshal," he sputtered.

"You don't know what I think," he countered, cold steel in his eyes. "People are dead because of you. My friend Johnny Ringo is dead… because of you."

"I had nothing to do with that," he gushed. "All I was supposed to do was to report back on what was happening. I —"

Mason cut him off with a flip of his hand. "So if I was killed, you were to report back mission accomplished. Is that it? Or were you to wait until all those I loved were killed?"

Roger licked dry lips, then swallowed hard.

Young Rebecca strutted up, placing the plate of steaming steak and potatoes in front of Mason, twisting the plate so that the steak was directly in front of him. She then placed the cup of coffee to the right of the plate, adjusting the handle for easy reach. Walking to his other side, she aligned the fork, knife and spoon to his left.

"Anything else, Marshal?" she dreamily asked.

Giving her a winning smile, Mason said, "That's perfect, Rebecca. Thank you."

"Anytime, Marshal."

Reluctant to leave, she stared longingly at him until another customer called out her name, asking for more coffee.

As young Rebecca walked away, Mason picked up his knife and fork then slowly leaned forward, holding Roger's gaze with his flinty eyes. "You've got 'til sundown to get out of town. Then one day after that to leave the territory. You know my reputation with a gun. If I see you or hear that you are anywhere in the territory, I'll find you and I'll kill you." He paused then added, "And if I don't, I have friends who will."

Roger's eyes widened.

Mason sliced a chunk of steak, stuck a fork in it and raised it to his lips. "If I were you, I'd be on my way by now." He plopped the meat into his mouth, chewing slowly as he watched Roger squirm.

Bolting up to standing, Roger shoved a hand into his pockets, withdrawing several silver dollars. Indecision assailed him as he debated waiting for change or hustling out to collect his things before the Marshal made good on his threat. Deciding his life was worth more than a few coins, he slapped the dollars on the table and ran for the door.

Young Rebecca approached the table just as Roger burst out the door. Frowning as she stared down at the plate still piled with food, she said, "What happened to him? He left half his food on the table."

"Lost his appetite," Mason said with a shrug.

Two weeks later, Mason and Belle emerged from the Bird Cage Theater in the wee hours of the morning, arm in arm. Standing on the sidewalk, Belle sighed happily.

"Let's take the long way home," she said, breathing in the pulse and the excitement of living in Tombstone. "I want to enjoy this experience for as long as possible."

"It all has to end sometime," Mason sagely replied, leading her out onto the street, away from the cribs on 6th Street.

"I know," she said, "but not now. Now I want to taste the fullness of living and excitement. I want to fall into bed each day exhausted from the experience of life."

They walked down Allen Street then turned onto 5th Street.

"So you want to burn the candle at both ends?"

"If that's what it takes," she said. "I don't want to look back and ruefully wish I had tasted more of life. The time to live is now."

With the heat of the day dissipated, the early morning air was pleasantly cool with a full moon and star-filled sky. Belle shivered and clutched Mason's arm tighter.

"So when do you plan to take a break and rest?" he asked.

"I can rest when I'm dead," she flippantly replied.

"Let's hope that will be a long time from now," he said with a chuckle.

Turning on Safford Street, they quietly strolled, each lost in thought. Mason noted they were approaching St Paul's Episcopal Church.

"Every time I pass by the church, I can't help but think of the first time I met Caleb and de la Fuente there. Talk about being shocked."

"I can only imagine," she replied. "We haven't seen them since we left Annie in the Dragoons. I wonder if Ringo ever came back."

"We might never know," he answered. "They have a way of disappearing for a while then showing up when you need them. As it stands right now, our lives are pretty calm, especially compared to a few weeks ago. I imagine we won't see them for a while."

As soon as he said it, he noted the door to the church opening slightly then closing. The action repeated several times before the door closed.

"What?" Belle asked as he guided her to the church.

Mason said nothing but opened the door. "Who's in here?" he said, his voice firm.

Moonlight through the stain-glass windows cast muted colors on the pews. Noise in the dark shadows caused him to twist his head to the left. "Come on out."

He stepped back, Belle in step with him.

Wrinkling his nose at the smell, he said, "Caleb? De la Fuente?"

Stepping back through the door into the moonlight he waited until a figure appeared.

"Johnny?" he sputtered as Ringo emerged.

"Johnny," Belle exclaimed then brushed past him into the church. "Annie?" When no response came, she hustled back to stand before Ringo. "Where's Annie?"

Ringo looked at her then at Mason and shrugged.

"What?" Belle blurted. "Annie should be with you. That's why we left her in the Dragoons."

Ringo awkwardly twisted his head to stare at Mason then at Belle then back to Mason.

"Slow down, Honey," Mason said then focused on Ringo. "When did you get back?"

Ringo held up an index finger and made an arcing motion.

"Yesterday?" Mason said.

Ringo nodded.

"I'm getting better at charades," he chuckled. "Darling," he said to Belle. "He doesn't know."

Silence thickened as Belle pondered how to tell him what happened. Deciding the truth was the best way, she said, "You know Annie loved you more than anyone."

Ringo nodded.

"She loved you so much that she couldn't stand the thought of not being with you. When she found out that you had been killed, she decided to follow you."

Ringo stiffened then tilted his head.

"Yes, Ringo. She killed herself. When we discovered her, we took her to Caleb and de la Fuente, hoping they could help her. She's there waiting for you."

Without hesitation, Ringo burst between them and in a mad staggering dash hobbled away towards the mountains.

"I hope you're right," Mason mused aloud. "We don't know for sure she's alive… or half-dead, or whatever."

"She is," Belle smiled. "I'm sure of it."

"I hope he finds her."

"He'll find her. Love has a way of finding what you need."

As they watched him disappear into the night, Mason said, "I never had a chance to thank him for saving my life."

Slipping an arm around his arm and hugging it to her, Belle said, "I'm sure there will come a time when you can tell him. For now, let's be happy we're here, alive, and together." Reaching up she stoked his smooth strong chin.

Holding his eyes with hers, she winked then flicked her eyebrows. "I'll show you a good time, sailor."

Laughing, he shook his head. "Somehow I think life with you will never be boring."

Wrapped around each other like young lovers, they walked on, the sounds of Tombstone fading in their unspoken desire.

Thank you for choosing to read this story! If you enjoyed this book, please leave an Amazon Review.
Thanks for reading!
-pdmac

WEBSITE
www.pdmac-author.com

FACEBOOK
www.facebook.com/pdmacauthor/

OTHER BOOKS

The Wyvern Master Chronicles

The Sixth Kingdom
A Spy in the Court
Raising the Dead
Wizard King

Bridge Quest: A GameLit Adventure Series

Bridge Quest
Orc's Bane
Lord of Innis Torr

Steampunk Western: Tombstone Trilogy

Fool's Gold
An Ounce of Lead
The Devil's Disciple (Coming Soon)

Viking Time Travel Romance

Beyond Her Touch

A Dystopian Novel

Rebirth of Angels

A Time Travel Novella

Ctrl Z: The Do Over Stone

Poetry

a young man no more

CO-AUTHORED BOOKS AND ANTHOLOGIES

Teen & Young Adult Coming of Age Fantasy: Dragons of Isentol

Throne of Deceit
Rune Marked
Empire of Serpents

www.ingramcontent.com/pod-product-compliance
Lightning Source LLC
Chambersburg PA
CBHW020536020726
47494CB00006B/1791